D1430284

HERO UNDER FIRE (SPECIAL FORCES: OPERATION ALPHA)

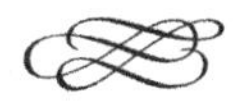

TRISH MCCALLAN

Dear Readers,

Welcome to the Special Forces: Operation Alpha Fan-Fiction world!

If you are new to this amazing world, in a nutshell the author wrote a story using one or more of my characters in it. Sometimes that character has a major role in the story, and other times they are only mentioned briefly. This is perfectly legal and allowable because they are going through Aces Press to publish the story.

This book is entirely the work of the author who wrote it. While I might have assisted with brainstorming and other ideas about which of my characters to use, I didn't have any part in the process or writing or editing the story.

I'm proud and excited that so many authors loved my characters enough that they wanted to write them into their own story. Thank you for supporting them, and me!

READ ON!

Xoxo

Susan Stoker

AUTHOR NOTE

I'm a recent convert to Susan Stoker's world of hot alpha heroes and smart heroines, but once I found her work, boy did I glom on. I kind of wrecked my health with so many late nights of reading. LOL

Once I discovered her Operation Alpha fan fiction world, it was natural to gravitate in that direction. I'll be forever indebted to Susan for allowing me to work in her world and play with her characters from the author side of the computer screen.

I've really enjoyed my stint in Susan's sandbox and fully intend to play in there some more.

Hero Under Fire incorporates Tex, Rocco, Gumby and Ace. I hope you enjoy reading this story as much as I enjoyed writing it!

Trish McCallan

ACKNOWLEDGMENTS

Many thanks to the following people for their help in producing this book!

Copy Editing: Jennifer Jakes, Killion Publishing

Proofing: David Steele

Proofing: Patti O'Shea

Susan Stoker: For her help with *everything*!

Mr. Stoker: For his patience in answering all of my medical questions!

Riley Edwards: For her patience in answering my questions about RPGs.

Any mistakes within this book are mine and mine alone.

CHAPTER 1

"Fuck." With a muffled groan, Devlin Russo rolled off the sweaty, soft body he'd just pounded into the mattress. What the hell was his cock trying to do to him? Kill him? He was forty years old for Christ's sake. Too old for this shit. His lips twitched. Although...as deaths went, dying because of sexual exhaustion wasn't a bad way to go.

Madeline huffed out a breath, the muted sound full of satisfied amusement. "I believe we already took care of that. Multiple times, I might add."

The low hum of the air conditioner across the room accompanied their heavy breathing as they lay side by side. The room smelled like air freshener and sex—an odd combination, but probably standard for motel rooms.

Satisfaction swelled as he listened to her ragged breathing. There was no doubt she'd found her release. All six times. He'd made sure of it. Made sure she was flying before letting himself go. But then, it wasn't hard pushing her up to the cliff and over the edge.

Hell, she was the most responsive lover he'd ever had. Open, without shields in bed. There was something damn addictive about that, about the way she quivered at his touch, the way her flesh heated and twitched beneath his lips, the way her head would arch back and her eyes would close, like she was focused fiercely on what he was doing to her.

The woman was dynamite in bed.

Of course, he reacted just as explosively to her. Six times for fuck's sakes, in 24 hours. Three times alone in the last three or four. He couldn't remember ever being so hungry for a woman. Not even back in the horny days of his adolescence. Sure as hell not with Sharon. Pain threatened at the thought of his ex—and everything they'd lost. But he didn't let it grab hold of him. Didn't let the memories sweep him from the here and now.

Another first.

His reaction to Madeline in bed shouldn't have surprised him. There'd been clues after all. Like how she'd fractured his concentration as soon as he caught sight of her in that parking lot three days ago. Even back then, when he should have been solely focused on keeping Tag alive long enough for the EMTs to arrive, he'd been aware of her—of the way she'd filled out that red lacy bra she'd been wearing while she'd used her shirt to staunch Tag's bleeding. Of the subtle fresh scent drifting from her. She'd smelled like rain after a long drought. Hell, the fact he'd even been able to smell her over the metallic stench of fresh blood had stunned him.

"I'm thinking a shower and some dinner. It's only eight. There must be some places in town that will still deliver." She paused a beat before adding casually, "You want to join me?"

"For the shower, or dinner?" His sweaty skin cooling beneath the chilly air of Madeline's suite, Devlin shifted onto his elbows to stare down at her face. Her eyes were closed, a faint smile curving her lips, flags of red still painting her cheeks and forehead. His chest tightened. Christ, she was beautiful with her tangled, brownish-black hair spread across the ivory white pillow like that.

"Both." Her smile broadened. With a flutter of dark lashes her eyes slowly opened.

"I could be persuaded," he said absently, his breath catching at the dazed look still glazing her eyes. Fuck, she was so damn... gorgeous...like this. Replete. Relaxed. Vulnerable. He ran a hand up the curve of her belly to cup her tit. The nipple instantly tightened, poking into his palm.

Responsive.

His cock stirred, mimicking her reaction.

You'd think after two days of fucking like a pair of horny rabbits, they would have satiated the hunger by now. But apparently not.

A shadow of unease drifted through him. This ramped up horniness wasn't normal. Not for him. And this weird sexual insatiability wasn't the only abnormal thing about his reaction to her. There was his inexplicable possessiveness too.

Last night at dinner, when he'd caught the appreciative look their waiter had turned her way, he'd wanted to rip the bastard's eyes right out of his head.

His reaction had blindsided him. He'd never been a jealous man.

Hell, when Jess, his last casual hookup, had started flirting with every man in sight trying to inspire jealousy and force a commitment from him, he'd shrugged and walked away.

"What's wrong?" Madeline asked, the hazy look in her eyes sharpening.

That was another thing he liked about her. How upfront she was. The way she jumped in headfirst. No tiptoeing around. No feeling the situation out. If she wanted to know something, she asked. There was no guessing with Madeline, no wondering what she was feeling or thinking. Which meant no holding resentments back and anger in.

"Nothing. I'm just surprised the bastard hasn't settled down yet." He waved a hand over his hardening cock. "Apparently the damn thing doesn't have an off button."

Her laugh held rueful amusement. "I'm not complaining. However, without some immediate sustenance, I'm not going to have the energy for a fourth round. As you can see, I'm barely recovered from round three."

Fair enough.

Dev dropped back to the mattress and worked his left arm beneath her back, dragging her against his side. Bare flesh to bare flesh. Her damp, flower-scented hair tangled across his chest. There was no reason recovery had to be a solo affair.

"On the other hand," she sighed, snuggling into him, "it won't hurt to rest for a bit before jumping in the shower."

Thank God she didn't want to go out. The last thing he needed was a repeat of his reaction from the night before. Besides, he liked the idea of having her to himself.

Which was another weird reaction. This obsession with having her close, particularly after sex, was strange. His usual post-sex urge to cut and run hadn't struck. Hell, the warm weight of her against him didn't even feel claustrophobic. It felt…natural…right. He'd shared her bed last night without getting antsy, the entire fucking night, without wanting to bolt.

Hell, he hadn't spent the night with a woman since his marriage had fallen apart. Yet not only had he cradled her close through the previous night, waking at dawn for a long, lazy fuck, followed by a long, lazy, shower, but he wanted a repeat.

Madeline was different.

Special.

"Any idea yet when you'll have to head back to Phoenix?" he asked absently.

She was vice president of hospitality and quality control for the Best Western corporate headquarters and had been sent to Dark Falls to assess the performance of the three Best Westerns in town. She'd finished her assessment and checked out of the motel just before Mitch had set off his smoke bombs and shot Tag. The fallout from the incident had kept her in town longer than she'd expected, as she organized and smoothed the transfer of the damaged hotel's guests to the remaining Best Westerns in town. But that had been days ago. She must have facilitated all the transfers and refunds by now.

"I'm not sure." Another relaxed sigh broke from her as she melted into him.

He ran a hand down her sleek back, around her rib cage and up her chest to cup her tit again. He gently squeezed and released, his cock hardening with each pulse of his fingers against her full, swollen flesh. Apparently, his libido didn't need feeding. At least not with food.

Phoenix, where she was based, wasn't that far from Coronado. Barely a five-and-a-half-hour drive. Or an hour by plane. It would be easy to shoot on down for a visit when he had time off. The idea was attractive. While he'd never been interested in pursuing a long-distance affair, there was something simmering between them. Something strong. Something unique.

He wanted to see where it led.

"I'm good through tomorrow. But I need to get hold of Ronnie. See what his plans are after that."

"Ronnie?" Dev kept his face blank but couldn't stop the tension from seeping into his muscles. He forced himself to relax. She was probably talking about her boss, or hell, Ronnie could be a woman. Madeline wasn't married or involved with another guy. It was the first thing he'd asked, before inviting her to dinner.

"My ex-husband."

He frowned. That was a surprise. She hadn't mentioned being divorced. But hell, he hadn't mentioned Sharon either. Except...he didn't have to check in with his ex when it came to his schedule. The less contact he had with Sharon, the better. It had been what? Five? Maybe six years since he'd talked to her?

"You and your ex are close?" He fought to keep his tone level...unconcerned. But his hand went still against her tit.

It didn't matter if Madeline and her ex remained on good terms. He didn't own the woman. No matter how much the caveman lurking within him wanted to claim otherwise. Of course she'd had a life before they'd met. Hell, it was admirable that she kept in touch with her ex.

"Pretty close," she said on a long, languid stretch, a move that made her muscles ripple and her skin shimmer and her tits jiggle.

For a moment, Dev's attention fractured, zeroing in on the way her skin glowed beneath the bright wash of light coming from the lamp on the nightstand beside them.

But all too quickly, the possessive jealousy reared up again. Along with the unpleasant realization that she kept in contact with someone who'd shared her bed...who knew the contours of her body…who'd probably seen her naked skin glowing countless times in the past.

Grimacing, he battened down the ugly green monster trying to ambush his brain with a sudden injection of the primitive beast.

"We've kept it civil for Cassidy's sake."

It was her tone that caught his attention first. The forced casualness. The caution. But then the name registered.

The implications of that name hit him hard. A vicious punch to the gut. He froze.

Fuck. Fuck. Fuck.

"Cassidy?" Let it be a dog. Let her ex be watching her dog. He could live with that. He could live with a dog.

"My daughter. Ronnie and I share custody."

Her explanation was a second jab to his gut. Only harder. Crueler.

She wasn't as old as him, maybe in her early thirties. Which meant this daughter of hers couldn't be that old either. The realization lit a fire in his chest. Like he'd been hit with an RPG.

His cock wilted. He rolled away from her, onto his back, and stared at the shadowy ceiling with burning eyes.

A daughter. She had a daughter.

He dragged his arm out from beneath her back and laid it across his eyes, trying to lock the memories down…but one squeezed through.

"One more time, Daddy!" Shrieks of childish laughter climbed the air. The flash of raven black hair. A Christmas tree twinkling in the corner of the living room. Sparkling eyes of such a deep, dark brown they often looked black locked on his face. Chubby white arms wrapped around his neck. The scent of baby powder...and pine sap.

He shut the memory down. But not fast enough to prevent the bolt of agony…of raw, burning loss.

"Are you okay?" Madeline asked, concern in her voice.

The hand she settled on his chest burned. Only not in a good way. Not with erotic fire. But with corrosive, acidic grief.

His lungs felt seared, like each breath was coming through a vat of flames.

More memories crowded the edges of his mind. He grimly forced them back. Sealed off the crevices. Fortified the cracks.

Fuck. I have to get out of here.

He didn't say anything because there wasn't anything to say. Instead, he rolled away from her, swung his legs off the mattress and stood. She watched him dress in silence. But he could feel her eyes on him. Feel her questions throbbing in the charged air.

It wasn't until he grabbed his boots and headed for the bedroom door that she spoke. "That's it? You're going to walk out without a word?"

Her voice was sharp. Full of disgust and disbelief. Hell, he couldn't blame her. Two nights of sex followed by a silent bailing was not cool. It was a dick move. He knew that.

But he couldn't stay here, not one second more. Not with the memories threatening to break through the walls and drown him. Not when she was off limits now.

He paused with his back to her, not wanting to see the disgust in her eyes. Not wanting that memory to haunt him, along with all the others. For a while she'd held the nightmares at bay. Now the memory of her would just add to his nightly cargo. Which made him want to pound something, slam his fists against the wall until they were bloody and broken. Until the physical pain superseded the mental and brought him some relief.

If not relief, at least peace. At least for a while.

But he owed her something. A hint of explanation.

"I don't do kids." His voice was flat…cold…empty, the words echoing through the yawning pit inside him.

"You don't even know her, you ass." She didn't sound pleading. More like pissed. Utterly furious. "She's a great kid."

He didn't doubt that. But it didn't matter.

Without looking back, he walked away.

He didn't do kids. Not even great ones. Not anymore.

* * *

Every inch of Madeline Roux felt scorched, liked she'd been dragged behind a car for miles and the road rash had shredded her skin and burned right down to her internal organs.

"What did this new PI say?" her sister Marguerite asked. Her brown eyes, which were the exact same shade and shape as Maddie's own, were stormy with worry and helplessness. "Are they going to take the case? Will they go in and get Cass out?"

"They're a security firm. But yes, they will." Her fingers trembling, Madeline lowered her cell phone, carefully setting it on the motel's wobbly table, afraid that the slightest sound it made as it settled against the wood might shatter her. "As soon as I come up with the thirty-five grand they require for a retainer."

Which was way out of her reach. She'd never be able to scrounge up thirty-five thousand dollars. Just coming up with the five grand retainer for the initial private investigator had pretty much bankrupted her.

Margie groaned, shifting from foot to foot. The worry lines on her forehead dug in deeper. Madeline knew her own anxiety was etched into her face as well. Looking at her sister was like looking into a mirror. Stress furrows and everything.

"I'll give you what I have, Mads. But it's only a couple thousand. I used most of my savings for the down payment on my condo," Margie said, her eyes darkening to black.

"Thanks," Maddie managed. She crossed her arms, clasped her elbows, and hugged herself, trying to stave off the quaking.

She was so cold. Icy cold. Which had more to do with fear than any chill in their motel room. The temperature in Belgrade, Montana had hovered around seventy-five since their arrival. But she'd been feeling cold and desperate for weeks now. Three weeks to be exact. Ever since she'd realized Ronnie and Cass had disappeared.

"Why can't your PI go in and get her? He only asked for five thousand. Which is a lot cheaper than this other place you called," Margie said. "If he wanted another five, we could probably come up with that between the two of us. Maybe he even has some of the money you gave him left over, so it won't be as much this time."

Maddie shook her head. "Niko said he used up the entire retainer finding them."

When the last word came out mangled and choppy, she swallowed, trying to ease the tight dryness in her throat. It had taken Niko Aubrey ten days to track Ronnie and Cass down. Plus another four days working with the local sheriff's department to get inside the cult. But still, five thousand dollars in two weeks? Was that normal? Or was he scamming her.

"Okay...but why can't he go in? If we gave him another couple grand—"

"He said I needed a specialist," Maddie broke in, her voice stiff. "He said he doesn't do cults, particularly dangerous ones."

Releasing her elbows, she stared down at her phone, trying to think. The cops had been of no use. She'd gone to the Phoenix police three weeks ago when she'd returned from Dark Falls to find that Ronnie had disappeared with Cassidy. After a week of no progress, she'd hired Niko Aubrey, a private investigator out of Phoenix, who'd tracked her ex and daughter to Belgrade, Montana. Although technically the Children of the Second Cycle weren't located in town. Their compound sat between Belgrade and Three Forks.

"Maybe this private investigator is wrong." Margie paced to the room's tiny kitchenette and back. "The cops didn't find any sign of them when they searched the property, right?" She drew up in front of Maddie and stood there, tension radiating from her.

"Nico is sure they're there. He has photos of them with other members. He said they were probably hidden when the sheriff's department went through."

"Well they should go through again." Margie's voice picked up heat.

Which was exactly what Maddie had said when she'd talked to the private investigator earlier that morning.

"They declined." Maddie twitched, her muscles tense and jumpy. "The State Patrol say they won't get involved since the sheriff is already investigating and the local FBI office isn't returning my calls. And the local cops are out. Apparently the property the cult inhabits is outside city limits, so it isn't within the Belgrade Police Department's jurisdiction. "The only shot I have of getting Cassidy back is hiring this security firm Detective Aubrey recommended."

Which meant she needed thirty-five thousand dollars.

Which she didn't have.

A flash of panic heated her, chasing aside the cold. For a moment anyway. When the heat vanished and the chill roared back in, she was colder than ever.

"Can you take out a second mortgage on your house? I can't on my condo—not enough equity yet," Margie said, her thoughts apparently racing in the same direction Maddie's were. How to get that thirty-five thousand. Not a surprise. They often mirrored each other's thoughts. Sharing a womb had given them a special bond. Although not as special as other twins shared. They couldn't hear each other's thoughts or feel each other's pain. But they did have similar thought patterns and tastes in things.

"The bank said they can't help me." Maddie's voice was grim. She grimaced and forced the confession out. "Ronnie and I took out a second mortgage on the house before we split. That's how we got the money to buy the repair shop."

A look of disgust clamped over Margie's face. "Oh hell. And you're still paying that off, aren't you, since you took over the debt on the house when you divorced?" Margie spun around, stalking to the far bed and back. "If that isn't just like him. Force a massive bill on you, and then lose interest and walk away, leaving you holding the bag."

The disgusted rage on her twin's face was exactly why she hadn't told Margie about the second mortgage at the time. Her sister had never liked Ronnie. She'd even tried to talk Maddie out of marrying him. Margie had called him shifty, and spineless and irresponsible. Which wasn't far from the truth. Being married to Ronnie had often felt like raising another child. But she didn't regret the years she'd spent with him. He'd given her Cassidy. And her daughter was worth every ounce of frustration associated with her ex.

The whole second mortgage fiasco had been her idea anyway. A last-ditch effort to force Ronnie to grow up. If he owned his own shop...was his own boss, like he was constantly dreaming about...maybe he'd settle in and work to keep it. Maybe he wouldn't keep job hopping as soon as he got bored.

He was a good mechanic. One of the best around. He could have made something of himself.

It hadn't worked, of course. You couldn't force Peter Pan to grow up. Rather than settling in and buckling down, he'd stopped paying bills and working on cars and bringing in clients. After a couple of months, the shop had been closed more than it was open as Ronnie jumped from one distraction to another. Within six months it had been closed for good.

It wasn't that Ronnie was a bad guy. He didn't do drugs or alcohol. He wasn't cruel. He didn't have a temper or play games. And there was no question he loved his daughter. While he might be periodically late with his child support payments, he always caught back up when he got a new job. He went all out for her birthdays and Christmas. Showed her every second they were together how important she was to him. And while he might be irresponsible when it came to his own life and career and wellbeing, he'd *never* been irresponsible with Cassidy. When she was with him, he made sure she ate right, that she went to bed on time, that she did her homework.

In the seven years he'd been a father, he'd never given her cause for concern. Hell, up until three weeks ago, it hadn't even occurred to her that their dual custody was something to worry about.

"What are we going to do, Mads?" Margie asked, a distinct catch to the question.

Madeline poked aside the plaid curtain covering the window next to the table and stared out the glass at the acres of knee-high grass drying in the field across from their window. A plan slowly took shape. When everything else was impossible, then you went with the only option left on the table.

She didn't have the money to pay anyone to get Cass out.

But she couldn't leave Cassidy in there, either. Not if what the private investigator had told her was true.

"I'm going to join The Second Cycle." She tested the plan out loud, ignoring her sister's scoffing laugh.

When Madeline didn't join in with the laughter, Margie's voice stopped mid chortle. "You can't be serious!"

Maddie turned to face her. "What other choice do I have? I

don't have access to thirty-five grand. Neither do you. But if they'll take me in and I find Cass, I can bring her back out."

"Didn't Detective Aubrey say the cult was dangerous? There must be a reason that security company you talked to charges thirty-five thousand to bring her out. There must be a reason why it's so expensive. Try something else first. Hell, go to your boss. He probably has the money."

Oh, he did. But he wouldn't loan it to her. She'd already known that, but she'd contacted him anyway. He'd summarily dismissed her request. He was still pissed she'd gone to HR when he wouldn't stop touching her. That last time he'd squeezed her butt as he walked past had been the final straw. And while HR hadn't done much in censoring him, at least he'd stopped hitting on her and started treating her with chilly distain.

"He's not going to give me the money, Marge. I already asked him," Madeline said, exhaustion crashing down over her. She hadn't realized how alone she really was until the last three weeks. Oh, she had Margie, for sure, but her sister wasn't any more capable of handling this situation than Madeline was.

"Fine. If your boss is out, what about that guy you met in Dark Falls? You said he was a SEAL, right? SEALs are trained for situations like this. Rescuing someone from a cult would be right up his alley. If he won't do the job himself, maybe he knows someone who will. Someone who won't charge thirty-five grand. Maybe they'd even do it pro-bono."

Wouldn't that be nice.

"I already tried that. He never called back," Maddie admitted with a flinch.

She drew a shaky breath and ran tense fingers through her hair. Even though the thought of asking him for help made her stomach churn, she'd done it for Cass. She'd done it for her daughter. She'd called twice. Left messages both times. And he'd ignored her cry for help.

What a good judge of character she was. She'd thought there was something special happening between them. That what they were sharing was unique.

While he'd been looking for a weekend fling. A round of sex

while he was in town.

"I don't do kids."

The memory of his cold, flat explanation still scraped beneath her skin. A combination of hurt and rage heated her face. He'd rolled away from her and walked out the instant Cassidy's name hit the air. A guy like that? He wouldn't put himself out for some kid he didn't even know. He'd made it clear when he walked away that he wasn't interested in her.

He'd made it even clearer when he'd refused her call for help.

"Then what are we going to do? You can't be seriously considering joining this cult, Maddie! There has to be another option!"

"Is there?" Maddie asked. "I'd love to hear it."

She waited. And waited some more.

Finally, Margie stirred. "What if we start a GoFundMe? Ask the public for help."

Madeline groaned beneath her breath. She hadn't planned to worry Margie with the rest of this. But her sister needed to understand the gravity of the situation, and why she needed to get Cass out now. Not later. Not after the money dripped in through a charity campaign.

"I can't wait for that, Margie." She paused and forced the rest out. "Niko said the cult leader is a suspected pedophile. And he's choosing his victims among the cult's children. The police have tried to shut him down, they've brought charges against him multiple times before, but they've never had strong enough evidence to make anything stick. I can't leave Cass in there. Not if there is even the slightest chance…"

"Oh God." Margie's hands flew up to her mouth and her eyes pooled with tears.

Madeline knew exactly what her sister was feeling. She'd had the exact same reaction on hearing the news. But that initial shock and horror had hardened into resolve. Into pure determination. She was going to get Cass out of there. And since no one had stepped up to help her, she'd do it on her own.

She was resourceful. She was smart.

She'd work her way into the cult and rescue Cassidy. She just had to be careful and clever about it.

CHAPTER 2

The sudden sound of raised voices outside his office snapped Devlin's head up from the incident reports stacked on the precision-shined mahogany desk in front of him. Raised voices in HQ1's inner sanctum was an abnormality. The men under his command had better control than that. The fact that one of the voices was his administrative assistant's was even more of an anomaly—he'd never heard Anderson so *loud* before. But of even more interest was the other voice. It was female. There weren't many women associated with HQ1—well, other than the CIA analysts—but hell, those women were even more buttoned down than his men. There would be no raised voices coming from that quarter.

"I told you," the woman's voice climbed, "I'm here to see Lieutenant Commander Russo. He's expecting me."

He was? Dev's eyebrows arched. That was news to him. There was no meeting on his docket for this morning.

"If the Lieutenant Commander was expecting you, I would be aware of it."

Anderson's voice flattened. Apparently this supposed meeting was news to his formidable assistant too.

And Anderson would know. Hell, he handled Dev's schedule. Not that the woman trying to storm his fortress backed down in the slightest. He'd give her credit for that. He'd seen badass spec-ops warriors crumble beneath Anderson's icy demeanor.

It wasn't just the man's attitude; it was the bubble wrap of scarring that tracked down the left side of Anderson's face and neck. The scars were damn gnarly and intimidating. So was the prosthetic arm that started at his left elbow and ended in three steel prongs. That missing arm was clearly visible since Anderson was dressed in his short-sleeved summer BDU's. His prosthetic left leg was less visible, hidden as it was beneath his pants. Still—when faced with Anderson's face and arm, followed by his icy demeanor, most people backed off fast.

Not so this woman. Hell no—she battened down.

"Trust me. He'll see me." The woman's voice turned breezy, carrying a don't-you-worry-your-pretty-head-about-it tone that was sure to set a match to Anderson's temper. The man hated being patronized.

Dev frowned, tilting his head slightly. There was something familiar about that husky female voice, although he couldn't pinpoint where he'd heard it.

"I'll just mosey on in there and let him know I'm here. You can go back to doing whatever—" Her voice stuttered to a stop. When it cranked back up, it had lost its airy dismissiveness and dropped several octaves into pissed. "Take your hand off me right *now*. You don't have permission to touch me."

"And you don't have permission to be here. How did you get on base?" Ice invaded the flatness in Anderson's tone.

"None of your business," the woman snapped, completely unintimidated. "And trust me. Your boss is going to want to hear what I have to say."

"If you're on base illegally, it *is* my business. The MAs will make it their business as well."

Which was true. The Master-at-Arms—or naval police—didn't fuck around with trespassers on the base.

"Try...like really hard... to pull that stick out of your butt so you can hear what I'm saying," the woman said in a suddenly quiet voice. "I need to see Devlin Russo. It's a matter of life and death."

Which sounded pretty damn dramatic, except...Dev

frowned. The woman's voice was completely void of drama and deadly serious. And even more familiar.

Who the hell was she?

Curious, he pushed back his desk chair and rose to his feet. By the time he'd skirted the edge of the desk and stepped into the middle of his office, the quick fall of footsteps sounded behind and to the right of the open doorway.

"God damn it." Anderson's voice climbed explosively.

The woman must have darted around him. His administrative assistant wasn't as agile since that RPG had taken out his Jeep and limbs back in Afghanistan. But circumventing him wouldn't earn her any favors.

"Swearing," the woman offered with a voice full of snark, "is the sign of someone with weak intelligence."

Dev shook his head, amusement rising as he headed for the door. If that was the case, then every operator he worked with was a fucking moron.

He reached the doorway at the same time as his unexpected visitor. His first sight of her stopped him in his tracks and then rocked him back on his heels. Thick, shiny, brown-black hair hit her shoulders. Deep brown eyes. An oval face. Full lips. Perfect little ears that played peekaboo through the shiny waterfall of hair. A petite, voluptuous frame.

Instinctively, his gaze skimmed down her fitted lace blouse to her dark gray slacks, and finally dropped to her feet, looking for sparkling, crystal studded sneakers. Plain white ones met his gaze instead. This woman might look like Madeline from the top of her dark, glossy head, to the soles of her plain white sneakers, but looks were definitely deceiving.

This woman was not Madeline.

How he knew that, he wasn't sure. Maybe because of his complete lack of response to her. No fire. No hunger. No craving. No possessiveness. Nothing. She looked identical to the woman he'd walked away from two months ago, but she left him cold. Which meant she wasn't Madeline.

She couldn't be.

"Who are you?" His voice came out flatter and more suspicious than he'd intended.

His tone didn't alter the stranger's forward motion. Although she wasn't quite a stranger now, was she? Not with that face and those eyes. Hell, even her voice had been recognizable. That's why it had sounded familiar. There was a difference in tone—Madeline's was slightly throatier—but there was enough similarity to tickle his memory.

Her eyes flared and lightened at his question—more cinnamon than dark chocolate now. She was pissed. He could see it in the press of her lips and the lines digging into the corners of her mouth.

Did Madeline's eyes take on that golden flare when she was furious? Had they turned to cinnamon the night he walked out on her?

"You don't recognize me?" she snapped at him, absolute loathing in her voice. "After spending a whole damn weekend—"

Dev raised his eyebrows. "You're not Madeline."

His comment shut the tirade off in mid-stream. She was obviously related. Probably a twin. Not that Madeline had mentioned a twin in the two nights they'd spent together. But then, she hadn't mentioned a kid either. Not during that first night, anyway. Who knew what secrets she would have spilled if he hadn't split.

"You know I'm not Mads?" This time, the rounding of her eyes carried surprise rather than fury. "Wow. That's a first. Most guys can't tell us apart."

"You're twins?"

"Yeah. Identical." She stepped into the room, her gaze scanning the office before landing on a framed photo of the USS Gerald R. Ford, the navy's newest and largest aircraft carrier.

"I've reported the situation to the MAs, sir," Anderson said tightly from the doorway, his gaze locked on their surprise visitor with frustrated suspicion.

"Call them back and cancel the report." Dead silence greeted his order. He glanced up, catching the resistance in his assistant's gaze. "I'll find out how she got on base." It went without saying it wouldn't happen again. When Anderson didn't budge from his spot in the middle of the door, Devlin hardened his voice. "You're dismissed. Close the door."

Looking like he'd swallowed a shit sandwich, his secretary stepped back and closed the door with excruciating care. Anderson hated losing control of a situation, no doubt because of losing so much back in Afghanistan. He clung to control now, like a drunk afraid one sip would send him on a three-day bender. The fact this woman had outmaneuvered him wouldn't be forgotten or forgiven.

Normally, he would have backed Anderson's call. It had been the right one, after all.

But Madeline's twin had claimed her visit was a matter of life and death. And Madeline wasn't with her. Nor could he imagine the woman who'd haunted him since driving away from Dark Falls condoning her sister tracking him down. She had too much pride for that. She wouldn't seek out someone who'd made it crystal clear they had no interest in her sans sex. Giving her his back, as he walked out the door, and then ignoring her phone calls, would have told her exactly that.

So, what the hell was going on? Why was Madeline's twin here? And whose life was in danger? From the tightness restricting his lungs and the hard thump of his heart, he was afraid he knew the answer to that last question.

Fuck. He had a bad feeling that he should have listened to Madeline's messages instead of deleting them unheard.

"You want to fill me in on what's going on?"

His surprise visitor spun around to face him. "Mads needs your help."

She didn't dither around, thank Christ. "Why?"

"You know about Cassidy, right?" From the disgusted look that darkened her eyes, she knew he'd walked out after hearing about the kid. "After returning home from that weekend in Dark Falls, she found Ronnie and Cassidy gone."

Dev frowned. If her ex had bailed with the kid after that weekend, then they'd been gone for six weeks—give or take. "She went to the police?"

"Of course," the twin said with a snap. "They were useless. So she hired a PI. The guy tracked them to Belgrade, Montana and a cult called The Children of the Second Cycle. Ronnie—" her lip curled in derision, "—joined a cult." She paused to scowl. "And took Cassidy in with him."

Devlin tipped his head to the side, studying this woman who looked so much like the woman he'd spent the past two months fantasizing about. Nights full of erotic dreams. Mornings sporting fucking wood and fisting off in the shower.

He forced his mind back on the situation. "The PI didn't get them out?"

With a frustrated sigh, his visitor ran long, slender fingers through her dark hair. "The cult members claimed they weren't there. That they'd stayed for a few days—long enough for the PI to snap his pictures—then took off. The PI convinced the sheriff's department to go in and look for them, but when they walked through, they didn't find them. Maddie's private investigator was certain they were there, hiding when the deputies went through. But the sheriff's department refused to do another surprise drop in."

"What's the PI's name?"

"Niko Aubrey, from Aubrey Investigations out of Phoenix." She waited, studying him, as though she were expecting him to say something. When he remained silent, she continued. "When the sheriff's department was a bust, Niko told her she needed a cult specialist and referred her to a firm out of California. But they wanted thirty-five grand up front, just for starters. When we couldn't come up with the money and Niko refused to go in and get Cass out, Maddie decided to..." She trailed off, fear shining in her eyes.

"Fuck." Dev went rigid. "Tell me she did *not* go in there to rescue her kid."

The fear tightening the twin's face, along with her tense silence, were clear indications that the damn woman had indeed done just that.

"Jesus Christ. I thought she had better sense than that." Turning on his heel, he stalked around his desk.

"We're talking about Cassidy," the twin snapped defensively. "Maddie would do anything for that kid. No way is she gonna sit back and let Cass disappear into a cult, especially not when the leader is a suspected pedophile. She didn't have a choice. There were no alternatives."

"Bullshit. There are always options."

"Really?" The twin's shoulders pulled forward as she sneered, her face twisting in derision. "Like calling you for help? Which she did—twice. She asked for help from multiple people but surprise—no one stepped up, including you. So she tackled the problem herself."

Devlin flinched, his scalp tightening beneath a wave of shame. The sister was right. He had a hell of a lot to answer for. He should have taken Madeline's calls—or at least listened to her messages. Instead, he'd taken the easy way out…the cowardly way out…and hit delete.

He should have known she wouldn't have called him for a weekend redo. He should have known she'd have too much pride for that. But then, he hadn't been thinking rationally. At least not when it came to Madeline.

Fuck…he couldn't stop thinking about her and how good the sex had been between them.

He'd been afraid that if he heard her voice, if she asked to see him again, his cock would wrest control from his brain and he'd have hot-footed it down to her for another weekend of multiple orgasms.

But then what? He couldn't be trusted with her kid. Nor would she bounce the kid whenever he was in town—he'd known that instinctively.

And he'd been right. A woman who would join a cult to get her daughter back wasn't going to drop the kid just because the opportunity for sex arose.

Sure, they might have managed a short-term sexual relationship when the kid was off with Dad. But eventually things would get complicated. They always did. And there was no long-term gain here. Just a quick path to obsession.

The signs were already there that Madeline was a fixation waiting to happen. If that weekend had taught him anything, it had taught him that. There Tag was, in the hospital…and Mitch's arms dealing associates were alive and kicking and still dealing their stolen military weaponry…and what had he been thinking about? Yeah, getting it on with Madeline. She had all the makings of an obsession.

And he didn't do obsessions any more than he did kids.

Even so…he'd handled that badly. He shouldn't have ghosted her and forced her into rash decisions. Grimacing, he punched the intercom button on his desk phone.

Not much he could do about his previous asshole choices, except get her out of the mess she was in now.

"Yes, Lieutenant Commander Russo?" The rigid formality in Anderson's voice was a clear indication the man hadn't forgiven him for siding with their trespasser.

Tough fucking shit. There was more at stake than his assistant's pride.

"Get Nico Aubrey of Aubrey Investigations out of Phoenix online," Devlin ordered curtly. "When did she go in to get the kid?" He remained standing behind the desk while he waited for the call to patch through.

"Almost three weeks ago." For the first time, the sister's voice cracked, and Devlin caught the ragged edge of fear. "It was supposed to take a week. Two, tops."

Son of a bitch.

Three weeks?

"Have you heard anything from her since she went in?"

The twin shook her head, her shoulder length hair swaying. "The police won't do anything. They said the cult property is outside the city limits, which puts it in the sheriff's department's jurisdiction. So I went to the sheriff. A couple deputies knocked on their door, looked around. When they couldn't find her, they gave up."

Frustration joined the fear in her voice.

Devlin frowned. The locals hadn't done more than a simple walk through? Even after receiving multiple reports of missing people associated with the cult? Normally, law enforcement was suspicious as hell about cults and cult members. They tended to harass rather than hang back. With three people missing after visiting the place, the locals should have been swarming over the compound.

Fuck, something was off. Way off. It damn well reeked.

Could the locals have been bought?

"Nico Aubrey is online." Anderson's quiet voice came over the intercom. That icy formality was gone. He must have picked up on the grim undercurrents emanating from the room.

Devlin snatched up the receiver to his landline.

"Nico Aubrey?" He barely waited for the confirmation on the other end of the line. "This is Lieutenant Commander Devlin Russo from HQ1, out of Coronado." Tossing his rank around often jumpstarted intel. "I need to know everything about the case you're running for Madeline Roux regarding her missing daughter."

Surprised silence traveled down the line before the man coughed. "Mr. Russo. I'm afraid I can't go into the details of the case. Client confidentiality you know—"

"Lieutenant Commander Russo," Dev broke in, dropping the temperature in his voice to arctic. "I'm well aware of client confidentiality. Are you aware your *client* is missing?"

"Missing?" The smooth voice fractured.

"Yes. Missing." Dev's voice turned deadly. "When you refused to help get her kid out, she went in to retrieve her daughter herself. Nobody has heard from her since."

Or at least the sister hadn't.

Dead silence engulfed the line. Then— "That's unfortunate. I advised against that."

No shit, Sherlock. Of course, he fucking had. "I'm taking over. I need everything you have on the case. The pictures you took, the intel you gathered—everything."

More silence. "I need client authorization for that."

"Your client," Devlin laid the derision on thick, "is missing."

You mother fucker.

"I understand that, but—"

"I have Madeline's sister here. She'll give the permission." The bastard was covering his ass. He didn't give a shit about Madeline.

"The sister is *not* my client. You need to understand—"

"Oh, I understand," Devlin drawled, "and I'll make sure that your agency's recommendations, reviews, as well as my testimony to the licensing board will reflect just how *accommodating* you've been."

No question the bastard picked up on the subtext. Dev hung up as protests and excuses rolled down the line.

Fucking asshole.

He punched the intercom button hard enough to send shards of pain into his knuckle. "Get Tex on the line."

It was barely ten hundred hours here, which put it thirteen hundred hours in Pennsylvania. Hopefully, Tex wasn't sitting down to lunch with Melody and his girls. Although...it was September and a weekday. Hope would be at school and Akilah at college...if she was going to college. Fuck, it had been ages since he and Tex had played catch up.

A wraith of a face pushed into his mind. He slammed the door on it. Locked it down tight. The memories always tried to wrap their tentacles around him when he thought of Tex and his girls, particularly Hope.

He grimaced. Tried to rub the burn from his chest.

Focus, damn it...focus.

He should have hit Tex up first. The guy was a fucking genius with computers. When his buddy had taken that IED hit and lost the lower half of his leg, Dev had worried. Some guys couldn't transition off the teams, even if they retired whole. And Tex—hell, the guy had been a first-tier operator. With killer instincts. One of the best warriors Dev had worked with. To lose his spot in the beach boat, along with most of his leg and his fucking mobility...to see the pity in people's eyes... Yeah, that shit would burn, eat most operators alive. But not Tex. Fuck no. His buddy had squared his shoulders, strapped on his boots, and got down to business. He'd traded his ballistics vest for a computer. He'd started gathering intel. Forging connections. Making himself indispensable to fucking everyone. All these years later, those killer instincts were stronger than ever and saving lives with the intel he provided. Which meant he was overrun with requests for help.

Thank Christ Tex was also loyal as fuck and would pull Dev's request to the top of his queue.

If anyone could get the down and dirty on this cult Madeline was tangled up with, it would be John—Tex—Keegan.

"Tex is on line one." Anderson's voice came over the intercom.

Devlin snatched up the phone. "Yo, buddy, thanks for taking—"

"Don't fucking go there, Hoss." Tex's southern drawl thickened with each word, which meant he was amused or annoyed. Devlin guessed the thickening was due to annoyance this time. "Your call's always good. What's up?"

Dev coughed the grit from his voice. At one time, way back, before Tex had taken the IED hit and limped away from the teams, they'd been beer and barbeque buddies. Hell, even after Tex had left California for Norfolk, married Melody, and then moved to Pennsylvania, they'd stayed in touch.

It wasn't until Gracie…fuck…until seven years ago that the calls had gotten sporadic…the visits non-existent.

Hearing about Tex's girls…watching them grow…that shit burned…was pure acid.

Of course, Tex knew why the calls had stopped, why the visits had ceased. He didn't hold it against Dev. Hell, he'd stopped by a couple of times when he'd been out west visiting Wolf and Caroline, or Abe and Alabama, but Dev had made sure to be *busy*. The whole goddam lot of them had kids now…and yeah, he didn't do kids.

Not even his buddies'.

"Hoss? You still there?" Tex's southern drawl crawled down the line.

"Yeah. I need a favor."

Tex was the only one who called him Hoss these days. Most of the guys on the teams had never even heard his old moniker. With Tag and Tram gone now, that old nickname was sure to wither and die. Not that either one of them had used it in years.

Just as well. Hoss belonged to a different man…a different life.

"You got it." Tex didn't bother with questions.

That was team bonds for you. Alive and well after years of atrophy.

"I need everything you can find on a cult called The Children of the Second Cycle. I need you to crawl so far up their ass you'll know what time they shit in the mornings. Nothing is off limits."

"On it," Tex's southern drawl smoothed. "Priority?"

Devlin paused. His overwhelming instinct was to classify the request as high. Priority one. Get to Madeline and her kid and get them out as fast as possible. But he couldn't. Not when Tex was constantly called on to extricate one team or another from one clusterfuck or another. Team intel came first. Tex's work saved lives. Hell, half the teams that Tex ran intel for were outside of JSOC, but they were all fighting evil, protecting those unable to protect themselves.

They had the priority.

He wasn't even sure Madeline was in danger, or that she needed protecting. Although every fucking instinct inside him screamed that he needed to find her, get her out fast.

"Secondary." He forced the word out his tight throat. Christ, he wanted to set the priority to high. Get the ball rolling. But in good faith, he couldn't. "It's personal. If you can't take it, pass it on to one of your hacker friends. I need the intel fast, but not at the expense of your other…" he glanced at his visitor, "clients."

Tex barked out a laugh. "I got time. The world is surprisingly chill at the moment. Won't last long so I'll dig into this before shit starts raining down." He paused. "Personal? As in Sharon?"

"No." Devlin scowled at the hope in his buddy's voice. But there was no going back there. No patching up what had been shredded and bloodied. Too much pain and blame for that. Too many recriminations.

His marriage had ended long before the divorce.

Still, Tex deserved to know who he was helping.

"It's for a friend. Her ex took her kid and disappeared into this cult. Madeline went in to get her kid out. Nobody's heard from her since. No sign of her or her daughter when the locals walked through." He hesitated, glanced at Madeline's twin who was listening to his half of the conversation with narrow eyes. "Something is off about the locals' response. We're talking three people who just up and disappeared after coming in contact with this cult. The locals should have been all over this case. Instead...nada. Check into them while you're at it."

"Will do." The lack of inflection in Tex's voice was a sure sign he was reading more into the request than Dev intended. "This Madeline, is she—"

"No," Dev interrupted flatly. "She's just someone I know. Her sister came to me for help."

"Damn." The disappointment in Tex's voice weighed down his drawl. "I'd hoped—" He broke off, and Dev could almost hear the shrug. "Digging into this now." His southern accent was back. "Shouldn't take too long."

And with that he was gone. Dev listened to the dial tone for a moment, before lowering the receiver. The sister, when he turned to her, was almost vibrating with tension.

"Who was that?"

"The man who's going to help me extricate your sister and niece," Dev said calmly.

"So, you're going to help. You'll get Maddie and Cass out?"

She hadn't mentioned Madeline's ex. Apparently the sister didn't care if he made it out or not. Devlin studied her, easily reading the fear and doubt on her face.

"I'll get them out. What's your name?"

"Marguerite..." she hesitated, frowned, finally shrugged, "but everyone calls me Margie."

Was the offer of her nickname her way of inviting him to be friends? If so, too damn bad. They would never be friends. He wouldn't be around long enough for that.

"I'm going to get Madeline and Cassidy out," he assured her, forcing the kid's name off his unwilling tongue. "You can trust me on that."

And once they were free, he'd walk away.

Again.

She could trust him on that too.

CHAPTER 3

Tex's timeframe of "Shouldn't take long" was off by hours. Six hours after hanging up the phone, Dev was jumpy as hell and ready to crawl out of his skin. He'd tried Tex's number again, multiple times, but his buddy hadn't picked up. With the guy's hacker skills and contacts, he should have chased down the intel Dev needed by now. Since he hadn't called back, he'd either gotten another assignment, or what he was finding was bad…FUBAR bad.

Thank Christ he'd sent Marguerite back to her motel. Already freaked by the situation her sister and niece were in, the woman didn't need to watch him tying himself into knots too.

When his phone finally rang and Keegan lit up the caller ID window, he snatched the receiver up before Anderson had a chance to answer it.

Finally. "What did you find?"

"Brace yourself, brother." Tex's voice was grim. "This shit is fucked."

Of course it is.

Devlin grimaced. There must be a reason Nico Aubrey had refused to infiltrate the cult, and the security firm out of California had quoted Madeline thirty-five thousand to get the kid out.

"Give it to me." Dev tensed and waited.

"For starters, The Children of the Second Cycle is what's known as a Doomsday or Apocalyptic cult. The leader goes by Apostolos, which is Greek for Messenger."

"Let me guess." Devlin rolled his eyes. "He's a messenger from God."

"That would be correct. He claims to have the gift of prophecy. And he's prophesizing the imminent end of the world."

"Don't they all?" Dev asked dryly.

"Apostolos—whose real name by the way is Stanley Gibbens —preaches that his followers have been chosen by God to repopulate the world after the earth has been *cleansed* of humanity. And that his descendants will rule what's left of humankind. He's called the Divine Ruler by his people."

Yeah…delusions of grandeur much? But then something Tex said niggled at him.

"Cleansed? How?" Devlin narrowed his eyes, a cold draft feathering his spine. Something about that term set his radar on high alert.

"By a reign of fire and blood. But we'll get to that."

Tex's voice tightened, and for the first time Devlin realized his Southern drawl was missing, which was a sure sign the guy was tweaked.

"This asshole further preaches that since his disciples are tasked with repopulating earth, that his female member's divine obligation is to reproduce, and it doesn't matter with whom. Word is the women are required to… accept… whoever requests them, *whenever* they are requested. Which makes this cult an incel haven and one of the reasons his male followers are so loyal. He recruits these assholes through incel chat rooms and forums and pitches the cult as their wet dreams come true. A harem of women available at their whim, with no fear of possible rejection."

Devlin froze, his blood pressure spiking at the thought of Madeline being pimped out to this asshole's disciples.

Like fucking hell…

"Apostolos, though. He doesn't partake of the cult women. No, he uses his female followers to keep his incel army loyal. But when it comes to the Divine Ruler, God has purportedly told him that his *wives* must be pure. Chaste. That they must cleave only to him. He claims that it is through his seed and his wives' purity that civilization will be reborn, with his descendants, of course, in control."

The cold contempt in Tex's voice told Dev clear as day that there was more to the cult leader's proclamations. A lot more.

"As for Apostolos's brides, and yeah, that would be plural, they are young. Like pedophile young."

"Jesus." Devlin scowled. Marguerite had mentioned something about a pedophile too. He flinched. Christ...no wonder Madeline had rushed in to get the kid out. "How young?"

Marguerite had said her niece was seven.

"The youngest mentioned was ten." Tex's tone had darkened. Resonated with disgust and fury.

No surprise there, Tex had two daughters.

"The feds say he targets incels, runaways, and vulnerable women with children. Once a prospective member enters the cult, they don't leave. The only person who successfully fled the cult disappeared immediately after going to the police.

"Only one? Is that normal?"

"Hell no." Tex's explosive response rolled down the line. "The feds think he's killing anyone who makes waves and tries to get out. After that one escapee, he locked the place down tighter than Knox."

Devlin's scalp tightened, his gut clenching. Why in the motherfucking hell would Madeline's ex take their kid in there? Was the guy fucking deranged?

"Why haven't the feds shut this guy down?"

"They've tried. But they haven't been able to make any charges stick. This guy's Teflon. Everything slides off. And they don't have any actual evidence tying him to anything, just the ramblings of an ex-member who up and disappeared soon after. Whenever the feds raid the place, there are no children present, even though several of the members are known to have kids. All the feds have found are a bunch of brainwashed men and women."

Which matched what Marguerite had told him. Madeline's

daughter hadn't been on site when the sheriff's department did their walk through.

"It doesn't help that the bastard moves his people around. A lot. A dozen times in the last five years. Before they arrived in Montana, they were in South Dakota. Before that, Oregon. Every time the feds get a lock on them, Apostolos pulls up stakes and they move on. They survive by offering internet-based services. Graphic design, mostly. Which means all they need is an internet connection and they're in business." He paused, the derision heavy in his voice. "Apparently these incel bastards are quite computer savvy"

Devlin ignored that last comment. "But the feds are onto him?"

"Yeah." Tex hesitated, and a cautious tone entered his voice. "This is for your ears only, but my contact at the FBI says they have a man inside. He's been deep cover for a couple of months, and he's reported that the compound has a military grade arsenal. Everything from APC9K submachines to RPGs."

"How the fuck did they get their hands on those?" Devlin's voice rose in shock. "Christ, why would they even need that kind of fire power?"

"Yeah, about that." Tex's voice wavered, as though he'd turned away from the phone. When it came back, it was tighter than ever. "Remember the fucker's prophecy of blood and fire? Apparently when the apocalypse comes, it's going to get ugly. Like neighbor against neighbor ugly. People killing each other for food, supplies, whatever. He claims they'll need the arsenal to survive. However, he has also warned his incel army that they may be required to initiate the cleansing. And if the bastard targeted the right chat rooms and forums, he'd have found plenty of men from that particular subculture who would be thrilled with the prospect of killing everyone they can get their rifle scope on. Most of the incel communities are misogynistic, encourage violence, hold extreme views, and radicalize their members. My contact at the FBI says that multiple mass shootings have been carried out by men with incel ties. The feds consider the sub-culture a terrorist threat."

Fuck...fuck...fuck...

Devlin massaged his suddenly pounding temples. "Motherfucking hell. This has the elements of another Waco."

"No shit. And it sounds like the FBI plant has collected enough evidence to make a raid imminent," Tex added quietly. "My contact says the warrants and approval are being expediated. They want to grab this asshole before he pulls up stakes again."

"And how the fuck are they going to grab him with that fucking arsenal inside?" Dev scowled and dropped his hands.

If the feds fucked up, which was a good possibility, Madeline and her kid would be caught between two lethal forces. Seventy some cult members had died at Waco, many of them children.

Fuck...he needed to get Madeline and her daughter out of there, like yesterday. But how the hell to do that with the arsenal this guy had on hand?

"Does this asshole ever go off reservation?" Maybe he could grab him off the compound and use him to get Madeline and her kid out.

"Doesn't sound like it. Sounds like he surrounds himself with warm bodies for protection."

Of course he did. A warm body barrier would make the feds think twice about raiding the place.

"Hang on. I got a call coming in."

Devlin worked up a rescue scenario while Tex concentrated on his other call. He'd have to tap Tag and Tram. Both men had put in their papers and left the teams now, which would give them some protection. At least they wouldn't be in violation of Posse Comitatus. Dev on the other hand, as an active duty Naval officer, would be in flagrant disregard of the statute...which just meant he better not get caught.

With Tram's contacts in the security company he'd recently joined, they should be able to grab a couple more guys, at least enough to round out a team. God knew Tram's firm was chock full of former special ops guys who knew their shit.

He took a deep breath, forcing the image of a struggling Madeline beneath some fucking incel aside. He couldn't go there. He needed to throw all that violent energy into what he could do. Which was get in. Get Madeline and her kid out. And if some of those incel bastards got in his way—that would be damn fine with him.

Time to reach out to Tag and Tram. Get things moving before the feds raided the place and blew everything to hell and back.

When Tex came back online, Devlin knew instantly something had changed…and for the worse. The line practically crackled with frustrated tension.

"What?"

"They're gone."

"What do you mean *gone*?" The question shot from him like a bullet.

"The bastard pulled up stakes again." Rage ate at each word. "The feds have no fucking idea where they went." He paused and a deep breath squeezed down the line. "I'm on it, brother," he finally said. His voice tight. Filled with focus. "I'll find them."

The line went dead before Dev could blast him with questions. Like how the fuck could the cult be gone? Hadn't the feds had eyes on them? What kind of bullshit operation were those fuckers running? When his jaw started throbbing, he realized he was grinding his teeth. He forced his jaw to relax.

Tex will find them.

Dev had no doubt of that. Hell, Tex could hack into anything —traffic cameras, toll bridges, government drones, even SAT feeds. He'd follow the crumbs that cult had left behind and find them. With kids and pedophiles involved, Tex wouldn't rest until he'd hunted those bastards down.

But fuck…how long would it take? And what kind of soul-crushing hell were Madeline and her daughter going through while he sat on his ass and waited?

* * *

Well that hadn't gone according to plan.

Marguerite had to be frantic by now.

Madeline cradled Cassidy closer to her side, finding comfort in the warm, soft weight of her daughter's slight frame anchored against her. Their bodies swayed on the narrow metal bunk. Or rather the bunk swayed, taking their bodies with it. When she'd first woken from the drugged haze those bastards had reduced her to, she'd fought the movement of the bunk, tensing her muscles, trying to remain alert and stationary beneath the rocking. But fighting the movement just led to fatigue and aching muscles.

She was almost certain they were on a ship. While the windowless room they were locked in was fully enclosed, with metal bunkbeds riding three of the four walls, when Rebecca and Leah had unlocked the door earlier and allowed her to use the tiny bathroom down the narrow hall, she'd caught the fresh, briny smell of the ocean swooshing down the metal stairs to the right. And then there was the dampness of the mattress and bedding they were lying on, and the smell of mildew permeating the room.

But the clincher was the deep vibration emanating through the walls and floor of their prison. The vibration seemed to travel through her flesh and jitter against her bones, numbing her body.

Yep, they were on a ship that was under power. Where they were headed, she had no clue. Nor did she know how she was going to get them out of this mess.

She had to be the world's worst rescuer. She should have been more careful about accepting the food and water the cult members provided. There must have been something in that last meal. She remembered getting so sleepy, and then...nothing... until she awoke in this bunk with a splitting headache and dry mouth.

Grimacing, she turned slightly, cuddling her sleeping daughter closer. She buried her face in the brownish-black hair spread across her shoulder and breathed in the minty scent of the shampoo the cult members used. The smell was as foreign as the room they were locked in and the thin, white cotton sheath that clothed Cassidy's small frame. The garment indicated purity, according to Rebecca, one of the friendlier cult members. The plain sheath shouldn't have inspired terror, but it was a constant reminder that she had to free Cass from these people and the bastard who preyed upon the children of the Second

Cycle. And she needed to escape with Cass soon, before Apostolos stole her childhood and introduced her to the evil that walked the world.

She'd had no idea how dangerous these people were when she'd put together her harebrained plan and knocked on the compound's doors. She'd had no idea they were armed to the teeth. If she'd known, she would have gone down to Coronado and cornered Devlin in person to ask for his help. It would have been harder for him to shrug off her pleas if she were right there in his face, nagging him unmercifully. At the very least, he could have given her options, even people to contact.

But no—she'd thought she could extricate Cass on her own and now she was in over her head with no rescue in sight.

How could she have been so stupid?

She joined the cult three weeks? Maybe even a month ago. She wasn't certain how much time had passed. They'd taken her cell phone and watch and there were no calendars on the cult grounds. But this was the first time they'd left Cassidy with her unattended. Probably because they were at sea, with nowhere to go. In the Belgrade compound, which according to Rebecca had once been a tech company's retreat, she'd never been left alone with Cassidy. At least half a dozen cult members had always been in attendance, including several men with guns. Almost all the cult men were armed. Lord, she'd never seen so many guns in her life.

She should have done something sooner to get Cassidy out. But the men guarded the entrances, the windows were boarded shut, and Cassidy was taken away from her at night to sleep with Rebecca, while Madeline was locked in a different room.

There had been no opportunity for her to escape, let alone escape with Cassidy. So she'd chosen a different tactic. Tried to convince them she was seriously contemplating joining them. Tried to assuage their suspicion. If she could escape their vigilance and act when an opportunity presented itself, maybe she could get Cass out... only nothing had presented itself and now she was stuck.

Damn you Ronnie.

She was almost certain Ronnie was dead. He hadn't been on

site when she walked through the compound doors. The cult leader—creepy Apostolos—had told her Ronnie was out spreading God's message, as all new disciples were required to do. Except she didn't believe a word of that crap. Ronnie might have been stupid enough to join this cult, but there was no way he would walk away from his daughter.

Sure as hell not if he'd gotten a whiff of the horrifying deviant vibe Apostolos shed when he watched the children, especially the little girls. No, he must have realized what kind of a depraved people these cultists were, and he'd tried to get Cass out. And they'd killed him for it.

But even knowing that, knowing he was probably dead, she couldn't forgive him for his colossal stupidity. *What had he been thinking*? He'd put a bullseye on their daughter's back.

Maddie could see it every time Apostolos looked at Cass. The douchebag didn't try to hide it. The only reason Cass hadn't already been assaulted was because she was undergoing the ninety days of purity. A bogus ritual Apostolos had enacted to give a thin veneer of propriety to the marriages of young girls—of *children*—to that disgusting pig of a pedophile.

Somehow, he'd convinced the other cult members that God had ordained these appalling marriages of his. Or at least he'd convinced the women. The men probably didn't care, not if in exchange for their silence they were given their fill of guns and women.

But the women? How could they do this to their daughters? How could they believe that God would require them to give their baby girls over to a sexual predator? It made Madeline furious that anyone could fall for such manipulative bullshit in this day and age.

But they had. The whole lot of them.

Which was unbelievably heartbreaking for their daughters.

Maybe if the women weren't so isolated, they wouldn't have been so easily brainwashed. But no one was allowed outside contact, and that included with family or friends. And while there were computers onsite, they were solely the providence of the men and the room was guarded twenty-four seven.

There was no way to get word out to the police about what

was going on in here when everyone was watched constantly, when members spied and reported on each other.

Plus, they hid the children when cops did show up. Which explained why the sheriff's deputies hadn't found Cassidy when they'd done their walkthrough. The Belgrade compound had a huge, soundproof, secret room. According to Rebecca, it had been the safe room to protect the tech company's executives if a kidnapping attempt was made. A while back, she, along with all the children, had been herded into the room and locked inside for hours. When they'd finally been released, she'd heard whispers that a couple of sheriff's deputies had done another walkthrough.

"Momma?" Cassidy stirred beside her, lifting her head. Huge, dark brown eyes peered over Madeline's chest and scanned the room. "I have to go potty."

Maddie sat up and swung her legs off the bunk. Once on her feet, she stood there swaying, clutching the side of the bunk for balance. Her stomach cramped. She waited for it to calm. She'd been nauseated since awakening. Probably because of the ship's rocking. Or maybe the lingering effects of the drug they'd given her.

"Okay, sweetie. Let's get you to the bathroom." She waited for Cass to scramble out of the bunk and join her on the floor.

The engine vibrations were even stronger while standing. They penetrated the steel through the cheap canvas shoes the cult had provided and tickled the soles of her feet. She slung an arm across her daughter's fragile shoulders and staggered to the door.

It only took one round of pounding her palm against the steel door before it opened with a grating squeal. Rebecca's beaming face greeted them. Rachel and Leah stood stoically behind her, their simple blue dresses hanging on their thin frames. Their skin looked sallow, their eyes dull, their hair lank.

"Everything okay?" Rebecca asked, with what appeared to be actual concern.

The woman was an anomaly. She was more pleasant and cheerful than the other women. According to Cass, the woman had been nice to her and taken care of her when Ronnie had disappeared.

"Cass needs to use the restroom," Madeline said.

"Of course!" Rebecca said cheerfully and stepped away from the door.

The other two, taller women shuffled back as well.

After a quick glance toward the metal stairs to her right, she steered her daughter down the hall to the tiny bathroom she'd been shown to before and waited outside for her to finish her business.

"Are you and Cass hungry? Would you like some water?" Rebecca asked, as they waited for Cassidy to rejoin them.

Madeline thought about it. While she was leery about eating or drinking anything these people gave her, she couldn't afford *not* to eat either. She had to keep her strength up. She needed to be clear headed. Besides, why would they bother drugging her again? They already had her, and Cass, where they wanted them.

"That would be nice." Maddie shot a quick look at the armed guard in front of the stairs. The other two women were still waiting back by the bunk room, which gave her a bit of privacy with Rebecca. "Are we on a ship?" Madeline lowered her voice.

A flicker of something crossed the woman's face as she stared back.

"Yes," she finally admitted, followed immediately by—"You're awfully pale. Are you feeling sick? We have some Dramamine on hand if that would help."

"No thanks." Dramamine would just make her drowsy. She needed to stay focused and alert.

"Where are we headed?" Madeline asked.

"Apostolos is keeping that a secret so he can surprise us when we reach our new home." Rebecca offered with a beaming, confident smile. As though she had total faith in the Divine Ruler's decisions.

That blind, adoring look on Rebecca's face stayed with Maddie long after she and Cassidy returned to their bunk. Long after Rebecca returned with water and soggy sandwiches. Long after Rebecca, Rachel, Leah and two other less familiar women entered the bunk room and settled down for the night.

As the soft snores and snorting breaths of the women surrounded her, Madeline laid awake, desperately searching for a way out of this mess. But Rebecca's look of blind devotion kept interfering with her plans—or more like lack of plans. They were surrounded by dozens of Rebeccas. Dozens of brain-washed, heavily armed crazy people.

How was she ever going to free Cassidy from this cult?

CHAPTER 4

It came as no surprise that the shit started flying as soon as the East Coast guys walked into the command center. Also no surprise—it started with that damn calendar. Only the new one this time. The one with the pit bulls.

"Well, fuck me..." Jacob Moore paused just inside mission control's doorway, his gaze flicking from Rocco, to Ace, and then Gumby, "...if it isn't Fabio and the pinup boys."

Gumby, Rocco and Ace, all West Coast operators, swiveled in their chairs to face the newcomers.

"I'm concerned you know who Fabio is," Ace lobbed back, his voice dry.

But it was Rocco, a smirk riding his face, who ratcheted up the insults. "Jealous, are you?" He laid the derision on thick. "Maybe if you put more time into PT, you would have gotten an invite to the photoshoot."

"Not a chance." Ace linked his fingers behind his neck and performed an exaggerated up and down assessment of the East Coast team leader. "Who wants to look at all that pasty white skin? Sure as hell not the ladies."

Devlin ground his teeth and fought back his impatience.

Three weeks. It had been three fucking weeks since Tex had filled him in on the cult of the Second Cycle, only to discover the whole damn lot of them had slipped past the feds and disappeared. Three more weeks that Madeline and her daughter had been stuck among those crazy motherfuckers. You add these last couple of weeks to the three that Madeline had already spent with them and that made six weeks that she'd been at their mercy.

Jesus, anything could have happened to her by now. They didn't have time for this kind of bullshit.

"Trust me, brother," Dylan King, who'd bugged out of Belize with Moore, pushed his way past his teammate and dropped into one of the empty chairs scattered around the sitrep table, "Squish does *not* have trouble attracting the ladies."

"No? You realize his hand's not a lady?" Ace's lips twitched at the middle finger Moore flashed him. "Your boys call you Squish? How the hell did you get stuck with that?"

"That's need to know," Squish shot back as he took a few steps forward and claimed a chair for himself. "How'd you get roped into doing another pinup calendar, anyway?" There was as much curiosity as derision in the question.

Rocco shrugged. "Gumby's woman works at a pit bull rescue. The place was having some funding problems. Long story short —they no longer have a cash flow shortage."

Devlin scoffed beneath his breath. Of course, there was more to it than that. The rumor was Gumby's wife, Sidney, had been heartbroken about how many dogs the rescue organization was turning away. Without rehabilitation, most of the animals had to be euthanized. But there just weren't the resources or room to take them all.

So, Gumby and his teammates had decided to do something about that cash flow problem. They'd spearheaded the calendar campaign and convinced a bunch of their West Coast brothers to participate. After hooking up with a professional photographer who'd donated his services for free, the whole lot of them had posed—bare chested—with pit bulls that were up for adoption. Once the calendar had been created, the team women had taken over, getting the damn thing into practically every store imaginable, both physical and online—with the proceeds from the calendar sales going to Sidney's pit bull shelter.

Gumby's wife and the rest of the team's women managed the

calendar now, and rumor had it business was booming. The damn thing was on its twentieth printing and bringing in more money than anyone had imagined—enough for the shelter to open two new wings and add a dozen more people to their staff.

Apparently SEALs posing with dogs were crack to women far and wide.

Squish shook his head in mock disillusionment before dropping into the chair he'd spun to face him. "I thought you surfer dudes were smarter than that. Didn't you learn anything from your last foray into mommy porn?"

Devlin grimaced. That was a very good question.

Back in the late eighties the west coast teams had agreed to do a charity calendar for...hell...Dev couldn't even remember what organization had spearheaded the original calendar. And all these years later, they were still paying for that decision with constant razzing and calendar related practical jokes. Fuck, a couple years back, some comedian had even produced and internally distributed a dick of the month calendar—full of glossy, close up, dicks.

Talk about disturbing.

Gumby and his crew had to have known they'd be opening themselves up to endless ridicule and practical jokes with that calendar. Yet they'd done it anyway. What the hell had they been thinking?

As if in answer to Dev's silent question, Gumby offered an unconcerned smile, followed by a shrug.

"It was for a good cause. All the dogs in that calendar were adopted, and the place has enough money to rescue every animal that walks through their door for years to come. But the best thing? My wife falls asleep every night with a smile on her face, and that, my friend, is priceless." Gumby winked. "We're looking to produce a new calendar for next year. Hit me up if you're interested."

From the constipated look that seized Squish's face, his answer was a firm motherfucking no, but before he or any of the other self-styled comedians lounging around had a chance to jump on Gumby's comment about the smile on his wife's face—and why it was coming from dogs, when Gumby was in bed beside her—and you just *knew* that shit was coming—Commander North appeared in the doorway.

Fifteen chairs were shoved back, and fifteen men launched to their feet as the men bullshitting around the table came to attention.

Thank fucking Christ.

They could finally get the damn ball rolling.

"At ease, gentlemen." North skirted the chairs on his way to the front of the table, while his assistant passed out thick file folders. He waited until everyone sat back down before nodding toward Squish. "As you're aware by now, Chief Moore, and Petty Officer King from SEAL Team 4 will be joining us for this operation. They both have numerous deployments through South America and are fluent in Castellano and Quechua, which are common languages in the Amazon Rainforest." He gave a chin lift toward Devlin. "Lieutenant Commander Russo, from SEAL Team 7, will be joining us as well."

ST4's geographical area of expertise was Central and South America. The fact that this operation hadn't been assigned to one of ST4's platoons was a clear indication something big was in the works down there. Something that required the entirety of ST4's resources. But at least they'd been able to loan them these two jokers. God knew they'd need their knowledge of the terrain, language, and local dynamics.

Fuck, if Tex hadn't hooked the FBI up with HQ1, and the feds hadn't requested help in extricating their deep cover agent, it was doubtful a mission would have been considered at all. At least not one through JSOC.

Although, with rumors of children and a pedophile swirling around the cult, no doubt Tex would have reached out to one of the other teams he worked with—one of the ones outside of JSOC.

North took a seat at the head of the table and gave everyone a few minutes to read the files. The sound of rustling paper periodically broke the silence as everyone flipped their way through the file folders. Dev opened the folder North's assistant had placed in front of him and started scanning. Nothing on the pages surprised him. Tex had kept him updated over the past three weeks.

After a few minutes of silence, North started talking.

"Three weeks ago, a cult called The Children of the Second Cycle pulled up stakes and disappeared before the feds could raid it. The FBI had an agent inside, who disappeared along with seventy-five adults and fifteen children." North lifted his chin toward Devlin. "Around the same time, Lieutenant Commander Russo had been approached by —" he glanced down at his notes, "—one Marguerite Levine. Ms. Levine's sister, Madeline Roux, had disappeared inside this cult three weeks earlier in the hopes of rescuing her daughter. Nobody's heard from her since. Dev reached out to John Keegan for intel on the cult." He glanced up, scanning faces as though checking for questions.

"Hell, I haven't heard that name in years," Dylan King said, looking up from the folder spread open in front of him. "How is the old bastard?"

"You can ask him that yourself. He'll be joining us shortly via video," North said, and King went back to flipping the file pages.

King was slightly shorter and slightly broader than his team leader. His brown eyes were detached, his dark brown hair slightly wavy with glints of red. Devlin had never worked with the guy, but he knew him by his reputation as a calm, thoughtful operator with killer instincts and steel plated balls. The guy had saved the lives of his crew during his first deployment, or at least he would have if the grenade he'd dived on after it had been tossed into their midst had been live. The dude hadn't known the grenade was a dud though. He'd acted instinctively the moment that bomb had hit the ground and sought to defuse its carnage on his team brothers with his own body. If the damn thing had gone off, King's guts would have been liquified...he would have died on the spot. Which was something the SEAL brotherhood would never forget.

By all accounts, the guy was lucky. And not just with hand grenades, but with cards and gambling too. Which explained why he'd been dubbed Lucky.

After a few more minutes of reading, Lucky turned to Dev

with lifted eyebrows. "Why did this Marguerite go to you? Why not the cops?"

"She went to the locals first," Dev said. "A couple of sheriff's deputies did a walkthrough, but found no sign of her sister. When they refused to investigate further, she came to me."

He knew now that the locals had been told by the feds to back off, as they didn't want the cult pressured into running again. Not with their raid imminent. Not that the backing off had done a damn bit of good. The fuckers had run anyway.

"Okay…?" Lucky cocked his head, his eyes still questioning.

Right.

"Marguerite's sister, Madeline, the one who disappeared in the cult, is the woman who saved Lieutenant Taggart's life two months back. She stopped him from bleeding out after that fuckhole Mitch dropped him. Without her intervention, Tag would be dead. The incident made the papers, so both women know Tag, Tram and I are SEALs. Marguerite feels we owe her sister."

"No shit? That was her?" Lucky's gaze dropped back to the file folder, and the ten by ten glossy photo of Madeline. "Beautiful *and* smart. This op is looking up." His gaze was full of respect when it lifted again, and far too carnal for Dev's liking. "You can assure the sister we'll get Ms. Roux out of there."

Devlin stiffened, acid suddenly churning through his gut. Like hell was this bastard doing anything other than helping get Madeline out. The asshole's reputation with the ladies preceded him. He was as bad as his fucking team leader when it came to long term relationships. A drive by bang was more his style.

Shame twisted through him. Hell, he'd played the drive by game with her too. Madeline deserved better than that.

"That was some fucked up shit, man," Rocco said, shoving a hand through his dark hair. Contempt lightened his brown eyes. "Never trusted Mitch. Was glad to hear Sarah put him down. Although bleeding out in seconds was too good for the bastard. Dropping a brother like that…he should have suffered."

Nods traveled the table. Faces hardened in scorn.

Mitch Armstrong's betrayal of his country and team ties would never be forgotten or forgiven in the SEAL community. It wasn't often you found a traitor in the brotherhood, but when you did, their memory tarnished everything the community stood for.

"So our target is Madeline Roux, her daughter and this FBI chick?" Ace broke the lingering, distasteful silence with a frown.

"That would be correct." Commander North stepped into the conversation again.

"Sir." Ace's frown escalated to a scowl. "What about the rest of these kids? If their parents were willing to hand them off to a pedophile, who knows who else they'll hand them off to? The compound could end up being a pedophile haven."

He was probably thinking about what would have happened to his adopted daughters if he hadn't rescued them from Timor-Leste. They would have been looking at a similar fate as the kids stuck inside this fucked-up cult, to be used and eventually discarded by the adults that were supposed to protect them.

"We won't be," North assured him. "Keegan is working with a private organization. We'll evac the children. Get them to safety, where Tex's people will take over. They'll be united with relatives or fostered once they're stateside."

Devlin suspected extracting the children was going to be a major clusterfuck. But they sure as hell couldn't leave them there. Not when their parents were less than *parental*.

Lucky grunted, his head still down as he poured over the intel in front of him. "It's too bad they aren't still on that freighter. Insertion and extraction would have been easier by water."

No shit.

Devlin rolled his shoulders, trying to release some of the frustrated tension. Twenty-one days of waiting and wondering had wrecked his shoulders, neck and patience.

By the time Tex had realized that the cult had used container trucks to transfer their members, and tracked the trucks to the Port of Portland, the containers had already been hauled down to Callao, Peru and off loaded.

How the hell had the FBI missed those trucks? If they were planning to raid the place, why hadn't they had eyes on the compound? It was inconceivable that the feds could have missed two container trucks arriving and departing from the cult's compound.

Without eyes focused on the site, and with the compound far enough out of town that there weren't traffic cameras available to access, it had taken Tex forever to find the mode of transportation. How he'd figured it out was still a mystery. Tex wasn't talking...probably because whatever method he'd used had been illegal as hell.

It was a damn good thing Tex used his instincts and abilities for the good of mankind. If world domination had been on his mind, the world would be well and truly fucked.

"Tex tracked the cult from Callao to Tarapoto where they boarded two minibuses and drove to Yurimagua," North continued. "From there they took a river cargo boat up past Iquitos." He nodded toward Squish. "Chief Moore, take us through the rest."

Squish looked up, his black eyes narrow and intent. All sharp focus and professionalism now. "Tex's last location puts the boats twenty klicks upriver past Iquitos into the Tapiche Jungle Reserve. This region is wild and isolated and pocketed with guerrilla rebels associated with the Túpac Amaru Revolutionary movement. My team and I have spent the past two years posing as weapons dealers and establishing connections among the Amaru Rebels. The objective has been to draw out Alejandro Diaz, a major player in the Tapiche weapons cartel. Diaz is supplying the Amaru rebels with the latest and greatest in US military weapons, which has strained US-Peruvian relations. Our mission is to lure Diaz out, locate the conduit supplying him, and shut the pipeline down. With that objective, we've established relations with several rebel strongholds, posing as competing weapons dealers encroaching on Diaz's territory. Through these contacts, I believe we've found where this cult has gone to ground. They've taken over an old rubber plantation forty klicks northwest of Iquitos. My Amaru contact tells me the cult leader is seeking an introduction to Diaz. He's looking for more weapons. I've been pitched to this cult asshole as a cheaper alternative to Diaz. We'll walk in for a meeting to discuss our wares and remove Stanley Gibbens—AKA Apostolos—from God's plan, along with any cult members who resist."

North took over. "The rest of the cult members are not to be engaged unless they engage first. There is a good chance the rest of these yahoos will stand down once our boys show up." His stern gaze roamed the table to drive his point home before he continued. "Since Russo has had contact with Ms. Roux and she has reason to trust him, he'll accompany Chief Moore, and Petty Officer King, posing as an American weapons supplier."

His previous connection with Madeline was the *only* reason he'd been allowed to join this operation. Number one, he wasn't under North's command. And number two, he was executive leadership, which put him on the planning and briefing side of missions. He rarely saw any action these days. Most of the guys surrounding him were probably tweaked as hell that he'd been pulled on board. Which was too fucking bad. They'd just have to deal.

"According to the FBI, Gibbens is known to share the cult women with his lieutenants," North continued, looking up to scan the table. "Devlin is going to take a liking to Ms. Roux and request her company."

Dev flinched, rage hitting him like a furnace blast at the thought of Madeline being forced to accept anyone against her will. The whole thing was prostitution, but with power and favors as payment rather than coin.

"With luck, Roux and the fed will get the women and kids into a defensible position while our boys keep Gibbens occupied." North turned to Dev with a frown. "Team insertions will commence at zero hundred. Make sure those kids are locked down and out of harm's way when we breach the walls." North shifted his attention to Squish. "Gibbens needs to be neutralized prior to the insertion. His incel army are more likely to cut and run if the bastard's dead. Not to mention his aspirations of world dominance needs to be shut down ASAP." He scanned the table. "Questions?"

Rocco looked up; his laser sharp gaze locked on the Commander's face. "We're dropping directly into the compound?"

"Correct. We'll drop in with dual birds. The plantation sits on four cleared acres. Plenty of room for drop and lift. We'll go in, grab the kids, and get them out first. Offload them with Tex's people. If there's room, we'll take any women who want to bug out. If there are leftovers, we'll come back, grab the rest of them. The closest rebel encampments are over forty klicks inland. We'll go in in stealth mode. Avoid attention. Get in and out before the Amaru even realize we were there."

Approving nods went around the table. The helos couldn't accommodate all the women and children along with the assigned teams, so they'd have to evac in shifts. However, it was a safe bet that some of the woman would refuse passage, if they were as brainwashed as the intel showed.

Of course, they had alternative plans up the ass. A whole fucking alphabet of back up scenarios. That kind of over preparation was what kept operators alive to over prepare again.

Squish turned to Devlin, a flinty look in his eyes. "What about this gal? This Madeline Roux? Will she keep her mouth shut when she sees you? If she gives any indication that you're not who we say you are, the entire operation is fucked, and we'll be headed home in plastic."

An image of calm brown eyes and steady hands slick with blood rose in his mind.

"She's solid," Dev said, holding the flinty gaze, knowing from the flicker that crossed the guy's hard face that Squish had doubts.

Too fucking bad. The best shot they had of getting everyone out safely was getting to Madeline and enlisting her aid. She'd know the deep cover fed, or at least she'd recognize her picture. She'd be able to connect them with her— assuming the agent was still alive. And while Madeline might not like him much after that business in Dark Falls, she knew him, knew he was a SEAL. She'd realize that they were there to help.

On the other hand, she didn't know Squish. If she'd been abused over these past six weeks—Dev flinched, his gut clenching. He forced himself to think past the internal turmoil—if she'd been abused, then she wasn't likely to trust Squish. Not when the guy looked like the arms dealer he was portraying. The time it took Moore to convince her to trust him could be the difference between everyone climbing on those choppers alive or dying in a hail of gunfire.

Devlin held Squish's flat, hard eyes until the guy finally glanced away.

It was the right call, damn it. Madeline had been a rock while they'd fought to keep Tag alive. That kind of strength didn't just wash away. She'd be a rock now, too, when he needed her to be.

She damn well better be… everyone's lives depended on it.

CHAPTER 5

"Get a move on it," Brother Abraham snapped. Reaching beneath the mosquito netting attached to the brim of his hat, he mopped his streaming face with a handkerchief. "I'm tired of sweating my ass off out here."

He was sweating his ass off?

He wasn't the one breaking his back with a hoe in an effort to rip up the sod and loosen the soil below for the potato planting that Apostolos was demanding. And while Abraham was wearing pants, a long sleeve shirt, gloves, and a mosquito netted hat like she was—thank God she didn't have to wear that dress anymore—he wasn't doing anything physical.

Or at least she didn't consider standing around, carrying an automatic rifle, physical.

"I'd be happy to trade places with you," Madeline offered, her back going into spasms as she straightened from her hunched position.

The first few days after their arrival had been spent cutting the knee-high grass with scythes. Because why bother hauling in a mower when you could provide the women with ancient cutting instruments and tell them to have at it? Once the grass had been cut to a manageable length, the hoes had come out. Even with the leather gloves, she had blisters on top of blisters.

"How about you hand over the gun and I'll stand around

looking bored?" she added. She thought about adding a smile to ease the bite in her offer but couldn't manage it. Abraham, like the rest of the men here, were misogynistic worms. She wasn't going to pretend otherwise.

She took a second to mop her streaming face, although she couldn't do much about the sweat running down her sides and spine and between her breasts. Holy Mother of God, this was a miserable place. Hot and humid, with swarms of mosquitoes. Mosquitoes that always managed to find their way beneath the netting. They'd only been here a week, and she already hated every square inch of the Amazon.

"Smartass bitch," he sneered. "You won't be so full of yourself after tomorrow night. I've put my name in the hat for a chance to teach you some manners."

Maddie ignored the comment, although her belly tightened and churned. He must have picked up on her revulsion. His laugh was caustic as she turned back to the patch of soil she was hoeing.

If she could get her hands on one of those guns, she'd blow every single one of these people away. The men. The women. All of them. Every single one.

Except for the children.

The children were the only innocents among these people... these crazy, crazy people.

While the men of this cult were among the worst that humanity had to offer—preying on the women nightly—the women...holy hell, the women were just as bad.

While they weren't responsible for what was happening to them—no, the disgusting pigs patrolling the property and house with their guns were solely responsible for that—the women were complicit in what was happening to their daughters. They were the ones handing the girls over to that disgusting scum of a pervert who called himself Apostolos—the messenger of God.

How could they believe that utter crap?

How could they believe that God had ordained that their daughters be molested? Abused? How could they believe that God wanted *anything* like that for their *children*?

Her hoe slammed into the earth with much more force than

was necessary or wise, ripping up a clot of sod. She bent to grab it and tossed it toward the huge pile of ripped up sod to her right, then took a second to rest. Heat stroke was a real possibility out here, what with the physical workout beneath the boiling sun. Add in her simmering anger and she could be in real danger of stroking out.

But the sheer stupidity and blind obedience of the women to this morally corrupt con artist and his morally bankrupt henchmen made her want to scream. Made her want to wrestle one of the guns from her guards and start shooting. Made her want to gather all those poor babies tucked in the main house and run.

But she couldn't. Not yet.

She was watched...constantly...more now than ever. Even if she could overpower one of the men guarding her, there were another dozen nearby with their guns waiting. If she got herself killed, who would protect Cassidy? Who would stop her baby girl from joining Apostolos's child brides? Who would rescue the other children?

But things had gotten so much worse since that scumbag had moved his people out here. Into the middle of the freaking Amazon. Where there was no one who gave a shit. No one to stop his depravity. No one to prevent him from killing anyone who didn't bow down before him and submit to his will. There had been an underlying current of evil in Montana, but it was overt now. In your face. No need to hide it.

He'd dropped all the trappings of morality since they'd arrived.

Good God, he didn't even bother to hide what her fate was now. The cult women were simply sexual cattle and work horses. They accepted whatever man requested them in between taking care of the children, the cooking, cleaning, planting, tending and harvesting.

While the men strutted around with their guns playing the great protectors.

She'd suspected for a while that the only perk that kept the men loyal to their Divine Ruler was having their choice of the women—but the guns probably played into it too. They sure loved those guns. The only male here who abstained from the women was Apostolos.

And that was simply because his tastes ran so much younger.

The rest of the men, though, they shared the women among themselves.

It had been hinted to her, by both the men and women, that she needed to accept her place and her duty. That she needed to join the cult in spirit and body. But it wasn't until last night that she'd been ordered to do so by the Divine Ruler himself. He'd bluntly informed her that, as a female member of the Second Cycle, it was her duty to provide comfort to the men, and God willing, produce numerous children to repopulate the earth. It was her duty to accept whoever requested her. He'd told her that he'd gifted her with over six weeks to acclimatize to her new role, and he'd give her two more days to accommodate him, but it was time for her to stop resisting and join the cult fully—body and soul.

He'd also sternly warned her that if she was unwilling to accept this mandate, then she was a mouth to feed that provided no benefit and she would be expelled.

She wasn't sure whether expelled meant killed or banished from the property, but either way it was a death sentence. There was no place for her to go. No money to pay her way back to the states.

Besides, no way was she leaving Cassidy behind.

Which meant she had to find a way to provide value and earn her keep that wasn't sexual, or she'd have to submit to the cult's will. Which meant servicing whoever he sent to her, night after night.

The thought of any of the disgusting, perverted scumbags touching her, made her skin crawl. Made her want to vomit.

But she would compartmentalize and do it if she absolutely had to.

She would do it to remain on the premises and protect Cassidy. She would do anything for Cassidy.

When the plantation bell tolled, announcing the dinner break, Madeline straightened. Hot and dizzy, she pressed a hand to her churning stomach, hoping to calm the roll. After a few seconds of rest, she followed the women toward the house while their guards brought up the rear.

The property Apostolos had settled them on had once been a rubber plantation. It still had acres of rubber trees surrounding it, along with mango, banana, and coconut trees. The dozens of wood outbuildings had long since collapsed due to age and inattention. The generator didn't work, which meant lanterns for lighting and a wood stove for cooking. But the house itself, which had been constructed from a local limestone deposit, was still in good repair. The building was huge, rambling, with open arches along the front and sides that led to a nice cross breeze.

Apostolos had bought the property for pennies, thanks to the lack of electricity, the open, insecure structure of the compound, and the pockets of brutal revolutionary rebels that tended to swing through the area. The two previous owners along with their families had died bloody, terrible deaths. Not that their dear Divine Ruler was worried about exposing his people to such a possibility.

No sir. Not with God's providence on their side. Not with their ordained mission to repopulate and rule the planet. They had to be alive, to provide God with Apostolos's heirs, after all.

Still, the men were always on guard...always on watch. They took turns patrolling the area around the house, guarding the compound in batches of four or five.

Which made it harder than ever to sneak away.

The moment she pushed aside the mosquito netting from the center arch and stepped into the dim, lantern lit interior of the house, the temperature seemed to drop by twenty degrees. The inside of the house was always cooler than outside, less humid too.

She slowly shuffled her way toward the back of the open room with its flickering pockets of light thanks to the lanterns sprinkled around. She scanned the shadowy figures sitting at the tables for Cassidy's slight, small frame as she walked.

They'd set the main room of the compound up as the cooking and dining area, adding rows of folding plastic tables and chairs. The tables, all fifteen of them, along with the hundred and some folding plastic chairs had arrived on the boat with them. It must have cost Apostolos a fortune to ship the cult members plus the supplies all the way out here. How in the world had he managed to accumulate that kind of money?

While there had been rumors back in Montana that some of the men were tech savvy and worked online in the well-guarded and locked computer room, it was hard to believe their endeavors had brought in enough cash to buy this property and ship everyone to the Amazon. They had probably been involved in something high yielding and very illegal back in the states, although she'd heard no rumors of what that might be.

She grimaced when she caught sight of the food spread across the dinner table. Fruit...again.

It was too bad Apostolos hadn't splurged on a damn generator and a refrigerator to keep the food from spoiling. The lack of electricity for lighting wasn't so bad, as they had the lanterns. And cooking was easy enough on the wood stove he'd hauled in. God knew they had enough fuel to supply the stove since they were surrounded by rubber trees, which were perfect for firewood.

But the lack of any way to keep their food cold and prevent it from spoiling was a major problem. As was finding enough protein to keep almost one hundred people healthy and strong. There was plenty of fruit to keep their bellies full. Bananas, mangoes, and coconuts were plentiful on the plantation itself. They'd even had some luck in finding wild yams.

But meat...she sighed, eyeing the table of fruit distastefully... not much luck in that department. And she was already tired of eating like a vegetarian. They were several miles inland from the nearest river, which made fishing an all-day affair. On the few occasions the men had headed off to try their luck at catching one of those fabled 200-pound Amazon catfish they continually talked about, they'd returned with a dozen smaller fish instead. With almost one hundred people present, their offerings had barely provided a mouthful a piece. And while every morning several of the men went out on short hunting trips, about ninety-nine percent of the time they returned empty handed.

Apostolos said there were chickens, piglets, and goats arriving on the next boat, and the men were building pens for the animals. But it would take months, if not a year, for the animals to reproduce enough to feed the entire cult. What were they going to do for protein in the meantime?

She scanned the room for Cassidy again as she passed the initial rows of tables full of people picking at their fruit laden plates. This time she found her in the very back at one of the tables that had been set up for food preparation. There was a lantern in the middle of the table, shedding light over the people gathered. Cass was sitting slightly apart from the other children, next to Sister Abigail, one of the women who served as the compound's teachers—or more realistically, the babysitters. As far as she could see, there was no teaching going on.

More like constant indoctrination.

Cass noticed Maddie as she got in line at the drinking station and waved. Madeline smiled, waving back. But the smile faded when her daughter tried to get up from the table, only to be pulled back down by Abigail. When the woman leaned toward Cass, her face sterner than ever, her hand squeezing Cassidy's wrist, her mouth going a mile a minute, Cass shrunk into herself. Her shoulders curled as she hunched at the waist, her head bent.

Furious, Madeline stalked over.

The woman had no right to grab Cassidy like that. No damn right to lecture her daughter, sure as hell not for something as harmless as wanting to see her mother.

"Hey, sweetie." She stopped next to Cassidy's hunched form and ran a soothing hand down her daughter's tense spine, glaring at the hand Abigail still had wrapped around Cassidy's wrist. "How about you keep me company while I eat."

"Children sit at the—"

"My daughter will sit with me," Madeline broke in, ignoring Abigail's harsh, lined face and malevolent glare. "And if you don't take your hand off her this instant, I'll remove it for you," she added tightly.

Abigail stiffened, her graying head, with its ever-present bun, jerking back. But she dropped her hand. Which was when Madeline saw the white imprint of the woman's fingers on Cassidy's tanned arm. Fury flooded her, raising her blood pressure until she could hear her pulse pounding in her ears. She looked from the fingerprints into the woman's light blue, bitter eyes. But before she could let loose with the vitriol hovering on the tip of her tongue, Cassidy took her hand.

"Momma?" she whispered, her voice shaking.

Although she didn't say anything else, Maddie could hear the trepidation in Cass's voice. Unloading on the woman might make her feel better, but it would just worry her daughter. She carefully wrapped her hand around Cass's thin arm and lifted, easing her away from the table.

"Come on, sweetie, let's get something to eat."

"Spare the rod, spoil the child."

Madeline ignored Abigail's comment as she led Cassidy over to the water station.

Settling an arm around Cassidy's thin shoulders, Madeline drew her against her side as they waited in line at the drink station. "Did you get some food and water, baby?"

Her daughter simply nodded.

"Okay..." Maddie tried again. Cassidy had always been a sensitive but cheerful child. But she was becoming more and more withdrawn every day. "Are you still hungry? Would you like some more?"

Cassidy shook her head this time.

Madeline frowned, tightening her arm around Cassidy's fragile shoulders. "What's wrong, baby? If you're worried about what Sister Abigail said, don't be. She's a very unhappy person and unhappy people take their unhappiness out on those around them. You did nothing wrong, sweetheart."

"Okay." But the agreement was uttered in an unconvinced whisper.

Helplessness twisted through Maddie. Damn it, she needed to get Cassidy away from this place. The longer her daughter was stuck here, the more damage was being done to her soul. While Apostolos hadn't touched her yet, the cult members regimentation and expectations were already crushing Cassidy's spirit.

As they waited for the women in front of them to fill their plastic cups with water from the five-gallon dispensing jugs scattered across the table, Madeline considered and rejected numerous plans of escape. Nothing she came up with was viable. The sense of helplessness coiled tighter and tighter within her.

When they finally reached the water station, she drained two of the plastic cups of water to replenish her parched body, and filled a third one up for herself, as well as another for Cass.

While the place had running water since the pipes to the spring had been fixed, the pipes didn't feed into the house. The spring water fed into a 1000-gallon plastic cistern with a spigot. Whatever water they used was drained from the cistern by bucket and boiled before use. But at least they no longer had to hike to the spring and haul the water back like they'd done those first few days. That had been a miserable, back-breaking chore.

When the cistern was in danger of overflowing, they drained it by filling up the bathtubs. That was when they bathed. Which wasn't nearly often enough to scrub the stench of exertion off themselves.

She handed both cups to Cass while she filled a plate with bananas, guava, and coconut meat, then led her daughter to an empty table.

"Did you learn anything cool in school today?" Madeline asked after they sat down. There wasn't really a school, but whenever possible, she tried to act normal. Her daughter certainly didn't need to be reminded of the disruption in her life.

"No." Cassidy dropped her voice to a whisper and leaned over to Maddie, pressing against her side. "When can we go home, Momma? I don't like it here."

Madeline's chest tightened, the helplessness and rage coiling tighter and tighter until she felt like she might spring apart.

"Soon, baby. Soon." She hugged the slight, rigid body closer, feeling the fragility of each bone, and her heart squeezed with terror and pain. Cass felt even more fragile than she had last time Madeline had held her, like she was losing substance by the hour.

She needed to talk to Apostolos about providing some protein laden meals for the children. Since Cassidy was favored by him, maybe he'd do something to prevent her from getting weak and sick.

Brushing back the limp, black curls, she kissed the hot, slightly sweaty forehead, then tipped the small, chin up.

"Look at me, sweetheart." When dark, unhappy eyes met her own, her chest tightened even more. "Everything is going to be alright, baby. Just give me a little more time to figure out how to get us home. Okay?"

"Okay…" Cassidy's voice trailed off, but Maddie could clearly hear the reservations in the whisper. "Just…" She paused, her voice soft and trembling and barely audible. "Just don't make them mad, okay? They'll send you away, like they did with daddy."

Madeline's belly rolled at the plea. "I'm not going anywhere, baby. Not without you. I won't leave you here alone. I promise."

Ronnie wouldn't have left Cass alone either if he'd had a choice. He'd loved their daughter. He would have tried to protect her once he realized how bad the situation was.

Apostolos had told her that she could leave at any time, but she was pretty sure her departure would be accompanied by a bullet and a shallow grave. Besides, he'd also made it clear that he would not allow Cass to go with her. Which meant the gun wielding cult members wouldn't let her daughter accompany her either. The Divine Ruler was the law around here. Nobody challenged his decrees. And he'd signaled clearly that she wasn't to be trusted alone with Cassidy. She grimaced in frustration. She couldn't even take Cassidy outside by herself or to the bathroom. And at night she was locked into a windowless room along with Cassidy and the other children and the rest of the women.

Try as she might, there was no opportunity to free herself, let alone Cass, from this compound.

The sound of boots ringing out against the limestone floor brought her head around. Probably a change of guard or one of the hunting parties returning. The women didn't wear boots.

Three of the men walking across the great room were recognizable. Some of Apostolos's men with their ever-present guns. But the other three men were strangers. Dressed in dark pants and black, long sleeve shirts, even from across the room they looked intimidating. Tall, huge, with lethal auras surrounding them.

Even though the cult men had their guns trained on the strangers' backs, and the newcomers were outmanned a dozen to one, there was no question who was in charge—at least to Maddie—and it wasn't Apostolos's men.

A murmur went through the crowd. Nervous eyes and shifting bodies followed the strangers' approach.

Madeline frowned absently, there was something about the middle stranger…something about the way he moved, the way he held himself, the breadth of his shoulders…something oddly familiar. She shifted in the chair to get a better look at him, shocked by the tingle working its way down her spine and setting her nerves on fire.

Yes…there was something about him…something familiar…

"Where's Apostolos?" one of the cult guys taking up the rear asked.

"In the back." The call came from behind her.

Maddie didn't take her eyes off that middle stranger walking toward her.

Black hair. Tall—at least six two or three. Wide shoulders, lean hips. He was wearing black, dirty jeans, and a long sleeve t-shirt. Well-worn boots clipped against the limestone floor as he strode ever closer. Her gaze zeroed in on those boots. How odd…they looked familiar too. They looked like the boots that—

What the—

Her gaze flew up, landing on a hard, expressionless face. Black eyes, as black as his shorn hair, glittered a warning. He held her eyes, his dark gaze fierce…demanding.

She'd seen those eyes soften and blur above her. Watched that hard face redden as he pounded into her. Held his huge, muscled body as he quaked and emptied himself.

Her heart started slamming against her ribs…echoing in her head. She closed her eyes and counted to five. When she opened them again, he was still there. Closer than ever…. watching her with intense, hawkish eyes.

She caught and swallowed her shocked gasp, disbelief turning her skin cold and clammy.

Holy Mother Mary.

I didn't hallucinate him. He's really here. Devlin is here.

"Momma?"

She vaguely heard Cassidy's timid, frightened voice, but her attention was snared by the man walking past her. He held her gaze until the last moment, until he was past them. And then he walked away...no hesitation in his stride. No glance over his shoulder.

Watching him walk away, watching the strong length of his back as he left her behind, should have reminded her of the motel, of him abandoning her, of the way he'd shattered the fairy tale she'd spun around him—around them—in her mind.

But instead of pain, the sight brought relief. Pure, raw, unadulterated relief.

"Momma?"

She snapped back to the present at the tug on her shirt.

"What's wrong?" Cassidy whispered, her anxious gaze locked on Maddie's face.

"Nothing, baby. Everything is fine," she choked out, reeling her shock and relief back. She needed to bury it. Hide it from prying eyes.

Madeline drew a deep breath and glanced around the makeshift dining room. Had anyone noticed her reaction? It didn't look like it. Everyone was watching the men walk away, as absorbed by the sight of these three, dangerous strangers, as she'd been. Her reaction hadn't stood out.

Thank God.

If Devlin had wanted to acknowledge their connection, he would have said something to her. He hadn't. That, and the warning so clear in his eyes, told her she needed to keep her mouth shut. To watch and wait for his cue.

She had to keep his name and profession a secret. Apostolos and his men would not react well to the knowledge that a Navy SEAL was in their midst. Probably three SEALs. The two other men who'd been flanking Devlin had that same lethal, larger than life aura as Tag and Tram and Devlin.

Where exactly this development left her, she wasn't one hundred percent certain. But in a better position than she'd been in minutes ago, that was for sure. Devlin wouldn't leave her or Cassidy here. She just needed to wait for him to act and help him in any way she could.

The helplessness and uselessness she'd been drowning within drained away. Replaced by hope. For the first time she believed the promises she'd been filling her daughter's ears with for the past six weeks.

Everything was going to be okay. They were going to get out of this.

Devlin would make sure of it.

CHAPTER 6

As soon as Devlin stepped into the compound's dimly lit main room, with its weak pockets of lantern light, he spotted Madeline. She was sitting in front of a plastic table, with a platter of fruit and several cups of water in front of her.

The tension that had launched weeks of *what if* scenarios, evaporated. His muscles loosened. His gut unknotted. His stride and breath caught. She was here. She was alive.

She might have gone through hell. But she'd survived.

He scanned her as he walked. She wore powder blue pants, a matching long sleeve shirt, and white canvas shoes—like the rest of the women on site. While there were other brunettes in the room, his gaze had found her instantly, like she was a shining star on a cold, dark night.

He scanned her petite frame as he crossed the room. From what he could see, she looked thinner. Beneath the clothing, her hips looked slenderer, her shoulders and collarbone more pronounced. Her hair hung limp and dull. Her back was hunched, her chin dipping toward the table, as she listlessly picked at the plate of fruit.

She looked defeated.

Exhausted.

Slowly, heads turned, voices rose in surprise. A swelling murmur filled the room. She was slow to respond to the commotion, but finally she shifted in her plastic chair and looked right at him. Her gaze swept him from face to boots and back up. He was close enough to see her face now. It looked drawn, tinged with gray beneath the golden halo of the lantern in the middle of the table—like she'd been short on food and sleep over the past six weeks.

The possibilities for why she wouldn't be getting enough sleep hit him right between the eyes. Shards of glass dug into his gut. They twisted and churned, cutting him into bloody ribbons of rage. He was going to kill every fucking guy who'd touched her... every motherfucking one of them.

A frown crept across her face. Her eyebrows knitted. Vague recognition stirred in her dull gaze. Puzzled eyes dropped back down to his feet and lingered. Suddenly she stiffened, and her gaze flew back up to his face. He saw the recognition hit her hard this time, saw it rock her back in her chair. Disbelief followed. She closed her eyes, her mouth silently counting to five.

When she opened them again, he was directly across from her. He held her gaze, silently projecting caution. She blinked, understanding replacing the disbelief on her face and watched him without making a sound or indicating in any way that she knew him.

Thank Christ.

He'd known she was quick on her feet...able to adjust on the fly. But he'd also known that the shock and relief of seeing him could fuck up her reaction and blow their plan sky high.

Thankfully, she'd held herself together.

Since their strategy called for him to notice her, he didn't try to hide his interest. He needed to get her alone, and the easiest way to accomplish that was to pretend a strong physical attraction, followed by a demand for sex.

Tex's research indicated the cult women were not allowed to say no to the men. His hands clenched at the thought of Madeline being forced into sexual obedience. Of unwelcome hands wandering over her sleek, creamy flesh.

Before he boarded the chopper out of here, he'd break some

bones in those incel bastards' faces. But until then, he had to play a kindred spirit.

The kind of man who took instead of asked.

The kind of man who didn't care if his choice of female companionship was unwilling.

The odds were good that if he demanded a few hours of one on one with Madeline as part of the price for the weapons he was supposedly offering, that rat bastard Apostolos would be happy to oblige.

So he'd pretend instant lust, and use the cult's motherfucking prehistoric culture toward their women to his advantage.

He held her gaze the entire time he walked past, turning his head to keep her in view. It wasn't until he was well past her that he noticed the slight, dark-haired child tucked close to Madeline's side. Huge, dark, frightened eyes were fixed on his face. The kid flinched, her eyes skittering away when he caught her gaze. She pressed even closer to her mother's side.

There was no question they were mother and daughter. They shared the same petite frame, the same brownish-black hair, the same heart shaped faces and pert little noses. The same shape and color to the eyes.

Jesus... the kid looked like a mini Madeline.

He assessed her in a quick glance...she looked smaller than Gracie had been—

And just like that memories swamped him.

"Higher, Daddy! Push me higher." Black hair glistening beneath the San Diego sun. Ruffled pink sleeves plastered against pudgy, white arms. Dark brown eyes giddy with excitement...with joy. The silver flash of chains as the swing reached for the bright blue sky.

A fist slamming into his shoulder knocked him from the past. He wrestled his gaze away from Madeline's mini-me and kept walking. Christ, he couldn't afford that trip down memory lane. Sure as hell not now. Sure as hell not here.

"Now that's some mighty fine ass you got your eye on." Squish turned his head and leered in Madeline's direction. "You calling dibs? If not, I wouldn't mind hitting that. Hell, the old lady's tirade might even be worth it."

Their tactics called for him to show interest in Madeline, and for his buddies to notice. It didn't call for the rush of jealous rage that boiled up at the thought of Squish touching her. Or the bizarre urge to drive his teammate's teeth down his throat.

He wrestled his attention back to *the plan,* and drove his shoulder into Squish, knocking him to the left a few steps. Yeah, maybe he'd put a lot more *oomph* into the shoulder jab than had been necessary to sell it. But…

…Whatever.

"Best look elsewhere, brother." He didn't bother to lower his voice or smooth the sharp edge to his reply. He was supposed to be possessive, right? Maybe only pretend possessive, but still… "That particular lady is about to be occupied for the next few hours."

"Why you always got to hog the hot ones?" Squish complained loud enough for the guys trailing them with their guns at half-mast to hear.

"How's it my fault you're always slow on calling dibs?" Dev drawled back.

"You could at least give a brother a shot at one of the gals with the big tits and sweet ass." Squish looked over his shoulder, catching their guards' eyes. "Am I right?"

The scoffing sounds the guards made were full of superiority. Devlin's fingers itched to shove their laughter back down their throats. The bastards had no clue how fucking outclassed they were.

"No need to fight over tail around here," one of the guards said, his tone full of condescension. "We rotate the favorites. Eventually you get anyone you want beneath you."

A snicker came from one of the assholes. "Or on top. Variety's the spice of life—am I right?"

So were knives and bullets. Which they'd be finding out soon enough.

Devlin didn't look back at the comment; he was afraid his fist might get away from him and plug those smirky mouths. Christ, he was looking forward to shutting those bastards up—regardless of North's decree. But he needed to keep cool for the time being and stick to the God damn plan. Which didn't include slicing and dicing so soon.

He forced back the disgust and rage and kept walking, scanning the dining hall. None of the women sitting at the tables looked like the deep cover FBI agent the feds had sent them in to recover. Maybe she was already dead.

If she was, it was a pity, but her death wouldn't fuck up their plan too much. Madeline could get the children into position. And they sure as hell didn't need the fed to bring down the cult.

All these bozos swaggering around with their APC9K submachine guns were rank amateurs. Hell, he, Squish and Lucky were more likely to die from an accidental firing than one of those bastards trying to shoot them. They could have disarmed and dispatched the guards behind them in seconds.

But that wasn't the plan.

Taking out the cult leader was the plan. Getting Madeline off by herself so he could fill her in on the upcoming rescue was the plan. Locating and rescuing the FBI plant—if she was alive—was the plan. Getting the children to safety was the plan.

And so far, everything had been speeding along like a well-maintained submarine. They'd been dropped off by the Black Hawk in a clearing free of rebel activity. But even if there had been patrols around the insertion point, the thick canopy and jungle vegetation muffled the distance and location of the drop. As soon as he, Squish and Lucky had fast-roped to the ground, the chopper had bugged out.

Sure, they'd had to hike nine klicks beneath the thick canopy of the rainforest, but while the hike through the muggy, hot jungle hadn't been pleasant, it hadn't been bad either. The bug spray might reek, but it kept the mosquitoes at bay. And they'd avoided any rebel patrols.

They'd arrived at the compound for their appointment with Apostolos early, which had given them plenty of time to bury their packs, main weapons and comms just inside the forest. After winding their way through the plantation, they'd taken cover behind a couple of the trees close to the compound. Rubber trees, as it turned out, were huge. Easily three feet around, which made them great projectile catchers in case one of the cult's wannabe warriors freaked at Squish's hail and sprayed the entire area with his APC9K.

They were entering Amateur Hour, which was a lot like the Twilight Zone, only stupider.

At Squish's hail, the guards had converged on them, but without shooting. Thank Christ. They sure as hell didn't need the cult guys all amped up with adrenaline after a fake firefight. Their excited eyes and twitchy fingers were bad enough.

The plantation and house looked exactly like the pictures Tex had wrangled. The guards had been patrolling the exact route Tex had identified. Everything was exactly as expected, which made him nervous as hell.

Too fucking easy.

Never a good sign.

"Take a left," one of the bastards behind them said about three quarters of the way down the dining room. The shadows were thicker back here, bereft of sun or lantern light.

They swung to the left, entering a roomy, lantern-lit corridor that allowed the three of them to walk abreast. The interior walls and floor of the compound were constructed of the same pale stone as the outer wall. All pale, creamy bricks. No pictures or wall hangings, no color anywhere at all. Even the clothes the cult members wore were subdued. The whole damn place, along with the people it housed, looked washed out.

The air was downright cool back here—like it dropped a couple degrees with each stride forward.

They passed a couple of closed wooden doors, with ancient, tarnished, brass handles. When the corridor veered to the right, they followed it, passing more of those closed doors. Eventually the hallway emptied into a wide, lantern-lit room. This room was much warmer than the hall. No surprise. There were open, mosquito-netted windows everywhere, as well as an open archway. Streamers from the dying sun penetrated almost every corner of the room.

Four men turned to face them as they stepped inside. All four had guns strapped to their hips like some Halloweenish version of the wild west.

The cult leader—Apostolos—was instantly identifiable. He was the only one in white. The other three men wore the same pale blue pants and shirts as the guards behind them.

None of the men facing them reached for their weapons. They all looked slightly condescending, as though they thought they had the upper hand because of numbers and guns.

Amateurs.

He scanned the room for anything that might prove dangerous. But the place looked like a handyman's shed. Two sets of plastic tables—three each—were pushed together in the middle of the room. Saws, hammers, wrenches, pliers, wire cutters, bags of zip ties, plumbing pieces, small spools of wire, and cans of plumbing cement were scattered around the tables. Weathered wood panels and five-foot rolls of wire fencing were propped against the west wall. Stacks of rusty metal pipes were sitting on the floor against the east. The north wall hosted an array of shovels, rakes, hoes, machetes, and scythes.

"Welcome to the Children of the Second Cycle." Apostolos dipped his head, and spread his arms, his palms up, the wide sleeves of his white tunic dangling.

Devlin's eyebrows rose as he got a good look at the bastard. Holy shit, the guy looked like he was auditioning for Jesus Christ Superstar. His slightly wavy brown hair brushed his shoulders. His beard, mustache and sideburns were neatly trimmed. Hell, he looked like he'd copied the hair and beard directly from a promotional poster. Even his clothes, a simple white tunic that dipped slightly at the neckline and fell in a straight line to his ankles looked like it had been specifically designed to match the historical records of what Jesus had worn back in the day. And then there were his sandals. His dark brown leather sandals.

Fucking sandals?

In the jungle?

Yeah, this asshole didn't get out much.

The whole ensemble looked like it had been lifted directly from a movie or one of the pictures of Christ that graced churches and living rooms everywhere. No doubt the costume was meant convince his lamebrain followers that he was the new Messiah.

Squish stepped forward, his hand outstretched, no sign of surprise or distaste on his expressionless face.

"Jake Neely." He nodded toward Lucky and then Dev. "Lex Ashford and Cain Dervish." He casually rattled off their aliases.

Apostolos cocked his head, studying them one by one. Disappointment touched his face. "You didn't bring the guns?"

Had the moron really thought they'd haul the guns in today, without payment, into a compound where they were outmanned and outgunned? Where they could be eliminated, and the weapons appropriated for nothing?

Was he really that stupid?

Dev studied the Divine Ruler's disappointed face. Yeah...he really was that stupid. Fucking amateurs.

Squish scraped his chin with his thumb, cocked his head to the right, and studied the cult leader. "We don't bring weapons to the first meeting. The initial meeting is to set parameters... assess your weapon needs...agree on a price and delivery date." He paused, eyed the cult leader with a flinty black gaze. "Fifty percent due upfront, through bank transfer, when the merchandise is ordered. Remainder due on delivery, through bank transfer." He scanned the room. "No cash. Everything is bank transfer through the Caymans. You got an account set up there yet?" When Apostolos frowned and shook his head, Squish grunted. "I got a guy. He'll set you up, but you'll need access to the internet and this place doesn't appear to have any electricity."

When Apostolos didn't respond, Squish shrugged. "Word of advice," he reached into his front pocket and pulled out a SAT phone. "Get yourself one of these. An Iridium Satellite phone and prepaid SIM card. It will set you back about three grand if you go for the 1200 prepaid minutes, but you'll be able to reach your bank and transfer money anywhere. Even out in the middle of fucking nowhere like here."

He stuffed the phone back in his pocket and shrugged. "We all carry one. The GPS comes in handy too."

The goons behind them knew about the phones. They'd found them on the body search. Normally phones didn't accompany special operators on missions. Too big of a chance someone could hack into the cell server and track them. But they'd known they'd have to dump their comms while inside the compound, and they'd need access to command if things went south. Besides, the damn SAT phones they'd been given were tighter than the nuclear codes.

While the phones had made it through the guards' search, their guns hadn't. As expected, they'd been stripped of their secondary weapons back at the rubber trees. Or at least the weapons their guards had found during their careless pat downs.

They hadn't found the blade strapped to Dev's ankle. Devlin wasn't sure what Lucky and Squish had on them, but likely knives too. Knives were favored over guns when the kill needed to be silent.

"Before we get down to business," Squish drawled, driving an elbow into the right side of Devlin's chest, "Romeo here has a favor to ask. Consider it a gesture of good will."

Apostolos's eyes narrowed. "What favor?"

Devlin stepped forward. Show time.

"There's a certain lady back there I want to get to know better." He paused to leer. "*A lot* better. I'll throw in a couple units free of charge, in exchange for a couple of uninterrupted hours in her company."

Apostolos studied him skeptically. "You have the authority to make such a deal?"

Devlin folded his arms and rocked back on the heels of his boots. "I control the fuckin' pipeline. But the freebies will come out of my cut." He turned, dropped his arms, and offered a half-hearted jab toward Squish. "Wouldn't want these poor bastards to get their boxers in a twist."

The cult leader's gaze traveled between Squish, Devlin, and Lucky. "I can accommodate that request," he finally agreed. "Who's the lady you want to entertain?"

"Long dark hair. Nice tits. Not too big. Not too small. Brown eyes." There were several women in the room who matched that description, but he could hardly call her by name. Nor could he describe her height since she'd been sitting down. "She was sitting with a kid. A girl. They looked enough alike to be mother and daughter."

Apostolos's eyebrows snapped forward beneath a scowl. "The daughter's off the table."

Devlin forced his muscles to relax. Motherfucking asshole—he was balking at pimping out the kid? But not the mother? No doubt he wanted to keep the kid for himself.

"I'm not interested in the kid. I want the mother," Dev said, internally wincing as the response hit too close to home.

That was exactly what he'd decided back in that motel room, wasn't it? He'd been willing to go the extra mile to see Madeline...but the kid, hell—she'd been a deal breaker.

"He's talking about Sister Madeline," one of the bozos behind him said.

As if the cult leader calling dibs on the daughter hadn't proved he knew exactly who Devlin was referring to.

"I'll make the arrangements," Apostolos said.

"What about you two?" The cult leader's eyes traveled between Squish and Lucky. "Either of you interested in a similar trade?"

Squish hesitated, like he was really thinking about it before shaking his head, regret on his face. "My old lady is the jealous type and can smell pussy on me a mile away. Better not chance it. Last time she almost took my dick with her paring knife." He paused, raised his eyebrows. "Never piss off an Italian."

Apostolos switched his focus to Lucky. "What about you? Same terms?"

"The women? No." He turned to leer at the guard immediately behind them. "This little bitch though? I'd plow him in a heartbeat. And yeah, same terms."

It took a few seconds for Lucky's meaning to hit the guy he was leering at, but when it did, the moron's mouth fell open in horror and he backed away so fast he almost tripped over his own feet.

"No fucking way, man. That's disgusting." He backed up even further and sent Apostolos a panicked look.

Lucky shrugged, turning back to the cult leader. "His loss."

Devlin was struck mute by the exchange. He knew for a fact that Lucky didn't run in that direction. What would he have done if Apostolos or the cult guy had agreed to the deal? Probably broke the bastard's neck the second they were alone.

But the request was pretty fucking perfect, considering what these bastards were up to each night. And it had given Lucky a good reason for why he wasn't interested in any of the women.

"You want her before or after the negotiations?" Apostolos asked, his attention back on Devlin.

Devlin swallowed his distaste. Fuck, it would be a pleasure to slit this asshole's throat. But for now, he had to play his part.

Disgusting as it was.

"I'll have her now," Devlin drawled. "My boys here can handle the negotiation. I'll approve or disapprove once I've had my fill of her."

Which he'd draw out for hours. By the time he left her, his team would be minutes from insertion and her rescue would be at hand.

If everything went according to plan.

CHAPTER 7

Madeline watched Apostolos sweep out of the left corridor, with Sister Rebecca in tow. He paused as he entered the dining area, scanning the assembled members. Rebecca tentatively touched the Divine Ruler's wrist and pointed to Madeline, who braced herself as Apostolos headed in her direction.

"Momma?" Cassidy whispered timidly, reaching out to tug on Maddie's shirt. "What's wrong?"

"Nothing, baby." Madeline forced herself to relax. Her daughter had become far too accomplished at picking up on her tension.

"Ah, there you are Sister Madeline," Apostolos said.

He'd adopted a pseudo-fatherly tone, which was just plain creepy. Not only were they the same age...but there was nothing fatherly about the man at all.

"If you would accompany me please," the cult leader continued politely. "We are in need of a chat."

Her mind racing, Maddie slowly pushed back her chair. When Cassidy scrambled to her feet beside her, Apostolos beckoned Rebecca forward. "Sister Rebecca will care for our little princess while you are gone."

Madeline mentally gagged at the title the scumbag had given her daughter. He'd given identical titles to all of his child brides, as though dubbing them princess erased the horror he was introducing them to.

He waved his hand toward Rebecca. "Sister Rebecca, if you'll be so kind as to take Princess Cassidy to the chapel with the other children."

Cassidy cringed as he said her name, which was so damn wrong. What girl didn't want to be a princess? The bastard had completely ruined that fantasy for her daughter.

"It's okay, sweetie." Madeline bent to give her daughter a hug. "I'll see you tonight at bedtime. We'll finish the story from last night, okay?"

Storytime had become their nightly ritual when they were locked in for the night. She hoped that by mimicking what had been their routine at home, she could instill some normalcy into their current circumstances. Back in Phoenix she'd read to Cass before bed, but here...with no electricity and limited fuel for the lanterns, it was lights out at bedtime. So, she'd made the best of the situation and told Cass stories instead.

"Okay, Momma," Cassidy whispered, reluctantly reaching for Rebecca's hand. She glanced over her shoulder, her eyes dark and anxious, as the other woman led her away.

The sight of her daughter's dark, worried gaze usually filled Maddie with frustration and fear. Not today though. Devlin's arrival had changed everything.

Hang on, baby. We're getting out of here.

She silently followed the cult leader across the dining room, her soft soled canvas shoes whispering against the limestone floor. The interior of the compound was set up like a giant cross, with the main room split into dining and food prep areas. Two corridors sprouted off the main room. The corridor to the left housed the comfort and sleeping rooms, with work and supply areas around the corner at the back of the property.

But the corridor to the right—that one housed Apostolos's private quarters, along with the rooms his wives occupied.

The room where he met with his disciples was sparsely furnished. Someone had found an ancient, fan backed armchair and set it against the far wall. The upholstery had long since faded from red to pink, and was liberally splashed with stains, but he treated the damn thing like a throne. An image bolstered by the half dozen white plastic chairs spread out in a half circle before it.

"Please, be seated." He gestured toward the plastic chairs as he settled against the fan back of his armchair.

She did as told and waited for him to begin. Best to hold her tongue until she knew what this summons was about.

"My far too generous offer of yesterday has been rescinded," he told her, watching her face with distant, uncaring eyes. "Your personal services are required immediately."

Her recoil was instant. She jolted away from him hard enough to rock the chair beneath her, which almost dumped her on the ground. Her heart slammed against her ribs with such force it took her breath away.

Personal services?

He meant sex. He was requiring her to have sex. *Immediately.*

Her stomach rolled. What little she'd consumed for lunch rushed up her throat, threatening to spew itself onto the floor. She forced the vomit back down and regrouped.

"You said I had until tomorrow night!" The protest sputtered from her. Her voice rose in horror and outrage. "You said—"

"The situation has changed," he broke in, raising a hand to wave her objections aside. "One of our guests specifically asked for you. And we need his good will. We need the guns he can provide. We are vulnerable out here. This is a matter of life or death for all our brothers and sisters. You will do your part to protect our people. You will accommodate his request. Or you will no longer be welcome here."

Wait...what...?

"Guests...you mean the three men Brother Timothy and Luke escorted through the dining hall?" Madeline asked, the urgent beat of her heart settling into a rhythm that wasn't quite as suffocating.

He had to mean Devlin and the two men he'd arrived with. Devlin must have requested her, which would effectively get her aside, so they could talk privately.

Her breathing eased.

She needed to play this carefully. She needed to react as though the man who'd requested her was a stranger.

An unwelcome one at that.

It wasn't hard to mimic her earlier horror. All she had to do was think about one of the cult men touching her.

Tensing her arms and abdomen, she drew her elbows tight against her ribs. "I won't do it."

"Think carefully before you refuse again," he told her, his gaze as cold as death. "To reject this opportunity, is to turn your back on your brothers and sisters. Which makes you of no use to us."

"I will not sleep with someone I don't even know!" She raised her voice. "He could be sadistic for all you know. Or infected with some kind of disease. If he infects me, it could spread through the entire commune."

Although there was a good chance some kind of sexually transmitted disease was already working its way through the cult members. She doubted the members had been tested prior to fleeing the states, and rumor had it condoms were forbidden, as the supposed purpose of the coupling was to provide the cult with children.

"My Father will protect you," Apostolos solemnly intoned.

He meant God. That God would protect her. What a bunch of bullshit. He didn't believe in God. In actuality, the guy was a true atheist. He wouldn't be preying on children and women, killing off those who threatened him, if he had any worries of facing God's wrath in the afterlife.

He might mimic Jesus with his clothing and hair, but his eyes told the real story. They held no compassion. No spirituality. No sadness or grief.

They were reptilian. Cold. Callous. Manipulative.

The eyes of a predator.

Not a savior.

"Fine." She drew in a deep breath and pulled back her shoulders. "Cassidy and I will leave."

She already knew he wouldn't accept that. He'd made Cassidy's role in his fantasy clear. He'd never let her go. But he'd expect the response from her. He'd expect her resistance. To give him anything less would be suspicious.

"The little princess does not belong to you." He spread his arms wide in the worst Jesus impersonation she'd ever seen. "Her destiny is here. As my wife and the mother of the new order."

She's a child! You fucking monster. She is not your consort. She is not the mother of your monstrous get. She's a seven-year-old child.

"I'm her mother." It was easy to project seething rage. All she had to do was think about his plans for her daughter. "Her destiny is with me. Not you. Not as your broodmare."

He smiled faintly. She could see smug enjoyment clear as day on his face and in his predatory eyes. He enjoyed witnessing her impotence. The scumbag.

"Cassidy stays here." He paused, cocked his head. "And you are out of time. Our guest is waiting. Yes or no?"

Her plan, from the moment she'd been told Devlin had requested her—or at least she was assuming it was Devlin—had been to accept the situation after a hearty protest.

"If I agree," she switched tactics, "then I want some time before I can be requested again. A couple of days at least."

With luck she wouldn't need those extra days. But if Devlin's plan couldn't be implemented immediately, she needed to protect herself.

An ugly expression slipped across his face.

"You do not make the rules." He clipped the rebuke out.

"Not a rule," she countered. "A negotiation. If I go to him… if I please him…thoroughly. Then I want a couple of days to recuperate."

Cocking his head, he fingered his chin and studied her closely. "Please him?"

"Pleasure him. Thoroughly. Put him in such a good mood, he's amenable to whatever it is you want from him."

Thoughtfulness coasted across his face. He nodded slightly, apparently liking that idea. "If such were the case, I would accommodate you with two days off."

"Three." The counteroffer shot out of her.

"Two." His jaw set.

She grimaced. He was done negotiating. Devlin better get her out of here before her time ran out.

"Fine." She drew the capitulation out slowly, filling her voice with reluctance.

"Excellent." He turned his head toward the open door, his hair brushing his tunic clad shoulders. "Brother Nelson." He waited for Nelson to appear in the doorway. "Show Sister Madeline to our guest. I believe he is waiting in the first comfort room."

Comfort room.

There was nothing comforting about the rooms reserved for sexual trysts. At least not for the women. Few of the cult women looked heartened after returning to the women's sleeping quarters smelling of sex and sweat.

"You may leave now." He drummed his fingers impatiently against the armrest of his chair when Maddie didn't rise to her feet fast enough. He scowled and glanced at Brother Nelson. "Make sure she gets there promptly. No meandering. Our guest has waited long enough."

"As you wish, Divine Ruler." Nelson bent his neck in supplication, but there was nothing pious about the ugly enjoyment on his face.

Madeline rose to her feet. With pretend reluctance, she dragged her feet all the way to the open door. As soon as she joined him in the doorway, Nelson grabbed her elbow and marched her down the corridor toward the dining hall.

"About time you were put in rotation," he sneered at her. "Not so high and mighty now, are you, bitch? I'm looking forward to my turn with you."

Clenching her teeth, she held back her response. If she made any attempt to challenge him, he'd put some actual effort into hurting her. Twist her arm. Break a finger. This scum bag was the worst of the worst here. He enjoyed hurting people. The women he requested to comfort him returned hours later, bruised and shaking.

Apostolos had been informed of his brutal behavior numerous times, but rather than taking the bastard to task, the

Divine Pretender had counseled the women to show compliance and understanding.

As if compliance and understanding had ever stopped a fist.

Nelson dragged her across the dining room. Heads turned, following their progress. She saw understanding dawn along with pity on many of the female faces. They obviously thought she'd been given to Nelson for the evening. Thank God that wasn't the case. But she needed to make sure she and Cassidy were long gone before the two extra days Apostolos had granted her were up.

Her bully of an escort stopped in front of the first room on the right, opened the door, and thrust her inside. She stumbled into the room, almost hitting the ground beneath the force of her escort's thrust.

Devlin, who was lounging against the limestone wall, not far from a flickering lantern, straightened. Slowly, the arms he'd folded across his chest loosened and dropped. His face went still, his body rigid. An icy glitter flared in his black eyes.

He looked pissed and battle ready.

"She's all yours," Nelson drawled, turning to leer at Madeline. Ugly anticipation crept across his broad, brutal face. "This one needs to learn her place. If she gives you any lip, let me know. It will be my pleasure to teach the uppity bitch a lesson or two."

Maddie shot Dev a quick glance, heat flaming across her face. To be treated like a whore in front of this man, the one who'd given her the best orgasms of her life…somehow that just made the position she was in so much worse.

Since Nelson was staring at her, instead of the man silently watching from across the room, he missed the stillness that crept over Devlin's huge body…the poised, lethal, readiness. It reminded her of the immobility of a lion just before it attacked. The light from the lantern flickered across his face, painting him in brutal, murderous repose.

Instinctively, Madeline stepped between the two men. She didn't know what Devlin and his buddies had planned, but she was pretty sure it didn't include killing someone so soon.

"I'm Madeline." She took another step forward and held out her hand. "The Divine Ruler said you wanted to see me?" She held his glittering, furious gaze and willed him to take her hand, to follow her lead, to let Nelson go.

It took a second, but then he seemed to shake himself. His chest rose beneath a deep breath. When he glanced back at the open door, his eyes were cold, but controlled. The rage masked.

"You can leave," he told Nelson flatly. "I've yet to meet a woman I can't handle."

Nelson laughed, his tone companionable, as though he took that to mean they shared similar appetites.

"Enjoy her." He winked. "Just don't do too much damage. Leave some of the work for the rest of us."

Devlin waited, absolutely still, his muscled frame seeming to vibrate within the flickering lamp light. Once the door closed, he held up his palm in a wait gesture and strode to the door. He waited there, his hand on the knob for several seconds, before cracking it open and sticking his head outside. He looked up and down the corridor, then pulled back, closed it, and turned to face her.

"We're clear." He scanned her from head to toe. "He hurt you?" His voice was low and throbbing with menace.

She tensed at his tone, only to relax. This was Dev and his rage was directed at Nelson, not her. He'd never hurt her. At least not physically.

"Other than grabbing my elbow on the way here? No."

He glanced down at her arm and took a step closer, but to the side so he wasn't blocking the lantern's glow. A low, menacing growl broke from him. In a flash he was by her side, gently lifting her arm. "That fucker left his fingerprints on you."

"Trust me. I got off light." She forced a smile past the blockage in her throat, trying to ignore the way her skin tingled beneath his touch. Trying to think past how happy she was to see him. "You should see the bruises he leaves on the other women."

"He just got added to the list," Dev muttered, letting go of her arm.

"List?" He was so close she could smell him past the lingering scent of sex in the room.

He smelled like sweat and insect repellent. She took a deep

breath, drawing him into her lungs and holding him there. Letting his scent steady her, fill her with hope. He was here. Not a hallucination. Not a daydream. He was real and he was here.

The relief made her dizzy.

"The kill list." His voice was low and matter of fact rather than furious.

Kill list?

She should have felt horrified by the comment, but she didn't have it in her. Not after watching what these men had done to the women. Not knowing the damage Apostolos had inflicted on so many of the little girls...what he had planned for Cassidy.

Apparently the past six weeks had kickstarted her blood lust. She wanted Apostolos and his men to pay. Every last one of them. Leaning back, she scanned his big body. She didn't see any guns.

"Did you slip a gun past the guards?" She wouldn't be surprised if he had one hidden on him. Most of the guards were pretty lax.

Some of the tension on his face faded. An upward curve touched his lips. "Sweetheart, we don't need guns."

No...they probably didn't. She'd recognized the innate lethality of Dev and his two friends as they'd walked across the dining room. Apostolos had no idea that he'd orchestrated his demise by letting these three men into the compound.

"Those two men you came with." She glanced at the door and dropped her voice to a whisper. "They're like you?"

Meaning SEALs.

He simply nodded, then turned back to the door. Opening it, he took another look outside.

While he was checking to see if they had an audience, she turned to study the room. She'd been hearing about the comfort rooms for the past week. About how bad they were. The sex rooms in the old place had been actual bedrooms, with actual beds. But there were no beds or even mattresses here in the amazon, so the women had to make do with what was available.

Which was apparently nothing but a couple of stained blankets and an oil lantern. Disgust filled her. Good God, even through the flickering lantern light she could see how awful this room was. The stench of fading sex and old sweat was overwhelming.

This was what the women were forced to endure every night? Thin, filthy blankets and a hard floor? Not only did they have to deal with the unwelcome asshole on top and inside of them, but the cold, hard limestone against their back.

Why the hell would any of them put up with this? Their compliance was inconceivable.

"We need to keep our voices low," Devlin said in a whisper. "While the corridor is clear right now, someone could walk by at any minute and we don't know how far voices carry surrounded by all this stone." When she nodded, he reached into his pocket and pulled out what looked like a cell phone. "A buddy worked magic with my SAT phone. As long as it's on, it emits a frequency that interferes with electrical devices. It's been on since I walked through the door, so if this place is bugged, they haven't heard anything we've said. Nor will they. We can talk safely."

Madeline released a shaky breath. She hadn't even thought of someone listening in on them, but it made sense. Of course Apostolos would bug his disciples. How else would he know if someone was planning on leaving or staging a coup? Although monitoring the rooms out here would be harder, wouldn't it? Without electricity to power the listening devices? Of course, they could run on batteries...and it was better to be safe than sorry.

Thank God Devlin was well-versed in all this spy stuff.

"How did you find me?" she asked, more to start the conversation, because she was pretty sure she already knew the answer to her question.

"Marguerite came to see me." His voice was tight. His face even tighter.

She nodded. She'd figured that out minutes after seeing him walk across the dining room. Her sister must have been worried sick when Maddie hadn't returned. She knew about Devlin. Knew he was a SEAL. So her sister had gone to the one man who had the contacts and capabilities to help.

Thank God for Marguerite.

"But by the time she came to me," he continued, "your *Divine Ruler—*" pure sarcasm coated the title, "—along with his entire cult, had left the country. It took us a while to track you down."

Madeline drew a deep breath and let it out slowly.

He was here. He'd come for her.

"Thank you for coming to the rescue." Her voice trembled. She forced it steady again. She wasn't out of the woods yet. She could fall apart once she was back home. She hesitated, then forced what was doubtlessly unwelcome news out. Considering how he'd reacted the last time she'd brought up a kid, he probably wasn't going to like hearing this. "We need to get all the children out, though, not just me and Cass." He had to know she wouldn't leave without her daughter. He would have taken that into account. "Particularly the girls. The *Divine Ruler,*" she infused the term with as much sarcasm as he had, "is nothing but a pedophile, using the children of his disciples as his personal brothel."

"So we discovered when we looked into him." His voice tightened with disgust, his fingers curling into fists. "Trust me, the bastard's at the top of everyone's list."

He meant their kill lists.

She thought about that…the whole vigilante thing. Only to shrug. She was okay with that. At least he wouldn't be able to prey on children anymore.

It was amazing how one's entire attitude could shift in such a short amount of time. Six weeks ago, killing anyone without due process would have been morally repugnant. Now, knowing he'd be removed—permanently—from God's green earth was a relief.

One criminal's death in return for dozens, if not hundreds, of children's lives?

That seemed like a good trade to her.

CHAPTER 8

Madeline looked awful up close. While he'd seen the weight loss and the way her clothes hung on her when he'd walked past her table, he hadn't noticed the rest of it. Translucent shadows dusted the bottom of her eyes. Stress lines dug into her forehead and down the sides of her mouth. Even within the meager light that pooled in the room, he could see the gray tinge to her skin.

She looked weak and shaky. Like all her mental and physical resources had been used up.

He could not fuck this operation up. She'd be the one to pay the price if he did.

The room he'd been shown to was ...horrifying. The only light, a sputtering lantern. The only bedding, a couple of ragged blankets. The smell of semen permeated the air. The thought of her being forced onto those blankets—he cut the image off. Fought back the urge to kill...to maim...to destroy.

Someone needed to pay for what they'd done to her.

For what they'd made her do.

"So, what's your plan?"

Her voice came to him from a distance, even though she was barely five feet away. He grasped onto it and clung, used it to pull him free from the rage and regret.

"To get you out of here." He paused, before adding. "Along with the children and women."

She nodded and took a deep breath. "I'm not sure how many of the women will come," she offered after a moment, her dark, exhausted eyes clinging to his face. "He has them brainwashed. They believe he is a conduit to God." She grimaced and shook her head. "He's convinced them he's the second Messiah." She fell silent, her face twisting. "What they've allowed him to do to their daughters, to their own bodies, because of his twisted teachings —" She broke off, took a deep, steadying breath. "They're not rational."

"We're aware." Devlin rolled his shoulders, wanting to touch her, soothe her. But he wasn't sure how she'd react to his touch. Whether it would bring back painful memories. Maybe even send her into flight. He'd best keep his hands to himself. "We won't force anyone to leave. We don't have the time or resources for that." He studied her face for a moment. "How did you escape the brainwashing?"

The cult specialist had told them the programming usually started immediately, progressing every day. And Madeline had been with them over six weeks. Plenty of time for the cult's systematic brainwashing to take hold.

Maybe the difference was that she'd gone in with a purpose —to get her daughter back—while the other women had been enticed with something their lives had been lacking.

"I did a lot of research. I looked up everything I could find on cults, brainwashing, and cult programming before I knocked on their door. The articles and documentaries I found examined the way various cults manipulated their members. But I also found some articles on deprogramming, and the methods deprogramming specialists use to free cult members from mental manipulation. I used those tactics to keep my mind focused on why I was here." She paused. Shrugged. "I came in as prepared as I could." But a shadow crossed her face. "At least in that regard."

Well, thank Christ for that. The worst-case scenario had been if she refused to leave, and he'd had to haul her kicking and screaming back to civilization.

While their objectives were to extricate the fed, Madeline, her daughter, and the rest of the children.... the cult women were not a priority. If they wanted rescue...fine. If not, they'd be left behind. They were adults. It was their choice. His team didn't have the resources or manpower to force a couple dozen women to show some fucking common sense.

Besides, Tex had mentioned hooking the women's families up with extraction specialists. Eventually, help would arrive, whether these bimbos wanted that assistance or not.

Devlin glanced at his watch. "We need to go over some details. We have five and a half hours before the rest of the team inserts."

Madeline's eyebrows shot up in surprise. "The rest of the team? You talked a whole team into coming to get me and Cass?"

Devlin grimaced. "Not quite. Extracting you and your kid are part of it. But there's another life at stake."

When shards of pain ripped through his jaw, he forced his teeth to unclench. Thank Christ for that FBI agent. If Tex hadn't convinced the feds to ask NSWC for help in getting their FBI plant back, HQ1 would never have approved this mission.

Sure, he would have come anyway, likely with Tag and Tram. But they wouldn't have had the support and resources of NSWC behind them.

Which would have made extricating Madeline and her daughter much more problematic. Not impossible. But difficult. And they sure as hell wouldn't have been able to evac the rest of the kids, let alone the women.

"The FBI has a deep cover plant inside. When Apostolos pulled up stakes, their agent disappeared too. They want her back."

Madeline's eyes rounded in surprise. "Her?"

Devlin reached into his pocket, pulled out his SAT phone, and punched in his password to unlock the device. It took a second to find the FBI file in his email and type in the code to unencrypt it. He pulled up the agent's picture.

"Yeah. Her." He turned the phone in her direction. "You recognize her?"

Shock hit her face and rocked her back a good foot. "No. That can't be right."

He studied her. His eyebrows rising. "Why not?"

She took his phone between both her hands and leaned in closer, as if she couldn't believe her eyes. "Because that looks like Sister Abigail. But she's ancient and one of the nastiest people I've ever met." She paused. Shook her head slightly. "She's so devoted to Apostolos's agenda, I thought she'd been with him from the beginning."

Devlin had been surprised by the fed's picture too, but for different reasons. She was much older than he'd expected—in her late fifties maybe. Hardly a spring chicken. Not at all what he'd expected an undercover FBI agent to look like.

Which must have made her particularly effective.

Although Madeline was right, it did seem odd that the cult had taken her in. She didn't fit the proposed agenda. She wasn't of childbearing age; she wouldn't appeal to the incel crowd. She must have had other attributes that had made her inclusion acceptable.

"It's brilliant, actually," Madeline said, still staring down at his phone. Her eyebrows drew together as the shock gave way to thoughtfulness.

"How so?" he asked.

"How long has she been in the cult?"

He cocked his head, studying her reflective face with curiosity. "Eight months, give or take. Why?"

"Because if they'd sent in a younger, more attractive woman. She would have been forced into the comfort rooms months ago. Apostolos has been trying to force me to concede to the men's demands since two weeks after I arrived. He gave me an ultimatum yesterday. Accept the requests or leave—which I'm pretty sure doesn't mean walking out of here alive. But nobody has requested Abigail since I've been here. She's been left alone. Which makes sense. Why ask for her when there are dozens of younger, more attractive women to choose from? And if they'd sent a male agent, and he never requested any of the women, everyone would have suspected him of being up to something. Apostolos is a genius in connecting with men who believe women were put on this earth solely to provide sex, cooking, cleaning, and children." She handed the phone back. "The limitless sex is what draws them, so anyone who abstained would stand out, and not in a good way."

"That's because he's recruiting his male members from incel chat rooms," Devlin said absently, still stuck on her comment about The Divine Asshole *trying* to force her into the comfort rooms, and how she'd been given an ultimatum the *previous* day.

Did that mean she hadn't been forced to service the men yet? Had she escaped that fate?

Christ, he hoped so.

Forcing his attention back to her, he saw her grimace.

"Well that explains where all the Neanderthals here come from."

"Do you think you can get to her? Explain to her in private what's happening?" Devlin asked.

"I think so. All the women are locked in the women's quarters with the children at night. The popular ones come and go as they're requested and returned by the men. Since Abigail doesn't get requested, she'll be there all night. If you release me before your team's arrival, I should be able to talk to her and let her know what's happening."

But there was hesitancy in her voice, and beneath the flickering shadows in the room, he could see the reservation on her face. He shifted closer.

"What?" he asked, and swore he could feel the release of her breath against his neck when she sighed. Heat exploded at the point of contact and shot down to his cock, which predictably hardened.

And if that wasn't disturbing as hell. That he'd gotten so fucking hard, so fucking fast, in such a despicable place.

What the hell was wrong with him?"

"What if I'm wrong and Abigail isn't your agent? If I tell her what you have planned and she's not who I think she is, she'll go straight to Apostolos. You and your team will be screwed."

He shrugged off the risk. "You'll need to wait until just before my team inserts. At that point, nothing she does will affect the outcome. Apostolos will already be dead." He scowled as another problem occurred to him. "I'll have you back at the women's quarters half an hour before my team breaches the compound. Plenty of time for you to connect with Abigail. Plenty of time for me to get in position. But what are the chances you'll get requested by one of these other assholes immediately after I release you?"

The smug anticipation on the face of the man who'd tossed her into the room still raised Devlin's blood pressure. He wouldn't put it past the man to snag her the moment Dev left the room and force her back inside. Which meant he'd have to hunt the bastard down and kill him.

"I should be okay." Madeline sighed, swaying slightly. "I negotiated a deal with Apostolos. If I please you thoroughly, I'm comfort-free for the next two days." She shrugged lightly. "Say what you will about the Divine Ruler, he does keep his promises. And his word is law. I'm off limits for forty-eight hours. Nobody will dare touch me until then." She paused, staring up at him with her huge, exhausted eyes, and he saw her throat tremble. Her voice dropped to a hoarse, shaking whisper. "We'll be out of here before then, right?"

Helpless beneath the gloss of fear on her face, he drew her into his arms and tucked her against his chest. She smelled sour—of sweat and dust—but she went easily, melting into him without making a sound. As he held her, his pounding heartrate settled, his muscles loosened, the urge to kill and maim subsided.

"Nobody is going to touch you, Madeline." His voice was tight, turning the words into a pledge. "Trust me on that."

And he'd keep that vow, even if it meant killing every fucking asshole in this place.

He felt the movement of her head against his chest as she nodded. She felt so fragile in his arms. Her bones pressing through the loose cloth of her shirt, and into his skin. He thought back to two months ago, to how she'd felt in his arms then. She'd lost even more weight than he'd realized.

"We've got over a five hour wait. Might as well get comfortable." He pulled back, but kept an arm around her fragile shoulders as he led her over to the wall beside the lantern. "Let's sit down. I'll find something to cover the floor."

He glanced around the room on the way over. He needed a pad for her to sit on.

"Don't even think about it," she said, her voice full of revulsion when she saw him glance at the blankets.

There was another choice, thank God. He stripped off his shirt and spread it out. It might not be all that thick, but at least it was sweat, rather than semen, stained.

"Devlin, I can't take your shirt." She made no move to sit.

"You're not. We're sharing it," he lied. She didn't look convinced. "Having a barrier between us and the floor will keep us warmer. It might be eighty degrees outside still, but the temperature drops fast once the sun goes down. It can get down to the mid-sixties, and we have five hours of inactivity before the boys insert," he told her flatly.

While sixty-five degrees wasn't exactly arctic weather, Madeline had lost a lot of weight. That, along with the stress and exhaustion, would leave her vulnerable to the cold. He'd considered tucking her into his shirt, but knew she'd object. Besides, his body heat would keep her top half warm.

"Sit," he finally ordered when she just stood there looking at him.

She stuck her tongue out at him, but sat with a weary sigh. "Just so you know, I'm too tired to get annoyed at you for treating me like a dog. But don't make a habit of ordering me around."

Whatever.

At least she was off her feet. He settled beside her and tugged her against his bare chest. Her weight barely registered as she settled against him with an exhausted slump.

It was a damn good thing evac was happening out front. She didn't have the physical or mental reserves to battle her way through the rainforest. He dug into his front pocket and pulled out a protein bar. He was lucky the guards hadn't confiscated the two energy bars he'd had on him when they'd performed their pat down. They'd sure as hell looked interested in them, but had eventually passed them back. Probably afraid to jinx their Divine Ruler's deal and suffer the consequences.

"Here. Eat." He pressed the protein bar into her hand.

She lifted the plastic wrapped object and peered down.

"Oh wow! Thank you. You have no idea how hungry we are." But rather than ripping the wrapping open, she shifted and shoved it into her pocket.

He scowled. "Madeline—"

"Cassidy needs it more than I do." She slumped back against his chest, exposing the lie. She was obviously a great mother, putting her daughter first, but she was in desperate need of the energy the bar would provide too.

"I've got another one. You can give that to her. Hell, I've got a whole supply of them, along with several MREs in my rucksack." Which was buried outside of the plantation perimeter along with his ballistic vest, NVDs and headset. He'd grab everything before they evac'd. Madeline and her kid could eat on the bird. "Your daughter won't go hungry." When she made no attempt to reach into her pocket, he pulled the second energy bar free, ripped open the packaging, and held it to her mouth. "Eat."

When she reached for the bar, he pulled it away, knowing it would just disappear into her pocket along with the other one.

"You're going to need all the energy you can muster to get your daughter on that helicopter. You'll be doing her no favors if you're too weak to help her." He eased the bar back up to her lips. "You need to eat."

He relaxed as she finally took a bite. When she took another and then another and finally reached up to take the bar herself, he leaned back against the wall.

"What are MREs," she asked between bites.

"Ready to eat meals—although their technical name is Meals, ready to eat," he answered softly, content just holding her. "They're combat meals. Used during missions." Since she seemed interested, he continued talking. "It's a full meal package that contains an entree, side dish, dessert, powdered drink, along with everything you need to prepare and eat it."

He barely paid attention to what he was saying, simply enjoying the feel of her in his arms again.

"Really?" Her head didn't lift from his chest. "You eat it cold?"

"Nope." He settled more comfortably against the wall. "The package includes a flameless heater."

"Wow." She sounded half asleep. "That's kind of ingenious. Do they taste good?"

"Some of them." He kept his voice soft, soothing, conducive to sleep. It would do her good to grab some *zzz's* now, while she had a chance. It was going to be a long night. He'd wake her up an hour or so before insertion and go over everything.

With the hope of lulling her into sleep, he kept talking, his voice low and soft...intimate. "American MREs are the most in demand at the Bagram Airfield MRE swap in Afghanistan. That's where military forces from around the world meet up to swap packages. The French meals are second. But among our teams, the chili mac is hands down the favorite, with the strongest trading value."

"Chili mac?" Her voice was slurred and vague. "Is that like a chili hamburger?"

He smiled slightly, letting his lips brush the top of her head. She must be thinking of the Big Mac or something. "Nope. It's macaroni and chili. Comes with a pound cake, crackers, and candy."

She lifted her head, offering a moue of distaste. "That sounds terrible. The chili and macaroni combo I mean."

He stroked a dark swath of hair back from her face. "No—terrible is the veggie burger, or the veggie omelet, or God help us, the chicken a la king."

Leaning back, she peered into his face, as though she thought he was teasing her. "Chicken a la king doesn't sound so bad."

He smiled back at her. "You wouldn't say that if you ate one. It's called chicken a la death for a reason."

He tucked a tendril of hair behind her ear, his chest aching at the dirty, gritty feel of it against his fingers. She'd had the most beautiful hair back in Dark Falls—thick, glossy, healthy. Now it looked and felt unwashed, malnourished, just like the rest of her. What the hell had these bastards been feeding her?

"What have you and the others been eating out here?" he asked. The rainforest was full of food if one knew where to look.

Snakes alone were plentiful and made a solid, protein-packed meal.

"Fruit." She grimaced. "It will be years before I'll be able to look at a banana, mango, or coconut again."

"No meat?" He frowned. No wonder she looked so fragile.

"There's no electricity, so no way to refrigerate food. What they should have done was bring in a bunch of canned food. But I guess they thought the rainforest would provide all the protein we'd need. Except the men are lousy hunters. Small groups of them go out every day, only to come back empty handed." Her stomach rumbled as she said the last word, and she laughed. "I'd kill for a juicy cheeseburger or a steak."

"Deal," he said without thinking. "That will be the first stop we'll make when we get you back home."

He tensed as soon as the offer left his lips, realizing too late that she wouldn't leave her daughter's side anytime soon. And his spur of the moment offer didn't include her kid.

She must have felt him tense because she laughed softly.

"Relax." Her voice was wry. "I'm not going to hold you to that."

What if I want you to?

But all it took was the memory of her dark-haired, dark-eyed daughter peeking around Madeline's waist to remind him of why that wasn't a possibility. Why a relationship with her wasn't an option.

Her having a kid was bad enough…a daughter even worse… but a baby girl the same age and same coloring as his Gracie had been on that God awful day he'd lost her? Yeah, that was something he couldn't climb past. He flinched as the memories tried to roll up and claim him.

He'd done the right thing two months ago; he was certain of that. The only thing he regretted was how he'd gone about it.

"I'm sorry for just walking out back in Dark Falls," he said, his arms tightening convulsively around her. "I should have explained."

"It's okay." She sighed, snuggling in closer. "I'll admit I was furious and hurt at first. But you came all the way out here to get me and Cass. That makes up for everything. I was out of options."

Which reminded him of her earlier comments. "They hadn't pressed you into the comfort rooms yet?"

He tensed as he waited for her answer.

"No. Apostolos claimed he was giving me time to adjust to my duty. But I think he had so much on his plate back in Montana, he didn't have time to enforce the demand. But out here, with no one checking in on him, no one enforcing the rules of morality or ethics? I became free game the moment we left US shores."

"You said he gave you an ultimatum? What were you going to do?" He suspected he already knew, and it made his gut clench.

Her shoulders stiffened. She lifted her head and looked him right in the eyes. Her gaze was firm and unapologetic. "Whatever he wanted. Whatever he demanded of me. What I was not going to do was give him cause to get rid of me and leave Cassidy here on her own."

"Shush." He tightened his arms around her and dropped a kiss on top of her head, wincing at the greasy, gritty feel of her hair against his lips. "I get it. Trust me. I'm not judging." But then something she'd said registered. "You said leaving your daughter on her own? Is your ex not here?"

"No." She blew out a breath and collapsed back against his chest. "Ronnie wasn't here when I arrived. Cassidy had been alone for weeks. At least two, maybe even longer. Alone with these horrible people. They were already grooming her to be that scumbag's next bride."

"Your ex-husband just left her here? Alone." Devlin's voice started to rise. He caught it and forced it back down.

"Not on purpose, I'm sure. Apostolos said Ronnie left on a mission to spread the word of God." Madeline frowned and shook her head. "But there's no way he would have left Cass alone here. Ronnie might have been immature, irresponsible, and flighty on occasion, but he loved Cass. He would never have left her here to fend for herself."

She was using the past tense. He considered that. "You think he's dead?"

"I'd bet on it," she said on an indrawn breath. "If he were alive, he'd be here. Protecting her as much as he could." She sighed...shook her head. "Maybe he tried to escape with her, or maybe he tried to get help. Either way, I think they killed him. Apostolos is obsessed with adding Cassidy to his harem of child brides. Ronnie would never have allowed it."

She didn't sound all that broken up by her ex's possible death. But then, she'd had weeks to get used to the possibility. Either way, the ex's disappearance meant he didn't have to worry about interference coming from that quarter.

CHAPTER 9

Madeline awoke slowly, desperate to remain in the dream. She was secure in there. Warm. Safe. Comfortable. She groaned softly, flinching as her body rocked back and forth. No…just let her hide in this dream, where she was protected from horrifying choices and the fear in her daughter's eyes.

"Madeline…sweetheart. Wake up. We need to get moving." A voice whispered in the distance.

And Devlin was in her dream. She didn't want to leave him either, not when he was murmuring to her in such a gentle, soothing voice.

"Come on, babe. Wake up."

Her body rocked again. Was she still on that horrible boat, getting tossed around in her bunk?

"Madeline. Wake up." This time the dream-Devlin's voice was demanding.

Her eyes snapped open. A bare chest with a light dusting of hair met her blurry gaze. What happened? Where was she? Had they finally forced her into the comfort rooms? Her mind in a dull haze, her head shot up, slamming into something hard.

"Fuck." It was Devlin's voice.

She rocked back and looked up, the events of the day flooding her memory. Devlin's arrival...the comfort room request…the looming rescue…everything.

Devlin, she realized guiltily, was rubbing his jaw. She must have slammed the top of her head into his face when she'd jerked up.

"Are you okay?" At the last minute she remembered to lower her voice to a whisper.

"Yeah. My fault." He dropped his hand. "I should have known better than to lean over you while shaking you awake."

He was talking fine, and his jaw seemed to be working okay, so she must not have hurt him.

"What time is it?" she whispered. How could she have fallen asleep on him?

"Half past twenty-three hundred hours," he whispered back. "I let you sleep long as possible, but we need to go over some details before we head out."

Maddie groaned beneath her breath. Cassidy would be frantic by now. She hadn't meant to stay with Devlin for so long, just long enough to give their fake tryst an air of realism. Five and a half hours was way, way past her original estimate.

"I'm sorry I fell asleep on you," she said. He must have been sitting there for hours, holding her, keeping her warm. He must be exhausted. Not to mention stiff.

"You needed the rest."

When she pushed off his chest and tried to scramble up, he tightened his grip around her arm and tugged her back down.

She settled against him again, almost in his lap this time. "What about you? Did you get any sleep?"

Something haunted flickered across his face and his smile looked forced. "I'm used to going without."

Before she had a chance to question him about that odd statement—for some reason she didn't think his lack of sleep had anything to do with him being a SEAL—he continued.

"You said the women and children sleep in the same room?" At her nod, he grunted with satisfaction. "When we leave here, we'll go there. But wait until zero hundred hours before approaching the fed."

He meant Abigail. She nodded again. He was talking military time. "That's midnight, right?"

"Right." He touched her cheek lightly. "Team insertion is set for midnight. Squish, Lucky, and I will take out the Divine Asshole just before the boys breach the compound. You need to get the kids and women—"

"How?" Her voice started to rise, she forced it back down. "He has guns. You have nothing."

His scoff was low and full of amusement. "Sweetheart, we're not the ones you should be worried about."

She swallowed her reservations and hung onto the knowledge that SEALs were considered lethal—with or without weapons. But …. still…they had no weapons, and every man in the compound wore their guns like a badge of honor. She had good reason to worry about him.

"As I was saying..." Humor gleamed in his eyes. "Get the kids and the women into a corner. Away from the door. You should be fine, but just in case. I'll come and get you as soon as the compound is secure. Don't open the door unless you hear my voice."

"We can't open it anyway," she told him tightly, the worry escalating now that the rescue was at hand. "We're locked in at night. There's a guard on the door. He has the keys."

Apostolos claimed that the guard on the women and children's room was for their protection. Which was bull crap. Everyone knew it was to prevent anyone in the room from escaping.

He frowned thoughtfully. "Is this guard armed?"

She nodded. "Always."

"Good to know." He didn't seem concerned. "Where are you kept?"

"Down this corridor and to the right. Third door at the end of the hall."

He looked surprised and then pleased. "Next to the work room, with the fencing and tools?"

It was her turn to look surprised. "Yes, how did you know?"

"It's where we met Apostolos." He shrugged at her look, as though he knew what she was thinking. "It pays to keep track of rooms and locations. Tex got us blueprints from the original construction of this place."

Before she had a chance to ask who Tex was, he continued.

"I'll get the keys off the guard. But don't come out until I call for you."

She took a deep, calming breath and fought to cast the worry aside.

"We aren't allowed watches, and there are no clocks in the room. I can count the minutes off in my head, but…" she grimaced, "it won't be that accurate and it's kind of like counting sheep don't you think? What if I fall asleep again?"

His lips quirked. He lifted his arm and unbuckled his watch, handing it to her. "Take this."

She took it hesitantly. "How will you know when your team is coming in?"

He smiled slightly. "Squish and Lucky will be with me. They'll have my six."

Squish and Lucky? He must mean the two huge, hard-faced men he'd arrived with. What odd names. She slipped his watch into her pocket. "Okay."

"How many men are in the compound?" he asked, his gaze sharp and focused. "The FBI's estimate is thirty-seven men. Is that correct?"

She counted names and faces off in her mind, before nodding. "That sounds about right. I mean, I may be forgetting a couple, but I think that's right."

"Good." He studied her, then cupped the side of her face with his palm.

She leaned into his hand. It felt so good against her skin. Warm. Strong. Protective.

"You ready?" he asked, his voice steady. Like he had total faith in her capabilities.

She wished she had as much faith in herself.

Because she was pitiful. Even now she was dithering. Avoiding a subject that had to be broached. She cleared her throat. Her face was probably so red it glowed brighter than the lantern. Which was pathetic. She'd had sex with this man, multiple times. She knew his body intimately, as he knew hers… so why was it so hard to bring this subject up now?

"What?" His voice was low, concerned.

She swallowed and forced the observation out. "Anyone who

walks into this room will know we didn't have sex. Fresh sex smells...pungent. Particularly without condoms—which aren't allowed here. Everyone knows by now that we spent hours in here, and if—"

"Relax." There was the oddest look on his face. Half resignation and half...well, not exactly embarrassment...more like awkwardness. "I'm aware. I'll take care of it."

"You will? How?" And then it hit her what he meant.

Fire rushed up her neck and exploded in her cheeks. If she'd thought her face had been red before...jeez. Before she could release the *never mind* trembling on her tongue—he scoffed softly, his hand dropping from her face.

"Trust me sweetheart, every man over the age of puberty knows how to take care of himself when the need arises. Hell, there are dozens of myths warning unwary teenagers of the dangers involved in jacking off." Amusement hung on each word.

Her shoulders squared. She forced her embarrassment aside. She was an adult woman for God's sake. She'd had no inhibitions with this man two months ago.

She could face this discussion head on.

"Do you need any...inspiration?" She mangled the last word —because holy hell, what if he said yes?

His eyebrows shot up. Dry humor touched his face. "After having you on my lap, rubbing your ass into my crotch, and grinding those perfect tits into my chest for the last five hours? Nah. I'm good."

Instinctively, her gaze shot to his crotch. Even in the flickering light she could see the huge bulge down there. Choking on a breath, she jolted to her feet. Okie-dokie, she was not ready for this conversation after all.

This time, he let her go and followed her up.

When she tried to sidle to the door, he caught her elbow and held her still. "Hang on." The amusement had disappeared from his voice. "Wait for me out in the hall. I don't want you heading back on your own."

"I'll be fine." Her voice was noticeably high, at least to her ears, and she was having a devil of a time keeping her eyes on his chin. They kept trying to roam downward. "It's not that far from here."

"Still." He scowled. "I don't like you out there on your own, so wait for me. I'll be done in a few seconds and walk you to the women's room."

Wait for him outside? Knowing what he was doing in here? Yeah…that was not an option. She couldn't think of anything more uncomfortable than that.

He must have picked up on her reservations because he shrugged. "The other choice is to wait in here while I take care of business."

Her gaze followed his hands as they dropped to the waistband of his jeans, and slowly started to unbuckle his belt.

He wouldn't.

With slow, deliberate movements he pulled the belt loose and took hold of the zipper. Mesmerized, her gaze followed the slow, sensual slide of the metal tab down.

"I take it you want to watch?"

She was so hypnotized by the bare skin he was exposing and the husky, aroused tone of his voice, it took a second for his words to register.

With a choking breath, she forced her eyes away from the downward slide of that zipper. And …she'd been wrong…there were far more awkward experiences than standing outside the door, knowing what he was doing behind the wood.

Turning, she fled.

"Coward." His husky, aroused taunt followed her to the door. "Madeline?" His voice rose slightly. "Check the hall. Everyone should be asleep, but make sure the hall is clear." He paused, his voice lowering. "And wait for me. The guard at your room needs to get a whiff of sex. He needs to smell it, otherwise it will raise questions we can't afford. He won't know who the smell is coming from. He'll just know it's there."

She grimaced, her hand twisting the doorknob. He had a point. The women did smell like semen when they returned from these rooms. If she didn't, it would raise questions. At least with the guard. The women might wonder, but she could fob them off with some kind of excuse. She almost pointed out that there were other signs associated with sex. Like swollen lips, messy hair…but the men around here didn't offer the women kisses or hugs or any signs of affection. Penetration was all they cared about. The women were just a step up from a blow-up doll.

"Fine," she said tightly. "I'll wait for you."

She eased the door open to peek outside, her focus more on the man behind her than the corridor in front. The hall, thankfully, was clear and she was able to slip out of the room.

Surprised that he'd actually let her wait in the hallway, she settled her back against the wall beside the door and tried not to think about what he was doing inside. To distract herself, she scanned the hall again, praying that none of the other comfort room doors would open and disgorge their occupants. There weren't nearly enough rooms for the demand, so occupancy was staggered throughout the night. Devlin had kept her in this room quadruple normal, which must have led to ceaseless speculation.

Before the worry that someone was going to catch her standing out here had a chance to make her do something stupid, Devlin opened the door and stepped into the hall.

And *holy hell*—she took a long step to the side, away from him, because yeah, fresh sex had an *extremely* pungent smell.

"What did you do, roll in it?" she hissed, the question bursting from her without thought.

His stride caught for a second, but he quickly recovered. "Good. You can smell it."

Of course she could smell it. Everyone within a ten-mile radius would be able to smell it and they'd all assume… She gulped back a huge breath and beat the humiliation back. That was the whole point of what he'd done in there, wasn't it? They needed everyone to believe they'd spent the past five hours humping like a pair of horny rabbits.

Kudos to him for throwing himself into his role with such fervor.

"Kind of above and beyond the call of duty, isn't it?" she muttered, as he closed the door and joined her in the hall. She didn't think he was going to respond, but then he shot her a glittering look, with a bit too much of the devil in it for her comfort.

He scanned the hall, then turned back to her, dropping his voice until she barely heard it. "You know what SEAL stands for, right?"

Since she'd looked it up after she'd read in the paper what he did for a living, she knew exactly what it stood for. Sea. Air. Land. Not that she was going to admit that to him. "No. What?"

"Sex. Any. Location." His voice was dead pan.

She sputtered, her mouth dropping open. "No way!"

"Right." He tilted his head, studying her face thoughtfully. "You must have heard the other acronym. Sex. All night. Long." He slid her a quick glance and she clearly saw the teasing glitter in his dark eyes. "Just wanted to do the SEAL reputation justice."

With a wry snort, she shook her head. "Right. Although… based on previous experiences with you…that last acronym might not be too far off."

He'd certainly kept her entertained all night long back in Dark Falls. At least on that first night…not so much on the second one.

Dead silence followed the comment. A silence tinged with heat. With hot as hell memories. She cleared her throat, the discomfort back. That had not been the smartest thing to remind either one of them of.

"Madeline…" His voice was soft, full of…something…

Something she couldn't quite place. Something she didn't want to place. Certainly not right now. Not right here. Turning, she headed down the hall. "We should go."

They didn't have time for this.

He fell into step beside her. They walked in silence, side by side, an emotional gulf the size of the Grand Canyon spanning the foot or so between them. A lantern flickered against the wall at the end of the hall, haloing a ten-foot radius in yellowish light. There was another lantern behind them, at the other end of the hall, and they'd already passed the lantern in the middle. But the light the three lamps emitted didn't travel far, leaving large swaths of the hallway in darkness and shadows.

When they reached the end of the corridor, Devlin suddenly

stepped closer and draped his left arm over her shoulders, tugging her firmly against his side.

She started slightly and slid a glance toward him. "I doubt the guard will be expecting any intimacy between us."

He didn't say anything, just swung her around the corner, his focus on the lantern and guard at the end of the hall. "Don't get between me and the guard. I'm right-handed, so stay to my left."

The amusement and sensuality were gone. In its place were the narrow eyes and single-minded focus of a predator. He was intent. Fully engaged. In warrior mode.

Which was much sexier than it had any right to be.

He shot her a quick glance, his face hard, his eyes flat. When his eyebrows rose, she realized he was waiting for a response.

"Okay," she whispered.

Suddenly, what was about to happen hit home. Hit hard. She should have been nervous. Scared. He could get hurt. She could get hurt. They could both die. The compound was bristling with guns. Anything could happen. But instead of the worry intensifying. It vanished.

She felt safe with him.

Protected.

He'd make sure nothing happened to her or Cassidy.

She was so serene even the wrinkled nose of Brother Luke—the current guard—when he got a whiff of Devlin didn't bother her. Neither did the gloating smirk he shot her. Another hour or so and she'd never have to see him again. She wouldn't have to see any of them.

"I see you rode her hard." Luke grinned at Devlin, camaraderie in his voice.

Devlin went still. Dangerously still. The arm around her shoulders fell away.

He was about to do something...something he shouldn't.

"Would you just unlock the door and let me in?" Maddie broke in. She started to step between Dev and the asshole taunting her, only to remember her earlier promise. But if Devlin went after the guy, everything could fall apart. "I'm tired."

"I bet you are. Five and a half solid hours..." He started to high five Dev, but whatever he saw in Dev's eyes caused him to drop his arm and take a giant step back.

"Let her in." Devlin's voice was flat. Cold. Empty.

"Sure…sure…" The guard pulled a batch of keys loose from his belt and hurried forward to unlock the door.

Devlin leaned over to brush his lips against her ear. "Half an hour. Be ready."

His words were so soft, she barely heard them herself. There was no way Brother Luke had heard anything. With a slight nod, she slipped through the open door and into the dimly lit room.

CHAPTER 10

This asshole in front of him needed a few roundhouse punches to his face. Enough pummeling to knock some sense into him. Teach him a God damn lesson.

Men like him were a dime a dozen when it came to the sleazy, inhumane underbelly of life. Such men didn't care about consent or decency or basic human kindness. They only cared about proving their self-appointed superiority by taking what didn't belong to them.

But while it was frustrating as hell, he couldn't pound the guy into hamburger just yet. If this sleaze ball went whining to Apostolos, or hell, to anyone, he'd drag the entire mission into the gutter.

He curbed his impatience. "Where are Apostolos and my men?"

The work room, where he'd left Lucky and Squish, was dark. Silent. Obviously empty. A pity. It would have simplified things if they'd canceled the cult ruler next to the women's quarters.

But of course, that would be too easy.

"In the audience room," the guard said. "Go back down the hall, through the dining room. Take the hallway across from this one. It's the first door on the left."

Across the dining room? Which put Squish, Lucky and their target across the compound from the women.

Fucking great.

The thud of his boots on the limestone kept him company as he returned the way he'd come. He passed the room he'd spent the past five and a half hours in, almost all of them with Madeline nestled on his lap. He hadn't been lying when he'd told her he was hard as a fucking rocket, and just as ready to go off.

His cock had chosen the most inopportune time to remind him of how she affected him. Or maybe it had been the perfect time, considering it had barely taken two pulls before he'd shot his load.

He'd hated letting her slip out of the room to wait in the hall by herself, but she'd been so damn uncomfortable with the thought of him jacking off. Her reaction had been a big departure from her natural sexuality in Dark Falls. Whatever she'd witnessed between the men and women here had affected her deeply. Enough to straitjacket her sexuality. He hadn't had the heart to force her to remain inside while he took care of their problem.

The dining room was dark and empty. But the flickering lantern at the mouth of the right passageway was enough to light his way. The right corridor was set up identical to the left, with closed doors every fifteen feet or so. From the schematics Tex had found, this hallway curved to the left, marching around the back of the compound, with even more rooms and exits back there.

It was easy to see why this place had been so attractive to Apostolos. There were plenty of rooms for everyone. Particularly with the men all bedded down in one room and the women in another.

Apostolos was the only one with his own private quarters, and not just one room, but a whole fucking suite of them.

He identified the audience room the guard had mentioned by the warm yellow glow and male voices spilling into the hallway. Unlike the rest of the sputtering lanterns dotting the halls, there was no lack of fuel for the Divine Bastard's lamps.

Squish and Lucky turned to face him as he walked through the door. Both men were leaning against the wall, their tall, broad frames flickering within the lantern's yellow halo. The cult leader, flanked by two disciples—both of whom were armed—was sitting on a pink, fan back armchair.

Three to three. A bozo for each of them.

"About fucking time." Squish straightened. "What happened? It takes you that long to get it up?"

The frustrated impatience in his voice sounded genuine, even though he'd known before they'd stepped into the compound that Devlin would disappear for most of the hours they'd be there. Fuck, their entire plan had hinged on that.

Playing his part, Devlin smirked. "Can I help it if the lady didn't want to let me go?"

As he swaggered over to his two teammates, he saw Squish take a sniff, wrinkle his nose, and frown. The dark eyes that shot to his face lost their mock grievance and filled with surprise and questions.

Devlin knew exactly what his teammate was wondering. And fuck him for that. Did the asshole really think he'd spent the last five hours buried in Madeline? Taking his own pleasure while in the middle of a mission? While his men were waiting for him?

Squish should fucking know better than that.

"I take it Sister Madeline pleased you?" Apostolos asked, satisfaction on his face. No doubt he was reveling in the price break he'd received by pimping Madeline out.

Fucking bastard.

It didn't help that the cult leader's question reminded him of the deal Madeline had struck with the dickhole. How if she pleasured Dev thoroughly, she wouldn't be raped for the next forty-eight hours.

What a fucking disgusting pig of an asshole.

Rage flickered, threatened to flash through him like a forest fire. He ruthlessly squashed it, conjured up calm control.

"Trust me," Devlin drawled. "I couldn't be more pleased."

Although not about Madeline's supposed pleasuring. Nope—he was exceptionally *pleased* that this fucktard was about to breathe his last breath.

"Excellent." The satisfaction on Apostolos's face thickened. He smiled affably. "Then let's conclude our business and retire for the night."

No doubt the pervert was anxious to retire to his quarters and molest one of those poor kids he claimed as wives. At least his child brides wouldn't have to worry about that tonight—or any night to come.

Lucky straightened from the wall. "We should get moving."

Code for take them out now.

Devlin instinctively glanced down at his bare wrist to check the time. It felt a little early, but close enough. Moving now would give them extra time to free Madeline and the fed and get the kids and women rounded up for evac. His pulse spiked. His muscles tensed for battle.

Like a good little soldier, following their unspoken directive, Apostolos rose to his feet and stepped forward. His two incel guards—one on the right and one on the left—moved forward with him, although a step or two behind.

To avoid waking up the entire compound, these kills needed to be silent and swift. With that in mind, they'd already settled on knives or neck holds. Quick. Silent. Deadly. No mess…no fuss. Since they'd had no way of knowing how many men would be with the cult leader, or their positioning in the room, they'd kept the plan flexible. They'd each take out whoever was closest. Which meant Dev's target was the guard on the left.

Lucky was closest to Apostolos, which meant he'd get that honor. Looked like the bastard's luck was still holding.

"I'll contact my suppliers and get back to you," Devlin said, stepping forward and extending his hand, hoping to distract the cult leader as Lucky slipped away from the wall and slid in behind their three targets. "Pleasure doing business with you."

Apostolos and both his guards were armed—the weapons buckled into holsters strapped beneath their arm pits—but they were off guard, arms down, hands relaxed. No inkling of the looming danger.

Lucky eased into position behind Apostolos.

His pulse accelerating, Dev synchronized his movements to Lucky's. As his teammate stepped forward and wrapped a burly arm around the cult leader's neck, Devlin twisted, stepped forward and slammed his fist into his target's Adam's apple. The blow knocked the incel back several steps. Rather than going for his gun, both the guy's hands flew up to claw at his neck. Gargling, choked sounds spewed from his gaping mouth. His cries were muted though, thanks to the blow to his Adam's apple, which housed his vocal cords.

Dev moved in, pressing his chest and abdomen against the bastard's holstered gun, blocking any belated attempt to use it. From the corner of his right eye he caught Apostolos twitching and flailing beneath Lucky's neck hold. Low, grunting sounds were coming from that direction too, but nothing that would travel outside the room.

Pressing even closer to his target, Dev grasped the guy by his chin and the back of his head. He gave one hard, upward jerk to the right. A crack sounded. The gasping, choking sounds fell silent and the guy slumped. Dev dropped him and turned toward Lucky, who was already lowering a limp Apostolos to the floor and unbuckling the holster to remove the cult leader's weapon. A quick glance at Squish proved the second incel guard was down and unmoving too.

With all three targets neutralized, he helped himself to the weapon holstered beneath the left guard's arm and warped over to the door. He scanned the hall from right to left.

Nothing.

He waited for his pulse to settle. It didn't. His tension to dissipate. Instead, it settled in thicker than ever. The lack of relief was curious, considering that the take down had gone a thousand times better than he'd expected.

"We clear?" Squish asked quietly from behind him.

Dev scanned the hall again. Still empty.

"Clear," he confirmed.

"I don't like this," Lucky said, his voice tense. "That was too damn easy."

Devlin nodded in agreement.

"How many fucking deployments have we been on?" Squish's voice was just as tense. "We're due for an actual fucking easy day."

Why the fuck would he say that? Now? Here?

The stupid son of a bitch.

Everyone knew not to tempt fate. Fate was a nasty bitch.

With a nasty sense of humor. As illustrated by the sudden grating sound that started up from across the room.

Devlin turned to find a section of the wall behind the pink armchair sliding back. A pitch-black opening appeared.

What the fuck?

He dove for his knife rather than raising the gun he'd taken off Apostolos's guard. Gun fire could bring the whole fucking compound down around them.

A man in the baby blue pants and short sleeve shirts the male cult members wore stepped out of the pitch-black maw. The APC9K cradled against his chest was pointed down.

"Divine Ruler, there's a—" His gaze dropped to the floor, zeroing in on the dead cult leader and guards. His APC9K jerked up.

Dev aimed his knife, but before he could throw it, a flash of steel flew across the room. An MK3 buried itself in the new arrival's throat. The cult guy staggered backward, his hands convulsing around the submachine trigger.

A spray of projectiles peppered the room.

Fuck.

Dev hit the ground.

There went their silent attack. A single gunshot would have been bad enough. Thirty rounds from a submachine gun was worst case scenario. Scratch that—worst case would be one of those fucking projectiles hitting him or one of his teammates.

Dev rolled around the doorway and into the hall for cover. As the submachine sputtered to a stop, he crab-walked to the corner of the door frame. Based off the volume of projectiles that had hit the walls and floor, the cult guard must have spent his thirty-round magazine. Was he reloading...or dead?

It was freaky how often a target could survive a knife to the throat and cause unbelievable chaos. Usually not for long, but often enough to make the occurrence a nuisance.

Crouched next to the doorjamb, he thumbed off the safety of his newly acquired weapon. With a deep breath and steady hands, he stuck his head around the corner of the doorjamb and fired a couple of rounds into the black hole. At this point the damage was done. Maybe one of his rounds would take the bastard out—assuming the knife hadn't already done so. Four shots and he pulled back again. He needed to conserve ammo. No doubt there was a hoard of armed cult members thundering his way now.

Silence followed. No gunfire. No voices.

After a few more seconds of silence, he sidled closer to the corner of the door frame. Keeping his head low, he chanced a quick look into the room again, quickly pulling his head back out. No gunfire greeted him. He eased closer again and took a longer look.

In the distance came a chorus of shouts, the sound of boots hitting the limestone. That fucking submachine fire had awoken the whole goddamn compound and stirred the rats up. They needed to get out of here, like fucking now.

Lucky, the cult guard's gun in hand, was sliding along the edge of the wall toward the new doorway. Squish had dragged down a couple of the plastic chairs and was using them as cover—extremely tenuous cover. He glanced over at Dev and flashed him five fingers. The five by five sign.

Squish either wasn't hurt or wasn't hurt badly.

Neither was Lucky from the look of him. They'd gotten off damn light.

Devlin glanced down the hall toward the dining area. The shouting and pounding boots were closer.

Fuck—escaping in that direction was out. He glanced toward the other end of the hall. Doors were opening. He saw a young girl with long brown hair poke her head out of one of the rooms and slam the door again when she saw him.

Fuck...fuck...fuck...

Lucky had reached the open section of the wall. Still no submachine fire. Dev glanced back toward the dining area. A couple dozen shadows were racing across the cafeteria.

"Clear," Lucky said.

Devlin swung into the audience room as Squish gained his feet.

"Are we looking at a hidden room? Or a corridor?" The question shot out of Dev like a bullet.

"A corridor." Lucky's disembodied voice drifted back. "Can't see far though. Too dark."

"Look for the latch to close it," Dev ordered. He glanced at the lantern across from him. "Grab the lantern," Dev told Squish who was closer.

That lantern was throwing off too much fucking light, exposing the dead cult leader and guards, along with the secret door. If the cult members headed their way had picked up one of the hall lanterns, the empty fuel tank and withering light would work to Dev's advantage. It would take the bastards a few seconds to see their dead comrades.

"We're about to have company. A lot of it. They're coming from the south passage. If we got more coming from the north, we'll be pinched between them," Devlin said as he headed for Lucky. "This hidden passage is our best shot of getting out of here alive."

"We have no idea where it goes. Or who might be occupying it," Squish growled.

Devlin shrugged. "You got a better idea?"

Apostolos's cult members would reach them long before their team. And holding off an army of submachine guns with three handguns were shitty odds.

Dying in this fucking place was not on his bucket list.

"Find the mechanism to shut that door," Dev told Lucky again.

If that damn secret door was open when the cult army arrived, their odds of surviving this operation went straight down the crapper. The cult members would simply follow them in and pick them off one at a time. On the other hand, if the door was closed, they might assume the men who'd killed their Divine Ruler had escaped down the back hall.

Squish swooped down and snatched up the lantern. He and Dev arrived at the hidden passage and slipped inside in unison. The lantern and Lucky's flashlight app lit the interior of the corridor, illuminating a three-foot-wide, limestone-walled tunnel to the right and left. The right-hand section, which was currently blocked by the dead incel, probably continued to

Apostolos's quarters. Which made sense. The leader would want an escape route.

Not that it would do him any good now.

"Step back," Lucky said. "I think I found the mechanism."

As Dev and Squish eased back in the cramped space, Lucky pulled down on a silver lever anchored shoulder high next to the missing section of wall. That earlier grating sound started back up and the wall slowly inched shut. Behind the sound, in the near distance, came the thud of boots and a chorus of raised voices.

"Cut the light," Dev hissed.

Both the lantern and flashlight died, leaving them in darkness.

A low rattle sounded to his left.

"I set the lantern down," Squish whispered. "Against the far wall."

Good to know. They couldn't afford to trip over it and alert their pursuers to their hidey-hole.

He grimaced as the secret doorway slowly slid shut.

"Check the rooms," someone shouted, and close enough to hear each word. Could he hear the grating sound?

Fuck, this was going to be close. Damn close.

The wall sealed shut with a muted thud.

"Which way?" Squish's voice was barely audible. "Right or left?"

"Right." Dev made the snap decision.

From the looks of it, the right corridor headed toward the women's quarters...maybe. Regardless, they couldn't stand here dilly dallying. That fucking door could slide open again at any moment.

With Squish on point, Lucky in the middle, and Dev on their six, they headed down the pitch-black corridor without turning on their flashlight apps. Lighting the corridor to see where they were going would light them up like a fucking bullseye. Perfect target practice for anyone in front or behind.

He glanced over his shoulder, checking behind him. No yellow glow back there. Either the cult members hadn't entered the passage, or they were moving blind—like he and his teammates.

Then another possibility occurred to him. What if those bastards had NVDs? If so, they were fucking screwed.

"How the hell did we miss this passage?" Lucky growled.

Devlin shrugged. Obviously, the passageway hadn't been on the blueprints Tex had dug up. Which made sense. Why bother with a secret passage if you announced its location on the fucking blueprints? The whole purpose of a secret passage was—hello! Keeping it secret.

As they shuffled forward one slow step at a time, Dev tried not to think about his team, or Madeline, or the multitude of poisonous insects, spiders and snakes that called the Amazon Rainforest home and could be sharing the corridor with them.

After listening to Squish describe those fucking foot long poisonous centipedes, or the Brazilian wandering spider—which, according to Squish, was the most venomous spider in the world—he wasn't sure which was worse...poisonous snakes and insects or killer cult members armed with NVDs and submachine guns.

CHAPTER 11

Madeline slipped past Devlin and the guard into the women's room, only to stop dead as the overwhelming stench of body odor, sour sweat and God knew what else smacked her square in the face. She gagged as the door closed behind her.

My God does this place ever reek.

The smell of unwashed bodies churned through the stagnant, warm air, almost suffocating in its ripe, disgusting stench.

Had she smelled like this to Devlin? Heat singed her cheeks at the thought. God, that very real possibility was beyond humiliating. Daily showers were a luxury she'd never take for granted again.

An oil lantern hung next to the door, its meager glow lighting her way. She headed for the far-right corner and the piles of blankets she and Cassidy called their bed.

The room was windowless, with bare white walls. The stone floor was bare too, its hardness broken only by blankets. Everyone had been given two thin blankets. One to use as a pad against the floor and one to curl up under. She and Cassidy pooled their resources and slept snuggled together, using two of the blankets as a pad, one as a pillow and the fourth as covering.

The lantern allowed enough light to navigate around the blanket covered lumps stretched across the floor. But it didn't emit enough light to distinguish the facial features of the women bedded down. Which was too bad as she needed to find Abigail.

When she was close enough to see into the corner she and Cassidy slept in, she found Cass sitting up, her back against the wall. She couldn't see her daughter's face, the murky shadows were too thick for that, but she sensed the tension radiating from her baby's small frame.

Her chest instantly tightened, her belly clenching in sympathy and guilt. She'd known Cass would worry. If she'd returned when she'd planned, her baby would be fast asleep by now, replenishing her energy before the rescue unfolded. Now Cassidy was going to be exhausted as they fought to escape this place.

She stepped over a couple of women, sidled around a couple more, and quickly closed on the corner.

Cassidy sat up straighter, leaning forward. "Momma?"

"I'm here, baby. Everything's okay," Maddie whispered as she eased down beside her daughter and took her in her arms. Cassidy slumped against her, her rigid frame going limp.

"I thought you left too, Momma." The words were almost an accusation, and emerged on a hiccupping sob.

Madeline's chest squeezed. "Never, Cass. I will never leave you. I promise."

"That's what Daddy said." The response was raw and aching.

Maddie's whole body tightened beneath a wave of helplessness. While her daughter didn't realize what the cult leader had planned for her, she was a sensitive, observant child. She knew something was wrong. She sensed they were in danger. And with every day that passed, she seemed to become more timid and withdrawn.

"Hey." Madeline leaned back and cupped her daughter's cheeks between her hands. Cassidy's face was a vague blur within the shadows. Her eyes deep, dark pools that reflected the meager light. "I will never leave you. Never. No matter what happens. I will always be here for you. Always. I promise. Okay?" When Cass didn't respond, Madeline leaned down and kissed her forehead. "Do you hear me, baby?"

The slow, unsure bob of her daughter's head made Maddie

sigh. She could hardly blame her for her disbelief. Not with Ronnie disappearing. He'd probably told her the same thing... made the same promises...only to vanish.

Madeline wanted to tell Cassidy that rescue was at hand. Promise her they were about to get out of here, away from these people. But she couldn't. Not yet. There were too many people lying too close. If one of them heard her and went to alert the guard... no...she couldn't chance it. Not even for Cassidy's peace of mind.

Too many lives—including Dev's—depended on her keeping her mouth shut.

So, she crouched instead and shook out one of their blankets, then layered a second blanket on top of the first and rolled the third one into a long tube that they could use as a pillow. She needed to act normal, which meant bedding down for the night. She'd check the time from beneath the blanket, where no one could see the glow from Devlin's watch.

"Come on, baby. Lay down," she coaxed.

Cass crawled forward and curled up on the right side of the blankets, her head resting on their makeshift pillow. Maddie shook the last blanket out and draped it over her daughter's small frame, then lifted it and crawled in next to her. She let it fall back into place and shifted onto her back, cradling Cassidy against her chest. With gentle, soothing strokes, she ran her hand down the back of Cass's head and spine. With each glide of her hand, she could feel Cass relax further.

It was too bad she couldn't give her the protein bar in her pocket. But too many questions would accompany the treat. Best to wait until they were on the helicopter. She gave herself a few seconds to cuddle and soothe her fraught daughter before pulling the blankets up over her head and reaching into her pocket. She found the watch and pulled it out, pressing along the edges until the face lit up in a luminous blue glow.

Eleven fifty.

Ten minutes to go.

She felt Cassidy's head lift from her shoulder and instinctively covered her daughter's mouth with her palm. When she'd pulled the blanket up over her head, she covered Cass's head as well. The blue light from the watch was brighter than she'd expected; it lit up the entire space beneath the blanket. Of course Cassidy would notice it.

Before she had a chance to shush Cass, a distant *rat-tat-tattling* flooded the room. She froze, listening intently. The *rat-tat-tat* seemed to go on and on.

Her heartrate shot into triple time. Her breathing and pulse spiked.

The women and children surrounding her stirred, blankets and clothing rustling. Confused voices broke the silence.

She recognized the rhythm and metallic ping of that rattling sound. When they'd first arrived here, the cult guards had set up a target practice station and shot the hell out of a collection of cans. Then they'd turned their attention to obliterating towers of mangos and coconuts. They'd wasted so much ammunition, Apostolos had forbidden the use of the machine guns for anything except hunting and protection.

"What was that?" someone close to them asked.

Madeline's arms tightened around Cassidy's shoulders. What should she do? Should she find Abigail now?

"It sounded like a gun," another woman said, her voice more alert, sharp with worry.

But it hadn't come from outside. It sounded like it had come from inside, across the compound. Had Devlin's team already inserted? Were Apostolos's guards firing on them. But it was too early! Dev had said midnight. Her heart rate spiked. Devlin didn't have a gun…had someone shot at him? Or his teammates? Was he hurt?

"Who's shooting?" a woman asked, her voice strained.

More voices sounded, the rustling of feet and clothes, and blankets being thrown back as people climbed to their feet.

"More importantly, *who* are they shooting at? We could be under attack by rebels."

This new voice was grim. Focused. Maddie was almost certain it came from Abigail, and it sounded close.

With a snap decision, she shoved the watch back in her pocket and tossed off the blanket. She needed to find the woman. Talk to her.

"Momma?" Cassidy jerked up.

Madeline paused long enough to cup Cassidy's warm cheeks and kiss her forehead. "Hang on, baby. I'll be right back. I need to talk to Sister Abigail."

"No!" Cassidy's voice climbed. Panic lit her eyes. "Don't leave me! You promised you wouldn't leave me! You promised!"

The fear in Cass's voice stopped her cold. She hesitated, the need to calm her daughter battling with the need to find Abigail and fill her in on the rescue.

In the end, the chance of rescue won. She had to do everything in her power to make sure the rescue went off without a hitch. Not just for Cassidy and the rest of the children, but for Dev too. And that meant finding the FBI agent and filling her in on what was about to happen.

"I'll stay with her while you talk to Abigail," Sister Rebecca said, her blurry shape joining then.

Madeline relaxed. Thank God for Rebecca. At least Cass wouldn't be alone.

"Thank you." She thought about making up an excuse for why she needed to talk to Abigail, but nothing plausible came to mind. So, she settled on a vague. "I won't be gone long."

The first complication arose as soon as she climbed to her feet and started looking for Abigail. There were so many women standing, they blocked the meager lantern light. Maddie threaded her way through the bodies, scanning faces.

She finally found the woman she was looking for pounding on the door with her palms.

"Brother Simon?" Abigail paused, leaning her head against the doorjamb, and listening. "Hello? Brother Simon. Are you there?"

Madeline joined her at the door. "Sister Abigail?"

"Just a minute," Abigail said, and pounded her palms against the wood again. "Brother Simon?" When Madeline took hold of her arm and squeezed, Abigail absently shook her arm free. "He must not be there. He would have answered by now."

"Sister Abigail—" Madeline broke off to look around. There was no one close enough to hear. She dropped her voice to a whisper and leaned toward the other woman. "Agent—"

Before she had a chance to add the woman's real name to her title, Abigail jerked, then grabbed Maddie's arm and squeezed. Hard.

"Don't." The warning was a sharp hiss.

They were so close to the lantern; Madeline could see the chilly glitter in the woman's icy eyes.

Abigail turned her head to the right, then the left, and relaxed slightly. Apparently, she'd only just realized that no one was close enough to hear. She turned back to Madeline, her gray hair gleaming like steel wool beneath the lantern above them.

"What's going on?"

Maddie dropped her voice to a whisper. "We're about to be rescued."

Something flared in Abigail's eyes. "Rescued?" By who?"

Madeline forced a tight smile. "Apparently your agency wants you back so bad they sent a SEAL team to extract you." When the explanation came out surprised, as though she couldn't believe anyone would want this woman back. Maddie blushed. "I mean—"

Abigail absently waved the explanation away. Her forehead knitted and her eyes narrowed. She looked like she was rapidly putting everything together. "That man who asked for you..." She frowned; her gaze thoughtful. "You know him?"

Madeline nodded. "We have a…history. He's a Navy SEAL. My sister went to him when I disappeared."

Abigail shot a quick glance over the room. "Was that them shooting? The SEAL team?"

"I don't know. They weren't supposed to come in until midnight. Devlin and the two men he came in with don't have guns, so it couldn't have been them shooting." Fear for Devlin tightened her throat and voice.

"Not necessarily." Abigail smiled wryly. "These wannabe white supremacists Apostolos surrounds himself with are amateurs. Your Devlin and his two teammates could easily help themselves to the guards' weapons. Tell me everything he told you."

Madeline quickly ran through the salient facts.

"Midnight," Abigail repeated absently when Maddie fell

silent. "It must be close to that now." She turned to scan the women and children behind them. "Who exactly are they planning on rescuing? Me, you, your daughter, and...?"

"The children for sure. And as many of the women who want to leave. Two helicopters are on their way in."

"Most of the women won't go. They're blindly loyal to their Divine Ruler."

The loathing that coated the words shocked Madeline. Lord the woman was a good actress. Her earlier behavior had been so supportive and blindly obedient, this new persona was hard to accept.

"From what Dev said..." Maddie hesitated, then shrugged. If Abigail really was as contemptuous of their hypocritical Divine Ruler as she appeared, this news wouldn't phase her. If she were putting on an act, it wouldn't matter. Nothing the woman did would make a difference now. "It sounds like Dev's orders are to eliminate him. Maybe once he's gone, more of the women will walk away."

Abigail shrugged. "Maybe. I'm not surprised they're taking the bastard out. What did he expect with all his talk of holy wars and cleansing the earth? The number of weapons he's already accumulated makes him dangerous. The fact he's trying to get his hands on even more makes him a crisis about to boil over. Big government doesn't like anarchists. Not ours. Not Peru's. Cutting the head off the snake is SOP when they're faced with a charismatic megalomaniac."

Madeline nodded in agreement. *Charismatic megalomaniac.* That certainly fit the Undivine Ruler.

With a sharp, piercing whistle, Abigail faced the women and children. "Attention! I need your attention." When the room fell silent, she continued. "I can't reach Brother Simon and the door is locked. Considering the gunfire from earlier, we need to protect ourselves. Everyone head to the right corner. Away from the door."

Without questioning the instructions, the women started moving in the direction Abigail had instructed.

Now that she'd done her duty, and roped Abigail into the plan...now that the women and children were headed into the corner, as Devlin had directed, Maddie turned her attention to Cassidy. She was probably scared to death, afraid they were about to be separated forever.

Besides, she needed Cass next to her. Within touching distance. Close enough to protect if things went wrong.

She hadn't made it this far just to lose Cassidy in all the confusion.

* * *

Madeline had just collected Cassidy from Rebecca and settled down with Abigail and Cass in front of the huddled mass of women and children when a short, staccato *crack* sounded.

"Gunfire." Abigail stared at the door, her voice grim.

That first crack was followed by another and then another. It wasn't the *rat-tat-tat* of before, though. These new shots were deliberate. Sporadic. Like the shooters were more disciplined.

"I'd say your SEALs have breached the compound," Abigail said quietly.

Where was Devlin? He'd said he'd come and get her. Escort her and Cass to the waiting helicopter. Had those earlier gunshots been used on him? Was he lying dead out there somewhere? Had his attempt to rescue her and Cassidy gotten him, and his friends, killed?

Her chest tightened. She wasn't sure she could live with that…with knowing that her foolish choices had gotten three good men killed.

Maddie sat there, frozen, straining to hear, but the *cracks* were few and far between. It didn't sound like the SEAL team was finding much resistance. By the time footsteps and voices sounded outside the room, her entire body was one tight ball of nerves.

"Clear," a calm, baritone said somewhere down the corridor.

"Clear," another voice echoed.

"Ester Macmillan?" that first, deep voice asked from behind the door.

"Here," Abigail—or rather—Agent Macmillan called back, but

remained seated. "I take it you're with the SEAL team here to extract us?"

"That's right, ma'am. You can call me Rocco. Me and my team will have you out in a jiffy."

"We have the women and children on the floor, in the right corner, as far from the door as possible." Agent Macmillan filled them in matter of factly. "The door's locked. The guard, who had the keys, must have fled his post."

"Roger that," Rocco responded calmly. "Stand by." He was back almost immediately. "We're gonna blow the lock. Stand clear."

There were a few moments of silence, and then a muffled explosion. The door swung open—hard—slamming against the wall. A *huge* man, followed by a second and third, surged into the room, their tall, broad, dark swathed bodies and raised rifles stealing all the oxygen and heat from the room.

Several of the women and children screamed. All of them flinched back, cowering. To the left of the door, the oil lamp rocked violently against the wall, spewing yellow light and shadows everywhere.

Rifles scanned the room, sliding over everyone cowering in the corner—women and children alike.

"Hands up," someone ordered flatly.

Madeline's arms shot into the air. She was pretty sure everyone behind her had followed suit. Refusing to comply with these hard-faced strangers seemed like a very stupid thing to do.

"Macmillan?" The first man, with the deep voice—the one who'd said to call him Rocco—asked, stepping further into the room, his rifle moving from person to person.

"Here." Agent—Macmillan rose to her feet and stepped forward. "You can lower your weapons. There are only women and children here. What's the evacuation plan?"

The woman sounded so calm and casual. Not at all like the stern-faced, stern-voiced old battleax that Maddie was used to.

Rocco lowered his rifle. "The kids are coming with us, along with any of the women who want to leave." His helmeted head, with the band of tube-like protrusions that stretched across his eyes, moved from woman to woman and landed on Madeline. "Ms. Roux?"

Maddie climbed to her feet, keeping Cass's small body pressed close. "Yes?"

He gave her a chin lift. "Glad to see you in one piece, ma'am."

With a tight swallow to ease the dryness in her throat, she took a few steps forward. "Have you heard from Dev? He was supposed to come get us."

"We heard submachine fire," Agent Macmillan added quietly. "About ten minutes ago, from across the compound, toward the cult leader's personal quarters."

From within the shadows and light flung about by the swinging lantern she could see the SEAL's cheeks and jaw tighten.

He cocked his head and spoke into a mic next to his mouth. "Anyone got eyes on Alpha One?"

After a moment, where he seemed to be listening, he said, "Fan out. Find them." He turned his attention back to the FBI agent. "Chopper's on the ground. We need to move. Bring the kids forward. We'll load them first."

The agent turned to the women and children behind them. "Everyone, listen up. Apostolos is dead. His movement has died with him. There will be no apocalypse and reseeding of the planet. There will be no reordering of the earth." A cacophony of swelling voices joined together, rising in confusion and concern. Macmillan ignored the host of questions directed at her. "This is a dangerous land, full of dangerous people. These men are with the United States Navy and have been sent to escort us to safety. The children will be evacuated first, followed by those of you who wish to leave."

"You lie." A woman's voice quavered from the back of the packed corner. "The Divine Ruler cannot be dead. God would not forsake his chosen one." A chorus of "Amens" rose from around her.

Macmillan shrugged. "You can stay and see for yourself if you so choose. But the children will come with us." She raised her voice as argumentative voices swelled. "The United States will not allow you to endanger the lives of these minors. They will accompany us out of here. Those of you who wish to remain without your children are welcome to do so—but we will not leave the kids behind." She paused, waiting for the clamor to subside. "Children, come forward." When none of the kids stood. She raised and sharpened her voice until it cracked through the room. "Children, stand up and come forward. Now." She paused, softened her voice. "There is no need to be afraid. These men are our friends."

Most of the children stood, then crept forward.

"Those of you who wish to leave here, stand and move forward as well." Macmillan said as the last of the kids gathered around her.

"Where will they take us?" a woman timidly asked.

"To Lima. There are people waiting there who will get you passports and paperwork to travel back to the states. They'll reunite you with your families," Rocco said.

"This is our home. These are our people," a belligerent voice called back. "You have no right to take us anywhere."

The SEAL facing them rolled his shoulders and shrugged. "We're not forcing you to do anything. If you want to stay. Stay. But the children are coming with us. That's nonnegotiable."

"You have no right—"

Ignoring the interruption, Rocco turned back to Macmillan. "These all of them?'

"No. There are two girls in the cult leader's quarters," Madeline told him.

Rocco nodded curtly. "My men already have them. They're headed to the chopper."

"Mommy." Cassidy threw herself against Madeline's abdomen. "Is it true? Are they here to take us away?" Cassidy's voice was part worry and part relief, like she wasn't sure she should believe the news and get her hopes up.

Maddie lifted Cass into her arms and buzzed her cheek. "It's true, baby. They're taking us back home."

Cassidy sent the huge man blocking the door a wary look and dropped her voice to a whisper. "Are you sure?"

Madeline couldn't blame Cass for her reservations. The three huge men facing them with their helmets and guns and black camo clothing looked a thousand times more dangerous than the cult men. If Devlin hadn't vouched for them, she would have wondered about trusting them herself.

Which reminded her…

"Is there any word on Devlin?" she asked Rocco.

"Not yet." Rocco's helmet-clad head, with that weird band of tubelike protrusions covering his eyes, turned toward her. "Command says their trackers aren't registering."

"Which means what?" She didn't realize she'd asked the question out loud until he answered.

"The GPS trackers use a signal similar to a cell phone. For all three to be offline, there has to be something interfering with their signals."

She nodded her understanding and swallowed hard, forcing back the fear. The thick, limestone walls of the compound were probably blocking their signals. But Devlin was smart. Capable. He could take care of himself. So could his two friends. They would be fine.

"He said he was going to meet with the Divine Ruler. Which means he would have gone to Apostolos's private quarters," Madeline offered.

Rocco nodded. "I've got men sweeping the compound. We'll find them."

"How do you want to do this?" Agent Macmillan asked.

"We'll sandwich the lot of you between us. Make sure you keep behind my men in front and in front of my men behind."

The memory of those earlier shots rose in Maddie's mind. How many dead bodies were strewn between them and the helicopter? She needed to make sure Cassidy kept her eyes on the ground.

Rocco said something into his mic and the two men standing in front of the door turned and headed back into the hallway.

"Let's move." Rocco stepped back, giving the women and children room. "Macmillan, Mrs. Roux, you and the children go next. Stay behind the men in front of you."

"Children, follow me." Agent Macmillan followed the SEALS through the door. "Come on, you're safe." She urged the children over her shoulder.

Madeline waited for the last child to shuffle past her before steering Cassidy forward.

"Anyone else who wants to leave, fall into line now," Rocco ordered.

"Where are we going, Momma?" Cassidy's whisper was worried.

"These men have a helicopter out front. They're going to fly us home." Or close enough anyway. Maddie slung an arm across her daughter's shoulders and steered her forward, wincing at the fragility beneath her arm. Cass was going to need a lot of fattening up once they got home. "Keep your eyes straight ahead, Cass. No looking around." She stopped momentarily to give her a quick hug. "Hang in there, baby. Just a little bit longer and we'll be safe."

"It's true then?" Rebecca appeared by Cassidy's side. "These men are taking us back to the States? We've been rescued?"

"Yes. It's true." Madeline glanced over her shoulder. Most of the women were staying behind. Only a dozen or so were in line, shuffling behind her. She shrugged off her disappointment before turning to Rebecca. "Are you coming with us? There's room for you."

She hoped so. The other woman had been kind and friendly and tried to make things easier for them. She was one of the few cult women that Madeline liked. Hopefully, Rebecca intended to hop on that helicopter with them and start a new life.

"What about the Divine Ruler's wives?" Rebecca asked. "Are they coming with us?"

"Of course." Madeline glanced over Cassidy's head toward the other woman. "They're just kids. It would be criminal to leave them behind."

Apart from the faint *whop...whop...whop* of the chopper outside, the trip through the compound was silent. No shots. No voices. Just stillness and shadows. The men in front were moving in a half crouch, their weapons constantly up and scanning. Their vigilance should have made her feel safe, protected—instead, it illustrated the danger still surrounding them.

As they closed on the compound's entrance, the *whop...whop...*

whop of the helicopter got louder, as though the limestone walls had buffered it's noise.

She'd only seen a couple of huddled, still shapes in the shadows, so most of the cult men must have survived the assault. And they had guns. They wouldn't open fire on them, would they? Not with the children and women clearly visible. She thought of Simon. Of his cruelty. Of his disdain for women. He'd open fire on them without caring who he hit.

They were halfway to the big, black helicopter squatting across the yard when a familiar *rat-tat-tat* pierced the chopper's *Whop...whop...whop.*

"Down. Get down," yelled the half dozen men surrounding them.

The submachine fire was coming from the edge of the clearing, among the rubber trees. Maddie, Cassidy and the rest of the women and children hit the ground on their bellies as the SEALs closed around them, knelt, and returned fire.

Screams from the women and children within the circle of SEALs competed with the helicopter's noise and the barrage of close and distant cracks that followed the *rat-tat-tatting*. The rifle fire from the men surrounding them was deafening.

Good God those guns were loud.

Madeline crawled over Cassidy's prone form, pinning her daughter to the ground, hoping to provide as much protection as she could. She dug her fingers into the soft, freshly tilled earth and concentrated on the hard thump of her heart and the damp, gritty soil against her cheeks instead of the terror. The acrid smell of hot metal and fireworks surrounded her, adding to the churn in her belly.

It seemed to take forever—a lifetime—before the *rat-tat-tatting* fell silent. The SEALs surrounding them rose to a half crouch.

"Everyone up," Rocco yelled. "To the chopper. Move! Stay between us."

Maddie rolled off Cassidy, ready to grab her daughter and run for her life when something slammed into the side of her head and everything went dark.

CHAPTER 12

Devlin froze when a muffled rifle shot sounded behind the walls of the secret passage. That first crack was followed by a second. Gunfire. But not submachine.

Alpha Two must be sweeping the compound.

They'd hidden their headsets along with the rest of their gear in the tree line when they'd first arrived, so Dev had texted the location of the women and children to command on his SAT phone. At least the boys knew where to find Madeline and the fed.

"You hear that? Sounds like Alpha Two breached the compound," Squish whispered from somewhere in front of Devlin.

"This sucks," Lucky groaned softly. "We're missing all the action."

"Fuck man," Squish whispered back, derision thick in his voice. "Almost getting plugged a dozen times back there wasn't enough action for you?"

"That?" Lucky scoffed. "That was sloppy. The bastard got off, what? Thirty rounds? And didn't hit any of us. That's not action. That's a nuisance."

"How about you two assholes pipe down?" Dev growled softly. "You want someone to play target practice with your asses?"

So far, they hadn't run into any of the cult's incel guard. But it was black as fuck in here and they had no idea who was ahead or behind them.

"I'm good," Lucky drawled. "They'll hit Squish since he's in front...or you...since you're in back. But me? I'm golden."

Dev snorted. Fucking asshole. Like anyone would believe that bullshit after the bastard had dived on a grenade to save his teammates.

Within seconds, Squish spoke up again. "We've reached the end of the corridor. Let's see if I can find the lever to the door without the flashlight."

Seconds later, that familiar grating sound filled the air. A light gray hole widened within the pitch black. Silver moonlight pierced the gray. Devlin glanced back over his shoulder. Still no lights back there.

Fuck—they'd gotten lucky.

One at a time, they swung through the door and into the open, their weapons sweeping their deserted surroundings. Judging by their earlier recon, the tunnel had expelled them at the back of the compound.

He gave a fleeting thought to heading back inside the building to find Madeline, and her kid, but Christ—they had no NVDs or headsets. While they could reach command central on their SAT phones, the delay while command forwarded the info onto Alpha Two would leave them vulnerable to friendly fire.

They needed to retrieve their damn headsets before joining their team.

Devlin scanned what he could see of the area surrounding them. An endless, empty field lay ahead. Beyond that were the ghostly trunks of the rubber trees. Once they reached the tree line, they could use the trunks for cover as they made their way to where they'd ditched their packs and equipment.

"We need our comms," Squish said in a toneless voice. "Without them, we're as likely to get hit by our own team as those incel bastards."

"Agreed," Dev said. He scanned the field again. It looked quiet, peaceful, but looks could be deceiving.

Squish tilted his head toward Dev and Lucky. "Go. I'll cover you."

They didn't need to be told twice. In tandem, they broke into a run, headed for the silvery trees across the field.

They were too exposed for comfort out here in the open, silhouetted by the moon's silver glaze. Every step brought an internal curl and flinch as Devlin waited for the crack of a rifle, the rattle of submachine fire, or the burn of a projectile. But they made it to the tree line without gunfire lighting up their little neck of the woods. Once Squish joined them, they slipped through the trees until they reached the spot they'd stowed their packs and equipment.

The relief when Devlin finally pulled his headset and helmet on and flipped down the NVDs was sweet. The right equipment for the job made all the difference when it came to a successful mission.

"Glad to hear your voice," Rocco said as soon as Squish hailed him. "Sitrep?'

Squish filled him in on what had gone down, and where they were.

"Roger that," Rocco said. "Chopper's in bound. All targets have been acquired. We're headed for evac. Rendezvous in five."

Even as the team leader's words filled his earpiece, rotors beat the air in the distance.

Devlin relaxed at the news that all their targets had been acquired. Madeline and her kid were on their way home.

"Ten-four," Squish said. "We'll cover you."

They eased their way to the south tree line, directly behind the evac site, and settled in to wait. The sound of the chopper got louder and louder. Soon a big, black shadow swallowed the moonlight and dropped to the ground. The bird was flying dark, its running lights extinguished.

Devlin waited, his rifle sweeping from tree line to compound for any sign of trouble. Nothing.

Rocco and his team moved into the clearing. They'd surrounded the women and children in a tight circle as they advanced on the chopper. For a few seconds, it looked like the evac was going to go as planned.

But no—suddenly the rattle of submachine fire lit up the night.

"Shots coming from the east and west," Squish said into his mic. "Alpha One on it." He turned his helmeted head toward Lucky and Devlin. "They got our boys and their flock pinned down. Let's free them." His whisper was low and toneless.

Dev was already nodding. He knocked on his chest and pointed toward the west. Lucky pointed to the east. Squish pointed to the ground, indicating he'd stay and guard the chopper.

Every instinct on high alert, Dev wove his way through the trees toward the sound of submachine fire. The shooter was easy to find. The rattle of his weapon led Devlin straight to him. Even amid the green glaze of his NVD's, Devlin could tell the bastard was wearing the pants and shirt of a cult member. Which made him one of the incel guards. The dude was standing upright, partially hidden behind the trunk of a rubber tree, focused completely on the huddled group he had pinned to the ground.

Devlin settled the infrared laser pointer on the back of the target's head and gently pulled the rifle's trigger, sending the bastard to Apostolos. After checking for signs of life, he grabbed the submachine gun the bastard had been using and paused to assess. The gunfire from the east had died. Lucky must have silenced his target too.

He keyed his mic. "Alpha Two—shooter neutralized to the west of you."

"Hotspot to your east is down." Lucky's voice came over the com.

"Roger that," Rocco said. "Heading to evac."

Devlin waited, rifle at the ready as Alpha Two and their flock of rescues rose to their feet and ran for the helicopter. Or at least most of Alpha Two ran. Two of his teammates had remained behind and were crouched over a green-glossed lump on the ground.

What the hell? Had that asswipe managed to hit someone before Dev had neutralized him?

"Alpha One. Minnie Mouse is down."

Devlin froze. And then his heart slammed into double time. Adrenaline hit in a hard *whoosh*. He was hell for leather, racing across the field before Rocco's repeat hit his ear.

"Repeat. Minnie Mouse is down."

Minnie Mouse was the code name they'd given Madeline.

Madeline was down.

The words echoed through his brain, keeping time to the hard thump of his heart and boots. She must have been hit. If he'd gotten to the bastard a few minutes earlier, would she be on her feet and in the bird?

Christ…Madeline had been hit.

"I'm coming in hot to your west," Devlin warned Rocco as he shot across the field. Was she unconscious? Dead? He closed on Rocco at a dead run and skidded to a stop.

"Is she alive?" The question shot out as he dropped to his knees beside the limp body on the ground.

"Yeah," Rocco responded, straightening his back. "Her vitals are good. She wasn't shot." A muscle pulsed in his cheek, and his voice went tight and furious. "Looks like someone took a rock to her head." His head swung toward Devlin, who'd dropped to the ground across from him. "Which brings up another problem. According to the fed, Millie Mouse is not on the chopper."

Millie Mouse? That was the code name given to Madeline's daughter. Had someone knocked Madeline out so they could grab the kid? The kidnapper couldn't be one of those incel bastards, though. None of them had been close enough to hit Madeline or take the girl. The culprit had to be one of the cult women. "What about the women. Any missing?"

Rocco glanced toward the chopper. "The fed's doing a head count." He paused to listen. "Macmillan says a Sister Rebecca is missing. She was beside Millie Mouse when the hotspot popped up and we hunkered down. That chopper needs to get airborne, ASAP," Rocco continued grimly. "We're in stealth mode, but if we woke those rebel bastards on the way in—" He broke off to shake his head. "That bird's full of kids. Get Minnie onboard." Rocco climbed to his feet. "The medic can check her out once they're in the air."

"When's Whitehorse Two due to touch down?" Devlin asked.

The op called for two birds to carry everyone to safety. Madeline's daughter would have to take the second chopper.

"It's inbound. We'll load the leftovers once two is on the ground." Rocco scanned the field, before turning back to Devlin. "You and your boys sweep the compound for the kid. Me and my boys will sweep outside and hold the clearing for evac."

Nodding, Devlin bent to lift Madeline into his arms.

As his hands slid beneath her spine, her eyes popped open. Wedging her palms against his chest, she shoved him—hard. "Forget it. I'm not boarding the helicopter until we find Cass."

Her voice was firm, her eyes steady. The hands braced against his chest were confident. No sign of confusion or pain.

He scowled. Damn it… she'd been playing possum.

She must have seen the accusation on his face because she nodded and sat up. "Yes. I eavesdropped. I know Rebecca has Cass."

Devlin scowled. "You need to board that chopper. You need to get checked out."

"I'm fine. I was barely unconscious. I'm not leaving Cassidy behind." Her chin pointed toward the moon.

"You are *not* fine. People don't pass out for no reason." When her mouth tightened and stubbornness seized her face, he grimaced.

Fuck...

Since concern for her health, combined with strongarm tactics, wasn't working, he changed strategies. "I'll find your daughter. And I'll do it a lot faster without having to worry about you while I'm looking."

"I'm. Going. With. You." Her tone was flat. Her eyes determined as they held his gaze."

"That chopper needs to lift off," Rocco growled.

Fuck this standoff. Devlin bent back over her, ready to scoop her up, toss her over his shoulder and haul her kicking and screaming to the chopper. She scooted back, slapping his hands.

"Hear me out." Her voice rose. "Rebecca probably freaked when the shooting started and grabbed Cassidy, taking her back into the compound. She must have thought she was protecting her. She's panicked, scared out of her mind. You and your teammates are *huge,* scary dudes. She doesn't know you. For all she knows *you* were the ones shooting at us. She's not going to trust you, so she won't hand Cassidy over to you. Not willingly."

Devlin shrugged and leaned closer. No big deal. They'd just take the kid by force.

Madeline talked faster. "Rebecca will let me take her, though, without a fight. As for my daughter...she won't come to you willingly either. And if you kill Rebecca or incapacitate her in front of Cassidy, and then take Cassidy against her will, you'll traumatize her. Maybe for life. Cass will come to me willingly. I can get her out of wherever Rebecca has her stashed quicker and easier than you can."

"She has a point," Lucky said thoughtfully from behind him.

Devlin glanced over his shoulder to find both Lucky and Squish watching the battle unfold on the ground. "She was unconscious, damn it. She probably has a concussion," Devlin growled. "She needs medical attention."

"Allow me the courtesy of knowing what I need," Madeline snapped. She braced her palms against the ground and pushed herself up. "And what I need is to find my daughter."

The *whop-whop-whop* of the chopper blades across the field changed rhythm and picked up speed. Devlin rose to his feet and turned to face it. Planting his fists on his hips, he watched in frustration as a big black shadow climbed the air.

Fuck...there went plan A.

When he turned back to Madeline, he saw satisfaction on her face, as though she thought she'd won.

Not quite. She'd risen to her feet without any problem. Nor did she seem unstable now that she was standing, but that didn't mean a whole hell of a lot. "Can you even walk?"

"Of course I can." She mirrored his posture. Shoulders back. Hands on hips. Nasty glare. All without taking a step.

His eyebrows shot up. "Prove it."

"Fine." With a huff of breath so strong it popped a tendril of hair up; she took a cautious step. And then another.

Her third step was less cautious, with more stride. No wobble. No stumble.

Son of a bitch. There went that objection.

"Look. I'm fine and you need me. Let's go. We're losing time." She turned without wavering and headed back to the compound.

Fuuuck.

He could grab her, but what the fuck was he supposed to do with her then? Whitehorse One was already Lima-bound. Whitehorse Two hadn't set down yet. He couldn't cuff her and leave her out here defenseless. And while Rocco and his boys would keep an eye on her, they'd be out sweeping the grounds for the kid. Which meant she'd have to sweep with them.

Hell, if she was going to be out here anyway, she might as well be with him.

Catching up with her, he grabbed her elbow, dragging her to a stop. "A couple of rules first. You do what we tell you to do when we tell you. No arguing. And you do *not,* under *any* circumstances, run ahead of us, no matter what happens. Stay on my left, half a step behind, and don't interfere with my line of sight."

"I'm not stupid, Devlin." Her voice was quiet and surprisingly unannoyed. "I know you guys are the pros. I won't do anything that will put any of us in danger."

Frowning, he let go of her arm. Of course, she wouldn't *try* to put anyone in danger. But sometimes that didn't matter.

Anything could happen in a hot zone.

* * *

Madeline's head throbbed in time to her heart as she returned to the compound with Devlin and the other two SEALs beside her. She must have hit her head on a rock and knocked herself unconscious when she'd thrown herself on top of Cassidy.

If she'd been more careful, paid more attention to the ground, this wouldn't have happened, and she and Cassidy would be on that helicopter winging their way home right now.

They stepped through the giant, mosquito-netted arch. As they moved deeper into the building, the moonlight streaming through the main entrance gave way to darkness. By the time they reached the first of the tables in the dining area, the milky radiance from the moon had vanished.

The other two SEALs disappeared into the north and south corridors while Devlin and Maddie remained in the dining room, checking under tables and behind chairs. All but one of the oil lamps had burned out, and that one—at the mouth of Apostolos's private quarters—provided only a weak, feeble glow. The room was so dark she could barely see a foot in front of her face.

Dev though…he had no trouble seeing.

He reached out to snag her elbow and eased her around… something. Maybe an overturned chair.

"Those tubes across your eyes, they let you see in the dark?" she asked softly.

"Among other things." His voice was soft. Toneless. "No talking."

She grimaced. Right. Talking would give the bad guys a target. She pressed her lips together and tried to ignore the throbbing along the side of her head.

Instinctively, she reached up to finger her aching temple, only to lower her arm. Unlike her, Dev could see in the dark, and if he suspected how much her head hurt, he'd sit on her while his two buddies swept the compound.

It was hard to fault him for his concern. And sitting and resting sounded heavenly.

Except she couldn't. Not yet. She had to be there when they found Cassidy. And they would find her. They would. They *had* to.

When her lungs seized, she forced herself to breathe. Cassidy wasn't gone. She was around here somewhere. Rebecca would take good care of her until she was back in Madeline's arms.

Still…Cassidy must be terrified. Thank God Rebecca was with her.

A frown pulled at her forehead and the throbbing escalated. She was assuming Cass and Rebecca were together. Or maybe it was more like hoping. Cass holed up somewhere in the compound with nobody but Rebecca for protection was bad enough. But Cassidy by herself, with nobody protecting her? That thought was unbearable.

She glanced over at Devlin, desperate for something to concentrate on other than the pounding in her head and the fear constricting her chest. She could barely see him in the darkness, but she knew he was matching her pace with that smooth, easy stride she remembered so well. The clothes he wore were the same ones he'd worn in the comfort room. But the thick vest he had on, and the helmet with the band of tubes that covered his eyes, were new. So were the backpack and rifle.

Rocco had told her Devlin had checked in, and that he was fine before they'd headed into the clearing. She'd been so relieved. Certain that the rescue was finally coming together, and that everyone would be boarding the helicopter and heading home within minutes.

Only now Cassidy was missing.

With Apostolos dead and the men driven out of the compound, her daughter should be safe. Assuming the cult leader *was* dead. Agent Macmillan had told the women as much, but she'd gotten her information from Madeline. And while Dev had told her they were planning on *neutralizing* Apostolos, nobody had actually confirmed that the cult leader was dead.

Her chest tightened as her brain started bombarding her with *what ifs.*

"Is Apostolos dead?" The question popped out before she could stop it. Devlin paused. She sensed more than saw his head turn toward her.

"He's out of the equation. You don't need to worry about him."

The tension in her chest loosened. She took a deep, relieved breath.

Thank God.

Which might not be the most ethical response, but the man had been a monster. His death made the world a safer place, particularly for her daughter.

They moved forward one slow step at a time, the only sound accompanying them the whisper of their shoes against the limestone floor or the scrape of metal against stone as she brushed against a table or chair.

"Body to your left."

She jolted slightly, pain ricocheting through her head, as fingers clamped around her elbow and eased her to the right.

A body.

Maddie shuddered.

She'd known there must have been casualties when his SEAL team had entered the compound. Their controlled, deliberate shots had indicated as much. She'd even tried to shield Cass from the carnage as they'd been escorted to the evacuation site. She needn't have bothered. It had been dark then too. Plus all the big, broad bodies surrounding them had blocked their view.

But knowing they were walking among the dead made the darkness obscuring her vision almost comforting. She'd known the dead men. True, she'd loathed them, had even wanted to shoot them herself. But to actually see their blank, fixed stares and still bodies…that would be the stuff of—

A sharp *crack* echoed down the north corridor. A second *crack* followed. Devlin froze. So did Madeline.

Someone was firing a gun. But not the *rat-tat-tat* of a machine gun. Nor did it sound like one of the SEALs rifles.

"Copy that," Devlin said quietly from her right. He touched her elbow. "Squish found your daughter. She's fine," he added before she could ask.

After one moment of blinding relief, concern kicked in.

"Who's shooting?" Maddie asked as she blindly followed him across the room, letting his touch guide her.

"The good sister." His voice was dry and derisive. "She's targeting Squish."

He must mean Rebecca. The woman had probably grabbed a gun from one of the dead cult members. No doubt she was terrified.

"She's just protecting herself and Cassidy," Madeline reminded him. "Where are they?"

"North corridor. In one of your Divine Ruler's bedrooms."

Madeline scoffed at the *your.* The bastard had been nothing but a monster to her.

Once they reached the mouth of the north corridor, the visibility got better. The sputtering lamp's light traveled farther down the limestone corridor than it did into the dining hall. Plus there was a warm glow emanating from the cult leader's bedroom, enough to clearly see the broad figure lounging against the wall two doors down from the audience room.

"Madeline, meet Squish. Squish, this is Madeline," Dev said in a low voice as they joined Devlin's teammate.

Squish?

What kind of a name was that? Maddie shook the question off. Didn't matter. The only thing that mattered was getting her daughter out of that room.

Squish gave her a chin lift, before glancing back at the entrance to the bedroom.

"The damn woman starts shooting anytime I approach the door." His head, with those weird, tubular lenses, turned back to Madeline. "She's got your daughter behind her."

Madeline's breath escaped in a rush. "Let me talk to her."

Squish stepped to the side. "Have at it."

Vaguely aware of Devlin whispering into his mic, Maddie crept up to the edge of the doorjamb. "Rebecca? It's me. Madeline."

"Momma?"

"Madeline?"

"Yes. It's me." She took a step closer, but before she had a chance to step into the doorway, a callused hand wrapped around her arm, jerking her back.

A good thing too. A staccato crack pierced her ears, followed by the shriek of the doorjamb splintering. The hand tugged her back several more steps.

Maddie's mouth fell open. Had Rebecca just shot at her? No. She must have thought it was Squish.

"Rebecca." Madeline fought to project soothing calm. "It's me. Madeline. Don't shoot. I'm coming in."

"Don't come in. I'll shoot you. I will," Rebecca said, her voice full of determination.

Madeline frowned, trying to make sense of the other woman's reaction. She was probably afraid of Devlin and his two buddies. "You're safe, Rebecca. These men are friends. They're here to take us—"

"I know who you are," Rebecca screeched. "You're Judas. You're the betrayer."

Madeline rocked back in surprise. What the...? Had the woman lost her *ever loving* mind?

"What's going on Rebecca?" She tried really hard to cultivate that earlier, soothing calm, but the pounding in her head made it impossible. Besides, it was becoming increasingly clear the woman had been shooting at her, not Squish.

"I told you. I know who you are. You're the betrayer. You brought the Godless down on us. But you won't win. And you can't have her. They took all the other wives. She's the last of the chosen. Our last chance to reseed the world in God's image."

Maddie frowned. The woman *was* bonkers. How did you argue with a crazy person? Still...she had to try. "Apostolos is dead, Rebecca. There is no Divine Ruler. There will be no divine progeny to rule the world. There's just a dead conman two doors down."

Dead silence followed Madeline's proclamation, and then a shriek. "You're lying. You made that up. He's the messenger of God. God will protect him."

Madeline's mouth tightened, irritation adding a snap to her tone. "He wasn't a prophet. He was a pedophile. He wasn't God's chosen. He was a narcissistic monster intent on taking advantage of any little girls he could get his hands on," Madeline said, vaguely aware of Devlin whispering into his mic again. "I want my daughter back, Rebecca. Send her out." Demand hardened her voice.

"No. She doesn't belong to you. She belongs to the Divine Ruler. She belongs to all of us. She is the mother of the new world."

What utter bullshit. Maddie switched focus. "Cassidy. Sweetheart. Are you okay? Did Sister Rebecca hurt you?"

"She hit you on the head, Momma." Cassidy's aching whisper filtered into the hall.

She had? Madeline's fingers absently brushed her throbbing

temple. Seriously? That's what had happened? The bitch had knocked her out?

"She said you were dead. And that she was my momma now," Cassidy continued raggedly.

Madeline's throat tightened at the fear and confusion in her daughter's voice. She hadn't been the only one who'd thought Rebecca was a friend. So had Cassidy.

"She lied, Cass. I'm alive. We're safe now. We're going home."

"Okay." Cassidy's voice was small and unconvinced.

Maddie flinched at the lack of trust in her daughter's dull tone. At the acceptance, as though she'd already given up. As though Rebecca's betrayal had been the final straw to extinguish her spirit.

Grimacing, Madeline shook her head, only to flinch. How could she have been so wrong about the woman? She'd even liked her, for God's sake. Trusted her.

Suddenly, Devlin grabbed her arms and towed her several feet from the doorway. "We're moving in. Park your ass here," he said, his voice detached.

Both men squeezed past her and clustered next to the doorjamb, with Squish in front, Dev behind. She turned, looking behind her for the third SEAL who'd entered the compound with them, but the corridor was empty.

What were they planning to do? Storm the room? Her pulse skyrocketed. What if they missed Rebecca and hit Cass? What if Rebecca shot one of them? The fear jumped straight to a hard boil.

Before she had a chance to do something stupid, a low, gritty sound came from the room. Three…four tense seconds of silence ate at Maddie's nerves, and then came a staccato crack.

Devlin and his buddy swung into the room, their bodies in a half crouch, their rifles up.

Rebecca screamed.

So did Cass.

Her heart pounding in her throat, fear for Cassidy hijacking her sense of self preservation, Madeline threw herself into the room. "Cass?"

A small body slammed into her legs and abdomen, stopping her in her tracks. Arms wound around her waist and clung.

"Momma," Cassidy sobbed into Madeline's belly. "I want to go home. Can we go home?"

"Absolutely." The affirmation came with a sob. Forcing the tears back, she crouched and drew her daughter into her arms.

After kissing the top of Cassidy's head, she scanned the room for signs of danger. She could barely see Rebecca. The woman was lying on the floor, Devlin and his two teammates clustered around her.

Wait! Three men? Where had the third man come from?

"They shot her, Momma," Cassidy sobbed against her shoulder. "They kilt her."

They had?

But the shot had come before Devlin and Squish had even entered the room. So who had fired?

Movement between the huge, masculine bodies caught her attention, and she watched Rebecca struggling against the hands holding her down.

"She's not dead, baby." Maddie wedged a hand between her shoulder and Cassidy's face, and lifted the small chin. "See?" She gently guided Cassidy's face to the right. "She's moving. She's alive."

As if to illustrate Madeline's observation, Rebecca started shrieking. "Leave me alone. You have no right—" Her voice broke in mid shriek and turned into one long scream.

"Lie still," one of the SEALs growled. "Packing the wound will stop the bleeding."

Devlin straightened, ignoring the struggle taking place on the ground and turned to Madeline. "It's a clean shot through the shoulder. Barely even bleeding. She'll be fine."

"Liar," Rebecca panted. "You tried to kill me."

"Lady. If we wanted you dead, you'd be dead." Pure disgust coated the rough voice.

Devlin took a step closer. His gaze dropped to Cassidy, then shot back to Madeline's face. His jaw went rigid. His cheeks tight. She braced herself for his anger. She'd broken her promise after all. He'd told her to stay put—or words to that effect—and she'd bolted into the room without permission.

"How is she?" he asked tightly, his voice somewhere between gruff and hoarse.

The question shook her paralysis loose. She scanned what she could see of Cassidy's small frame. No blood. But when she tried to push her daughter back enough to get a good look at her, the thin arms clamped around her ribs, tightening with surprising strength.

"Cass...baby..." she said gently. "Did Sister Rebecca hurt you?"

The dark head pressed into her shoulder rolled back and forth. Slowly the thin arms lifted to twine around Madeline's neck, where they resumed their stranglehold.

Afraid that her daughter would lie to her, just to remain in her embrace, Madeline pried Cassidy's arms loose. "I need to see you better, baby. I need to make sure you're not hurt. Let go and step back."

"Don't want to." The whine in Cass's voice was more exhaustion than temper. "You'll go away again."

"I won't let go of you. I promise." When her daughter's arms, and the press of her body, didn't ease, Madeline forced steel into her voice. "Step back, Cass. *Now.*"

Cassidy instantly dropped her arms and trudged back several steps.

Maddie's stomach twisted when she caught sight of the tears pooling in the dark, exhausted eyes across from her. She forced herself not to haul Cass back into her arms. Not just yet anyway.

No blood anywhere on her front. Her arms and legs looked fine. She ran her hands up Cassidy's torso and then down her spine. No flinching. Finally, she cupped the small face and used her thumbs to brush the tears away.

"Are you mad at me?" Cassidy sobbed.

Madeline pulled her into her arms. "No, baby. I'm not mad at you. I just needed to make sure you weren't hurt."

"Okay." Cassidy wrapped her arms around Maddie's neck and her legs around her waist as Madeline stood.

The feel of her daughter's arms and legs clinging to her,

monkey style, was so normal it brought tears to Madeline's eyes. The storm of fear and uncertainty that had accompanied her every waking hour since she'd joined the cult finally calmed.

They were almost safe. They were unscathed. And they had three warriors to protect them.

The only thing better would be boarding that helicopter and heading for home.

CHAPTER 13

Devlin couldn't tear his gaze away from Madeline as she comforted her daughter. Their heads—both as dark as midnight with no moon—were pressed together, the black strands tangled and touching. The sight twisted through his chest and punctured his heart.

"Daddy? Will you come back for my birthday?"

That familiar, haunting voice rose from the depths of his mind, trying to seize his brain and drag him back to the past. Every cell in his body burned, with regret…with loss.

"Whitehorse Two closing. Evac in five." Rocco's voice came through Devlin's headset, snapping his attention back to where it belonged. On the mission and getting his charges to safety.

"Copy that." He turned to Lucky, who was crouched next to the cult woman. He'd patched her up best he could, poured some QuikClot in the wound to stop the bleeding, slapped on some gauze and a pressure bandage. He'd even immobilized her arm with a sling. She was good to go. "Get her up. Evac in five."

They could hardly leave the damn woman behind. Her injured arm put her at a major disadvantage. She'd have to come with them.

"I'm not going with you. The other man said we could stay if we chose to. I'll stay," Rebecca snapped as Lucky grasped her good arm and hauled her to her feet. "You have no right—"

"Lady." Lucky's voice was flat. "The minute you took my bullet, you lost your choice. I'm sure as hell not leaving you behind in the jungle. Get up and do what we tell you."

Devlin braced himself and turned back to Madeline. He skipped the kid clinging to her and locked on Madeline's green-glossed face. "We're heading for evac. You carrying the kid? Or should I?"

His scalp tightened as he forced the offer out. Christ—the last thing he wanted was that child in his arms, but Madeline looked weak as hell.

"I got her."

The giddy relief in her eyes tightened his throat. But it was the smile she shot him, the way it lit up her face, that penetrated his chest and filled it with aching pressure.

He briefly considered overriding her and taking the kid himself—hell, she was too damn thin and fragile to carry her daughter two feet, let alone through the compound and out to the chopper. Plus she was hurting, he knew it. The way her fingers were constantly touching the abrasion on her temple told him as much.

But the wariness in her daughter's dark, soulful eyes as they touched on his face and flitted away nixed that idea. The kid was terrified of him. Squish and Lucky too. Even with her mother vouching for them, the kid was afraid. Someone had taught her to fear men. And fuck, he wanted to bury whoever had put that look in her eyes.

Squish slipped past them to take point. Lucky hauled the cult woman forward and marched her out the door. Madeline glanced at him and fell in behind the others while Devlin took the rear, protecting their six.

As they headed for the evac site, the cult woman let loose with an endless bitchfest, no matter how many times Lucky told her to shut up. They should have gagged the woman. Every fucking word that came from her mouth opened them up to target practice. If she was so determined to die out here, in the middle of nowhere, they should let her. Her choice, her consequences. But Lucky had a major case of white knight syndrome and wouldn't go for that.

The compound sat silent around them, its darkness broken by the green shimmer of his NVDs. By the time they reached the front entrance, and the clearing stretched before them, Madeline's strength was flagging. Her strides were heavy and choppy, her breathing strangled.

"What's the ETA on evac?" Devlin spoke into his mic.

"Imminent," Rocco responded instantly.

Devlin cocked his head, listening. He could just make out the beating of the bird's blades. It would arrive within seconds. There wasn't time to drop his pack and grab a bottle of water and a protein bar to give Madeline and the kid. He'd have to wait until they were on board.

His gaze brushed the child's thin, fragile frame. Christ, she was even thinner than Madeline. She looked like a heavy breath would blow her away.

"You sure you don't want me to take her?" he asked Madeline quietly. "We'll need to clear the field at a run to board the chopper."

The *whop-whop-whop* of blades was directly overhead now, the rhythm and speed slowing. The bird was about to set down.

Before Madeline had a chance to respond, the kid jumped in with her objections.

"I want to stay with you, Momma," the daughter whispered, her legs and arms tightening around her mother in a visible protest to Devlin's suggestion.

"I've got her. It won't be long, now. Right?"

Even within the green glaze of his NVDs, he could read the exhausted determination in her eyes. Nothing was gonna pry that kid from her arms.

"Right." He shifted slightly to glance out the entrance. Whitehorse Two was on the ground.

"We are go for evac," Rocco said. "We've got you boys covered. Come on out."

"Let's move," Squish said, taking a step forward just as a muted white flash lit up the west tree line.

What the fuck?

Devlin recognized that flash, and it wasn't lightning.

Someone had fired an RPG. And it wasn't their boys, since a warning would have come before the launch.

Acting on instinct, Devlin launched himself at Madeline and the kid, pressing them against the wall, using his body as a buffer. The kid screamed as an explosion, followed by a weaker flash of light, rocked the limestone wall. A cacophony of submachine fire, from every direction, followed.

They were under attack.

"Alpha One. We have multiple hot spots," Rocco said, his voice never losing that calm flatness, even though he, along with the rest of his team, were right in the middle of those hot spots.

And Christ, it sounded like all hell had broken loose out there.

Devlin glanced through the archway as another RPG flashed bright white in the darkness. Another explosion. Devlin's heart tried to climb his throat. The chopper, along with Rocco and his team, were sitting ducks out there.

"Alpha Two, Whitehorse, bug out," Devlin yelled into his mic. "Repeat. Bug out."

There was no way anyone from Alpha Two would make it back to the compound. They'd have to cross the entire fucking field with no cover. And from the sound of the gunfire hammering the night, the trees surrounding them, along with the clearing itself, were crawling with hot spots—probably rebels. Which meant Rocco and his boys wouldn't be any safer among the trees.

Although how the rebels knew about this op was a big question. There hadn't been enough time following the first chopper's arrival and departure for those bastards to follow it in and set up camp.

Someone must have told them about the mission.

From the sounds of things, there were multiple rebel encampments out there, and the fuckers were well armed. Which meant the only chance his teammates had of making it home alive was throwing themselves into that chopper and getting the fuck out of Dodge.

Thank Christ the insurgents hadn't already taken Whitehorse Two out while it was on the ground.

Although...why hadn't they? The answer came immediately. They wanted the chopper intact. Securing a stealth modified Sikorsky UH-60 Black Hawk was the ultimate fantasy for virtually every terrorist organization in the world. They were deliberately holding back to keep the aircraft intact. Their mistake. Once the chopper climbed the air, the pilot would go evasive. Unless those bastards had a couple of anti-aircraft, surface-to-air missiles capable of targeting and tracking, they wouldn't be taking down that bird.

"We're bugging," Rocco said. "Evac two in effect."

Knowing his buddies had opted for the smart tactic—hell, the only tactic—was a huge relief. Of course, they wouldn't feel that way; leaving three teammates behind, even temporarily, would be eating at their guts.

He wanted to warp to the arch and cover the chopper, not that his MK16SCAR-L was a match for those RPGs. But his priority was protecting Madeline and her kid. Since the tree line and field were overrun by rebels, they would be headed into the compound next. He needed to get his charges someplace safe, someplace they could hunker down and wait. Some place the rebels wouldn't find.

Thank Christ, he knew the perfect hiding spot.

Squish was still at the entryway, his rifle up and ready, but silent. The battle was taking place too far away. Trying to provide backup would accomplish nothing, but give their position away.

"Falling back," Devlin said into his mic.

The gunfire raged on as he turned to face his two charges.

Another muted flash followed by an explosion. As tremors went through the limestone wall beside them, Rebecca suddenly surged to her feet. Lucky grabbed her t-shirt, but she wrenched away, the material ripping. In a flash, she was off, racing across the dining room.

"I've got her." Lucky—his white knight foolishness on full display—took off after her. Devlin let them go.

"Whitehorse Two is in the air," Squish said over the comm. "I'll cover you. Fall back."

His adrenaline in overdrive, Devlin hauled the kid out of

Madeline's embrace, anchoring her to his chest with one arm. The child let loose with a terrified squeak and started to struggle.

"Sorry, kid," he said, hearing the harshness in his tone. "We're under fire. We need to move fast, and your mom can't do that while holding you. You'll have to put up with me until we get you to safety."

He grasped Madeline's arm with his free hand, relieved that the kid had stopped struggling. She was as rigid as a board against his chest, unease radiating from her, but at least she wasn't trying to get away.

"I've got you," he told Madeline as he led her into the darkness. "I'll keep you clear of everything, just run alongside me."

He set a fast pace, towing her through the compound toward Apostolos's bedroom. She stumbled alongside him, almost falling a few times, her breathing labored and hitchy. But she didn't slow down. She didn't complain.

His chest loosened and warmed. Christ, this woman was something.

Something special.

Iron determination seized him. He would not let the insurgents catch them. Life in a rebel camp would make life in the cult look like the good-old-days. And that was assuming they weren't sold to traffickers after the rebels had their fill of them. The thought of what faced them if they were caught twisted Devlin's stomach and added urgency to his legs.

Constant gunfire rattled behind them. Another explosion hit as they reached the north corridor, this one so powerful it rocked the entire compound. The sound of rocks hitting stone echoed across the dining room. Apparently now that the chopper was out of reach, they were turning their frustrations on the building.

Devlin looked behind him. Clouds of dust swirled through the air. Through the curtain of dust, he could see that the archway leading into the dining room was buried in rubble. The entire roof had come down.

Jesus! Squish had been back there.

Fuck...fuck...fuck.

He didn't see Squish and he didn't have time to look. There were plenty of other access points into the building for the insurgents to choose from. He pulled Madeline into the north corridor, shifting the kid's weight to free up his hand so he could key his mic. "Alpha One-a. Sitrep."

As he rushed Madeline toward the sputtering glow that came from the bedroom ahead, he prayed to hear Squish's voice through his headset. But nothing disturbed the radio's silence.

"Alpha One-a—do you copy?" Silence followed his hail.

He let go of Madeline's arm as they closed on the lantern light ahead. There was enough visibility for her to see now. The kid had melted against his chest, her arms around his neck, legs around his waist, clinging to him. Apparently the danger they were in had finally gotten to her.

"Where are we going?" Madeline asked in something between a shout and a gasp.

The question came between explosions, so he actually heard her. Rather than answering, in case someone was close enough to hear, he caught her arm again and thrust her into the bedroom they'd found Rebecca and Cassidy in.

He pointed to the gaping black hole in the far wall. Thank Christ they hadn't closed the door to the secret corridor before leaving. At least they wouldn't have to search for the mechanism on this side of the wall.

"What the..." Her voice trailed off.

"Grab the lantern," he told her, closing on the secret passage fast.

Out of the corner of his eye, he caught the swoop of Madeline's body as she bent and snatched up the lantern's handle. He entered the secret passage with Madeline right behind him.

"Move back," he told her, as he reached for the silver lever attached to the wall. "Alpha One-a, alpha One-b. Copy?" He hailed Squish again, but tagged Lucky this time as well. "We are sequestered. Repeat. We are sequestered."

The grating of the wall moving back into place and Madeline's labored breathing were the only sounds that disturbed the silence.

Where was Lucky? He should have caught up with Rebecca by now. Maybe he was in a different part of the secret passage.

He tried again. "Alpha One-a, One-b, *do you copy*?"

Nothing.

Fuck.

The door sealed shut with a low thump.

"Are we safe in here?" Madeline whispered as a muffled explosion sent a round of tremors through the walls.

Good question. He answered honestly, "Safer than we'd be out there. This passageway isn't on any of the blueprints connected to this place. We found it by accident. The rebels shouldn't know it exists."

Which was gaslighting plain and simple. The rebels could have heard rumors. But there was no sense in scaring her more than she already was.

"But what if it collapses?"

Another good question. She was full of them.

He smiled at her, hoping he was projecting confidence and reassurance. "The walls are thick and strong. But even if sections of the corridor collapse, there are secret doors in multiple rooms, leaving us plenty of places to escape."

Which reminded him, when they'd subdued Rebecca, Lucky had entered the corridor from the outside door they'd escaped through earlier. Had he closed it? Damn it, if that door was open it would lead the rebels directly to them. He glanced at the sputtering lamp. So would the light from the lantern.

"We need to kill the lantern," he told Madeline, regretfully. "The light, if it bleeds through any cracks at the bottom of the door, will give away our hiding spot."

She swallowed hard. He watched her flinch from the thought of extinguishing her only access to light and visibility, but she nodded with resoluteness and leaned down to gutter the flame.

Fuck...she was amazing. Absolutely incredible. Terrified and exhausted, all but blind, and still she acted with courage and determination.

"You're amazing. You know that? Fucking amazing." The compliment broke from him without thought or planning.

Beneath the green gloss of the NVDs, her eyes rounded in surprise and disbelief.

"Me?" She laughed. "Right."

She obviously thought he was blowing smoke up her ass. He wanted to stay and explain—convince her. But he couldn't.

Leaving her and the kid while he checked on the doors to the passageway was a calculated risk. He hated—*absolutely hated*—leaving them alone and unprotected, but he didn't have backup, and he had to make sure the corridor was sealed tight. He could move faster on his own—without Madeline and the kid weighing him down. And everything counted on getting to those doors fast, on closing them before the horde outside found their way in.

If any of those doors were open and the rebels got to them before he did…yeah…they'd be seriously fucked. But first they needed to move deeper into the tunnel.

He shifted Cassidy to one arm and took Madeline's hand, guiding it toward his spine.

"We need to move until we're in between doors. I'll lead. Grab hold of the back of my shirt and follow me." Once her fingers took hold, he let go and moved forward ten feet or so. "This is good."

As soon as Madeline let go of his shirt, he shifted the kid and started to lower her to the ground. Startled, she grabbed his mic for balance and jerked it loose as she slid down.

There was a sputter of static, and then his radio went dead.

Son of a bitch. That couldn't be good.

"Damn it." The curse spontaneously slipped free. She must have done something to the radio when she jerked the mic loose.

"I'm sorry. I'm sorry," the kid cried, her voice pitchy and anxious.

Ah shit…

"Not your fault, Cass…Cassidy." He forced himself to relax and ran his hand over the kid's gritty hair. "My fault. I should have told you I was going to put you down. Besides, it's nothing that can't be fixed."

"What happened?" Madeline asked, her voice as anxious as her daughter's.

"Nothing important," Devlin said as he guided the kid back to her mother.

And wasn't that a pile of horseshit? If he couldn't fix his headset, they'd be running deaf. He had his SAT phone, so he could check in with command...at least until the battery died... but the damn thing had been on since he'd entered the compound.

No time to worry about that though.

His jaw tight, he delivered the first round of bad news. "I need to check the other doors. Make sure everything is sealed tight. You two wait here."

Through the NVDs he watched Madeline's throat convulse. "We'll come with you."

He forced his voice even. "I need to do this fast. The sooner it's done, the safer we'll be."

Translation, you'll slow me down.

He saw the realization register in her eyes, the flash of terror, followed by stoic acceptance.

"Okay." Her voice was thin, but firm. "We'll be fine. We'll wait here."

"Don't talk. Voices carry." He hesitated, second guessing himself. But damn it, he needed to check those doors.

Turning, he took off at a cautious lope, his NVD's green lighting his way. The trip, this time, through the dark passageway took a tenth of the time it had before and was a thousand times less nerve-wracking. He made a full circuit of the passageway, finding all the doors closed.

Thank Christ.

There was no sign anyone else was in the corridor with them, although dozens of voices, speaking some foreign language, could be heard behind the wall enclosing him.

The building had been invaded, as he'd feared.

The gunfire and explosions had stopped for the most part. Which meant the rebels had no one to target. Had Lucky and Squish found hiding places? Neither were in the corridor. He squashed the concern for his teammates—there was nothing he could do for them at the moment.

In stealth mode, moving silently and swiftly, he eased his way back to Madeline and the kid. If they wigged out and started screaming, or hell, even talked too loudly, they'd give their position away. And the rebels would start looking for them. Eventually, if they searched hard enough, the insurgents would find the mechanism to open one of the doors.

He found the pair cuddled together, sitting on the ground with their backs against the back wall. They were utterly silent, and even from a distance he could see the rigidity to their bodies.

No doubt they'd been worrying about the voices on the other side of the wall too. Praying that one of those doors that separated them from the monsters wouldn't slide open.

They'd kept their wits, though. Hunkered down in silence and waited for him to return. He approached them slowly, silently, listening as the outside voices drifted further away. When he hadn't heard another voice for at least a minute, he chanced a whisper.

"I'm back. Coming from your right." Best not to startle them into making a sound.

Madeline's head turned in his direction, her eyes blindly seeking him, and he saw some of the tension leave her face, but she didn't make a sound.

He eased up until he was across from them and shrugged out of his backpack. Opening it, he pulled out a bottle of water and a couple of protein bars, then took another minute to listen.

Still no voices outside.

Time to hydrate and get some food into them.

"Cassidy," he told the kid in a toneless whisper, as he twisted the cap off the bottle. "Here's some water." He leaned forward and pressed the plastic bottle into her hands. "Drink."

The girl took the bottle hesitantly, her face blindly tilting up toward her mother.

"Momma?" The word was so low he could barely hear it, and clearly a question.

"It's okay, baby," Madeline said, her voice as low as the kid's had been. "Drink."

Hesitantly, the kid lifted the bottle to her lips and took a couple sips.

"More," he insisted quietly when she lowered the bottle.

Another hesitation and the bottle lifted again. The eyes that turned in his direction were solemn and timid. The dark coloring, he remembered from earlier, was close to the color Gracie's eyes had been, but the expression was opposite. Gracie had never had a timid day in her life.

Gracie had been full of confidence and sass. Too much confidence.

"Higher, Daddy. Push me higher. I wanna go higher."

The memory was a knife thrust to his chest, leaving him raw and breathless. Everything had been higher, faster, more with Gracie.

He shook the memories and comparisons aside and ripped open one of the protein bars as the kid handed the water bottle to her mother. She hadn't drunk much, at least three quarters of the bottle remained, but he didn't push her to drink more. He'd just give her another chance to hydrate later.

"Here," Madeline whispered, holding the bottle out in Devlin's general direction. "You should drink too."

He frowned; she hadn't drunk much either. The bottle was still over half full. Maybe she thought that was the only water he had.

"I've got more water in the pack," he told her, keeping his voice to a toneless whisper. "Drink as much as you need."

Relief flashed across her face, but rather than drinking again, she fumbled around with her free hand until she caught her daughter's fingers.

"Drink more, sweetie." She pressed the plastic into Cassidy's hand.

The kid drank another quarter of the bottle before sending it back to her mother. "You too, Momma. You drink too."

Devlin absently rubbed his aching chest. Christ, the kid was trying to take care of her mother. How old was the girl? Seven? Whatever—that caretaker impulse was already strong in the kid.

At that age, Gracie hadn't worried about other people. She'd been too full of life and energy. Too determined to rush through the day as fast as she could, incapable of slowing down and assessing the people around her. Not that she'd been selfish. Hell no, his baby girl hadn't been spoiled. She'd just been...insulated...inoculated against worry and fear.

His throat tightened and ached beneath a fresh surge of sorrow. Even now, so many years later, the grief still caught him off guard and unprepared.

With a deep breath and an internal shake, he shoved the heartache aside, and ripped open one of the protein bars. Before passing it over, he listened hard. Still no explosions, gunfire, or voices beyond the wall.

Catching one of the kid's hands, he passed the unwrapped bar to her. "Here's a snack."

Her fingers felt along the plastic, lingering on the open end of the bar. Longing furrowed her brow.

"I'm not supposed to have candy." The hesitancy was back.

"It's not a candy bar," he assured her solemnly. "They're called protein bars. They're healthy. It's just wrapped like candy."

"Healthy? I think not," Madeline scoffed softly, amusement in the sound. When his gaze lifted to her face, he found her smiling in his direction. But then her gaze dropped to where the kid was tucked against her side. "But we're going to break the rules for now. Go ahead, baby. Eat it."

The kid's face lit up and she devoured the bar, stripping the plastic down as she ate. She was acting like she hadn't eaten in weeks.

Fuck...maybe she hadn't.

Ripping open the second protein bar, Devlin turned from the ravenous child to her mother. Would she eat it if he passed it to her? Probably not. She'd pass it on to her hungry child instead. Which was admirable. But she was going to need the energy it would provide far more than her kid.

"I'm going to give you a protein bar, and you need to eat it," he told her quietly.

"Cassidy needs it—"

Just as expected.

"Cassidy is eating one." The kid's name felt awkward on his lips, uncomfortable.

"But—"

"Madeline," he broke in, "you're going to need the energy. I can carry you, or I can carry your daughter. I can't carry you both."

He watched her examine the statement, watched her eyes widen as realization set in, watched anxiety flood her face. "The helicopter isn't coming back?"

"It is. Just not here. We'll have to hike to catch it." Through the jungle, in the dark, while avoiding both four-legged and two-legged predators. "I'll carry the kid. But you'll have to walk. You *need* this protein bar."

The fear that flooded her face was stark. Even beneath the green tint of the NVDs. he could see her face lose color. Her mouth opened, and he braced himself for her questions, wondering how much to tell her, how much she could handle.

Except, she glanced down at her daughter, and her mouth snapped shut. He could almost see the effort it took to force her body to relax. It was the kid. She didn't want to scare the kid.

"If you're going to carry Cassidy, you should eat this instead. I had one earlier, remember?"

Jesus…he shook his head in disbelief. She was worried about him?

"I've had three square meals a day for months. I ate good last night." Which wasn't true, but, whatever. "I'm good."

She frowned. "How many of these do you have?"

"Enough to get us through. Plus the MREs. But we want to hold off cooking those until we're sure the rebels have left. The smell of cooking travels."

She nodded, and determination landed on her face. "Okay. How about this. I'll eat one if you'll eat one."

"That works," he agreed. Anything to get her to eat. Besides, it was dark, she couldn't see him. She wouldn't know if he ate it or not."

"And I want to watch you eat," she added dryly. "Hand over those goggles that allow you to see in the dark so I can make sure you keep your side of the bargain. For every bite you take, I'll take one. Deal?"

Damn.

There went that work around.

He considered it. He'd packed a dozen bars. Which meant

there would still be seven left if he ate one. Three and a half for each of them—four if she hadn't given that one in her pocket to the kid yet.

"Agreed," he said, loosening the chin strap to his brain bucket. The NVD bar was attached to his ballistics helmet. She'd have to take the whole thing. But if this deal got her to eat, it was worth it.

She was going to need the calories, because things were looking downright ugly for their immediate future. No Squish. No Lucky. No radio. No one to help him get these two to evac B—which was three days and sixteen fucking klicks away, through the densest part of the rainforest.

Yeah...they were both going to need the energy the protein bars provided.

CHAPTER 14

It felt like they'd been entombed in the darkness forever.

When she'd given Devlin his helmet back, with those strange goggles that turned everything green, she'd given him the watch back too. Without his watch, or access to the sun, she had no idea how long they'd been stuck in this secret tunnel. The gunfire, explosions and men speaking in fragments of foreign languages had fallen silent eons ago. Or so it felt.

"You should get some sleep."

Devlin's deep, raspy whisper scraped against her spine. Electricity scurried up and down her arms and legs, leaving goose bumps and tingles behind. There was an intimacy to listening to his voice in the darkness. If she tried, she could almost conjure up that motel room in her mind, with the tangled sheets wrapped around their sweaty entwined bodies. Which was not something she needed to be thinking about with Cassidy's slight weight pressed against her side.

"What time is it?" she asked, he at least had a watch.

"Zero three hundred." He paused. "Three a.m."

Barely an hour since she'd handed back his watch, then. Wow…it felt like a full day had passed. The long rasp of a zipper being pulled came from her right. He must be opening his backpack.

"I've got a couple of Heatsheets in here. You two can lie on one and use the other as a blanket."

"Heatsheets?" Maddie cocked her head, listening to the rustling and scraping as he dug through his pack. She was already relying on her ears, and fingers to navigate this new, dark world. "Is that like a space blanket?"

"Pretty much. Only more durable and lightweight."

"What's a space blanket?" Cassidy asked timidly.

Madeline's eyebrows rose in surprise. Cass hadn't spoken at all since she'd devoured the protein bar, preferring to hang back and listen. Madeline hadn't been sure she was even awake.

"It's a thin, lightweight polyethylene sheet with a metallic coating. It's designed to reflect your body heat back and keep you warm," Devlin answered matter of factly, as if Cass had been talking to him all day.

"What's poly…lane?" Cassidy's voice was stronger, as if Devlin's casual response had emboldened her.

"It's a kind of plastic." The sound of boots scraping against stone accompanied his voice.

"Why is it called a space blanket?" Cassidy asked, her voice filled with curiosity.

"Because the technology was originally developed by NASA for use in space," Devlin answered patiently.

"Really?" Fascination infused Cass's voice. "Like with astronauts?"

Cassidy's reaction didn't surprise Maddie. Her daughter had always been intrigued with spaceships and astronauts. She'd dressed up in a spacesuit the last two Halloweens.

"Well that, and for use on the spacecraft as well," Devlin said. "I'll spread this one on the floor. Crawl onto it and lie down and I'll cover you with the second one. You can use my pack as a pillow."

"Momma?" Cassidy's voice was awed. "We get to sleep on a space blanket."

"I know." Madeline infused her voice with enthusiasm, and hugged the fragile body nestled against her chest. After a few seconds of simply enjoying Cassidy's interest, she turned her head in Devlin's direction. "Dev, you should keep one of the blankets for yourself. Cass and I will be fine with one."

He was silent for a long time. "I don't need one. I'll stand guard."

She could hear the shrug in his voice. "But if you get cold—"

"I won't."

A rustle and pop sounded, like he was shaking the space blanket out, and then a bunch of crinkling.

"Okay. Crawl over to your right. It's right next to you, flush against the wall."

With one hand feeling her way, and the other tugging Cassidy along with her, Maddie crawled onto the slick material and scooted forward until the slickness gave way to stone. She shuffled back until she hit the wall, giving Cassidy more room.

"Lie down, baby." Once Cass was stretched out beside her, she scooted forward again, until they were huddled together.

"It feels…slippery," Cassidy observed.

"That's the metallic coating," Devlin explained. "It will keep you warm."

That rustling pop sounded again, and more crinkling. The Heatsheet was so light Madeline didn't feel it settle over them. The only way she knew it was there was the building warmth and the scratchiness against her cheek.

Sighing in contentment, she relaxed, soaking in the slow build of warmth. She hadn't realized how chilled she'd gotten. The sound of Devlin's boots scraping against the stone came again.

"Lift your heads."

She expected to feel part of the bulky pack wedge into place beneath her cheek, but it was something rough and round instead. She fingered the material, it felt like cloth. "What is it?"

"The extra shirt and pair of cargo pants I packed. Figured they'd make better pillows then the pack." The shrug was back in his voice.

He'd obviously given her the rolled-up pants. Had he tucked the shirt beneath Cass's head? Her fingers stretched out to check, stroking her daughter's smooth cheek and the soft cloth beneath it.

Her chest went all squishy and weak. He might not *do* kids, but he sure knew how to take care of them.

"Cassidy, thank Devlin for taking such good care of us," she said, and felt her daughter roll her head in his direction.

"Thank you." Cassidy's voice was whisper soft. "I never slept on a blanket from space before.

"You're welcome," he said gruffly.

Maddie relaxed, listening to Cassidy's gentle breaths turn increasingly long and slow as she fell asleep. The long day and terrifying night had finally caught up with her. She waited a few minutes, concentrating on the sound of her daughter's breathing. When the rhythm didn't change, indicating Cassidy was still sound asleep, she turned her attention to the man sitting next to her.

She couldn't see him, but she knew he was there. She'd heard the scuff of his boots against the floor as he walked around them and the scrape of his back against the wall as he'd slid down to sit.

"She's asleep." Madeline paused. She didn't want to know the answer to the next question. But she suspected she *needed* to know what she was in for, that she needed to prepare herself.

The tension in his voice when he'd told her to eat that protein bar still echoed in her mind.

"You said the helicopter isn't picking us up here, that we'll have to walk to the next evacuation site?"

"That's right." His voice was tight. "It can't come back. Not when the rebels are using RPGs."

"RPGs?"

"Rocket propelled grenades. They're shoulder fired rockets equipped with explosive warheads. We're lucky they didn't take the chopper out when they attacked. Mission command won't chance sending the bird back in to get us."

"Okay." Madeline braced herself. "How far do we have to walk?"

Silence beat the air between them. His exhale was long and slow. "Roughly sixteen klicks."

Which told her nothing. "What's a klick?"

"A kilometer. We're looking at ten miles." His voice sounded tight and rough, like he'd delivered bad news.

Ten miles? A burst of relief hit. She felt a hundred pounds lighter. Ten miles wasn't that far. She and Cass could hike ten miles. "When will the helicopter be there?"

"I'll need to verify. Make sure evac two's location hasn't changed. But plan B called for a three-day turnaround."

"Three days?" The question burst from her, ripe with horror.

Hiking ten miles was one thing. But hiding out in the Amazon rainforest for three days was something else entirely. Three days of avoiding rebels and snakes and spiders and panthers and all the scary things that could kill a person.

"Most likely," Devlin confirmed, his voice so grim it tied her belly into knots.

If he was worried about it, she should be too. She took a deep breath, held it. Regrouped.

"Maybe your commander will move the evacuation up," she offered tentatively.

He grunted. "Let's hope not. We'll need every one of those days to reach the evac site before the deadline."

Her anxiety increased at the frustration in his voice. Maddie started to sit up, only to freeze as Cassidy stirred.

"Momma?" Cass's voice was groggy, still half asleep.

"Sshhh, baby. Everything is okay. Go back to sleep." Madeline settled back down, cradling Cass against her, waiting for her daughter's muscles to soften as sleep reclaimed her.

"You said the new rescue site was only ten miles away," Maddie whispered softly as soon as she heard the deep, regular breaths that indicated her daughter was deeply asleep again.

"Yeah." If anything his voice grew tighter. "Ten miles through the jungle. In the dark. Avoiding both animal and human trails."

In the dark?

She mulled that over. He must mean they'd be walking at night.

"Why can't we walk during the day?"

"Because that's when the Amaru revolutionary rebels, drug traffickers, and human traffickers are most likely to be moving around. We *do not* want to run into any of them. Since they hunker down at night, that's when we hike." He paused, before adding flatly. "We won't be able to use a flashlight either. The beam would light us up like a firecracker. I've got the NVDs, so I'll be able to see what's ahead of us. But you'll need to follow behind in the dark. I'll hook up a tether for you to hold onto, so you don't lose me."

Three days, through the thickest part of the jungle, in the middle of the night. No wonder he was so grim. His concern wasn't for himself though, she knew that instinctively. It was for her and Cass. He'd be able to make that trip in half a night without breaking a sweat if he were alone. But he wouldn't be alone. He'd be carrying Cass, and towing her, both of which meant frequent stops to rest.

"So we need to cover around three and a third miles a night?" She broke the milage down, hoping to make the distance sound more feasible. Three miles a night didn't sound so bad. They could do three miles. No problem.

"More like five. We'll have to wait until the rebels clear out before we can get started. We've already lost most of tonight."

True...his voice was looser now, less tense, as though the fact he'd gotten all the bad news out had relaxed him. Maybe he'd been afraid she'd freak out, start screaming or something.

While he might be more relaxed, her anxiety had just shot sky high. Somehow that extra one point seven miles had moved the needle from *can do*, to ...*oh shit.*

Five miles, in the middle of the night, through the dense underbrush, seemed much, much harder.

"Will we make it in time?" She could hear the worry in the question.

"We'll make it." Determination hardened each word.

Right...maybe she was worrying over nothing...but just in case... "If we don't make the second evacuation site, will they set a third one?"

"Of course." His voice sounded tired now. "But it will be in a different location. The sound of the chopper will bring the rebels in. The next evac will be miles away."

Which meant more nights of tromping through the jungle.

"And..." he started hesitantly.

She grimaced; she really didn't like the sound of that *and.* Devlin was the most confident man she knew. She'd never heard him so hesitant before. "What?"

His exhale was long and slow. "The kid asleep?"

Uh... "Yeah." ...Why?

"My radio is dead." He dropped his voice to a whisper. "When your daughter grabbed my neck, one of her hands caught my mic and ripped it loose, which either bent or snapped something in my headset. The whole damn thing's dead."

Even as the anxiety tried to strangle her, Maddie's chest warmed. He'd wanted to make sure Cassidy wouldn't hear what she'd done. He didn't want Cass to feel bad.

Regardless of what had happened between them back in Dark Falls, Devlin Russo was a good man.

"I have my SAT phone, so I can still contact command central, but the battery is almost shot and there's no way to recharge it out here."

"What about your two friends? They must have radios?" They'd also missed their ride out, so they had to be around somewhere.

Silence. Followed by a flat— "They didn't answer my hails before the radio died. Nor have they shown up here, which they would have, if they were able to. We can't count on them."

He sounded so bleak...

She wanted to reach out and comfort him. He had to be worried about his friends and frustrated with the situation. Here he was, stuck babysitting her and Cass. He probably wanted to go look for his teammates, help them if they needed it.

"You should look for them." She forced the suggestion out.

She hated—absolutely hated—the thought of Devlin leaving, of her facing the dark on her own. What if something happened to him? What if he didn't come back? What would she do then? She didn't even know where this second evacuation site was, or how to get there.

But such concerns were selfish and cruel.

If Devlin could help his teammates, maybe even save their lives, then he needed to go...no matter how much she wanted to keep him by her side.

* * *

She didn't want him to go, that fact was clear. Her voice was taut with misgivings.

Her cheek was resting on his cargo pants, but she was looking up toward him, the tension on her face and the wrinkles digging into her forehead clearly visible within the green glow of the NVDs. The thought of him leaving terrified her. Yet she'd told him to go anyway.

It was one of the bravest, most selfless things he'd ever seen.

His fingers itched to smooth the creases between her eyebrows. He forced his hands to remain still.

"They can take care of themselves," he told her quietly. "I'm not leaving you."

Which sounded like an eternal promise and not what he'd meant to imply. He tried again. "You're stuck with me until you're back home."

He saw the relief wash across her face and the spasm of her throat as she swallowed.

"Are you sure? You seem…I don't know…edgy…" Her voice was soft, conflicted.

The edginess she'd picked up on had nothing to do with his teammates. He hadn't lied; they were experienced, well trained, fully capable special operators. They could take care of themselves. There were any number of reasons why they'd gone radio silent and ditched the rendezvous point. He wasn't about to put Madeline and Cassidy's life in danger by taking off to find them.

Sure as hell not when he was the only thing standing between his charges and full on horror.

What she'd picked up on hadn't been because of his teammates, it had been because of her daughter. The kid was a magnet for regrets, and guilt, and a mountain of anguish.

Every time he looked at her, Gracie swam up from her grave, accusing him of betrayal with her black, water drenched eyes. And whenever Madeline's kid turned her dark, timid eyes on him, the memories flooded in—of his own baby girl, with the same dark beautiful eyes. Only Gracie's eyes …they were full of condemnation.

And fuck...he deserved that censure. He deserved the accusations. He *had* betrayed her. He'd spent all his time saving others —his men, civilians who'd gotten themselves into trouble, diplomats who needed protection, foreigners who needed the expertise of someone well versed in operational strategy.

He'd spent so much time out of the country, focusing on saving others, he'd let his daughter slip away. If he'd been home, he would have stopped it. He would have found her in time. He would have saved her.

She wouldn't have died.

"Dev? What's wrong?"

He shook his head to clear the memories.

"Nothing." He coughed to clear the ache from his throat. "Just thinking."

Which wasn't even a lie, at least the last part of the claim. He *had* been thinking, about things he couldn't change and couldn't control. Time to focus on stuff he could do.

"Okay." Her voice was doubtful, like she didn't believe him.

He ignored her misgivings. "In another hour or so, before sunrise, I'll head outside and call into command central to make sure evac B is still in effect. I'll do a quick recon at that time too, assess the rebel presence." He suspected the Amaru had pulled out, or at least most of them. There had been no gunfire or voices for hours.

"Can't you call from here?"

"No signal," he said simply. "I need to be in the open." When she didn't respond, he continued. "Afterwards, I want to test something. We'll crank the oil lamp back up and I'll check the rooms on either side of our position. If the light doesn't seep through the cracks in the secret doors, we can leave the lantern on until we bug out." Or until it ran out of fuel.

Her breath stuttered out. "That would be nice...being able to see again, I mean."

"Yeah." He left it at that. Not being able to see, when she was stressed and afraid, had to be hard as hell. Yet she'd handled the situation like a pro. He shouldn't be surprised by that. She'd proved her mettle in that motel parking lot when she'd fought to save Taggart's life. She'd stripped off her shirt for Christ's sake, to use as a compression pad, and knelt there in her bra, in front of a crowd of useless men, applying pressure.

Tag would be dead if not for her quick action and calm reason.

"You should sleep." He kept his voice soft. "I'll wake you before I head out."

She apparently decided to take his advice. Her side of the conversation gave way to deep even breaths, leaving him to his darkness and disfunction.

Two hours later he woke her. It was zero five hundred, which meant the sun would be rising above the jungle canopy soon. He needed to sneak out now, while there was still darkness to cloak him.

But first, they needed to go over a few things.

"There's a 9 mm in my backpack, so keep your daughter out of it." He pitched his voice low, to avoid waking the kid. "Do you know how to handle a gun?"

Her breath caught. "Yes. I own a gun. Both Cassidy and I took gun safety lessons in Phoenix. But I took shooting lessons too."

Her voice was steady now. Maybe too steady. He sensed she was hanging on by a thread.

"The weapon is in the bottom front right of the pack. Safety is on. It's loaded." He left it at that. Didn't offer to pull it out and give it to her. She knew it was there…if she needed it.

God help them both if she needed it.

He hesitated. Giving her the coordinates to the evac site would mean nothing without the SAT phone's GPS system. And he needed the phone to reach command central so he couldn't leave it with her. But she needed a plan in case something happened to him.

"Do you remember how I closed the secret door?" The lantern had been on, and she'd been watching him.

"Yes." Her voice wobbled.

"Good. To open it, push up on the lever. Give me your hand." He pulled his watch off, caught the hand she offered him and gave her the watch. "If I'm not back in three days, head down to the river." Three days would give command central time to arrange for another team to insert and collect them...assuming he had a chance to call their location and the situation in. "Hide in the tree line until you see a cargo boat and wave them down." She'd traveled up on a cargo boat, so she'd be able to identify one. "Move around at night as much as you can. Take whatever you need from my pack. The cargo boat will have a SAT phone. Once you're onboard, ask to use it and call this number." He unzipped a pocket on the side of his pack and pulled out a pen and pad. After jotting down Tex's number, he pressed the slip of paper into her hand, next to the watch. "Tell the man who answers who you are. He'll get you home."

The cargo boats only delivered supplies once a week, which meant she'd be alone, with the kid, out in the jungle for God only knew how long. As plans went, it was shitty as hell. The water's edge carried the most human activity too, which would put her and the kid at risk. But it was the best he could give her under the circumstances.

He wished he could leave her his helmet with the attached NVD bar. If the situation went belly up, at least she'd be able to see what she was doing. But he couldn't. He'd need the damn thing while he was out there. It was his best defense against walking into an ambush.

"Three days?" Her voice spiked. "Why...why are you telling me all this?"

Her voice shook so hard he could barely make out the words. Great. He scowled. He'd terrified her.

"It's a *just in case* contingency plan, that's all. During mission prep, we work up a whole alphabet of contingency plans. We always have another plan to fall back on."

"Like a second evacuation site if the first one falls apart?" Her voice was steadier, but the glaze in her eyes spoke of terror.

"And a third and a fourth. That's all we're talking about. I fully expect to be back within half an hour. But it never hurts to plan for the unforeseen."

"Okay." She took a deep breath and then another.

"When I get back, we'll crank the lantern up, and I'll check to see if we can use that safely." He could at least offer her that carrot.

"Okay," she said again. "Be safe out there."

He watched her throat tremble as she swallowed and grimaced. He could have handled that better.

"Always." He hesitated, hating to leave her like this. Her face looked too still and tight, like she was about to shatter. But he suspected trying to reassure her would just scare her worse. "Madeline...I *will* be back. I will."

Turning, he headed for the exterior door that entered out into the field behind the compound. The building urgency kicked him into a jog. The sooner he checked in, the sooner he could return. He didn't like leaving Madeline and the kid any more than they—or at least Madeline—liked him being gone.

He listened for a minute at the exterior door. No voices. No gunfire. Good so far. The door slid open with that familiar grating sound. He parked himself next to the wall and waited. Once it was fully open, he swung through in a half crouch, his rifle up and ready. As he scanned the still landscape, he searched the limestone wall beside him for the outside lever. He found it in the same spot as the inside lever, just on the opposite side of the wall.

As the limestone door slid shut behind him, he exhaled in relief. At least Madeline and the kid were safely sealed inside their hidey hole. After powering the phone up, he checked the battery—ten percent.

Fuuuck...

He waited to call command central until he'd found a good spot to hole up—a partially constructed animal pen a quarter way down the back field.

Commander North answered on the first ring. "Devlin, am I ever happy to hear your voice. Sitrep?"

Devlin filled him in on everything from Lucky taking off after the cult woman, to Squish covering for them and the roof coming down. He paused to clear the grit from his voice. "My comm is out thanks to a mishap with Millie Mouse. Alpha One a and b didn't respond to my hails before the radio died. Nor have they showed up at the rendezvous point. Any intel on them?"

Given names were never used in the field. Too big of a

chance that some terrorist asshole would track them down stateside and help themselves to a little payback.

North sighed. "Yes and no."

What the fuck did that mean? Devlin lassoed his impatience and waited.

"Alpha One-a's tracker shows him moving erratically. He's approximately twelve klicks to the west of you. He appears to be heading in the general direction of evac two. But his movements are irregular."

Fuck...

Devlin digested that news. Alpha One-a was Squish. Erratic could mean anything. "Are there any Amaru encampments where he's wandering?"

Could Squish have been captured?

"According to Alpha One-a's commander, that's a negative."

Well ol' Widdy—Commander Widmer—would know, as he headed up ST4's operations.

"What about Alpha One-b?"

Tight silence greeted the question. Not good. Not good at all.

"One-b is off the grid."

Lucky's tracker was dark? How was that possible? "Wasn't he chipped?"

While GPS chipping wasn't a command requirement, it was *highly* encouraged. And most of the guys accepted the chip. There had been too many occasions where those tracking chips had saved operators' lives, or recovered their brethren's bodies, for the teams to go all conspiracy nutty and refuse the protection the tracking technology supplied.

Of course, the fact the trackers were removed between missions helped alleviate some—although not all—of the suspicion directed at the technology.

"Yes, he was chipped. But his tracker is dead. There's no data stream."

What the hell...

Devlin swiped a hand over his head and scowled. The lack of data transmissions didn't mean Lucky was dead. The tracker would continue transmitting regardless of the health of its host.

They'd located several dead operators through data transmissions.

"Could the chip have malfunctioned?"

"It's possible," North said. But there was something in the flatness of the commander's voice that made Devlin think he didn't believe that was the case.

A darker scenario occurred to him. If someone knew where to look, the chip could have been removed and destroyed.

"This is sheer speculation, sir. But the Amaru rebels wouldn't have had time to follow Whitehorse One in. And they sure as hell wouldn't have had time to follow it in and set up shop so they could try to take Whitehorse Two. They held off attacking until that second bird landed. They knew it was coming. Someone must have tipped them off."

"We're aware." North's voice was flat, but Devlin could sense the rage in the reply.

So he wasn't the only one thinking they had a traitor in their midst. Had that traitor targeted Lucky? If so, why? And where had he been taken?

"What about Alpha Two, sir? Did they and their rescues make it back to base?"

"They did. They're itching to head back out and provide you with some much-needed support, as well as track down your missing crew. However, all operations have been grounded pending a thorough investigation."

Devlin nodded in agreement. They sure as hell didn't want more mission details ending up in the wrong hands. Of course, that left evac B hanging. The location had already been picked and sent up the chain. If their mole had sabotaged evac A, chances were he, or she, knew the details about evac B too.

Of course, North already knew that. He would have pivoted.

As if he'd read Devlin's mind, North started talking again. "You'll be receiving a text from a mutual friend momentarily. It's encrypted. The same friend ran a z-scan on your phone and inserted a digital blocker."

He had to be talking about Tex. Tex was the only one with those kind of computer chops. Although what the hell a z-scan was he had no idea. He'd have to ask Tex next time he talked to him. The digital blocker was easy enough to figure out, and a huge relief. Tex must have done some of his magic to block anyone from digitally accessing Devlin's SAT phone. At least no one would be eavesdropping on any of his upcoming conversations.

"Understood."

"Do not call into command central again. Call our friend with your updates."

"Copy that." Fuck...the situation must be even worse than he'd suspected if North had bypassed HQ1 mission control in favor of Tex.

"How are your two rescues holding up?" North sounded tired now, maybe even dispirited.

Devlin didn't blame him. Every time their boys stepped off that chopper, or out of a boat, they were putting their lives on the line for their country and fellow citizens. To have one of their own not just spit on that sacrifice but sell them out... fuck...the notion wasn't just disheartening, it was depressing as hell.

"They're holding up like a pair of troopers," he told his commander.

Too often extrications went south because of the rescues themselves. The amount of entitled pricks walking the world were astronomical and God knew they ran into their unfair share.

He signed off not long after and waited for Tex's message. Evac C wouldn't be among the contingency locations that had already been hammered out and sent up the pipeline. It would be new. He could only hope the new location and timeframe wouldn't add more stress to the load Madeline and the kid were already carrying.

CHAPTER 15

The warm glow of the lantern brought a primal sense of relief. She'd never been afraid of the dark, but there was a primitive wariness there. An instinctive understanding that darkness masked danger and death.

Now that they had light again, Devlin had even taken off his helmet with the night vision goggles.

He'd returned from his excursion outside much sooner than she'd expected. Which had led to a different kind of relief. The knowledge he hadn't been hurt, or taken, or killed, had launched a dizzying bout of euphoria.

After telling her the rebels had cleared out, he'd fired the lantern up and snuck back out to see if the light could be seen from the other side of the wall.

When he'd returned, he'd told her they could leave the lantern on.

"When do we head to the evacuation site?" she asked.

"At deep dusk. Eighteen hundred hours." He consulted his watch. "Twelve hours from now." He paused, his intent gaze fixed on her face. "Evac B's been canceled. Evac C is in effect." Before she had a chance to worry, he added, "Timeframe remains the same. So does the distance. Our plan doesn't change."

Okay… "Why did it change?"

He shrugged. "Command decided the new location was a safer option."

She suspected there was more to it than that, but she let it go. "Geez, you weren't kidding when you claimed SEALs have a whole alphabet of contingency plans, were you?"

A smile touched his lips and lightened the darkness in his eyes. "Hell. Option number three is nothing. Try option eight or nine."

She smiled back at him. "Well, hopefully this will be the final option in our case."

"I've got some aspirin if your head still hurts," he said quietly.

Madeline dropped the hand that had been absently fingering the knot on the side of her head. Of course he'd notice what she'd been doing. He noticed everything. "That would be nice."

He pulled a first aid kit out of his pack, popped the lid and grabbed a bottle of aspirin. After shaking two tablets into his palm, he handed them over, along with a bottle of water.

"What about your two teammates? Did you get hold of them?" she asked after swallowing the aspirin. After a couple sips of water, she screwed the cap back on and passed it over. She still wasn't clear on how much water he had.

"They haven't checked in." His voice was gruff, his gaze guarded.

Maddie took the hint. He didn't want to talk about them. Moving on.

"Did you see any of the cult members out there?" She'd been wondering what had happened to the women who'd stayed.

"No." He eased down to the floor on her right and leaned back against the wall. "The compound is empty. So are the fields surrounding us."

Madeline looked over at Cassidy, who was lying beside her, to the left, still fast asleep between the space blankets.

"What do you think happened to the women?" she asked, lowering her voice.

She was pretty sure most of the men were dead…if not from Devlin's SEAL team, then because of the rebels. The gunfire had continued long after the helicopter, and the rest of the SEAL team had taken off. The rebels must have been shooting at someone.

She tried to feel bad for them but couldn't work up much sympathy. Their treatment of the women, their attitude toward her...it was still too fresh in her mind.

"Nothing good." Devlin's voice was grim. So was the gaze that brushed against hers.

"You don't think they killed them?"

He leaned forward and shot a glance toward Cassidy, before leaning back again. "No. There were no female bodies."

So the rebels had taken them. Or maybe some of the cult men had, after the SEAL team had cleared out. It wasn't hard to figure out why the women had been taken. Madeline shuddered. While the women were used to being treated as sexual conveniences by the cult men, they'd tacitly agreed to that situation. There would be no consent with the rebels…

Which reminded her. "I want a gun."

He had extras. There was a pistol strapped to his hip, and the rifle hanging from his chest. Plus—he'd mentioned the other gun in his pack. He had at least one spare.

He was silent for a few seconds, but the eyes studying her face were sharp with questions. "Will you be able to kill someone if you need to?"

She thought about that and offered a decisive nod. "Absolutely."

If killing someone would save their lives, she'd do it without hesitation.

Turning, he snagged his pack and dragged it over to him, the canvas scraping the floor as it moved. Maddie glanced at Cassidy, but her daughter hadn't stirred. With luck she'd sleep for a while yet, make up for all those sleepless nights they'd shared.

When she turned back to Devlin, he was holding a big, black gun. He looked from her to Cassidy and his eyebrows rose.

"Are you sure? You won't have a holster. You'll have to carry it or stick it in your waist band." Frowning, he looked at Cassidy again.

Clearly, he was worried about Cass getting hold of it. "Cassidy took the gun safety classes with me. She knows guns are off limits. She knows they aren't toys. We've discussed safety protocols repeatedly."

Still—she frowned. While her daughter was an obedient child, even dutiful children had occasional lapses of judgement. But all it took to convince her that she needed the gun was how vulnerable she'd felt without Devlin beside her. If something happened to him, she needed the means to protect Cassidy. She'd be extra vigilant. She'd make sure that Cassidy knew the gun was not to be touched under any circumstances.

"I'm sure," she told him, holding his dark, probing gaze.

He didn't question her further. Just handed the gun over and showed her where the safety was. "See if you can tuck it in your waistband."

They both rose to their feet.

The waistband of her pants, it turned out, was way too loose to hold the gun in place. The minute she let the pistol go, it started sliding. "Well, that's not going to work."

"Hang on." He bent back over his pack and pulled out a long-sleeved t-shirt.

Bending, he lifted the cuff of his jeans and pulled a knife from a thin holster strapped to his calf. He sliced the shirt from the top down on both sides, until the cloth had been cut in two.

After setting one of the pieces aside, he crouched and spread the second piece across the floor. "Hand me the gun."

She handed it down, watching as he placed the pistol into the middle of the fabric square and folded the cloth over it before cutting the sleeve off at the seam. He sliced at least two dozen thin strips of fabric off the second piece and punched a series of holes around the outer edge of the square with the gun. Once the strips and holes were ready, he set the pistol aside. As he worked the thin slips of cloth through the holes along the sides and bottom of the square, and tied them off, a pouch formed.

He slid the gun inside the pouch and shook it. Nothing unraveled, nothing came loose.

She coughed back a laugh, her lips quirking at the look on his face. Good lord, he looked pleased with himself.

Grabbing the sleeve, he rolled it into a rope, and tied the

strips around it until it held its shape. Then he attached the rope to the pouch with more ribbons of fabric. By the time he'd finished, he made her a belt and holster.

"Let's see if this works," he said.

Impressed with his ingenuity, Maddie took the rope he'd made and tied it around her waist, adjusting it until the pouch hung against her right hip. "You're the real MacGyver, aren't you?"

"Hell, no." There was amusement in the gaze that met hers. "MacGyver hated guns." He scanned the assembly and nodded in satisfaction. "You'll have to hold it down when you run, otherwise it will flap."

"Who cares if it flaps, when it looks so rustically chic?" She struck a cocky pose. "Before you know it, all the gunslingers will want one."

His face softened with humor, at least until his gaze dropped to her mouth and lingered. The amusement in his eyes vanished. Desire crept in, burnishing the dark brown of his eyes until they glittered. For a moment, he seemed to lean toward her...his head dipping. And then he froze. Pulled back.

He cleared his throat and took a long step back. "You should try to get some more sleep. We'll crack open a couple MREs after you two wake up. Get some grub into you before we head out."

Obviously, their moment of connection was over. Equally obvious—that sexual connection they'd discovered in Dark Falls was alive and well and trying to insert itself at the most inopportune times.

"Are you sure it's safe to cook?" He'd been worried about the smell attracting attention earlier.

He shrugged. "I'll check before we open the MREs. But if the tangos have cleared out, then the smell won't attract anyone." He paused, studying her face. "Try to get some sleep."

She must look pretty bad, judging by the worry in his voice. But he was right. She did need to catch up on her sleep. Untying the makeshift belt, she handed it to Devlin, holster, and all.

Lifting the top space blanket, she eased herself down next to Cassidy and drew the silver-lined blanket over them again. Her daughter turned toward her, mumbling something indecipherable, and fell back asleep in Maddie's arms.

With a deep sigh, she relaxed as the warmth seeped into her. And then, knowing that Devlin stood over them, protecting them, she fell into a deep, easy sleep.

* * *

Devlin folded the space blankets and stowed them away. The backpack was getting lighter each time he opened it. But it was still too heavy. He'd need to lighten the load even more if Madeline had to carry it.

He'd slipped outside to call Tex after Madeline had woke up. No sense in heading toward the new GPS coordinates if the evac site had changed again. Tex had filled him in on the current situation. Evac C was still a go. Squish was still wandering all over the damn place, on a loose trajectory for evac B, which wasn't in effect any longer. And Lucky's tracker was still out of commission.

Worry over his teammates was getting stronger. Not that he could do a damn thing for them. He sure as hell couldn't go out and look for them. There was too much mileage between him and Squish. He wouldn't be able to get to him and still make it to evac C in time. Not with Madeline and the kid in tow.

And fuck...nobody had a clue where Lucky was.

"I don't like it." Cassidy frowned down at the bowl of beef stew Devlin had slid in front of her.

Madeline, who was sitting next to Cassidy, plucked the spoon from the bowl and wrapped her daughter's fingers around the handle. "You like beef stew, that's why Devlin cooked it for you. You need to eat, baby. Take a bite." Glancing toward Devlin, she nudged the bowl of chili mac that he'd set in front of her back toward him. "There's plenty here for both of us. We should share it. You need to eat too."

"I'm good." When her mouth opened in protest, he shook his head at her. "I'm not the one with depleted energy stores. I can go a couple of days without eating. It won't affect me. You, on the other hand, are too thin. You need the calories. Eat."

He'd considered cooking just one of the MREs, but the pair desperately needed the energy the meals would provide, so he'd decided not to ration the packages. There were two MREs left in his pack, plus the protein bars. When those ran out, he could forage. He looked over at the kid, who was still staring suspiciously down at her bowl. Considering the kid's finicky reaction to her food, even though she had to be starving, he'd have to butcher and disguise the meat before he brought it back to camp, maybe tell her it was chicken or something.

"Cassidy, I'm not playing with you." Madeline dropped the coaxing tone. "Devlin gave up his dinner so you could eat. You *will* show your appreciation by eating it. *Now.*"

Devlin's head shot up, his instincts telling him that Madeline's order was not going to have the desired effect. Sure enough, the kid dropped the spoon back in the bowl and shoved the meal toward him.

Leaning against the wall, he studied Madeline's daughter thoughtfully. The kid had awoken grumpy as fuck. Belligerence sat in the jut of her chin. Her eyes were filmed with exhaustion. She had the look of a child too tired and too stressed. Neither of which he could do a damn thing about, but she'd feel better with a meal warming her belly.

She'd been fascinated by the space blankets after he'd told her the technology had been developed for astronauts to use in space.

He could work with that.

"Did you know that these packaged meals were developed for space travel?" he asked casually. Not true, but she wouldn't know that. The kid's head came up. From the frown on her face she wasn't buying it, so he laid it on thicker. "They were starving up there. Nothing to eat but paste from a tube. No way to heat food. So, the scientists came up with this." He waved at the bowl sitting on the ground between them. "The astronauts love the meals. Especially the beef stew."

A skiff of fascination nudged the misery from her eyes. "Really?"

"Yeah, really." Devlin nodded solemnly, holding her gaze. "In fact, they like these things so much, my buddy Buzz Lightyear says they eat them at home too."

Her forehead furrowed, skepticism touching her face again. "Buzz Lightyear isn't real. He's make-believe."

"Well, Buzz in the movie is make-believe." Devlin instantly pivoted. "But you know they patterned that character off a real astronaut, right?" He paused for impact. "The real Buzz Lightyear is called Buzz Aldrin, and he was the second man to walk on the moon."

The kid's mouth rounded. "Really?"

"Yes. Really." He'd hooked her now. Her eyes were as round as her mouth. "He's one of the most famous astronauts alive, and he's a buddy of mine. He's also a big fan of that dinner in front of you."

Her gaze dropped to the bowl. "He is?"

Devlin nodded solemnly. "He sure is. The only reason I even have these meals is because Buzz gave me some. See, civilians aren't allowed to eat these, they cost too much money to make. Only astronauts are allowed to have them."

Some of the timidness returned to her face. "What if the space police arrest us for eating them?"

He kept his voice completely sober. "Nah, since Buzz gave them to me, and I'm giving them to you, we're good. Buzz will vouch for us." He rubbed his mouth to hide his grin. Christ the kid looked completely enthralled. "Just think, you and your mom are the only civilians in the whole world who can say they've eaten a space meal." He moved in for the kill shot. "But heck, if you don't want it, I'll eat it."

Her hand flashed out and snagged the bowl, drawing it back toward her. "I want it."

"Are you sure?" He put on a concerned face. "If you don't want it, you don't have to eat it..."

"I want it." She picked up her spoon and dug into the bowl. After a few seconds of chewing, she nodded enthusiastically and went to work shoveling the stew into her mouth. "I like it. Buzz is right. It's really good!"

Mission accomplished.

Devlin was mentally dusting his hands when it occurred to

him that Madeline might not appreciate the con he'd just run on her kid. He shot her a cautious look. She caught his glance and sent him a smile, before mouthing *thank you.*

Five by five on that op then...

The first couple of spoonfuls of stew seemed to jumpstart the kid's appetite and she dug into the meal with ravenous gusto. Madeline followed suit, eating the reconstituted meal with the same appreciation she'd eaten that hundred-dollar lobster and steak dinner with back in Dark Falls.

While Madeline and her daughter devoured their meals, Devlin started strategizing. He'd already decided they'd make better time if he carried the kid on his back and Madeline carried the pack. But he'd need to jettison at least half the contents of the pack and lighten the load before handing it over. He considered Madeline's thin frame, and white, lined face. She was already weak. Carrying the pack, even a lighter one, might be beyond her current capabilities. But it was the best shot they had, so he got to work.

Once he'd unloaded everything but the essentials—the space blankets, an eight by ten, lightweight plastic tarp, water bottles, MREs, protein bars, bug spray, toilet paper, a coil of nylon rope, the med kit, plus boxes of ammo for all three weapons—the pack was a good twenty pounds lighter. Hopefully Madeline could carry it without much effort. If not, he'd improvise.

By the time he was finished streamlining the pack, Madeline and the kid were done eating and silently watching him.

"Here's our plan," he told them calmly. "We're looking at a long slog through the jungle. It's gonna be tough, even on a grownup like me. A little bit like you...?" He lifted his chin toward Madeline's daughter. "You're gonna need some help keeping up. So, I'm gonna give you a piggyback ride." He held the kid's huge, worried eyes. "You know what a piggyback ride is?"

The small dark head bobbed. "I think so."

"Good. That's good. All you have to do is climb onto my back and hang on. Wrap your arms around my neck and your legs around my waist. Think you can do that?"

The kid's forehead pleated, but she bobbed her head again.

"That's great. You got spunk and strength, kid. Which is exactly what you need to become an astronaut." The last bit had been a shot in the dark, but the kid's face lit up like he'd paid her the best compliment *ever.* "All you have to do is hang on."

She nodded with more enthusiasm. "I can hang on."

Devlin smiled at her in approval. "Good, that's good."

"I'm going to carry the backpack?" Madeline asked, her gaze skipping to the items he'd pulled out and lined against the wall, including his extra pair of boots. Hell, he hated leaving those behind, he'd just broken the damn things in, but they were heavy as hell and too big for Madeline to wear.

"That's the plan." He picked the backpack up by the strap on the top and handed it to her. "Do you think you can carry it?"

"I can carry it," she said before she even took it.

From the determined cant to her chin, he didn't doubt it.

"When are we leaving?"

"Now." When she looked at the lantern, he shook his head. "We can't afford the light. I'll lead. You follow." He handed her the tether he'd whipped up while they'd been sleeping. The sleeves from the shirt he'd cut up to make her belt and holster had come in handy. After tying the two pieces together, he'd made another length of rope. "Tie this to the back of my belt and you can hold onto it so you don't lose me."

She swallowed hard, her determination dimming. But then her chin shot up and stayed there. "Sounds good."

"Okay then." He split his attention between his two charges. "Are you two ready to head out?"

Madeline nodded, her shoulders going up and back. Cassidy, on the other hand, her eyes dropped to the floor and her shoulders drooped.

Houston, they had a problem.

He crouched, dropping to her level. "Cassidy?" He gentled his voice. "What's wrong, sweetheart?"

The endearment slipped out without warning and slashed him to the quick. He rocked back on his heels, almost losing his footing, about to straighten and turn away.

Only one child was entitled to that endearment. And she was dead.

But one look at Madeline's daughter's white, dismayed face told him he couldn't afford to push her away and burrow into his pain. He couldn't afford to flee the present in favor of the past. He couldn't afford to shut this kid out. Not now. Not yet. Not if he wanted to keep her alive.

"Cass?" he asked softly.

She peeked up at him, a flood of red darkening her cheeks, and instantly ducked her head again. Lifting her foot, she nudged the floor with the scuffed toe of her canvas shoe.

"I gotta go potty," she whispered.

Oh…*oh*…

He rose to his feet. Crossing to his pack, he pulled out a roll of toilet paper and handed it to Madeline. "How about you two take the lantern and do your...uh...business down the corridor. We'll head out when you get back."

"Toilet paper?" Her eyebrows rose in amusement as she plucked the roll from his hand. "You consider this a necessity?"

She'd obviously picked up on the reasoning behind all the items he'd abandoned against the wall.

"Hell, yes, it's a necessity." He grimaced and added, "If you've ever wiped your ass with leaves, you'd know that."

"Momma," the kid whispered as she reached for her mother's hand. "He said one of your no-no words. Are you gonna make him put money in your jar?"

Ah hell, he'd forgotten about little pitchers and big ears. Before he had a chance to apologize for his loose lips, Madeline slung an arm over the kid's shoulders and turned her around.

"Not just one no-no word," Madeline said, in a conspiratorial whisper, as she bent down to grab the lantern. "There were two bad words in there. He owes us two quarters now."

The smile she sent him over her shoulder was teasing and went straight to his cock like she'd brushed against it, bare skin to bare skin. He waited for the glow of the lantern to fade as they walked farther down the corridor, and then reached down and adjusted himself.

The good news? They'd be shutting the lantern off soon, and walking into the dark, so nobody—meaning Madeline—would see the machine gun tenting his crotch.

Not that his erection would last much longer anyway…not with the five-mile slog ahead and the child he'd be carrying on his back.

* * *

After they reached the end of the corridor, Devlin donned his helmet. Madeline set the lantern next to the wall and pulled on the pack, adjusting the straps to tighten it down. The tether was already dangling from Devlin's belt, waiting for her to grab it as soon as the door slid open. With Cassidy's hand in hers, Madeline forced deep chunks of air into her lungs and fought back the fear.

She wasn't looking forward to what the night would bring once they stepped outside. Neither was Cass, judging by the trembling fingers grasping Madeline's hand. Would Cassidy climb onto Devlin's back? Or chicken out at the last minute?

"Before Miss Cassidy climbs on board, we need to go over some rules." Devlin's voice subtly hardened. "Rule number one. No talking. Sound carries. Voices will attract attention. We don't want that. We want to slip through the rainforest without detection. So, no voices. Got it?" The gaze he settled on Cassidy was firm, but calm. "Cass," he added, "look at me. Do you understand what I said?"

Her gaze skimmed his face before flitting away. She nodded but stared at the ground. "I'm not supposed to talk."

"That's right." His smile looked forced. "If you need to talk to me, lean over my shoulder and whisper in my ear."

She glanced up. "I can whisper?"

"That's right. If you need to, but only if you *really* need to." He fell silent and glanced from Cass to Madeline. When they both nodded, he moved on. "Rule number two. If I kneel, then you climb off. Kneeling means I need you to climb off my back." When they both nodded again, he continued. "Rule number three. If I must leave, you two stay exactly where I left you. *Exactly.* Got it?"

Instead of nodding this time, Cassidy jolted. Her fingers

clamped so hard around Madeline's hand they ground the bones together and caused pain.

"Leave?" Cassidy asked. Her voice turned shrill, slick with fear. "You're going to leave us?"

The reaction startled Madeline. Cass was reacting to Devlin's theoretical leaving like she'd reacted to Madeline's possibility of disappearing. Terrified and clingy.

"He's not going to leave us, Cass."

Liquid, anxious eyes lifted to Madeline's face. "But he said—"

"What I meant," Devlin broke in calmly, "was that if I have to leave for a moment, like...say...if *I* need to go potty, you need to climb off. But if I do leave, I will always come back. Always."

Chewing on her lip, Cassidy thought about that. "You promise?"

He didn't hesitate. "I promise."

The stiffness left Cassidy's body. "That's okay then."

"Glad you approve." Devlin's voice was solemn.

Madeline remained silent, letting the two work it out, knowing full well that if Devlin had to leave, it wouldn't be for a bathroom break and he might not be able to come back.

"How will we know it's you when you return and not someone else?" She had no intention of idly waiting and praying nobody else found them first. She'd have the gun out and on standby. It would be a shame if she shot him by accident.

"Right." His gaze dropped to the pouch with the gun nestled inside. "I'll whistle before joining you. If you hear this—" He made a sound that was more bird call than whistle. "Then I'm back."

She frowned and leaned in closer. "Do that again." He repeated the bird call and she committed it to memory.

"So those are the rules." Devlin looked down at Cassidy and raised an eyebrow. "Are we clear on them?"

While he'd used plural, there was no doubt the question was directed at her daughter. It was also clear that he was waiting for a response.

"Cass." Madeline nudged her shoulder. "Do you understand what Devlin told us?"

The dark head bobbed.

"Repeat what he told us," Madeline said.

Cassidy's head popped up, her solemn gaze skating between Devlin and Madeline. "I'm not supposed to talk, but I can whisper, but only if it's important." She paused, her face wrinkling in thought. "Like if I have to go potty. Or throw up."

Devlin's eyes widened at that last insight and his lips quirked. "Exactly. If you're about to throw up, whisper in my ear, and I'll let you down."

He didn't look particularly appalled at the thought of Cassidy vomiting all over him. Maybe he didn't think she would actually do it.

"Uh, Devlin. Cassidy has a ...weak...stomach. She can vomit at just the thought of *vomiting*. So this is a real concern..."

He shrugged and winked at Cassidy. "How about we don't think about puking then. Can you do that?"

"I guess..." But there was uncertainty in the soft reply.

Devlin studied her worried face before shrugging. His voice was unconcerned when he finally responded. "A little puke never hurt anyone, right?"

"I guess?" Cassidy's voice rose on the last word, turning it into a question.

Ignoring her doubts, Devlin planted his fists on his hips. "Okay then. I'm going to kneel so you can climb on my back. You ready?"

When the small, dark head nodded, Devlin turned and went down on one knee. To Madeline's shock, her daughter scrambled onto Devlin's broad back without hesitation and wrapped her arms around his neck. When he stood, she wrapped her legs around his waist. He shifted the rifle hanging from the strap around his shoulders until it was hanging from his right side, and wrapped his forearms around her legs to stabilize her.

"Good little monkey," he told her teasingly. "You think you can hang on?"

"I'm not a monkey, I'm a girl," she said with a giggle, her thin arms tightening around his neck.

"Really?" He jiggled her lightly, until she giggled again. Her arms tightened around his neck until she was squeezing him so hard, she had to be cutting off his air supply. Not that he showed any discomfort. "The way you scrambled up, I bet you're part monkey."

As Cassidy giggled again, he turned to Madeline, lifting an eyebrow. "You ready?"

Madeline nodded, her throat tight. Tears tried to form in her eyes. She blinked them away. It had been so long since she'd heard Cass giggle, she'd forgotten what it sounded like.

She cleared her throat. "Ready."

He studied her a moment. His eyes confident. Reassuring. "Gutter the lamp and move three feet or so to the right. You don't want to be in front of the door when it opens."

After the lamp had died and she'd shuffled over to where he'd directed, she felt his hand guide her fingers to the tether attached to the back of his belt.

"Hang on tight," he said softly. "We'll need to take the clearing in front of us at a run. Without cover, we'll be exposed by the moonlight, so we need to get to the tree line ASAP. If I go too fast, and you can't keep up, tug hard on the rope. I'll slow down."

The breath she hauled into her lungs stuttered.

"Okay." Did she sound as terrified as she felt?

"Hey, we got this."

Fingers stroked her cheek, followed by the brush of his thumb against her trembling lips. She felt the moist heat of his breath against her face, just before his mouth touched down in a kiss more comforting than sexual.

When he pulled back, it took her a moment to notice the grating sound, and the slice of moonlight flooding into the darkness.

The sliver slowly expanded as the door slid open.

CHAPTER 16

Once the door stood open, Devlin eased into the doorjamb, feeling the tug on his waistband as the rope attached to his belt went taut. He waited just outside the corridor, monitoring their surroundings, listening for voices or footsteps or anything that might indicate trouble.

Nothing.

His forearms clamped around Cassidy's legs, he eased into the open. The kid was clinging to him like the monkey he'd called her. Her arms wrapped around his neck, her legs around his waist. She was lighter than he'd expected. Like her bones were hollow.

He waited a few seconds longer, scanning the field that stretched before them for signs of movement...signs of life. Once he was satisfied their path was clear, he broke into a ground-covering lope.

The light pull and release of the fabric tether assured him Madeline was on his heels. If the rope went loose and started bouncing against his legs, he'd know she'd let go.

That first leg of their journey seemed to take forever, although he knew—rationally—that they'd only been in the field for a couple of minutes. Time fluctuations were a byproduct of being completely exposed and waiting for the burn of a bullet.

Life either sped up or slowed down or sometimes alternated between the two.

When they reached the edge of the rubber trees, he dropped back to a walk, and wove a path through the tall, straight trunks decked out in their eerie green glaze. The branches started two thirds of the way up the trunks and blocked some of the moonlight. But not all.

They silently slipped between the trees, following the compass on the watch he'd retrieved from Madeline. Later, he'd fine tune the direction they were traveling with the GPS on his phone, but for now they were moving in the right direction, and it was more important to retain their cover.

Once they entered the rainforest, cover wouldn't be a priority, they'd be surrounded by vegetation.

He could hear the kid's hard pants against his neck, like she'd run that quarter mile at breakneck speed alongside he and Madeline, but she hadn't made a sound. And Madeline...hell... she was keeping up with him, hadn't slowed him down at all. Plus, she was doing a surprisingly good job of avoiding the twigs and sticks that would snap and expose their position.

They'd made it through most of the plantation trees when a crack sounded to the right. He froze, bracing himself as Madeline bumped into him. The kid didn't make a sound as they were jostled by the collision.

Thank Christ.

He reached out to stabilize Madeline as he scanned the trees to their right. A flash of movement lit up his NVDs. Waist high, so too tall to be an animal.

They weren't alone.

He eased up beside a massive tree and guided Madeline to the back so the trunk stood between her and their new neighbor. Once she was steady and still, he knelt, exhaling in relief as the kid instantly released her hold on him and slid to the ground. By the time he rose to his feet, Madeline already had her arms around her daughter's shoulders and was holding her tight.

Without thinking he flashed her the hold sign—palm up—and relaxed when she nodded. There was obviously enough moonlight for her to see his hand signal…equally obviously…she knew what was happening.

The kid, though. He glanced at the slight frame pressed against her mother's torso. She probably thought he was off to take a piss or a shit. The thought brought a flash of humor. Let her keep thinking that.

By the end of this mission, she'd probably think he had the weakest bladder and bowels on earth.

He closed on their unwelcome neighbor tree by tree, silent as a cat about to pounce. If he'd been alone, he would have ghosted past the guy and kept going, secure in the knowledge he could outmaneuver and overpower pretty much anyone. But this time, he had precious cargo on board and in tow.

He wasn't taking chances.

The interloper needed to go.

The guy didn't seem worried about discovery. He was meandering, leaving a trail of cracks and snaps, and rustling behind. So... not Lucky or Squish...special operators weren't that careless.

When the unmistakable smell of burning tobacco drifted to him, Devlin rolled his eyes. Unbelievable. Even a banana, fresh out of SEAL school, knew better than smoking while on recon. The smell of cigarettes floated for yards and let everyone in the vicinity know they were sharing space with a moron.

He eased closer. When the guy finally came into view, he was wearing the pants and shirt of the cult men. So…they'd stumbled across one of Apostolos's defunct guards…

Hell, the bastard wouldn't have been worth dropping, except he had a submachine gun propped against the tree beside him.

Christ save him from amateurs. The smart operator *never* set his weapon down. Not in a warzone. Not when the few seconds it took to grab it could mean your life. Special operators wore their weapons like an extra appendage—one ready for immediate use.

Seconds later, he had his arm wrapped around the bastard's neck and was squeezing, cutting off the air and blood flow to his brain. The guy barely struggled, simply dropped his cigarette, and tried to pry Devlin's arm from his neck.

Once the guy went limp, Devlin let him go. He'd wake up with a headache and a missing submachine gun, but he'd wake up. Once the guy was down, Devlin searched him. No pistol. No holster.

Damn. He'd hoped to present Madeline with an upgrade.

Shrugging the disappointment off, he grabbed the submachine gun, slipped the strap over his neck, and adjusted it so the gun hung beneath his rifle.

Several tree trunks from where he'd stashed Madeline and the kid, he stopped to whistle. After a second, for good measure, he whistled again. He'd barely taken a step forward when a whistle hit him back.

He stopped again.

What the fuck? A return whistle hadn't been on the books. He frowned; Madeline was the cautious type. She wouldn't deviate from the program unless there was a damn good reason...like—

In the still of the night, a man cursed, followed by the sound of flesh striking flesh. Madeline cried out.

Son of a bitch...

There was someone with her. She'd tried to warn him. And the bastard had hurt her because of it.

The hair on the back of his neck lifted. He switched directions, coming in hard from behind where he'd left her. He was still several trees out when he finally caught sight of them.

All fucking *three* of them.

The man behind her was backed up against a tree, an arm around Madeline's neck above the pack and a gun to her head. The kid stood still as a statue slightly to the left of them...at least she was out of harm's way.

He locked down the spike of fear and focused on his target. His adrenaline crested, sharpening his muscles and mind. Obviously, this second guy knew that Devlin was out there. He was scanning the trees, all the while holding that fucking weapon to Madeline's head.

As Devlin eased his knife from the holster on his hip, he ran scenarios and outcomes through his head. Approaching from the rear was out. So was approaching from the front. Cassidy was in the way on the left. He'd have to take the bastard from the right. To complicate things, the asshole's finger was on the trigger, which made freeing Madeline...tricky. Almost any strike could cause that damn finger to spasm and the gun to discharge.

He needed to get that gun away from her head.

Right now, his best strategy was to distract and attack.

But not with his weapon. They couldn't afford gunfire—fuck—shots would bring everyone running.

He eased in behind the tree they were huddled against. Knife in hand he crouched to pick up a couple of walnut sized rocks and straightened. With a flick of his wrist he tossed the rocks to the right. Two hollow *thunks* as the rocks struck wood sounded, as Devlin whipped around the trunk.

As he'd hoped, the asshole behind Madeline had turned his head, and gun, toward the right. Devlin grabbed the bastard's hand and slammed it against the tree trunk hard enough to snap his wrist.

A clipped crack exploded as the weapon discharged, then slipped from limp fingers and fell to the ground.

Fuck...while the muzzle was pointing up, so no one was in the line of fire, the fucking report would act like a homing beacon. He needed to finish this and get his charges out of here pronto.

Madeline wrenched herself free before the report faded and fell back, grabbing the kid as she moved. It was only then, with both his charges safe, that he took the time to actually look at the guy. Well, fuck him, it was the bastard who'd thrown Madeline into the comfort room and left his fingerprints on her arm. He'd regretted letting him walk away intact. Sometimes fate actually did come down solidly on his side.

He drove his knife into the side of the bastard's neck, slicing through the carotid artery. He'd bleed out in seconds, but dizziness and loss of motor skills would come even faster.

The asshole wouldn't be going anywhere.

Before pulling his knife free, he kicked the fallen gun to the side, out of range of the bloody faucet he was about to turn on. There was no place to bathe out here, and he hated the thought of being coated in this guy's blood.

It might scare the kid.

Stepping back and to the side, in the hopes of avoiding as much of the geyser as possible, he yanked the knife loose, and warped over to the gun. He ejected the mag and stuck it in a side pocket on his cargos. The extra gun he tucked into his waistband. His weapon's holster was already occupied with his Sig-P226.

It took two seconds to reach Madeline and swing the kid up into his arms. No time for her to climb up. They needed to get out of the area—*now*.

"Is he dead?" Madeline asked. Her face looked empty and eerie, ephemeral. Like she'd turned into a ghost since he'd left her.

"Yep." If he wasn't already, he would be shortly. "Let's move. That shot is sure to catch someone's attention." He clamped onto Madeline's arm with his left hand and adjusted the kid in the crook of his right elbow.

For the first time, he realized that Cassidy hadn't uttered a peep as he'd grabbed her and swung her into his arms. Hell, she'd clutched him tight instead. The arms she'd wrapped around his neck were in danger of strangling him.

Apparently he'd passed some kind of trust test since the last time he'd grabbed her.

Why the hell that would hit his heart like a nuclear bomb and rock him down to his soul was something he had no answer for.

Nor did he want to examine it too closely.

* * *

Ignoring the throbbing in her cheek and temple, and the way her pulse hammered in her head, Madeline stumbled alongside Devlin as he rushed her through the trees. The moon had crept behind a bank of clouds, so darkness obscured her vision. She couldn't see where they were going, couldn't see what was beneath her feet, had to trust that Devlin was skirting any tripping hazard.

Trusting him was easy. He'd saved her life repeatedly over the past twenty-four hours. He'd emerged from the darkness back there like the warrior he was and taken that rat bastard

Simon out in four, maybe five seconds. She didn't feel any sympathy for Simon. He'd planned on killing Devlin and Cass, and raping her. Simon had gotten what he deserved.

Thank God Devlin had picked up on her warning, even though she'd paid for it with a fist to her face.

She forced breath into her tight lungs and kept her legs moving. Her knees were shaky, so were her hands. Man, every muscle in her body quaked. She hadn't been shaky when Simon had stepped up behind her, pressed the gun against her temple and dragged her to that tree. She hadn't been shaky when Devlin had whistled and she'd whistled back, even though Simon had said he'd kill her if she made a sound.

But she was trembling now.

Not that it mattered, as long as she kept up.

With each step, her skin crawled, her scalp tightened and she expected a hard hand to land on her shoulder. But the plantation sat quiet and calm around her. No voices. No gun fire. No sign that they had company. But then she hadn't known Simon was behind her, either, at least not until he'd grabbed her.

When Devlin's fingers squeezed her hand and he slowed his pace, as though he knew her strength was flagging, she sighed in relief. Devlin wouldn't leave her behind. She knew that. He'd remain by her side no matter what. If her legs gave out, he'd try to carry her along with Cass. And when he couldn't, because even superheroes had limits, they'd all stop walking and die together.

That couldn't happen, so she forced one foot in front of the other and kept running.

She couldn't think of anyone she'd rather have beside her. He was the most competent man she knew. Certainly the most deadly, although she knew he'd never turn those skills on her or Cassidy. He'd use his training to protect them instead. To keep them safe in an unsafe world.

When they reached the last row of rubber trees and the dark tangle of the jungle loomed before them, he pulled her to a stop and bent to set Cassidy on the ground. He immediately pivoted and knelt, giving her his back.

"Up you go, little monkey." His voice was toneless, more

breath than substance. He waited for Cassidy to scramble up, anchored her legs with his forearms and rose to his feet. "We'll take a break in another hour or two. After we're deep in the jungle. Grab the rope, Madeline. It's gonna get dark."

Catching Madeline's hand, he guided it to the tether dangling from his belt.

The instant they slipped into the rainforest and the vegetation closed behind them, the darkness consumed her. The tree canopy, or maybe it was the clouds, had swallowed the moon, cutting off even the slightest glimmer of moonlight. She could barely see a foot in front of her face. Without the rope tethering her to Dev, she would have gotten lost instantly.

While he'd warned her about the darkness, he hadn't warned her about the freaky eerie factor. The dank, moldy smell of decay and moist earth. The sensation of movement around her, like something was ghosting past the corner of her eye. Or the shiver of leaves brushing against...things...and the rustling of tree branches above. And then there were the hooting shrieks rising into the night sky.

She thought the hooting and shrieking were coming from monkeys. But then...maybe not. Jaguars lived in the Amazon, too. And they were known to scream. Although, based off the wildlife documentaries she and Cass had watched back home, they didn't hoot. Their call was more like a deep, raspy cough.

Her fingers so tight around the rope connecting her to Devlin they started to cramp, she automatically ducked whenever she felt his tall frame bend. Or stepped over the fallen trees he guided her across. However, all the while she listened for that distinctive raspy cough she remembered from the documentaries.

Jaguars liked to hunt from above too. They'd lie in wait among the tree branches and ambush their prey from overhead. Was that the rustling she kept hearing? Of course snakes slithered their way from branch to branch too...maybe they were causing all the noise.

She grimaced. It was too bad she'd watched all those anaconda movies. Now that they'd slowed down to a walk and her brain didn't have to concentrate on keeping her moving and upright, her imagination was going a mile a minute.

Maybe Devlin had some kind of snake and jaguar repellant in that magical backpack of his. Something like grizzly or shark repellent, but formulated to prevent big cat and snake attacks.

Yeah…she really needed to stop thinking about all the things in the jungle that could eat her…

After switching the rope from her right hand to her left, she shook her fingers out. She concentrated furiously on that task, as well as slogging forward one step at a time.

Time lost all reference as they worked their way deeper and deeper into the jungle. The moon came out off and on, and fingers of silver filtered through the canopy above. Somehow, the streamers of moonlight turned the jungle even more threatening as they frosted the shrubs and bushes with an eerie, ghostly glow.

She had no idea how long they'd been walking when Devlin finally stopped, and she crashed into him. The impact sent her reeling backwards. She would have hit the ground if his hand hadn't shot out and stabilized her.

"Thanks." She blew out a breath.

"We'll rest here for a bit," he whispered.

Man…did that news sound good.

There was the sound of clothes rustling, followed by a light thud. Seconds later his hand guided her to Cassidy.

"Wait here while I check the ground for insects."

It was eerie how quiet he was. She didn't hear his footsteps, or twigs breaking beneath his weight, or anything.

"We're good," he said after a few minutes. "You can drop the pack."

She felt along her waist until she found the buckle to the backpack straps and pressed the tabs to release it. When he stripped the pack from her back, she instantly felt a thousand pounds lighter.

She heard him rustling around in the pack. And then a swoosh.

"The space blanket is down." He took her hand and guided her over to it. "Sit."

Madeline did as he suggested, settling cross-legged on the crinkly material. The scrunching of the space blanket sounded again. Devlin took hold of her hand, and she felt Cassidy's small fingers grasp her thumb. Blindly, Madeline reached out, snagging Cass from around the waist, and pulled her into her lap.

A few moments later, he handed her two tablets and a bottle of water. She tossed back the tablets, took a small sip of water to wash them down and passed the bottle to Cassidy. After her daughter had drank her fill, Madeline took the water back and drank more. When it was down to what felt like a third, she handed if off to Devlin.

He might argue about it, but Devlin needed to drink too.

Content for the moment, she just sat there, cradling her daughter close, thankful they'd stopped walking. Thankful they were still alive.

Heavier crinkling sounded, and then a toneless whisper. "There's bug spray in the pack if you need it."

For the first time, she heard the buzz of mosquitoes around her face. While she'd been obsessed with the big predators attacking them, the smallest marauders were feasting on their blood. She'd probably be a mass of welts, with chronic itching by the time they crawled aboard that chopper.

Lovely.

"Here." He pushed a round metal object into her hand. "Bug spray."

She fumbled around as she uncapped the can and found the nozzle, more fumbling as she covered her daughter's eyes with her palm and then Madeline closed her eyes and doused them both with the repellant.

Capping the can, she handed it back to him. "Any chance you have jaguar or snake repellent in there too?"

He chuckled, but Cassidy recoiled.

"Snakes? Are there snakes here?" Fear tinted the question.

"Yes, there are snakes in the rainforest." Devlin's voice was a calm rumble in the darkness. "But you don't have to worry about them. That smelly stuff your mom sprayed on you will keep them away. Jaguars too," he added as an afterthought.

"Really?" Cassidy's voice dropped an octave.

"Really." Devlin's calm baritone assured her.

Suddenly, it occurred to her that they were talking a lot, when Devlin had asked them to keep silent. "Baby, we should stop talking. We promised Devlin we'd be quiet, remember?"

"You're okay," Devlin broke in, though he kept his voice low. "There's no one around. The monkeys will warn us if intruders arrive."

That's when Madeline realized the hooting and shrieking had stopped. So had most of the rustling.

"Monkeys?" Cassidy leaned forward in Madeline's lap. "Where are the monkeys?"

"Way up in the trees above us. Remember all that howling and screaming that scared you back there? Those were the monkeys warning each other that we were invading their home. They aren't screaming at us now, because we didn't hurt any of them. But they're still there. They're still watching us."

"How come they're watching us?" Cassidy whispered, stiffening in Madeline's arms. "Are they gonna hurt us?

"Nah," Devlin said, his tone calm and casual. "They're just checking us out. Making sure we aren't going to hurt them. They've got babies up there, so they're protective." He paused a beat, and his tone turned teasing. "Maybe they're even a little confused by you. Baby monkeys ride on their mother's backs like you've been riding on mine. Maybe they think you're one of them."

"They think I'm a monkey too?" Cassidy giggled, relaxing back into Madeline's arms. "But you're not my momma."

"Well, *yeah.* But they don't know that." There was a smile in Devlin's voice, like he was enjoying the conversation.

Madeline almost told him he was wrong. That there was no way anything—even a tribe of monkeys—could mistake him for female. He was too masculine, too rugged, too damn sexy to be anything but male.

"You said the stuff Momma put on me will keep the snakes away?" Cassidy suddenly backtracked to their earlier conversation.

"That's right," Devlin assured her in the gravest of voices. "It's an all-purpose repellent. Formulated to keep all sorts of scary creatures away."

"Like ghosts?" Cassidy asked, her voice so serious it made Madeline straighten.

Why was her daughter asking about ghosts? That seemed an odd fear to have in their current situation. Devlin apparently thought so too.

"Ghosts?" he repeated with obvious surprise. "Do you think we have a ghost problem?"

"I don't know," her voice dropped. "It's just that..." She rushed the explanation out. "They live in the woods."

"They do? Where did you hear that?" Devlin prodded.

Madeline was happy to let him handle the questioning. She was too surprised by what Cassidy was saying to know where to start.

"I saw it on TV." The guilty tone in Cassidy's voice made the announcement sound like a confession.

"You saw it on TV," Devlin repeated. "Like a movie or a show?"

"No. It was real," she insisted, her voice rising. "My friend Mandy's mom had a tape of it. Like the tapes mom made of me when I was little. And the ghosts, on the tape, they killed all of Mandy's mom's friends."

What the heck...?

Madeline's jaw dropped. Mandy was Cassidy's best friend back in Phoenix. What the heck had the two of them watched? She obviously needed to have a conversation with Mandy's mother.

"I see." Devlin sounded thoughtful. "And these ghosts. They lived in the woods?"

"I think so." Cassidy's voice quivered and she was stiff as a board in Madeline's arms again.

"Well, then it's a dam—er—*darn*—"

"That's still a no-no word. Momma will make you put another quarter in her jar," Cassidy broke in.

"Right..." Devlin coughed. "As I was saying. It's a good thing that the repellant your mom sprayed on you scares ghosts away too."

"Are you sure?" Cassidy whispered, and for the first time there was skepticism in her tone.

"Absolutely," Devlin said. "You know how bad that stuff smelled when your mom sprayed you?"

Madeline felt her daughter's head bob against her chest.

"Well that's because it has sage in it. And sage stinks something fierce." He made a pew sound. "But it's a well-known fact that sage repels ghosts. So the scientist had to put it in there."

"It does smell stinky," Cassidy agreed, the doubt gone. "But if it keeps the ghosts and snakes away, we better keep wearing it."

Madeline bit her lip, amazed at how easily Devlin had assuaged Cassidy's fears.

"I think you're right," Devlin said gravely.

Silence fell. Madeline's eyes grew heavier and heavier as she listened to the light rustling overhead.

"Why don't you two get a nap in?" Devlin whispered. "I'll wake you when we need to head out."

"Okay." Cassidy crawled out of Madeline's lap and laid down.

"How much farther do we need to go tonight?" Madeline asked, as she stretched out beside her daughter.

"Another two or three miles, depending on camping spots." Devlin's voice was almost directly overhead.

She heard the *swoosh* of the second space blanket being shaken out, felt the slick metallic coating cover her hand.

Two or three miles. Madeline internally groaned. Every muscle in her body already ached, throbbed, or burned. Another three miles might just kill her.

But then she thought of the alternative. Devlin couldn't carry her *and* Cass. Nor would he leave her behind. So...she set her jaw. She'd walk those three miles, and even more if he needed her too.

She wasn't going to be the one who prevented them from climbing on that helicopter and going home.

CHAPTER 17

Sitting cross-legged on the edge of the space blanket, Devlin watched Madeline and Cass sleep. The jungle sat quiet and dark around them, or at least quieter. The sounds were oddly hypnotizing—the leafy whisper of the tree branches, the occasional croak of frogs, the buzzing or chirping of insects.

The pair had surprised him today. Both of them. They'd met the challenge of the jungle and the grueling pace he'd set with determination and grit.

Madeline—fuck. She'd been amazing. He'd seen the swelling on her cheek from where that bastard had hit her. He'd seen the wobble to her knees, the whiteness of her face, the exhaustion, pain, and terror in her eyes. If they'd been anywhere else...if it had been any other time... he would have let her rest.

But he couldn't, because her life depended on them running. On avoiding another confrontation.

And then there was her kid. Christ, she was something too. Forged from the same grit as her mother. No whining there, either. Even though she had cause to complain. Her little legs and arms must be aching like hell after hanging onto him for so long. She'd held on for three miles...way, way past his expectations. He'd thought they'd have to break every mile or so.

They'd made it much farther than he'd expected, almost as far as he'd expected to camp during this first day of travel.

Particularly after that incident with the cult asshole. But Madeline had stuck to his six and maintained his pace. No matter how often she stumbled, or even fell, she'd just kept walking. She hadn't slowed down or begged to rest.

Nor was she treating him like he was a monster after he'd killed that guy in front of her and the kid. Why that struck him as unusual, he wasn't sure. Maybe because he'd never killed in front of a woman before. Maybe because Sharon had always treated his profession with subtle distaste, like she wasn't sure how his profession differed from your run-of-the-mill serial killer.

If it hadn't been for Gracie, Sharon and he, they would never have stuck. The differences between them had been astronomical.

But Madeline...he'd taken a life in front of her....in front of her kid...and she hadn't flinched. Not only had she accepted what he'd done, but there had been gratitude in her eyes. Why that knowledge made his pulse weaken and his cock rise was something he was afraid to examine too closely.

Fuck—he shouldn't be so hungry for her out here—in the jungle—with miles of hiking ahead and behind them, with death lurking behind every tree. It wasn't like she was trying to tweak his libido. Hell, he was insane for even finding her so damn irresistible. They both reeked. She was sweaty and dirty and hurting. But there was something about her that zapped his cock to life, no matter what she looked like, no matter where they were.

His thoughts crashed to a halt when a childish sob erupted from the kid. He zeroed in on her, caught the kick of her legs and swing of her arms. A nightmare, then. Much more of that and she'd wake her mother. He was moving before he thought it through.

"Hey, little monkey," he whispered, leaning over the child. He flinched as the kid started crying in earnest, although her cries were mostly silent. Tears streamed down her face. "Cass, you're dreaming, wake up, baby."

He didn't cringe at the endearment this time—one that he'd reserved for Gracie. There wasn't time for backpedaling or regrets, not with the kid crying like her heart was breaking...not if he wanted to keep her from waking her mother.

Leaning down, he pulled her into his arms. He jiggled her up and down, stroking her delicate back, crooning softly to her. He knew she was awake now by the press of her wet face against his neck. Her tears soaked his neck, dampening his t-shirt.

He let her cry. Let her drain the fear and stress.

"I'm sorry," she finally whispered on a hiccup.

"Don't be," he whispered back, gliding his hand up and down her spine. "Sounds like you needed a good cry. Nothing wrong with that. Sometimes crying is the best way to get all the sadness out."

"Really? Do you cry too?" Her head lifted from his neck and she peered at his face. Even within the green glaze of the NVDs he could see the curiosity in her eyes.

"Sure," he lied. "Everyone cries."

Although he never had. Not even for his little girl, for the life that had been cut so short. Not because he was too proud, or too ashamed—but because the emptiness sank too deep. He would have welcomed the tears. The chance to cleanse the anguish.

And Christ knew, Gracie deserved his tears. Just as she deserved his grief, guilt, and regret. His little girl deserved everything he'd had to give her.

Apparently satisfied with his lie, the kid tucked her face back into his throat and released a huge sigh.

"It was a really bad dream," she offered after a few seconds of companionable silence.

"I figured." He kept his voice non-judgmental and kept stroking her back.

"They took Momma," she whispered, the hiccup back in her voice. "Like they took Daddy, and she didn't come back either."

*Ah...hell...*the kid probably knew at some instinctive level that her father was gone.

"They?" he asked softly, although he already suspected he knew who she was talking about since her father had disappeared from inside the cult.

"The bad brothers." Her voice went tight and high.

Everyone had been sister this or brother that in the cult. She must mean Apostolos's incel guard.

"I'm going to make you a promise, right here, right now, little bit," he said solemnly. "No one is going to take your momma away. I won't let them."

There was so much doubt on her face, he knew she didn't believe him. He could hardly blame her. The disappearance of her father had obviously rocked her sense of security.

"Okay." She paused to frown, and a hint of accusation entered her voice. "But I'm not a little bit. I'm a little monkey. Remember?"

She lifted her head again to peer intently into his face, as though she suspected he'd lost his memory or some shit.

He laughed softly, his chest warming. "You can be a little bit and a little monkey, right?"

She considered that solemnly before shaking her head. "I don't think so."

He laughed again, the warmth spreading up and out.

"Okay, little monkey it is. Anyway, I promise, on a pinky swear, that I won't let anyone take your momma from you," he said again, hoping to restore her sense of security.

Her brow furrowed. "What's a pinky swear?"

"I'll show you. Give me your hand." He adjusted her weight until he held her with one arm and gently curled his pinky around hers. "I won't let anyone take your mom. I swear this on our pinkies."

Her gaze didn't budge from their joined pinkies. "Is that special?"

"Absolutely." He kept his face straight, his expression solemn. "SEALs put a lot of stock in the pinky swear. It's an unbreakable promise."

"Really?" She sounded impressed. "I saw a walrus once. The person who took care of it said it was a seal."

"Yeah, not the right kind of SEAL, monkey breath."

She giggled. "I don't have monkey breath!" She leaned closer and dropped her voice, whispering in his ear. "Cause I'm not really a monkey."

"Are you sure?" He worked skepticism into his voice. "'Cause you sure hang on like a baby monkey."

She suddenly changed the subject. "How come SEALs have pinky swears when they don't have pinkies?"

She was back on walruses again.

"I'm talking about a different kind of SEAL. I'm a Navy SEAL," Devlin told her as he eased her down. He loosened his arms once she was on the ground, in case she wanted to be free, but she clung to his chest even tighter.

"What's a Navy SEAL?" she asked on a jaw-cracking yawn.

"They're superheroes," Madeline's soft voice said.

Devlin looked over to find her sitting up on the blanket, staring in his direction.

"Hell, I don't know about that." He shied away from the soft look on her face as much as her compliment.

"Really?" Cassidy breathed, her eyes huge. "Like Superman?"

"Better than Superman." Madeline stretched, and slid a teasing glance in Devlin's direction. "Although they don't compare to Batman."

The insult caught Devlin off guard, and he barked out a laugh.

"Batman is overrated. If you stripped him of all that snazzy equipment, he's just a nerd in a costume. He sure as hell wouldn't passed BUD/S."

"You said two more no-no words," the little monkey warned him in a conspiratorial whisper.

When the impulse to tickle her struck, Devlin took a mental step back. Christ. They were sucking him in fast.

Time to regroup, rewind and refocus. He wasn't looking to replace the family he'd lost, and it wasn't fair to Cassidy or her mother, to let them think that he was.

* * *

Something had Devlin's boxers in a twist.

Madeline trudged along behind him, the fabric rope still in hand, as the jungle slowly revealed itself to her. First in murky, gray-green shadows, then rose-tinted bursts of green as the dawn broke over the canopy and ribbons of sunlight crept down through the tree branches to silhouette the dense shrubbery.

Before long, she wouldn't need the tether to keep track of him. Or his whispered warnings of low hanging branches to duck under, decaying tree trunks to climb over, or the endless tripping hazards—like roots, rocks, and uneven ground. With each stride forward, their surroundings got lighter. Soon, she'd be able to follow him by sight.

Which meant he'd break for the day and set up camp. And didn't that sound lovely? She was ready to call it quits for now and give her body a break. Get some food into her hollow belly and bed down for a good sleep.

What she wasn't ready for was more of his cold treatment.

Seriously, what was all the ice about?

While it was subtle, the distance was noticeable. Not only could she sense the gulf stretching between them, she could hear it in the flat monotone he'd adopted. While he was still taking care of them, protecting them, he felt more like a stranger now, rather than a friend—impersonal professionalism rather than warmth.

It was such a shame too. He'd been so good with Cass before, went out of his way to put her at ease. For someone who'd claimed he didn't like kids, he'd been wonderful with Cassidy. Patient. Gentle. Encouraging.

The observation brought a flash of insight. Maybe that's what was going on. Maybe he was worried that she and Cassidy were developing feelings for him, so he was warning them off with this icy impersonal demeanor, warning them that he was here for the short term, not the long.

That made sense. He'd made it crystal clear in Dark Falls that he wasn't father or husband material. He was probably trying to head off an uncomfortable situation once they returned home.

She got it. She did. They were a temporary responsibility. One he didn't want and planned to dump as soon as they climbed on that helicopter. Fine with her, she wouldn't try to change his mind. The last thing she needed was for Cass to get too attached to him, only to watch him walk away.

Her daughter had already lost her father. Losing another

father figure, one she'd developed feelings for, would destroy her crumbling sense of security.

A short time later, he stopped walking.

"We might as well camp here," he finally said. He pointed to three trees clustered together. "We can use those to string up the tarp, in case it rains."

The spot he'd picked wasn't exactly a clearing, although it was wider than the path they'd been pushing their way through. The ground was dirt instead of grass. Several trees circled it, their trunks soaring straight above, their branches weaving into the canopy, trapping most of the sun overhead. Palm-like shrubs and thick, lush bushes with huge broad leaves surrounded it. The vegetation out here looked strangely familiar, like house plants that had gone wild and thrived.

Devlin knelt, and Madeline lumbered over to help Cassidy down. Her daughter stumbled as her feet hit the dirt, as though her legs were numb. Madeline knew how she felt. Her legs were numb too. She unbuckled the backpack, wincing as Devlin pulled it off. Her shoulders felt bruised and raw, like the straps had rubbed a good chunk of skin off.

She held the tarp up while Devlin tossed the nylon rope over branches, and strung it through grommets, before tying it off. When he was finally satisfied the tarp was pulled tautly, sloped from the left to the right, and was high enough for them to stand upright, they laid down the first Heatsheet, anchoring it in place with multiple rocks. As Madeline and Cassidy collapsed on the blanket, he carried the backpack over, slid his machete into one of the loops on the side, and pulled out a bottle of water and two MREs.

"You should eat before you sleep," he said in that impersonal voice he'd become so proficient at.

"Okay," Madeline said without looking at him. Her chest ached every time she heard that monotone, seeing the coldness on his face would just make things worse. Opening the water, she passed it to Cassidy. It felt good to see her daughter's face again. It felt normal. "Do we need to start rationing water?"

If she remembered correctly, drinking this one left only two bottles in the pack, and they hadn't come across any rivers or streams.

He glanced up at the tarp and frowned. "It feels like rain is rolling in. The water will slide off the tarp. I'll collect what I can and fill up the empty bottles. We've got plenty of purification tablets in the pack."

So that was why he'd been so persistent about rigging the tarp on a slant. He'd already been preparing to take care of their water needs.

Once the MREs were finished cooking, Devlin slid the two bowls and their side dishes in front of Madeline and Cassidy.

"Devlin!" Madeline's voice rose in protest when she realized he didn't intend to eat now, either, but she broke off with a shrug and dug into her meal.

Fine. He was an adult. A Navy SEAL. If he wanted to starve himself for no reason, she'd let him.

Her annoyance dissipated when he finally settled onto the space blanket across from her, and she got a good look at his arms and face. The long sleeves of his t-shirt were ripped in places, scuffed in others. Brownish stains that looked like dried blood sprawled across his skin beneath the ripped patches. There were a couple of raw looking scrapes across his cheeks too, and what looked like a bloody gouge on his chin.

He'd obviously taken the brunt of the branches as they'd forced their way through the jungle…or rather as *he'd* forced his way through. He'd cleared most of the branches out of her way with his machete through the night. She'd seen the flash of the blade coming down when the moonlight had crept through the branches above and flickered across the blade. At other times, when the vegetation had been thick and heavy and the darkness so complete she'd been blind, she'd heard the *swish* and *thwack* as he sliced at something.

The branches they'd plowed through had obviously torn the hell out of his arms, whipped him in the face. Yet he hadn't complained. Hadn't grumbled. Hadn't sworn.

He'd just kept walking and whacking and protecting her. Tears stung her eyes. He might have taken a giant mental and emotional step back at some point during the night, but physically, he'd been right there in front of her, keeping her safe.

"Do you have antibiotic cream?" she asked. "I can wash and treat those scratches."

He shrugged without looking at her. "I can do it."

She swallowed hard, blinking the tears back, words of appreciation tip-toeing around on her tongue. But she swallowed them. Judging by the flinty tone to his voice and the way he avoided looking at her, he didn't want her appreciation.

With the MRE warming her belly, Madeline stretched out beside her daughter and tucked the second space blanket around their bodies. She fell asleep with regret and loss hollowing her chest, intimately aware of the man silently guarding them from across the blanket.

She awoke much later to the sound of rain pummeling the tarp above. Warm and dry, she lay there for a few minutes, enjoying the sound of the rain thundering overhead. It sounded almost musical, in the weirdest of ways. Eventually she stirred, instinctively lifting her head to look for Devlin. She found him outside in the rain filling the empty bottles with the water streaming off the tarp.

The spot he'd chosen for their camp was level, but the ground sloped sharply to their left. The tarp extended out over the slope, so when the rain slid off the plastic, it continued downhill. While the outer edges of the space blankets were wet, it was surprisingly dry in the middle.

Once the water bottles were full, he carried them over to the pack. He opened one of the outside pockets and removed a Ziplock bag with sheaths of plastic wrapped tablets. After ripping five of the packets open, he dropped the capsules into each bottle of water.

"Water purification tablets," he said quietly upon noticing she was watching. "It will taste funny. But the water's safe to drink. If you're thirsty, drink your fill. I can refill it again."

She cocked her head quizzically. "Why isn't the rainwater clean enough to drink as it is? I can understand purifying water that comes from a stream. But this came from the sky."

"Because the rain came down through the trees. Whatever

bacteria was on the leaves and branches is also in the water. As damp as the rainforest is, it's best not to take chances."

Okay, that made sense and she *was* thirsty. Sitting up, she scooted out from under the second blanket and took the bottle he handed her. It did taste weird—kind of chemically—but she drank until the bottle was empty and her thirst was gone. He took the plastic container she handed him back into the rain and refilled it, then added another purification tablet to the bottle.

Madeline debated waking Cassidy and having her drink too but decided against it. They were stocked back up on water, and there was a good chance it would rain again. While October was the dry season, it still rained—a lot. They'd been lucky they hadn't had to hike through a deluge. During the two weeks she'd been here, it had rained nearly every day.

"What about the kid?" Devlin asked, his gaze fixed on the slight lump beneath the space blanket. "We don't want her to get dehydrated. There are still two bottles of normal water. We'll save those for hers. She won't like the taste of the purified water."

He was right, Cass wouldn't like the chemical taste at all. But Devlin appeared accepting, rather than annoyed by Cassidy's finickiness.

"I know you don't like kids, but you're really good with them," Madeline absently said.

When he stiffened, she sighed and shook her head. While she'd made the comment innocently, he might construe it as proof that she was forming expectations...*Family* expectations. Before she could correct that assumption, the oddest expression crossed his face. It was somewhere between surprised and guarded.

"What makes you think I don't like kids?"

Madeline's eyebrows rose. Seriously? "You said so. Back in Dark Falls," she reminded him carefully.

"You misunderstood." He frowned, his voice absent, his gaze unfocused, turned inward. "I like kids. They're just safer if I'm not in their life."

It was the last thing she'd expected him to say.

"What?" Her mouth dropped open in disbelief. "What on earth would make you say that?"

His gaze refocused, locked on her face. "Because it's true."

There was a clear warning in the flatness of his voice, and the flinty look in his eyes.

Good God, he actually believes that nonsense.

"No. It's *not* true." Her response burst from her, full of certainty.

He rose to his feet so fast he made her dizzy. "Yeah? Tell that to Gracie."

Gracie?

"Who's Gracie?" Confusion swarmed through her. She felt like she was in a conversational funhouse, where everything was topsy-turvy and off-balance.

"My daughter." His voice was a gritty rasp.

She hadn't thought he could surprise her again. She'd been wrong. She reeled back, digging her fingers into the space blanket for balance. "You have a *daughter*?"

"Had." His voice went raw, anguished, as though all the agony of the world had coalesced within him. "I *had* a daughter. She died because of me." Rigid, he stared up at the tarp and thundering rain. "So take it from me. Or hell—take it from Gracie. I am the *last* guy you want hanging around that little girl of yours."

She didn't remember rising to her feet, crossing the space between them, or sliding her arms around his ribs and hugging him tight. If anyone needed a hug, it was the man holding himself so rigid against her.

"I don't know what happened to your daughter, Devlin. I don't know why you blame yourself for her death. What I do know—with *absolute certainty*—is that there is no way you were responsible. No way."

His stillness turned into stiffness. "You don't—"

She squeezed him tighter. "Here's what I know for sure. I know you came all the way to the Amazon to rescue us, even though you didn't have to. Even though we meant nothing to you. I know that when everything went to shit, you didn't bail and leave us to fend for ourselves, you saved us instead. Repeatedly." When he started to pull away, she squeezed him so hard her arms and shoulders burned. "I know that over the past forty-eight hours you have done everything you possibly can to keep us safe and healthy. I know you gave us all the food and most of the water. And I know you killed a man for us. I know for a *fact* that Cassidy is alive right now because of you."

She pulled her head back and looked into his face, seeing the rigidity that spoke of pain and doubt. "If you would do all this for two people you don't even care about, there is no way—no damn way *at all*—you would not have done the same for your Gracie…for someone you loved. Whatever happened to her *was not your fault.*"

Cupping his face, she leaned up on her toes and kissed the gouge in his chin, urging him to believe her. "Any child would be lucky to have you in their life."

He stirred against her, his body losing some of the rigidity, his hands rising to cover hers.

"I care. You were all I could think about when I got back to San Diego." The confession was rough and raspy and full of frustration. "You're an itch that got under my skin, and I can't scratch it out. I don't want to care. But I do. That's why I came. That's why I'm here."

And if that wasn't the *least* romantic declaration of …. something…. It certainly wasn't love. She was an *itch?* He didn't want to care about her?

Before his confession had a chance to sink in and start to sting, he leaned down and took her mouth. There was nothing romantic about his kiss either. His lips were hard. Demanding. His tongue insistent as it forced its way into her mouth. He didn't sip or savor, he marauded. He invaded.

He tasted like frustration and grief and the chemical after-taste from the purification tablets.

There was nothing, absolutely nothing, in his mouth, or taste, or on his lips that should have brought her arms up to curl around his neck or lured her tongue out to duel with his. But that didn't seem to matter.

He smelled like stale sweat, fresh soil, and dried blood. He was hurting and grieving, full of frustration and the remnants of rage. But she wanted him. Even here—after hours of hiking, exhausted and achy, with danger pressing in on them from every side—she still wanted him.

Maybe that itch description wasn't so wrong after all. Maybe she had the same itch—only for him.

Before the kiss got too out of hand, and she forgot where they were and that Cass was sleeping behind them, a chorus of hooting and shrieking shook the canopy above.

His head shot up and he stepped back, his hand flying to the holstered weapon against his hip. He eased over to the pack and swooped down, grabbing his rifle in one hand and her fabric belt and holster in the other. After handing the pouch over, he gestured toward Cassidy while holding a finger to his lips.

Shaking from fear now, rather than desire, Madeline tried to focus, regroup. The swing from carnal hunger to absolute terror was discombobulating.

Which was the greater threat? Making her way to Cassidy and alerting the intruders to their presence by the crinkling of the space blanket…or Cassidy waking up and saying something?

They'd gotten way too lax about the no-talking rule.

The clash of branches and rustling of leaves, along with the flash of brown and black fur, long arms, and tails, came from above as the monkeys swung from tree to tree. Their screams gained strengths, drowning out the thundering rain.

All this noise was certain to wake Cassidy, which elevated her daughter to the bigger threat.

Trembling harder than ever, Madeline slipped as quietly as possible to her daughter's side, praying the screams from above and the sound of the rain would mask her crinkling footsteps.

CHAPTER 18

Devlin stood still, his rifle up and ready, straining to hear. Christ, the racket the monkeys and rain were making drowned out everything else. A stick snapping or cloth ripping would have given him a location to zero in on, but no such luck.

Since he couldn't rely on sound, he'd have to rely on sight. Not that his eyes were doing him much good at the moment, no matter how often he scanned the area. Everything bled together in dripping shades of green—from the fluorescent green moss climbing the trunks, to the bright green fern-like fronds, to the deep green bushes ringing their camp. If someone were wearing a green poncho or windbreaker, they'd blend right in.

So did their tarp, though. Blending in was the whole fucking reason he'd picked the forest green.

Slowly, as the rain slowed to a sprinkle, the cacophony of shrieks and screams fell into hoots and barks, which lengthened out until they disappeared into silence.

Devlin relaxed. Whatever the monkeys had found threatening was gone.

He glanced over at Madeline and the kid, surprised to find that Cassidy was still asleep. Fuck, apparently the little monkey could sleep through Armageddon. Or the jungle equivalent, anyway.

Madeline, on the other hand? He suspected she wouldn't be

sleeping anytime soon. At least not until they climbed on that chopper. Her eyes were huge, drenched with worry. She sat beside the kid, her gun clenched between her white fingers.

Letting the rifle hang, he eased his way to her side and crouched down to reassure her. "It's gone."

"What do you think it was?" She didn't sound relieved. Hell, she sounded more nervous than ever. Like she'd gotten a sharp reminder of the danger that surrounded them.

Devlin shrugged at the question. "Doesn't matter. It's gone now. Try to get some rest. It's gonna be a long night."

He didn't expect her to take his advice. She was too damn frazzled for that. So was he. His gut was tight, his chest knotted, his pulse jittery—like he'd just guzzled a half dozen energy drinks back to back. But she slid the gun back into the pouch and handed it back to him, then lifted the top space blanket and crawled in next to her kid.

As the hours ticked past and the heat climbed, her fear gave way to exhaustion. Eventually her eyelids closed and her face relaxed. By mid-afternoon it was warm enough the second space blanket had to be smothering. According to his research on the Peruvian rainforest, October temperatures tended to hover in the high seventies. It felt warmer than that, though. Closer to the mid-eighties. As soon as he saw sweat beading on Madeline's forehead, he eased the second blanket off and folded it.

That's when the second problem presented itself.

The kid was all twisted up. She looked like a fucking pretzel. Her shoulders pointed in one direction, her hips in another. Her legs and feet in yet another. He stared down at her. That could not be comfortable. Sure, kids were more supple than adults, their joints laxer. But there was a big difference between supple and torturous.

You should straighten her out, good Dev whispered.

Nope. Not your kid. Not your responsibility. Keep your distance. You take that first step and the next thing you know you'll be reading her bedtime stories and participating in tea parties, the asshole inside him warned.

His instinct for self-preservation kicked in and he took a step back and started to turn.

It wouldn't kill the kid to sleep like that. Worse case she'd be sore come night. Maybe a little achy. Except...his feet paused... sore muscles might shorten how long she could cling to his back. Might even lead to more rest stops, which would slow them down.

That rationalization was all he needed to turn back, hunker down, and straighten out her twisted body. Fuck, her limbs felt thin and fragile beneath his hands, like a gentle tug might snap them. Once he had her straightened out, he refolded the t-shirt she'd pushed aside and slipped it under her cheek. A stiff neck might impede their progress tonight too...*right...*

Even good Dev had to admit that was reaching.

He retreated as far from the kid as he could get and still remain beneath the tarp. While the deluge had died, it was still lightly sprinkling. As he applied another layer of bug spray to his hands and face, he was reminded of the conversation the night before.

His lips quirked. He'd forgotten how literal kids took everything. Like the little monkey's explanation for how she knew ghosts were in the woods. She must have watched some horror movie portrayed as a pseudo-documentary—something like the Blair Witch Project or Paranormal Activity—and because it looked like a home video, she'd thought it was real.

Tenderness nudged aside the humor. He'd known from the way her arms had tightened and flinched around his neck last night that she'd been terrified of the shrieks and hoots that had greeted them from the canopy. But it was only when she'd told him about the ghosts living in the woods that he'd put those flinches in perspective.

She'd thought the monkeys were ghosts. Yet she hadn't screamed, hadn't cried, hadn't asked to get down. Hadn't said a damn word. Hell, she'd been pretty damn amazing...like her mother.

Forcing his mind off his two charges, he glanced at his watch. Just after three. He'd give Madeline another hour of sleep and then wake her to stand guard while he slept. He needed to catch a cat nap himself. He'd been up over seventy-two hours now, and while he was used to operating on very little sleep—sometimes only two or three hours a night—this long without sleep was not optimal for peak condition.

He'd needed to be alert, battle ready, which meant he needed to replenish his brain cells.

The urge to check in with Tex was strong, but concern over the dying SAT phone battery even stronger. The current seven percent wouldn't last long. He'd have to ration his calls, wait until just before they headed out to call in. If the evac site had changed again, he'd still have time to adjust his trajectory.

What the hell was he going to do if the site had changed, and they were tasked with even more days and nights in the woods? They had no MREs left, and only a handful of protein bars. Of course, he could hunt if he had to and collect water off the tarp when it rained.

But what he couldn't pivot around was that damn battery. Once it died, he'd have no way to contact Tex for updates. At that point they'd have to hunker down and wait for a team to come in and find them, then escort them to the next evac site.

Which would increase their time in the jungle, along with the chances that they'd run into a pocket of rebels or traffickers, or that one of them would sustain a life-threatening injury.

* * *

"Are you sure you don't want to sleep longer?" Madeline asked.

"I got two hours in." Devlin stretched his right arm above his head and then his left. "I'm good."

He was the one with the watch, so he should know, but it hadn't felt like two hours had passed. Of course, that might be because she'd been so distracted with watching him sleep.

There was an intimacy about watching a man sleep. Particularly with Devlin. It had something to do with the way his big body and face relaxed, a vulnerability he exposed during sleep that wasn't there when he was awake. He was so confident and self-reliant; it was easy to think he had no weaknesses. But sleep brought a softness to his face.

Which reminded her of Dark Falls.

Of *them* in Dark Falls. Before he'd walked away. Before he'd shattered the what-ifs brewing in her heart. He'd been...not so much gentler...as easier with her back there. No fences. No distance between them. No complications.

She'd loved watching him sleep in Dark Falls too, so it had been easy to imagine they were back in her motel room, lying naked and entwined.

This man did things to her. Brought primal emotions to the surface. Heady, delicious, sensual feelings. It didn't matter where they were, or the circumstances they were in. He made her tingle and twitch and melt.

And lose track of important tasks—like listening to what he was saying.

"—still on."

She almost asked him to repeat what he'd said, but then he'd know she hadn't been listening. And as tuned into her as he was, he'd probably figure out why, and from there, *what* she'd been thinking. Which was the last thing she wanted. He didn't need to know she was still hung up on him.

Besides, it shouldn't be hard to figure out what he'd said, based on what little she caught of his comment.

"What time do we have to be there tomorrow?" She started fishing. He'd said still on, so he must have been talking about the evacuation.

"First light," he responded instantly.

So, his comment *had* been about catching the helicopter. "Will we make it there in time?"

She had no idea how much distance they had left to travel. While Devlin had told her they'd covered more ground than he'd expected, he'd never mentioned how much ground they'd covered or how much was left to go.

"We should make it in plenty of time. There's about four miles left to go." He paused to frown thoughtfully. "From the map Tex sent, the terrain looks similar to what we've been traveling through. Assuming our progress matches last night's, we'll arrive well before dawn."

If the helicopter were picking them up at first light, they'd be on their way home within sixteen hours. The realization brought a huge gust of relief. Showers, food, fresh clothes, and a comfortable mattress crowded her mind. Four things she'd never take for granted again.

But then her relief dimmed. There was a downside to their imminent rescue, too. Once that helicopter landed...Devlin would walk away. She'd never see him again.

Desolation pierced her at the thought. She shook it off. She'd known that was how this trip would end. He'd made no secret about that, given her no reason to expect him to stay. He'd called her an itch, true. But he'd also said he didn't want to want her. When it came right down to it, she and Cassidy were simply a mission. Two people who needed rescue.

SEALs were notorious for rescuing people from difficult situations. Heck, Devlin wasn't the only SEAL involved in making sure they arrived home safely. He might be the only one physically on hand, but he had a whole crew working alongside him from a distance. Like this Tex person he kept mentioning.

"You've mentioned this Tex before. Is he on your SEAL team?" she asked, hoping to take her mind off how much it was going to hurt to watch him walk away.

"He used to be. Now he does consulting and computer stuff." His voice was vague, like he didn't want to reveal too many details. "We were posted to the same platoon back in the day."

If he'd known Tex that long, had the other man known his daughter? His wife? Had he been around to support Dev, to comfort him, when he'd lost his baby girl?

Her chest ached at the thought of him grieving alone. Had there been anyone around to comfort him? She suspected not. She suspected he'd isolated himself and buried his sorrow. She suspected he hadn't gotten over his daughter's death yet.

Not that she could ask him any of this stuff. He'd made it clear his daughter's life and death were off limits.

"You were right," he said out of the blue, his gaze on her sleeping daughter.

"About what?"

"About your little girl being amazing." He suddenly shifted his gaze to Madeline. "Like her mother. The apple didn't fall far from the tree there."

She knew what he was getting at. She'd told him Cass was a

good kid back at the hotel...just before he'd walked out the door. Just before he'd said he *didn't do kids.*

She understood why now...

While his words were sincere and obviously a compliment, they didn't have the effect he'd probably expected. They pierced her heart like an injection of Novocain.

Numbness spread out in waves.

Because while she could see the respect in his eyes and on his face. His compliment sounded like a goodbye.

"Yeah...she's pretty amazing," she managed, her voice thick, clogged with tears.

For the first time, she admitted to herself that she wanted more from him.

Much more. She wanted all of him. She wanted his heat and heft in bed beside her at night. She wanted his big body on the bleachers while Cassidy played soccer in the field below. She wanted his cool calm, and his capability, and his hot hunger every day of her life.

But most of all she wanted to share his memories of his daughter and create new memories together with Cassidy—as a family.

She wanted all of him.

Which he had no intention of giving her.

Suddenly exhausted, with tears lurking just behind her eyes, she stretched out next to Cassidy.

"I think I'll sleep some more while I have the chance," she said, hearing the sadness and loss and exhaustion in her voice.

He didn't respond. But then she hadn't expected him to. There was no question he'd noticed how his compliment had affected her. He must have sensed why. Yet he hadn't tried to comfort her.

Because he was still going to leave.

It was amazing how much it hurt to lose someone she'd never even had.

* * *

Listening to the slow, steady scrape of the machete blade against the whetstone, Devlin glanced at Madeline. She was still pretending to sleep. Her eyes were closed, but her face was tense.

His compliment had hurt her. He hadn't expected that... hadn't expected to see her flinch, or the brightness of pain to bleed into her eyes. He'd tried to tell her how special she was, how special Cassidy was...instead, pain had registered on her face. It seemed like he was always hurting her.

Of course, he knew the why of her reaction. Knew that she felt...something...for him. She tried to hide it, more for his benefit than hers, if he had to guess, but her shields were practically non-existent. While she hadn't expressed her interest verbally, the longing was clear in her eyes.

Her longing for *him.*

He wasn't an idiot or driven by false modesty. He'd been around the block a thousand times or so. He knew women found him attractive. Christ, he couldn't hit the Bottom's Up Tavern without some *frog hog* trying to follow him home for a roll on the mattress. In his guppy days, he taken them up on it. Then he'd met Sharon, gotten her pregnant during one of those mattress rolls, and put a ring on her finger.

While he hadn't loved her—at least not with all the bells and whistles—he'd been content enough in his marriage...because of Gracie.

Gracie made up for everything lacking in his marriage.

What he felt for Madeline didn't compare to what he'd felt for Sharon. With Madeline, there was a mental and emotional connection along with the physical one. He'd never had that with Sharon. Or any other woman.

It wasn't just the sex—although that had been hot as hell—but he *liked* Madeline. Liked everything about her. From her sense of humor, to her confidence and courage, to the way she didn't put up with shit from anyone...not even him. He liked her calm head and common sense, and her patience and devotion to her little girl. She put that child first every single time. He respected the hell out of that.

The feelings she instilled in him were unlike any he'd felt for another woman.

That connection between them had been strong even in Dark Falls, so strong he'd toyed with the possibility of trying to blend their busy lives.

Until he'd found out she had a daughter.

The strange thing was that the little monkey didn't dredge up his ghosts anymore. She had at first, every time he'd looked at her, he'd thought about Gracie, and the grief, guilt and regret would spew up. But the more time he'd spent with Cassidy, the less she reminded him of his lost little girl.

Somehow, over the past forty-eight hours, she'd set herself apart in his mind, carved out her own little corner, separated herself from Gracie.

But the even weirder thing was how the little monkey seemed to ease the grief and guilt he carried. Memories of Gracie were still there. He hadn't forgotten her. He'd *never* forget her. But recollections of her now didn't bring that cutting, debilitating agony like they had previously. The grief had turned to sorrow, a gentler pain.

He frowned slightly, staring down at the whetstone, listening to the slow, steady scrape of the blade against stone, and tried to imagine Gracie out here, in the jungle, on the run…

He'd loved his baby girl with every fiber inside him. Loved her so hard and so deep her death had come close to destroying him. He would always love her. Nothing would ever change that.

But he hadn't been blind to her faults. Just knowing her personality and temperament, he knew damn well that Gracie would have been total hell under these circumstances.

His baby girl had been a firecracker. With negative qualities as well as positive ones. She'd get crabby and stubborn when tired. She'd been loud. Impetuous. Impatient. Adventurous. She'd believed rules didn't apply to her and broke them as often as possible.

Those negative traits would have put her in danger out here and made the trip a thousand times longer and harder. His lips quirked. Hell, if Gracie was the child on his back, they wouldn't make it to the evac site at all.

A thoughtful frown took over, as he realized that those negative traits, combined with his absence, had ended up getting her killed.

Sharon had blamed him for that, claimed that if he'd been around more and taught their daughter discipline, instead of coddling her and catering to her, that she would never have snuck out of the house that afternoon. That she would have stayed put when she'd been told no.

Devlin flinched. Fuck, Sharon hadn't been wrong, either. He *had* coddled Gracie, tried to make up for all the missed birthdays and Christmases when he'd been home. He'd lost so much time with her, the last thing he'd wanted was to discipline her on the few days they shared the same space.

So yeah, he'd spoiled her, badly.

But fuck—Gracie had been easy to spoil. He'd have given her the moon and the stars if he could have, hunted down a unicorn if she'd asked. Sure, she might have had some negative traits, but everyone did, and her positive traits had outweighed her negative by three to one.

She'd been loyal, and loving, and affectionate. It never mattered to her what they did when he was home, as long as they did it together. She'd had the softest heart, hated to see anything in pain, even crying during the commercials the humane society would run.

During that final year, she'd begged him for a puppy and Christ, he'd wanted to give her one. But Sharon had refused to even consider the possibility, telling him she was a single mother for most of the year since he was gone so much. She wasn't going to be a single pet owner too.

He should have pressed the issue, given Gracie the puppy she'd craved. Hell, in retrospect, he should have walked away from the teams entirely and put his family first.

But he'd thought he had time. A couple more years tops and he'd jump rank. The higher one climbed in the leadership roles, the less one got deployed. Another four years in and he wouldn't be sent out on rotation as much. He could spend more time home, then get her the puppy she deserved.

Only she'd died years before he'd made Lieutenant Commander.

His gaze drifted to Madeline. Her face had relaxed, like she was actually sleeping now.

He'd bet his trident, that if Madeline's daughter asked for a puppy, she'd get one, but only after a lengthy lecture on responsibility and pet ownership. He smiled slightly at the thought. While Madeline was basically a single mother too since her divorce, he couldn't see her denying her kid something just to make life easier on herself.

Gracie would have thrived if Madeline had been her mother. Hell…maybe she'd still be alive.

As he started that slow, steady slide of the machete blade against the sharpening stone again, memories unfurled in his mind. Images of Gracie's small, heart-shaped face. The way the devil would dance in her eyes. Her unfettered, surprisingly deep laugh. The strength and love in her hugs.

Gracie had given the best hugs. No holding back…open hearted and open armed.

Christ. He missed those arms. He missed her.

The warm, salty slide of tears shocked him. Absolutely floored him. He sat there, his eyes blurry, while the grief oozed out of him, while he mourned his firecracker—the light that had burned so bright and so short.

The light he could never get back.

The light he hadn't been able to save.

CHAPTER 19

By the time Madeline woke up from her third nap of the day, the sun was setting, the shadows were thick, and something had changed. Not in their situation, or the location, or their plans. But with Devlin.

There had been a shift within Devlin.

She couldn't pinpoint exactly what she was picking up on, she just knew it was there. It was too dark to see his face clearly, and she only had a blurry sense of his body language. But she knew something had changed. She could feel it.

He seemed at ease...with her...with Cass...with...

Madeline shook her head. She had no clue what she was sensing.

But he was back to teasing Cass, calling her little monkey, or monkey breath, back to explaining things to her daughter, satisfying her endless curiosity. And that earlier distance she'd sensed between them had vanished. What this all meant, Madeline didn't know. Maybe it meant nothing.

Maybe everything. Maybe it wouldn't change anything at all.

He gave them each a water bottle. The fact Cassidy didn't complain about the taste was a sure sign he'd remembered to give her one of the regular bottles, rather than rainwater that had been purified. Before breaking camp, he stripped the plastic from two of the protein bars and handed her and Cass each one.

Then he stripped the third one and broke it in half. She instantly knew what he had planned.

No way.

She let him give one of the halves to Cassidy. God knew her daughter needed to eat. But when his arm extended toward her in the dying light, she waved it away. While she couldn't see the bar through the shadows wreathing his hand, she knew it was there.

"Eat it," she said. It wasn't much, but it was better than nothing. "When's the last time you ate something?"

She suspected it had been before he'd arrived at the compound. He hadn't eaten any of the MREs and only a protein bar the day before. She would have split the bar he'd given her in half and handed part of it to him, but she knew he wouldn't take it. Besides, he'd been right earlier. She needed the energy it would provide. She could not afford to weaken and slow them down. Reaching the rendezvous site by dawn was on her shoulders. She was the weak link.

"I'm—" He kept extending his arm.

"No. You're not good," she said, knowing what he was going to say. She could barely see his face in the dusky shadows, but she easily imagined the stubbornness sliding across it. Fine. She'd go straight to the blackmail then. "If you don't eat that half, I won't eat mine."

She folded her arms to show her seriousness. She could be stubborn too.

"And I won't eat mine, either," Cassidy piped up, her voice less sure than Madeline's had been.

Madeline felt the light pressure of Cass leaning into her side and looked down into the moon shaped shadow of her daughter's face.

"Can I give him my other half too, Momma?"

She considered it. It never hurt to reinforce generosity. But Cassidy needed those calories. "Not this time, baby. You have a long day ahead of you and need those calories."

"So do you," Devlin pointed out quietly.

"I'm not seven," Madeline retorted. "Plus—I have a full bar.

You need the calories too and that's barely a mouthful. For God's sake stop being a hero long enough to eat it."

A bark of laughter broke from him.

"Yes, ma'am." The shadow of a hand lifted toward his forehead, like he was saluting her. "Do you want to watch me eat it again?" The question was dry.

"No. I'll trust you to do as promised." Her voice was equally dry. She relaxed at the crunch as he bit into his bar and turned her attention to eating her own.

"Has anyone ever told your momma she's got a stubborn streak?" Devlin leaned in Cassidy's direction and lowered his voice to a staged whisper.

Cassidy giggled. "Daddy tells her that all the time. So does Auntie Margie."

Daddy...

Madeline flinched. At some point she was going to have to tell Cass that her father was gone...forever...but that could wait until they were home, surrounded by all the familiar trappings of their old life.

After finishing her protein bar, Madeline was hungrier than ever. The pangs in her stomach made her long for those fruit-laden tables back at the compound. At least they would fill her belly, satiate the rumbling.

It was kind of annoying actually. There had been bananas, mangos, papayas, and orange trees growing everywhere on the plantation. But they'd run across nothing like that out here in the jungle. Or she assumed they hadn't. At night, it was so dark beneath the canopy, she wouldn't have known if they'd passed right through a whole grove of fruit trees.

"Have you seen any fruit trees through those night vision things of yours?" Madeline asked absently.

"No," Devlin said. "Maybe there isn't enough sunlight. Or the thick vegetation choked them out." He paused, and his voice gentled as though he knew what she was thinking. Or possibly he'd heard the rumbling in her belly. "Eleven hours, give or take, and you can eat as much as you want. They'll have plenty of MREs on the chopper."

And if that didn't sound like heaven.

They broke camp next, or at least Devlin did, with Cassidy following him around like a blind puppy. It was so dark, Madeline could barely see, but the darkness didn't seem to bother Cass much. She chatted away, sharing the secrets of her short life, while Devlin made appropriate sounds, or teasing comments to prove he was listening as he untied the ropes and pulled down the tarp.

She almost reminded Cass about the no talking rule, but the monkeys were silent, so nobody else was around. And *God*—it was so wonderful to hear Cassidy chatter. She'd been such a talker back home. Madeline could swear she'd talked nonstop for the past two years. Sometimes she'd escape to the bathroom for longer than necessary just to avoid the constant talking.

She'd never thought she would miss Cassidy's chattering. Until she'd arrived at the cult, and found that Cass had gone silent.

Had Devlin's daughter been a talker?

If she had, the sudden, absolute silence must have been hard...heart breaking. It must have been devastating.

Madeline wanted to ask him about his Gracie, get to know his child through his eyes, through his stories. She wanted to ask how she'd died...what had happened. But she wouldn't. It wasn't fair to dig through his grief to satisfy her curiosity.

After the tarp and space blankets were packed and she donned the backpack, he powered up the SAT phone for a quick check in.

"We need to conserve the battery. But Tex would have messaged if the evac site has changed since this morning," Devlin said. "We're good," he announced a few seconds later as he powered the phone down again.

The breath that had caught in Madeline's throat as she waited to find out whether the evacuation had changed again, released itself in a rush. At least they weren't looking at more milage and more nights pushing their way through the jungle.

Tonight would be the last, hopefully. Lord was she ever ready for that helicopter to whisk them away.

"You ready, little monkey?" he asked.

Since Cassidy had already taken care of her potty needs, as had Madeline, they were ready to go.

She saw his shadow kneel and a smaller shadow climb onto his back—until the two merged into one, although he didn't look any bigger with Cassidy onboard.

"Madeline, you ready?" he asked, his shadow shifting in the darkness.

"Yep." She stumbled forward and patted him down until she found the fabric rope.

What would he do if she'd said no? She scoffed internally at the question. Her refusal to move wouldn't stop him from getting them to that helicopter. He'd carry her on his back and Cass on his chest because that's what a superhero would do.

And then they were off, the *swish* and *whack* of Devlin's machete as he cleared a path for Madeline keeping them company.

She expected her legs to be weak and shaky. Or achy. Or even numb from all the stumbling around last night. But they were surprisingly firm beneath her. Maybe all that hard-physical labor Apostolos had forced on her had toughened her up. Sure, she stumbled and tripped and got slapped in the face by a branch or two, but all in all the night passed easier.

Although she had no way to compare, it felt like they were making excellent time. Cassidy only asked to get down once, rather than twice like the night before. When the *swishing* and *whacking* paused, she was ready for Devlin's sudden stop, and quit walking to avoid bumping into him. It had taken a while, but she'd finally picked up on the rhythm of their journey. When the machete fell silent, he was about to stop.

"You up for another hour? Or do you need a break?"

"I'm good," she said, hearing the echo of his speech patterns in her words. And she wasn't even lying. She felt like she could go all night at their current pace.

"How about you, little monkey? Can you hold on for a while longer? Or do you need a break now?"

"I'm okay," Cassidy said, her soft, weary voice floating back to Madeline.

"You two are doing great." Devlin's voice was thick with praise. "We don't have much farther to go. Another two miles tops. Once we reach the evac site we can rest until the chopper arrives."

That was the best news Madeline had heard in days.

She could do two more miles easy.

"Okay, little bit, this next part has a lot of low hanging branches, and I'll need to use the machete a lot, so lay your head down on my shoulder and hold tight."

"You called me that before. What's a little bit?"

Cassidy's voice was drowsy, and Madeline frowned. While she had no doubt she could make these next two miles easily, maybe they should stop to let Cass rest.

"You are." Devlin's voice was teasing. "You're just a little bit of a thing."

A weak, exhausted giggle drifted to Madeline. But before she had a chance to ask Devlin to stop, so they could take a break, the rope in her hand jerked, telling her he had started walking again.

More *swishing* and *whacking* and *whacking* and *swishing.*

And then Cassidy screamed.

* * *

Devlin stopped dead, Cassidy's screams reverberating through his head. He started to kneel, but she'd already let go and was sliding off his back, her screams going on and on.

"Cassidy...Cass...baby..." Madeline's confused, terrified voice rose stridently.

What the fuck had happened? Had he hit her with the machete? He rejected that possibility instantly. Before rising or slicing, he always checked to make sure her arms and head were clear.

He hadn't hit her, so what had happened? There was no question the kid was in pain. Her screams made that clear. He spun as soon as he heard the thud of her feet hitting the ground and fished out the small flashlight he'd stuck in his pocket in case of emergencies.

And Cassidy's screams made this an emergency. He flicked the torch on, aiming it toward the screaming.

The kid was crouched, hunched over, still screaming, her hands tight around her neck. He scanned her trembling body with the flashlight beam. No blood.

A flicker of movement on the ground caught his attention and he swung the beam that way. A motherfucking giant centipede scurried across the halo of bright white. It was huge. At least twelve inches. Before he could bring his boot down on the motherfucker, it disappeared into the darkness.

From the way the kid was holding her neck, it looked like the centipede had stung her there, which meant it must have dropped on her when he'd sliced one of the branches. He shined the beam up, above them. Looking for more of the bastards.

Something moved in the branches above them, His flashlight swung in that direction.

Fuck.

Another one of those motherfuckers was crawling along the branch above their head. How many more of those bastards were lurking up there? He swooped down, lifting Cassidy into his arms. They needed to get out from under these branches.

"Back up, Madeline." He pointed the way with the flashlight.

"What—" Her voice was high. Thin. Her face a white blur as the beam skimmed it.

"Back up." He injected some snap into his voice to get her moving.

When she still didn't move, he lurched forward and wrapped his free arm around her waist beneath the backpack, towing her along with him. Once they were out from under the tree branches, he stopped and eased Cassidy to the ground.

The kid's screams had fallen into sobs. Deep, raw, pained sobs—which were almost worse than the screams.

"Hey there, little bit." Devlin flipped his NVDs up and crouched in front of her. "How about you let me see your neck?"

"It hurts." There was a world of pain in the sobbed complaint.

He'd researched the poisonous creatures within the Amazon before hopping aboard the helicopter, and that had included the giant, yellow-legged Amazon centipede. So he knew that, while extremely painful, a sting from one wasn't fatal...for an adult.

But for a small child, one as petite as Cassidy? One who, according to the medical reports he'd pulled, had a history of bee sting allergies...?

Fuck. Fuck. Fuck.

The one recorded human fatality attributed to a giant centipede in the Amazon had been a child. A four-year-old child. Cassidy was seven.... but tiny.

Madeline crowded in closer. "What happened?" Her voice was still high, shrill, panicked.

"She got stung. By a centipede. There's a med kit in the bottom right corner of the backpack. Get it for me."

He turned back to the kid, who still had her hands clamped around her neck. "Sweetheart, you need to let go of your neck. I need to see where it stung you."

"But it hurts." Tears were streaming down the small, white face.

His chest throbbed. "I know it does, baby. But I can't make it better unless you let me see it."

"You'll make it better?" The drenched eyes that held his beneath the flashlight beam were brimming with trust and tears.

He squirmed. He didn't deserve her trust. It was his fault the damn thing had stung her. But he forced the shame back and concentrated on what needed to be done. "I can make it feel better, make it so it won't hurt so bad. But I need to see it."

The heat would pull out the venom. The EpiPen would prevent an allergic reaction. Both needed to be administered immediately, and he didn't want to hurt her more by forcing her hands aside.

"Okay." Cassidy hiccupped out a sob and her small hands fell away.

Devlin gently eased her head to the side, his flashlight beam already locked on the exposed skin. His gut clenched at the two white puncture marks amid the red, swelling flesh. She was already having an allergic reaction. He needed to get that EpiPen into her stat.

"Madeline." He kept his voice calm. No sense in panicking

the kid or her mother. He was already panicking enough for both of them. "Did you find the med kit?"

Instead of replying, she dropped the red canvas bag onto his lap. He unzipped it and snatched up the EpiPen.

"Madeline, help her stand up," he said as he cupped the kid's wet chin. "Cass, sweetheart. I'm going to pull your pants down so I can see your thigh, okay?"

The epinephrine needed to be injected in the largest muscle in the body, which was the thigh.

"But it's my neck that hurts," Cassidy sobbed.

"I know, baby. I know. The medicine that will make the pain go away has to go in your thigh."

"Okay." With her mother's help, she straightened.

As soon as she was standing, he glanced at his watch to record the time, eased the waistband of her pants down to her knees and administered the EpiPen.

"There you go." He pulled her pants back up. "All done."

"What was that?" Madeline sounded strangled and terrified.

"Epinephrine. Same thing she got when you took her to the ER a couple years back after she was stung by that bee." Thank Christ he'd included a couple of EpiPens after reading the kid's medical record.

He swung the flashlight back up to the kid's neck. The welting and redness were even worse. The epinephrine would start working within seconds, or at worst, minutes. Heat would pull some of the venom out, and the venom was causing the reaction. But ice would reduce the swelling. And he needed to reduce the swelling before it closed off the kid's windpipe.

Fuck—what to do?

He made a snap decision. He needed to stop that swelling stat, so ice it was.

"Check the ground for insects, and spread one of the space blankets out so she can sit down." Devlin handed the flashlight to Madeline, who was standing there, looking lost and terrified. But then she shook herself and turned to the backpack.

He thought about grabbing his extra shirt and using it as a barrier between the ice and the kid's skin, but decided against it.

They needed to bring the swelling down stat, and applying the ice directly to the swelling would help with that.

By the time he'd snapped one of the instant ice packs to start the chemical reaction and plastered the cold compress to Cassidy's neck, Madeline had the blanket spread out.

According to what he'd read about centipede venom, it was much stronger than bee or wasp. Would that first EpiPen counter the allergic reaction enough to stop the swelling? The real danger was her trachea swelling shut.

Cassidy gave a soft, sobbing sigh as the ice pack touched her neck. Her hands came up to cover his. Devlin's gut churned even harder.

"That feel good, little monkey?" he asked softly. When she nodded and peeked up at him with those huge, wet, trusting eyes, his heart just about stopped right there in his chest.

Christ...he didn't deserve that look in her eyes.

"Let's get you over to the blanket so you can sit down." Keeping one hand pressed against the ice pack, he picked her up, and carried her over to Madeline, easing her down to the space blanket. "Scoot in behind her," he told Madeline. "We need her sitting up, and forward."

A sitting, forward position was the best option for keeping her trachea open. While she wasn't having any difficulty breathing—yet—that could change in a heartbeat.

He took the flashlight back from Madeline, crouched next to the kid, and lifted the icepack. Raised, puffy red flesh greeted the beam of light.

Fuck—the swelling was much worse.

He glanced at his watch. Four minutes had passed since the first shot.

According to what he'd read, conventional wisdom called to wait five minutes before administering a second dose of epinephrine. But the same articles had said that being proactive, rather than reactive, when administering epinephrine could prevent fatalities. As close as the swelling was to her trachea, they needed to shut the allergic reaction down fast.

"Get her back up and drop her pants," he told Madeline, before backtracking to his med kit.

He hauled the canvas bag over to the space blanket and grabbed another EpiPen. He gave the second injection in her other thigh and tugged her pants back up, then helped her sit down again. Madeline scooted in behind her. Devlin snapped another icepack and settled it over the new swath of red, raised flesh.

He needed to get hold of a paramedic or doctor and find out how long he needed to wait to administer a third dose. There had been plenty of articles that presented a timeline for two doses, but none had talked about three. He had another EpiPen. Would three be too many?

But of even more importance—if he couldn't control the swelling and the kid's trachea closed, what were his options? Would an emergency tracheotomy keep her breathing until evac arrived and the doc on board took over?

"Madeline." He forced calm into his voice. "Hold the ice pack on her neck. I need to make a call."

When Cassidy's fingers tightened around his hand, refusing to let him go, he cupped her left cheek. "Baby, you got to let go for a moment."

Her eyes filled with tears. "But I don't want you to go."

"I'll be right here. I'm not going anywhere. I just need to call someone who will tell me how to help you feel better."

Her fingers loosened slightly. "You promise you won't go away?"

"I promise. I'll be right here. You'll be able to see me."

"Okay." The small, hot hands covering his let go and Madeline's hands moved in.

As he transferred the icepack into her keeping, it slipped, giving him a glimpse of the flesh beneath it. The swelling might have slowed, but only slightly, and it sure as hell hadn't started to recede.

Relax. The second icepack has only been on for a minute. The second Epi was injected maybe two minutes ago. Give them time to work.

Which would be a fine and dandy strategy if this little girl's life weren't on the line.

Turning to the pack, he found the SAT phone and powered it up. Five percent left on the battery now.

Fuck.

His best chance of getting the information he needed was through Tex. He'd have to power the phone back down as soon as he sent Tex his questions. He'd give his buddy some time to hunt down the answers Devlin needed and then power the phone back up. Waiting on the line while Tex went to work would eat up too much juice.

Tex answered on the second ring. Thank Christ.

"What's wrong?" Tex knew that Dev wouldn't be calling unless it was an emergency.

"The kid got stung on the neck by a centipede. I've administered two doses of epinephrine, icepacks are in place, but there's still swelling." He glanced at Madeline and her daughter. They were both listening and watching him. He should have taken a walk. Gotten some privacy. Put some distance between them and this conversation so he didn't alarm them.... except he'd promised the kid that he'd remain in sight.

"On the neck," Tex repeated. "How bad is the swelling?"

"Enough," Dev said tightly, hoping Tex would pick up on the subtext. Which he did, as proved by his next question.

"She having trouble breathing?"

"Not yet. I need to know when I can get a third EpiPen into her if I need to." He lowered his voice and turned his back to Madeline and the kid. "And I need options if the last EpiPen doesn't work," he told Tex tightly.

"Got you." Tex paused. "How much battery?"

Devlin pulled the phone away to look at the screen.

Fuuuuuuck...

"Four percent." His voice was grim. Just powering the damn thing off and on to preserve its juice would take another percent. He'd be lucky to get Tex's report before he lost the phone completely.

But he needed that information. He needed to know if a tracheotomy was a possibility if she stopped breathing. Hell, he didn't even know if a trach was an option. If the swelling covered the entire throat, it could shut the wind pipe off in multiple places.

"Give me ten minutes and call back." The line went dead.

Devlin powered down the phone, checked his watch and headed back to the pair. He lifted the ice pack. The swelling was wrapping around the kid's neck now, way too close to the front.

Crouching next to her, he cupped her small face with his free hand.

"How you doing there, little bit?" He kept his voice soft, comforting.

"It hurts." Tears filled her eyes again.

"I bet it does." He rubbed the tears off her left cheek with his thumb. "Word is that a centipede bite is more painful than almost any insect around. It hurts really, really bad." He paused to rub her cheek again. "I'm going to give you something for the pain as soon as my friend calls back. He's finding out what will work the best for you. Okay? You are so incredibly brave, little monkey." His throat tightened. "Can you be brave a little longer?"

"I guess." But her lips trembled, and tears continued to seep from her eyes and down her cheek.

His chest was so tight it throbbed. Without thinking, he leaned forward to press his lips against her forehead...her hot forehead. Her *too damn hot* forehead.

Centipede venom could cause a fever. Was the heat in her face because of the venom, or emotion, or pain? Probably all three.

He glanced at his watch. Only two minutes had gone by since Tex had gone to work. For one long moment, he watched the pair sitting on the ground. Madeline was scooted as close as she could get to Cassidy's back, using her torso to brace the kid up. A constant stream of wordless, soothing sounds were coming from her.

"Madeline, I need both your hands on the ice packs," Devlin finally said.

As soon as her hands replaced his, he bent back over the med kit, taking stock of what it contained. There was one more EpiPen. A box of children's liquid Tylenol, as well as a bottle of adult aspirin. The Tylenol would help bring her temperature down and knock back the pain. He scanned the kit again. A rolled length of rubber tubing. A scalpel. Bandages. Disinfectant. He had what he needed for an emergency trach…if he had to do one.

He flinched, praying it wouldn't come to that, praying that he wouldn't have to cut open that poor kid's throat with nothing but a flashlight and a roll of tubing. He had nothing to knock her out, and only Tylenol to control the pain. Would she even lie still while he cut into her and inserted the tube?

But he'd do it if he had to, if it were the only way to keep her alive. Setting the kit aside, he turned back to Cassidy, focusing the flashlight beam back on her neck. Madeline instantly lifted the icepacks.

Son of a bitch.

He locked the reaction down, ignoring the way his muscles clenched. The raised red welts were barely visible beneath the puffiness circling her neck. Plus the swelling was inching into her cheek now.

Cassidy was just sitting there, perfectly still, staring at the ground, tears dripping off her chin. She wasn't making a sound. Somehow her silence made her suffering worse. It gutted him.

"Can you say something for me, little monkey?" he asked her softly. He needed to see if she was having trouble breathing. She wasn't gasping, but wheezy speech could be an initial indicator that the swelling was interfering with her breathing.

"What do you want me to say?" She peeked up at him with wet, dark, pained eyes.

But her words were clear, her tone strong. No slurring or rasp. He relaxed slightly.

"What you just said is perfect, baby." He glanced at his watch. It was close to ten minutes now. Tex should have something for him.

He powered the phone back up, groaning beneath his breath at the three percent charge indicator. His fingers twitched as he punched redial. The phone didn't even ring before Tex was on the line.

"How's the swelling?"

"Still going on. Should I give her that third dose of epinephrine?"

"Doc says a third dose can be given but give it at least ten minutes after the second."

That was easy enough. Ten minutes had already passed.

"She having trouble breathing?"

"Not yet." Thank Christ. "But she may have a fever."

"Aspirin will bring the fever down. Keep ice on."

"About the other thing I asked you…" Devlin glanced at Madeline, who was watching him talk.

"Yeah, that," Tex broke in. "You got what you need in your med kit?"

"Yeah." He mangled the word as his throat close.

He'd been trained in battle triage, including emergency trachs, along with the rest of his platoon back when he'd been in the field. But Christ, that had been years ago. He'd needed to brush up on the procedure…just in case.

"I'm sending you the Cliff's Notes." A ping hit Devlin's phone.

Dev instantly brought up the text, tapped the attachment and started reading. He needed to commit the instructions to memory before the phone died.

A pause beat the line. "Are you going to make evac?"

Still reading, Devlin's jaw set. "We'll make it."

They still had four hours to cover the last two miles. Even if he had to do the emergency trach, they'd make it. He'd fucking make sure of that. Make sure that little girl was onboard that chopper and under a doctor's care.

He hadn't quite finished reading the emergency tracheotomy instructions when the screen went blank and the phone powered down on its own.

The battery was out of juice.

Fuck...

He was on his own.

CHAPTER 20

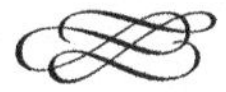

"Devlin?" Madeline heard the fear in her voice. Felt it in her tight chest, the hard beat of her heart, and the greasy sweat that broke out down her spine.

The centipede bite was bad. Really bad. If she hadn't already figured that out on her own, by Cassidy's reaction, Devlin's response would have clued her in.

Currently, he was standing across from her, still as stone, the SAT phone clenched in his hand. He wasn't talking to his friend. Wasn't reading the screen. Wasn't texting.

The phone's battery must have died. The fear wound tighter, edged into panic.

Where did that leave them?

The flutter of hysteria climbed, tightened her scalp, almost overwhelmed her...*almost.* She tightened her arms around Cassidy and held tight, let her daughter's heat and weight ground her.

Where that left them was with Devlin. With the most capable man she knew. He probably already had a plan. He'd know what to do. Hell, he'd already done everything, while she'd fallen apart. She'd done nothing to help, just stood there frozen and let him handle everything. Let him take care of her daughter.

She could do better.

She *would* do better.

Brushing Cassidy's hair aside, she lifted the ice packs and picked up the flashlight. Her heart stuttered at the sight of the bright red swelling puffing up her daughter's mouth.

"Devlin," she called out, trying to mask her anxiety. Cassidy was already scared enough. No need to add to that fear.

He jolted and walked over to kneel next to them. "Hey, baby girl. How are you holding up?"

"Did your friend tell you how to make it stop hurting?" Cass asked, her head lifting.

Maddie heard the hope in her voice, as well as the pain.

"He did." Devlin's voice was grave. He studied the welts pulling at her lips and frowned. The med kit was lying open to his right. He leaned over and snagged it, dragging it close, then glanced at Madeline. "We're good to give her the last dose of epinephrine."

Surprised, she straightened. "You have another EpiPen?"

He shrugged. "Being prepared is second nature."

And thank God for that.

She almost asked him whether three injections were safe. Two years ago, when Cassidy had been stung by the bee, she'd only had one shot. But Maddie brushed the concern aside. Back then, the swelling and welts had subsided within minutes of that one shot. Cass had already received two doses now, and the swelling was still progressing. That third EpiPen was definitely in order.

Besides, Devlin wouldn't recommend a third injection unless it was safe…and necessary. Nor would he trust someone with her daughter's health unless he believed in them implicitly.

"Okay, little one." Devlin cupped Cass's elbows and lifted her to her feet. "Up you go."

He lifted his chin at Madeline, and she tugged down Cassidy's pants. He administered the drug in the thigh he'd injected first, but lower down. As Maddie pulled Cass's pants back up and got her settled down again, Devlin went back to rummaging through his med kit. This time he pulled out a box of children's liquid Tylenol.

He had children's liquid Tylenol in his med kit? That could not be standard issue. He must have added it for Cassidy's sake.

Wow—he hadn't been kidding. He *was* uber-prepared. Since his original plan had called to install Cass on that helicopter immediately, he wouldn't have had any interactions with her. Theoretically, he wouldn't have needed that bottle.

Yet here it was. Relief curled through her. It was comforting to know he was prepared for any contingency.

He took the flashlight back and aimed it at the box, then bent his head, reading the instructions. "How old is she again?"

"Seven."

He bent back over the box. "10 ML then." After he opened it, took the bottle out, and ripped off the tamper proof plastic, he filled the plastic cup with the thick liquid and held it to Cassidy's lips. "Here you go, little monkey. Drink this. It will make you feel better."

She tilted her head back and opened her puffy lips, letting Devlin tip the medicine into her mouth.

"Madeline," he said quietly. "Grab some water. We need to keep her hydrated. The bottle we've been saving for her is in the back, behind the ammo."

But when Devlin held the bottle to Cassidy's lips, she was lethargic and whiny, and barely drank.

"I don't want it," Cassidy whined, weakly pushing the bottle away.

"Just a couple more sips," Devlin cajoled.

"I don't feel..." Whimpering, Cassidy jolted forward vomiting on Devlin's shirt and pants. Since there hadn't been much in her stomach, it was mostly the medicine and water that came back up. "I'm sorry. I'm sorry." Her voice climbed hysterically, sobs tearing through her again.

"Hey." He stroked her cheek. "It's okay. A little puke never hurt anyone. But you need to try really hard to keep the medicine down." He cupped her chin. "If I give you another cup full, can you do that for me, stop yourself from throwing it up?"

Tears filled her eyes. "I don't think so."

He sat back on his heels and looked at Madeline. "Do you think she'd be able to keep another dose down?"

Maddie shook her head. "Not after throwing up the first one. Her stomach needs to settle before we try again."

Concern touched his face, but he cupped Cassidy's cheek again and brushed her tears away with his thumb. A second or so later he recapped the bottle of Tylenol and dropped it back in his med kit, along with the plastic dispensing cup.

When he picked the flashlight up and directed it at Cassidy's neck, Madeline lifted the ice packs. The swelling didn't look like it had spread any more. It might even have come down a bit.

"It looks better, don't you think?" she whispered hopefully.

Devlin shook his head. "Better? No. But it's not worse. So that's something."

Madeline tried to take comfort in that, but there was too much concern in his eyes to delude herself into believing the danger was over. They'd used up all the EpiPens. If Cass's allergic reaction continued, they had nothing on hand to control the effects of the centipede venom. Nor could they get the Tylenol down her to control the fever and pain.

The big threat was that the swelling would interfere with Cassidy's breathing. What were they going to do if that happened? How were they going to keep her daughter breathing when they were hours from the helicopter and even more hours from a hospital?

The question filled her with terror. Swallowing hard, she focused on the one thing she did know, the one thing she knew for sure: Devlin would have a plan. He always had a plan. He'd find a way to keep Cassidy alive. Just like he'd kept them both alive since he'd arrived.

Just as he'd kept his friend alive back in Dark Falls.

* * *

The swelling around the kid's mouth was a bad sign.

If this last epinephrine injection didn't bring the allergic reaction under control, he could be looking at an emergency trach.

They were still almost two miles from the evac site. This was as good a place as any, when it came to performing the trach, at least when it came to the jungle and the actual procedure. But having to carry the kid to the evac site after the trach was another beast. He'd be better off hauling her there now and doing the surgery on site.

"Cass, can you say something for me?" He leaned closer to her, listening for indications that the swelling was affecting her trachea. She'd cried hard after she'd thrown up, and her breathing had been fine then.

She stirred, her head lifting lethargically.

"I don't know what to say." Her voice was cranky. So was her swollen face.

But there had been no wheezing, no gasping, no shortness of breath. He'd keep an ear on her while they were on the move, but they needed to get going...after he'd made a couple of adjustments to their hiking strategy.

He turned to Madeline who was still sitting behind her daughter, holding the icepacks in place. "We need to get to the evac site, stat."

She looked from him to the kid, and back to him. "We're not that far, right? And we've got time. Can't she rest for—"

"She can sleep while I carry her," Devin interrupted. He paused, glanced at the kid, then back at Madeline. "If I need to... ensure...that her airway remains open, she'd be better off at the evac site, where she can rest without being jostled."

He saw the instant she realized what he meant; fear burned bright in her eyes. For a moment, it looked like she was going to panic, but then she squared her shoulders and lifted her chin.

"Okay." She swallowed hard. "What can I do to help?"

He'd never been as proud of her as he was at that moment.

"We're going to make some adjustments. The trees ahead of us are full of centipedes. I'll cut a hole in the tarp for my head, then drape a good chunk of it down my chest to cover Cassidy." He'd have to carry her the two miles. There was no way she could cling to his back. "You'll need to keep right on my tail and keep under the back half of the tarp. If any of the centipedes drop on us, they'll hit the tarp and slide off."

His stomach churned beneath a wave of disgust. If he'd made that adjustment earlier, the kid wouldn't be facing emergency surgery in the middle of fucking nowhere.

"We'll need to move fast, cover the distance ASAP, so use the flashlight to guide you."

Hesitation hit her face. "But won't the flashlight beam give us away?"

Crossing to the backpack, he grabbed the tarp, and reached for his knife. "We'll have to chance it. The tarp will blunt most of the glow, so we should be good."

After unfolding the tarp and shaking it out, he cut a hole big enough to slip his head through about five feet from the front edge.

"What about you?" she asked, watching him pull another icepack from the backpack. "What if one stings you? Your head will be exposed."

True, but he needed to see where they were going. "I'll be fine."

She must have heard his dismissiveness because her tone turned sharp. "Devlin, you should protect yourself too. Why can't you use the tarp for protection? If you held it out in front of you, you'd still be protecting Cass, but it would cover your head too."

Her concern hit him like a shot of whiskey, warming him from the inside out. She must not have realized yet that her daughter's predicament was his fucking fault.

"I need to see what's up ahead. Where we're going. Holding the tarp overhead would cut down on my field of vision."

She didn't look convinced by his argument, but she stopped questioning him, which allowed him to return to weightier matters. He needed a way to hold the icepacks in place, without using his hands. He stowed the med kit and grabbed his extra shirt from the pack, then returned to the pair on the ground. After folding his shirt into a long flat scarf, he snapped the new icepack to start the cold and placed it at the end of the second pack. He held the new pack in place with one hand and wound his shirt around her neck with the other. Once Madeline pulled her hands free, he tightened the material and tied it off.

Cassidy sat there during the entire operation like an exhausted rag doll. No sobs, no whining, no talking—just complete apathy.

Shouldn't have happened. Shouldn't have happened. Shouldn't have happened.

The condemnation rolled through his head, an endless litany of remorse and regret.

When he lifted Cass into his arms and rose to his feet, she sighed and collapsed against his chest, her arms hanging limply at her sides.

He didn't have to ask Madeline to fold and stow the Heatsheet, or slip the hole in the tarp over his head and arrange the excess portion in front so it covered her daughter. She did that on her own. And then she brought his helmet over. He bent his head so she could plop it on top and freed an arm so he could adjust the chin strap as she struggled into the straps of the backpack and turned to face him with the flashlight in hand.

"Ready when you are." She offered him a tight smile. And then as if she couldn't help herself, "How is she?"

"Her breathing is good," he told her quietly, knowing that was the fear on both their minds.

She nodded. Took a breath, her throat trembling. "Good. So, we should probably get this show on the road then?"

Once Madeline was beneath the tarp, her flashlight beam peeking around the edges of the plastic, Devlin took off. Rather than using his machete, he ducked beneath the lower hanging branches and kept moving. He listened hard for indications that Cassidy was struggling to breathe, and stopped multiple times to retrieve the flashlight, lift the front flap of the tarp, and check on the child cradled against his chest.

The kid's breathing never faltered. Madeline's, on the other hand, he listened to her increasingly heavy breathing and frowned when it turned to gasps. They needed to slow down so she could catch her breath, or he needed to stop long enough to give her a break. Opting for the slow down first, since they'd still be covering ground, he cut his pace by half. It took a few minutes but her breathing finally evened out again.

The last part of the trip to the evac site passed in a blur of green-glossed vegetation, self-recriminations, and hard breathing. They were still surrounded by vegetation when the pedometer on his watched claimed they'd walked the final 1.8

miles. He didn't worry…at least not much. Between the GPS—when his phone had been working—and his compass, he knew his course had been true. The clearing the chopper intended to land in had to be around here somewhere.

It took another five minutes but they finally stumbled into it. One second they were pushing past shrubs and bushes, ducking around trees, and the next a good three acres of emptiness stood before them.

They'd made it.

They were at the evacuation site and in plenty of time for evac.

"Flashlight," he said softly, reaching behind his back.

The oblong weight of the torch settled into his palm. Folding the front flap of the tarp back, he shone the light down. Between his t-shirt with the bulky ice packs beneath and the way the kid's face was tucked into the crook of his neck, he couldn't see the swelling. But her chest was rising and falling. There was no gasping or wheezing. She appeared to be breathing just fine.

It took some juggling, but he managed to free a hand to lift the kid's chin. The welting had retreated from her mouth and part of her cheek. It looked like that third dose of epinephrine had done the trick. The relief about knocked him on his ass.

Maybe he wouldn't have to open her throat after all.

"How is she?" Madeline asked, her voice breathless.

"Her breathing's good," Devlin said as he handed the flashlight back and dropped the flap over Cassidy. "And the swelling is going down."

"Thank God!" The relief in her voice was audible. She took a couple of deep, raw breaths, like she was fighting back tears. But then her breathing stabilized again. "How much farther do we have?"

He smiled slightly, some of the tension dissipating. At least this would be welcome news. "We're here. We just need to find a place to hunker down and wait for the chopper."

"Really?" Even more relief crept into her voice, but without the threat of tears this time. "We're there?"

"Yep."

He needed to do a quick recon, find a camping spot that

would conceal them but still allow them quick access to the chopper. Since there was no way he was leaving his charges behind while he scouted the area, they'd have to come with him. The flashlight though, would light the tarp up like a giant, oblong glow stick without the jungle for cover.

"You'll need to grab the rope on my belt and follow me without the flashlight. But stay put beneath the tarp for the time being."

"I thought we were here?" There was exhaustion in her voice, as though that last request had finally broke her.

"We are," he assured her softly. "But we need to find a camping spot."

"Can't we just take the tarp off now?"

"We could," he kept his voice patient, "but we'd have to fold it. Which is wasted effort since I'll be shaking it out shortly to string up a shelter. It's going to rain again." He could feel the dampness in the air.

"Okay." The flashlight winked out and he felt the tug on his waistband as she grabbed the rope.

He found exactly what he was looking for a few minutes later. A wide spot, clear of vegetation but ringed by trees, on sloping ground.

Madeline borrowed his helmet and NVDs to check the ground for anthills, or centipedes, before dropping her pack and laying down the Heatsheet. Devlin eased Cassidy into her mother's arms, took his helmet back, and went to work stringing up the tarp. When he finished, they still had four hours to evac.

"Can we use the flashlight to check the swelling?" she whispered as he settled cross-legged onto the blanket next to her. She had the kid cradled in her arms, braced against her chest.

"No," Devlin whispered back. "It's too easy to see the beam without the vegetation and tarp in the way. I'll be able to get a sense of the swelling with the NVDs."

He went to work unwrapping his shirt from Cassidy's neck. The ice packs weren't nearly as cold as they'd been earlier.

"We'll need to swap out the ice packs." Once the shirt and ice had been removed, he took a good minute to assess the kid's neck. "I think it's better," he finally said.

Although it was hard to compare what the area looked like beneath his NVD's versus the flashlight. Still, the kid was sound asleep, with no indication of breathing problems. He grabbed his med kit from the pack, along with the second Heatsheet and several bottles of water. The first *plunks* of rain hit the tarp as he settled back down.

They'd been lucky with the rain at least; it had held off until he'd gotten the shelter up.

He traded out the icepacks and rewrapped the scarf, then pressed the back of his fingers against her forehead. She felt hot. Turning back to the med kit, he rummaged around until he found the no-touch forehead thermometer he'd packed.

Devlin held the wand against the kid's forehead and gave the thermometer enough time to register, before swinging it around to face him. A green one hundred and two flashed back. "She's running a 102 fever. We should try to get some Tylenol and water down her. She needs to drink," he added tightly. "We don't want to add dehydration to her condition."

While Madeline woke Cassidy up, Devlin poured the medicine in the plastic cup. The kid was half asleep and cranky as hell and tried to shove both the medicine and water away, but Devlin got all the Tylenol down her and some of the water.

Now it was just a matter of waiting to see if the little monkey threw the meds back up...and to see if the chopper showed up at five-thirty, as scheduled.

That last question was the big one. With the phone dead, he had no way of contacting Tex to make sure they were still on for plan B. If they weren't, if the evacuation had moved to plan C, he had no way of finding out the new location.

Nor did he have a fucking clue what he was going to do if that bird didn't show up.

Pivot...he supposed...but he had no fucking pivots left.

As the rain picked up speed, he shook out the second Heatsheet and tucked it around Madeline and her kid.

"Will the helicopter still come if it's raining?" Madeline asked. She sounded haunted. Like she didn't trust that they were getting out of here.

"You know the mailman's motto? Come rain or sleet or snow

—" He broke off with a heavy scoff. "Who do you think they stole that from?"

She laughed, as he'd hoped, but her voice dropped into seriousness immediately. "So they'll still come? Even though it's raining?"

"They'll come." She obviously needed reassurance, so he gave it to her, even though he had doubts himself...although not for the same reason. "Rain doesn't affect a chopper's ability to fly. It can affect the pilot's visibility, so it's the pilot's call whether to hit the air. Our bird is piloted by a SOAR aviator, they're the best pilots in the world. They're called Night Stalkers because they rule the night. A little rain won't stop that chopper from landing."

Which was true, rain wouldn't stop it, but other things might. Like a change in the evac plan. But he kept that concern to himself.

Now that they were here, situated, with nothing to do but wait, he started thinking about Squish and Lucky. Last he'd heard, Squish had been rambling his way toward the second evac site. Had anyone updated him? Was he on his way here now? Or was he already here? Shifting his position, he scanned the edges of the field surrounding them, only to shake his head in disgust.

What the fuck was he doing? He wouldn't locate Squish by looking. The guy was a special operator, for Christ's sake. Devlin wouldn't see him until the bastard stepped out of the forest to board the chopper—assuming he'd made it here.

He could go out and scout for him, but that would mean leaving Madeline and the kid alone. He glanced over at them and instantly ditched that idea. The kid was fast asleep, leaning back against her mother's chest, and Madeline looked half asleep herself.

Since Cassidy still wasn't having breathing issues and that last shot of epinephrine seemed to be working, she'd probably be okay lying down now.

"Why don't you and Cass lie down?" He rose to his feet and walked around the pair, easing the Heatsheet off of Madeline.

She laid her daughter down, curled up beside her, and he covered them.

As the rain picked up heft and speed, he sat there across from them, keeping guard while they slept. When worry about the chopper's arrival tried to wriggle up, he emptied his mind, focused on the pings and bangs overhead, and lived in the moment.

Living in the present, without worrying about the future, was something special operators excelled at. It was one of the traits that set SEALs apart, that allowed them to do what needed doing, when it needed doing, without stress depleting their strength.

By the end of the first hour, the rain had slowed and then stopped. An hour after that, the moon came out as the clouds dispersed, and lit the evac field like a ghostly landing strip. Madeline and Cassidy slept on. At the four-hour mark, the faint but distinct *whop whop whop* of blades beating the air reached him.

Their ride was headed in.

He closed his eyes beneath a wave of relief, and then leaned forward and shook Madeline awake. She sat up, brushed back her disheveled hair, and stared at him with hopeful eyes.

"The bird's headed in. We need to break camp." The relief that plastered itself across her face brought his first smile in what felt like a very long time.

By the time their camp, or what little there had been of it, was folded and stowed away, the chopper sounded like it was seconds out. He carried the kid, who was still sleeping, to the very edge of the tree line, with Madeline trailing behind him, and waited for the bird to drop.

Other than the Black Hawk's blades and the rumble of its engine, the clearing was silent. No gunfire. No RPG flares. No rebels. No Squish or Lucky either.

Damn it.

It was still dark, with the first hint of peach tiptoeing across the horizon, when a big, black shadow filled the sky. It whipped the shrubs ringing the tree line into a frenzy and flattened the grass as it dropped. Once it touched down, the door slid open and disgorged six, huge, camouflaged men.

So, North had sent a squad in. Why? To find Squish? Lucky? Both?

By the time they converged with the six men halfway across the field, Devlin had recognized them. Ace, Gumby, Phantom, Bubba and Rex sent him silent chin lifts and kept moving. But Rocco broke off and headed his way. Devlin shifted Cassidy to his left arm and reached for Rocco's outstretched hand with his right. The team leader pulled him in, kid and all, for a hard, fist pounding hug.

"Good to see you, brother," Rocco shouted in his ear. "Doc's on board. How's the kid?"

"Sleeping. She'll make it." At least she would now. The doc and the medicine he'd brought would make sure of it. The relief was almost overwhelming.

At least he wouldn't return home with another child's death on his conscience.

"You boys drop in to find Squish and Lucky?" Devlin asked.

"That's plan A." Beneath the green glaze of the NVD's, Rocco's face turned grim. "Still no word on Lucky's location. But Squish's signal stopped moving ten klicks west. The boys and I are gonna hunt him down. Bring him back for evac, then head back out...do some poking...see if we can get some intel on Lucky."

Devlin nodded his understanding and support. SEALs didn't leave their brothers behind. Ever. They'd find Lucky...one way or another.

Squish though...the fact the East Coast operator had stopped moving was bad. Very bad. That mission might be a retrieval rather than a rescue. Either way, they'd bring Squish home too.

He offered Rocco a fist bump. "Luck to you, brother."

Rocco nodded and turned, striding after his team, who were vanishing—one by one—into the jungle.

Devlin turned back to the chopper and broke into a jog, with Madeline beside him. The sooner they climbed on the bird, the sooner they could bug out.

When someone with the insignia of a medical professional

leaned out the chopper door and reached down for the kid, the craziest impulse hit. To refuse to hand the little monkey over, to hang onto the precious weight.

Which was fucking crazy. It would be harder to access the chopper with the kid in his arms. Not to mention the doc needed to check the little monkey out, stat.

He forced himself to hand the kid to the doc, waited for Madeline to scramble up, then hopped aboard himself.

The door rolled shut. The whine of the rotors, *whop whop whop* of the blades and vibrations of the engine accelerated as the bird climbed the air. He took one of the seats in the rear of the chopper and watched the doc examine the kid. He'd placed her on a blanket between the seats. His examination was swift, his hands sure. Someone had given Madeline a headset, and he could see her mouth moving. She must be answering the doctor's questions.

As he sat there watching, a dull, empty haze settled over him. Without the adrenaline of keeping everyone alive, the three days of physical labor without sleep or food were finally catching up with him.

But he sensed the emptiness spreading through him was more than that, that some of it had to do with the distance separating him from Madeline and her kid. The emotional distance. They didn't need him anymore.

Which was good. It was what he wanted. What they needed.

They were better off without him in their lives.

CHAPTER 21

Two days later, Madeline sat beside Cassidy's hospital bed, listening to the rhythmic beeps of the hospital equipment, while watching her daughter sleep. Cass had been sleeping more than not since her arrival and admittance to the hospital. The doctors assured her it was normal—a combination of the centipede venom, the three doses of epinephrine, and her weak immune system.

Apparently, the weeks of stress and improper nutrition had diminished her immune system, so she hadn't been able to fight off the effects of the venom.

If Devlin hadn't had those EpiPens in his med kit, her daughter would have died.

The swelling was gone now. So was the fever. Cassidy was eating and drinking well. If the swelling and fever didn't return within the next few hours, the doctors were going to release her, and they could head back home.

Margie, who'd been waiting for them at the North Island runway at Coronado Naval Base, had already booked them a hotel for the night. The plan was to get a good night's sleep and head home in the morning.

Madeline should have been relieved. Yet all she felt was...hollow.

Since her return from the Amazon, the world seemed too

busy, too noisy…too cold. Like she didn't belong in it anymore. She felt untethered, as if she'd lost her grounding.

The helicopter had flown them to a naval medical research facility in Lima, Peru. From there, they'd caught a military transport to Coronado. The ambulance waiting for them at the runway had whisked them off to Mercy Hospital in San Diego.

She hadn't seen Devlin since.

Not that he'd been much of a presence on the two flights back to the states. While he'd shared both flights with them, he'd made himself scarce, sitting as far from them as possible. She'd known within minutes of boarding the chopper that he was distancing himself. Preparing to walk away.

The hollow exhaustion filling her was more of an emotional one than physical.

What did you expect? He made it clear he wasn't interested in you and Cassidy. He made it clear that he didn't do kids.

While she might understand why now, that didn't change anything. He'd still walked away…again.

"Momma?" Cassidy asked.

Madeline leaned forward in her chair and ran the back of her knuckles down her daughter's clean, cool cheek. "How are you feeling, baby?"

She almost called her little monkey but swallowed the pet name at the last minute. No sense in reminding either of them of Devlin. Cassidy had asked where he was as soon as she'd awakened in the hospital, and then more sporadically through the next two days. But she hadn't asked for him at all today.

Cassidy at least, was moving on.

"I'm hungry." Cass pushed herself up further on the pillow and pouted.

"You are?" Madeline forced a teasing tone. "Does your Aunt Margie know you or what? She went to find you some chicken strips. How does that sound for lunch?"

The pout stalled as Cassidy's face lit up. "Really?"

"Yep." When the phone attached to the wall next to Cassidy's bed rang, Madeline waggled her eyebrows teasingly. "That's probably her calling. She wasn't sure whether you would rather have chicken strips—" she made an expression of disgust— "or liver." Leaning forward she tickled Cassidy's ribs. "We all know how much you *love* liver."

"Gross!" As her daughter broke into a flurry of giggles, Madeline reached over to grab the phone.

She didn't have a cell anymore. Getting a new one was at the top of her to-do list.

"Hello?" she asked, expecting Margie's voice.

"Madeline Roux?"

The voice was deep, male, with a hint of southern twang. She swallowed the disappointment that the caller wasn't Devlin.

"Yes. Who is this?"

Probably a reporter. They'd started harassing her within a day of arriving at the hospital.

"My name is John Keegan, but you might have heard me referred to as Tex."

"Of course. Devlin talks about you often." *Talks.* Present tense. She grimaced. Dev was in the past now. She had to accept that. "You're the one Dev called just before the battery on the phone died, after Cass was stung."

When Devlin had only minutes to get the information he needed to save Cassidy's life, he'd gone to this man.

"You helped save my daughter's life. Thank you," she said, her voice heartfelt.

"I wouldn't go that far." He sounded uncomfortable. "I just gathered the intel for him. Dev did the hard work."

Yes, he had. Tears gathered in her eyes. She blinked them away.

"I'm glad you called." Something had been prickling at her for the past three days. Ever since they'd landed and her mind was free to focus on things other than terror, and hunger, and thirst. "Did you download Cassidy's medical record?"

Devlin had known about the bee sting, along with the trip to the hospital when Cassidy had been five. Madeline hadn't told him, so he must have gotten it from somewhere. Devlin said that this guy was a computer whiz, so he was the likely culprit to have accessed her daughter's medical records.

"Dev asked me to track down you and your daughter's

medical histories. He wanted to make sure he had everything he might need in his med kit." Tex's voice turned cautious.

Did he think she was going to raise a stink about the invasion of their privacy? As if.

"Like an allergy to bee stings." She turned to look at Cassidy and tried not to imagine what would have happened if Dev hadn't been so thorough.

"Exactly." Tex's voice had lightened. He'd probably read the appreciation in her voice.

"So, he added the children's thermometer, the children's Tylenol, and the EpiPens for Cassidy," Madeline added. And by doing so, he'd saved her life.

"Well he added the second and third EpiPen. The first one is standard." He paused, and humor climbed his voice. "Did he use any of the sparkly unicorn bandages?"

"No." A smile spread across her face. "Did he really add those too?"

"He did." Tex broke into a belly laugh. "I'm not sure what it says about my character that I'm really, really hoping he forgets to take those out."

Her smile turned into a grin, only to fall into thoughtfulness. The only way Tex would know about the unicorn bandages would be if he ordered them. She seriously doubted Devlin would have mentioned them.

"Did you find all that stuff for him?"

When his laughter died and that earlier discomfort ate at the line, she knew she was right.

"Thank you," she said thickly. This man had helped keep Cassidy alive. She would be eternally grateful for that.

"Yeah." He coughed, the uneasiness clear in his voice. "That's not why I'm calling."

Of course it wasn't. Like Devlin, Tex was obviously uncomfortable with gratitude. Why was it that the men who did the most for people were the least likely to accept praise for their actions?

"I'm actually calling about Dev."

Madeline's smile died. Her hand tightened over the receiver. "I'm sorry. He's not here."

"I'm sure he's not. That's why I'm calling."

The uneasiness was back in his voice, but it felt different this time. She wasn't sure why.

"Has he contacted you at all since you hopped off the plane?"

"No." She left it at that.

"I figured." He paused and cleared his throat. "Look...I'm not one to intervene in a buddy's life, but for Devlin Russo I'll make an exception."

Her eyebrows rose. What the heck was he talking about. "Okay?"

"Yeah." He sounded thoughtful now. "Where to start?" The question sounded like it was directed at him, rather than her. "Did you know he had the hospital put the tab for your daughter's stay on his credit card?"

"What?" She jerked up, her mouth dropping open. "He can't do that. Why would he even do that? My insurance will cover most of the charges."

"He already did it. It's done."

Madeline digested that, knowing instinctively that Devlin wouldn't have told anyone what he'd done. Tex must have figured it out on his own. While she was still reeling from the hospital bill news, he asked his next question.

"Did he tell you about Gracie?" Tex's voice was guarded now, as though he wasn't sure how much to say.

Madeline's throat tightened. She glanced over at Cassidy, who was watching her with those big, dark eyes. Most of the stress had left her face. Her cheeks already looked fuller, healthier.

She couldn't imagine life without Cassidy, couldn't imagine losing her. Couldn't imagine what Dev had gone through after his little girl had died.

"Madeline?" Tex prompted.

She coughed the lump from her throat. "Yes, he told me his daughter had died. But not much beyond that."

Tex's voice turned thoughtful. "I'm surprised he even mentioned Gracie. He doesn't talk about her." And then he cleared his throat and continued briskly, but with an underlying echo of discomfort. "Anyway, I just wanted to tell you that Dev's a good man. One of the best I know."

Madeline frowned. She was well aware of that. "I know he is."

"Misguided of course," Tex added after a too-long pause. "But I suppose, under the circumstances, that's to be expected."

"Misguided?" That was an odd description.

"Yeah. Misguided." Tex's voice softened, until she could clearly hear the drawl. "For example, I bet he didn't mention that he blames himself for your daughter getting stung?"

Her jaw dropped in shock. "What? That's crazy! He saved her life!"

"Yeah," Tex drawled. "He doesn't see it that way. In his head, your daughter got stung because he didn't protect her."

The instant Tex said it, the insight made sense. Devlin had told her he was responsible for his daughter's death. She'd known back then, even without knowing the details, that he was wrong. Instinctively, she'd known he'd never behave so irresponsibly that he'd cause a child's death, or near-death.

Not Gracie's. Not Cassidy's.

Yet he blamed himself.

"He told me he was responsible for his daughter's death," Madeline murmured absently.

"He wasn't."

"I didn't think he was."

Tex cleared his throat, and when he started talking again, that warm drawl had tightened. "But yeah, Dev blames himself, even though he wasn't home when it happened."

"He wasn't home?" She frowned, thinking that over. "Was he out on a mission? Is that why he blames himself?"

"That, and because of Sharon." Distaste crawled through his voice. "Sharon blamed him. Constantly. Vocally."

"But he wasn't even there!" Her horrified disclaimer rang out in the room.

Madeline wanted to ask him about Gracie, how she'd died. But she didn't. That story was Dev's to share...if he ever chose to do so.

"Why are you telling me all this?" Madeline asked. While she appreciated the insights and information, it felt like an odd reason for him to be calling her.

"Because you're important to Dev. Your kid too, I suspect." Frustration throbbed in the reply. "But the dude is so stubborn and so indoctrinated in self-blame, he's not going to act on what he feels for you." He paused, before adding wryly. "Not without a good shove."

He cared about her? He cared about Cass?

She wanted to believe that. Really, really wanted to. But he'd given her no indication he cared. No indication she was anything more than a weekend stand, and a three-day responsibility.

Tex must have picked up on her reservations because he scoffed beneath his breath. "Trust me, sweetheart. I'm not wrong about this."

"How can you be so sure?" Madeline asked, wanting to be convinced, but too much of a realist…or…maybe…she was just too afraid of opening herself up to him again, only to get hurt.

"Because the minute he heard you'd gone into that cult, he called me for help. The guy hadn't talked to me in years."

She frowned, disappointed. "That doesn't mean he has feelings for me. He's a good guy—as we both know. He would have done the same for anyone."

"He covered the hospital tab," Tex reminded her.

True…but if he blamed himself for Cassidy's illness, that could be his guilt at work.

"But the real clue is in how he badgered Commander North until North allowed him to join the rescue operation." Tex continued. "He wouldn't have done that for just anyone. Dev hasn't been in the field for years. It's rare that an officer asks for, or is granted, field duty. Not saying that he hasn't been offshore while monitoring a mission. But he's always held a leadership role. He's always trusted his men to complete the objective." He paused, before adding simply, "Until you. With you, he badgered his way into the field. Because you were personal. The other operations? They weren't. When it comes to SEALs, they're hands on when it gets personal. When their emotions are involved. They don't trust anyone with the lives of their women, unless they're right there, supervising the action."

"I'm not his woman," Madeline whispered.

"Do you want to be?" Tex asked.

"Yes." She didn't hesitate. My God...did she ever want to be Devlin Russo's woman.

"Then you're going to have to make the first move. You're going to have to convince him to let go of his misconceptions and take a chance on a future with you. Trust me, he wants to. He's just a stubborn cuss locked in his own stupidity."

"But how do I do that?"

"Confront him. Badger him. Knock him upside the head if you must. Trust me. He's worth the effort."

"Yes. Yes, he is." Madeline squared her shoulders. "Where does he live?"

Finding Devlin's address would be impossible on her own; the Navy must scrub those kinds of details from the public record.

She grabbed the pad and pen on the tray beside Cassidy's bed and jotted down the address Tex rattled off.

"Go get him, tiger," he drawled and hung up.

Madeline slowly hung up the receiver. She'd wait until the doctor released Cassidy and they were safely ensconced at the hotel. But after Cassidy fell asleep, she'd ask Margie to babysit and head off to convince the man she loved to give life with her and Cass a shot.

The worst that could happen was he'd say no.

But at least she'd have tried. At least she wouldn't go through life wondering what might have happened between them if she'd let go of her fear and went after what she wanted.

* * *

Devlin ignored the knock on his door. It was closing on nineteen hundred hours—visiting time was over. Which reminded him of hospitals. Which reminded him of Madeline and the little monkey.

He'd talked to the kid's physician several times over the past three days. Turns out the doc was a SEAL groupie. After he'd offered to give the guy a tour of HQ1 and a chance to watch the boys training in the surf on Coronado Beach, the doc had agreed to update him once a day.

From today's update, he knew Cassidy had been discharged from the hospital. Courtesy of Tex's sleuthing, he knew Madeline and her sister were booked into the Hilton on Riverdale—for tonight anyway. The kid too, as they wouldn't be staying anywhere without her. Since they'd only booked the one night, they were probably heading off to Phoenix come morning.

Not that he was spying on them. Or had plans to do anything with the intel. The knowledge was more a form of mental self-flagellation...

The knock came again. He ignored it again. He wasn't in the fucking mood for God damn company. When would the motherfucker pounding on his door take the hint and bug off?

"Devlin?"

He froze. That was Madeline's voice. Madeline was here.

How the hell had she gotten his address? It was locked down tighter than Edward Snowden's location. The only way she could have gotten it was from someone who knew him, where he lived, or—had the computer chops to hack into a secure database and acquire it.

Fuck.

Tex.

That interfering bastard had all the skills needed to crack Devlin's address.

His feet carried him across the living room against the wishes of his brain. He yanked open the door as a third round of knocking landed, and almost took some knuckles to his chest. For a few long seconds, he simply stared at Madeline, as she stared back.

"Hi," she finally said, breaking the awkward silence.

He crossed his arms and rocked back on his boots, without saying a word.

"Can I come in?" The look on her face was full of challenge rather than entreaty.

He refused to notice that her hair was clean and shiny. Or

that it smelled of oranges or maybe lemons…something citrusy. Fuck, she smelled good. Too damn good.

"No." But he didn't close the door in her face. His first mistake.

She rolled her eyes and pushed past him. "Smartass."

She wore an ivory silk shirt and fitted, gray pants that cupped the curves of her ass. His fingers twitched, aching to cup and squeeze and lift…

Motherfucking Keegan. Talk about a dirty play.

He slammed the door and stalked after her. "Tex send you?"

She swung around to face him. "I wanted to thank you before we left for Phoenix. For coming to rescue us. For taking such good care of us. For everything."

He cringed. Yeah, right. He'd taken such good care of them, he'd almost gotten her kid killed.

"It was my job. No thanks necessary," he said brusquely.

She scoffed, and the oddest look crossed her face—half amusement, half frustration. What the fuck was that about?

"Why are you here, Madeline?"

"I told you. I came to thank you." The challenging look was back. "For everything. But most of all for saving Cassidy's life out there."

Every muscle in his body locked. So did his jaw. He bit the denial out. "I did no such thing."

Her eyebrows rose. "Sure, you did."

"Bullshit." He could feel the muscle ticking away in his cheek, knew from the way her gaze flitted to it, that she'd seen it too.

"Did you have Tex pull Cassidy's medical records and add two extra EpiPens to your med kit when you realized she was allergic to bee venom?"

He scowled, his shoulders stiffening. There was only one way she could have gotten that intel—Tex and his big fucking mouth.

"That was SOP. Nothing more," he growled.

She ignored the disclaimer. "It was that second and third shot of epinephrine that stopped the allergic reaction. If you hadn't ordered those two extra pens, she would have died."

"No." His voice tightened. "I would have done an emergency trach if I'd had to. She wouldn't have died."

No fucking way would he have let that kid die. Not on his watch.

"Yes. I know you would have." Her voice was quiet. Certain. "I know you would have saved her."

He scowled, suddenly seeing the trap she'd set.

"I wouldn't have needed the EpiPens, nor would she have been screaming in pain—" those screams, her tears, they still haunted him— "if I hadn't dropped that centipede on top of her."

"*You* dropped the centipede on her?" Madeline repeated, her eyes rounding in exaggerated surprise.

He set his jaw and spread his feet, feeling like he was headed into battle. "Well, it wouldn't have dropped on her if I hadn't whacked that fucking branch."

"Really?" The challenge was back on her face, heavy in her voice. "You saw it fall?"

That stopped him, but just for a minute. "No. But that's the most logical—"

"No. It's not," she broke in firmly. "There were a bunch of those things above us. That's why you had us wearing the tarp in case one *fell* on us. The centipede that stung Cass could have dropped from any of those branches. You can't be sure where it came from."

His jaw ached like a motherfucker, but he couldn't get his teeth to unclench. So, he spoke through them instead.

"Look, I should have *expected* something like that to happen. I should have had us using the tarp for cover the minute we entered the rainforest."

"Did you know they would crawl that high in the branches?"

"I knew they crawled onto branches," he hedged, trying to avoid an outright lie.

"Okay." Something flickered across her face. "If you knew they hung out in the branches, why didn't you have us using the tarp from the beginning?"

His gut cramped with guilt. Finally...finally...she was seeing why the whole fucking incident had been his fault.

"Because using the tarp would have slowed us down." He forced his failing out. "Made it likely we'd miss the second evac." He shook his head blindly and scrubbed tight hands down his face. "Since the damn things prey on small shit, like lizards, mice and bugs—and most recorded stings have been lower, around the ankles and feet—I weighed the risk of us getting stung and judged it small."

She nodded, and he relaxed. She understood now. She realized how he'd failed her...failed her kid.

"And because the branches the Amazon Giant Centipede crawl on are usually closer to the ground, where their prey are, we shouldn't have needed to worry about them being above our heads," she added, her voice complacent.

What the fuck? Devlin's eyes narrowed. She was setting him up.

She cocked her head and shrugged. "I read up on those centipedes after we got back. There has been only one case of a fatality because of a centipede sting. And that was a four-year-old child who was stung on the lip. The articles mention that people with bee sting allergies can have stronger reactions to the venom. But, although painful, centipede venom is considered harmless. The poison dart frog and Amazon Wandering Spider can be fatal to humans, but they are found on the rainforest floor too, near their prey."

"So?" He scratched his eyebrow. Where the hell was she going with this?

"So..." she echoed with a shrug and suddenly the challenging look was back on her face, "there should have been nothing above us that required using the tarp for cover."

Fuck...

He regrouped, circled her argument for a weak spot. "I knew Cassidy was allergic to bee stings. I knew if she got stung by a centipede it would be serious."

Madeline nodded again. This time he wasn't fooled by her apparent agreement, and braced himself for her counter point.

"Which is why you carried her, rather than letting her walk. Which is why you checked our rest spots and camping places thoroughly before letting her down. Which is why you added *three* EpiPens to your kit."

"I should have taken better fucking care of her." The words burst from him, so raw and full of pain, he mentally squirmed.

She took a step toward him but stopped when he backed up.

"How? You gave us almost all the food and water. You didn't sleep because you were watching over us. What happened wasn't your fault." She stopped, studied his face, and sighed. "Let me ask you something. If you were to do it all over again, without the knowledge you have now, without knowing that centipede was going to drop on her. Basing your decisions on the risk factors that were known to you back then. Would you make different decisions?"

He wanted to say yes. Fuck...did he ever want to claim that he'd have used that damn tarp as a cover from the moment they entered the jungle.

But he couldn't. Because it would be a lie.

Christ, making that second evac site had been the priority. He'd had two malnourished, weak charges. Lots of mileage and limited time. No headset, and a dying SAT phone battery. He'd been far more worried about missing the next evac appointment and having to drag them to a third. Which would have meant another two days in the fucking jungle with no food and more mileage to cover. And all the while trying to avoid rebels, along with human and drug traffickers. At some point, their luck would have run out and they'd have stumbled into somebody.

So, no... he wouldn't have done anything different. He'd taken the lowest risk option he could find.

And fuck.

He'd just walked into her trap. A logic trap. Which were the worst.

He blew out a tired breath and shook his head.

Instead of looking satisfied with his silent admission, she looked sad.

"I don't know what happened to your daughter," she said quietly. "But I suspect your self-blame in this case has more to do with what happened to your Gracie than what happened with Cassidy."

He started to express surprise that Tex hadn't filled her in on the details of Gracie's death, but swallowed the sarcasm when she held up a hand.

"I'm willing to bet money that what happened with your

daughter is the same kind of thing that happened to Cass, and you're blaming yourself for something that wasn't your fault."

"You'd lose money on that bet," he clipped out.

The situation was completely different. He hadn't saved Gracie. Christ, he hadn't even been in the fucking country.

"Maybe." She shrugged. "What I do know is that you're using her death, and your feelings of guilt, to isolate yourself. That's not just a shame. It's a crime. You deserve to be happy, Dev. You deserve a chance at another family."

She swallowed hard and he could see her throat tremble. "I'm sure you're aware that I have feelings for you. I've had them since Dark Falls. Those nights we spent in my hotel room? They meant something to me. I think they meant something to you too. At least I hope they did."

Each word was a poison dart to the chest. The pain flared out in waves, before going numb.

"They meant something to me." The admission broke from him. "But the kid..."

He trailed off, his breathing raspy and raw. Yeah—the kid meant something to him too. Now anyways.

"I know. You don't do kids." Her smile was full of sorrow and understanding. "I can't even imagine how deep the agony goes when you lose a child. But is sealing yourself away and wallowing in your grief the way you want to spend the rest of your life?" She shook her head. "I think you're braver than that."

When he didn't respond...*couldn't* respond...she sighed. Exhaustion and sorrow settled across her face and glistened in her eyes.

"I would love to have you in my life. So would Cass. But we'd want all of you. Everything you have to give. All of your love. All of your trust. We'd give you the same in return." She paused and held his gaze, her own bright with unshed tears. "If you think this is something you could give us…" She shook her head and took a deep breath, held it a second, then exhaled. "I'm staying at the Hilton on Riverdale. But we leave tomorrow."

Feeling simultaneously frozen and burned to a crisp, he stood there, still as stone.

"I'm aware," he said, his voice tight.

"Of course, you are." She suddenly frowned. "And just so you know, I've talked to the hospital and got the charges reversed from your credit card."

Fuck.

God damn Tex and his big mouth. Sure, she would have eventually realized she wasn't getting any hospital bills, but by then the charges would have been settled.

She stood there for a minute. Studying his face. Obviously waiting for him to say something. Agree to give them a chance. Offer up a future.

He clamped his mouth shut and locked down his need. She might be right about her daughter, but she was wrong about Gracie.

When he didn't respond, she gave him a small, unsurprised nod. "There's one other thing you need to remember."

She moved so fast he didn't have time to retreat. Or maybe he didn't want to. And then her arms were around his neck, she was stretching up on her toes and her mouth was on his. She licked his lips, then nibbled at them. But it wasn't until she drew his bottom lip between her teeth and suckled that she broke him.

Fuuuck...

His arms rose to shove her away, only to encircle her waist instead. He dragged her against his chest, leaned down, and took over. His mouth opened over hers, his tongue pushing its way into her mouth. She met him aggressively, everything from her thighs to her hips to her tits to her tongue shimmying against him.

The blood hit his cock so hard, his brain froze, like he'd taken a cold bite of ice cream on a hot day.

He slid his hands down her back to her curvy ass and squeezed. Christ, that sweet piece of real estate had been taunting him since she'd walked through the door. As their tongues dueled and their hands roamed and their nipples peaked, every ounce of him was focused on her—her tongue, her hands, her tits. The sweet, yet tangy scent that floated from her hair. The even sweeter taste of her mouth and lips, like she'd applied strawberry lip balm before knocking on his door.

The urgency spiked. Releasing her ass, he moved his hands back to her waist, ready to toss her over his shoulder and carry her to his bed.

Except she twisted and took a giant step back, her hand climbing to her red, puffy lips.

"Remember that kiss and those nights in my bed while you're making up your mind."

And then she was gone, the door softly opening and closing behind her, leaving him with her lemony scent and the taste of her strawberry lips, and the overwhelming sense that letting her walk out that door was the worst mistake of his life.

CHAPTER 22

Two weeks later, when Devlin's phone rang during his early morning run, he dug it out of his pocket and glanced down.

Tex.

Scowling, his thumb hovering over the dismiss icon, he debated canning the call. He had no interest in talking to the bastard who'd sent Madeline after him after they'd returned from the Amazon. Her visit and that fucking kiss had made it harder than ever to stay away from her. He'd come close, numerous times, to breaking down and heading to her hotel that night—and to Phoenix virtually every night since.

Except—fuck...what if the call *was* about Madeline, or the kid? What if something was wrong? What if there were long term repercussions to the venom and the kid was sick again?

He stopped there, on the beach, letting the cool San Diego breeze whisk the sweat from his bare arms and legs, and stared out over the ocean. Dawn was rising, swiping at the sky in blurry patterns of pink and maroon.

After hitting the accept icon, he lifted the phone to his ear. "What?"

Tex didn't bother with a greeting. "Guess who wins the award for the most stubborn son of a bitch in the history of stubborn sons of bitches?"

Sounded like a rhetorical question. Devlin started to lower the phone.

Tex's voice climbed. "Since you've proved that you don't want them, you won't mind if I send them someone who will appreciate what they have to offer?"

What the fuck?

Not want them? Every single fiber inside of him wanted them. He was staying away for their own fucking good. Not because he wasn't interested. And then the last half of Tex's absurd statement rolled over him, and the chilly beach breeze turned into needles of ice that punctured his skin.

The phone shot back up to his ear.

"What the hell are you talking about?" he bit out.

"I'm not just talking," Tex drawled. "I'm doing. Madeline and her little girl deserve a good man. Someone who will take care of them. Cherish them. Love them. Someone who will give Cassidy a little brother or sister, or both. Someone who isn't afraid to take what's offered." He paused, and a shrug entered his voice. "Since you're not interested, I'm sending them someone who *will* be."

What the fuck?!?!

"The hell you say!" The protest that erupted from him was breathless and hoarse, as though Tex had sucker punched him through the phone and knocked all the air from his lungs.

Tex ignored the interruption. "So, I'm sending Jacob Moore to her."

Devlin's jaw went tight. "Squish? You're sending Squish to her? Are you fucking crazy?"

Hell, to the fucking no.

"The guy's solid, as solid as they come." The shrug was back in Tex's voice. "He's also on medical leave and at loose ends. He needs a distraction before he breaks rank and heads back down to the Amazon to look for Lucky—against his doctor's and commander's orders. Madeline and her daughter will be good for him. They'll give him something besides himself and Lucky to focus on."

If Tex did it, if he made up some crazy reason and sent Squish down to Phoenix, Madeline would take him into her home and life with open arms. She'd feel guilty about Squish's traumatic brain injury, which he'd gotten when the ceiling collapsed on him, as he held the rebels off so Madeline and her kid could escape.

As for Squish... Tex was right...he *did* need something to focus on while his brain healed—but not Madeline and the kid. They were off fucking limits.

Tex would just have to come up with a different solution to keep Squish stateside. Maybe remind him that nobody even knew where Lucky was, and Christ knew they'd looked for him. For a solid week they'd had squads combing the Amazon, only to return to evac empty handed.

And if Squish thought that knowledge wasn't eating at every single special operator on the teams—particularly the ones who'd been involved on that fucked up mission—then he'd forgotten team code. In the entire history of JSOC, they'd never left a brother behind. Never.

Until now.

Until Lucky.

And fuck—that betrayal wasn't sitting square with anyone. Whoever the fucking bastard was who'd sold them out, and set up that FUBAR situation, would answer to all of them...once they flushed him out.

"—Madeline's type."

"What the hell did you just say?" Devlin barked, disliking intensely what little he had caught of Tex's last comment.

"I said that Squish seems to be Madeline's type, and hell, women are a sucker for those wide shoulders and fierce black eyes."

Rage erupted through him. "No. Fucking. Way."

"Why not?" Tex shot back. "They're perfect for each other. Just think of the beautiful babies they'll make."

Devlin could hear the gloating in the bastard's voice...and he knew the asshole was playing him....but God damn, son of a fucking bitch, the needles of ice were sinking deeper with each word until they were deep inside him, ripping his guts apart.

Because the worst part—the absolute worst fucking part—

was knowing the bastard would do it. He'd send Squish down to Madeline without hesitation.

"What's the problem? You don't want them. You should expect some other guy to grab what you were too fucking stubborn to claim for yourself."

And with that last taunt, Tex hung up.

The rage turned volcanic. Devlin drew back his arm and hurled his phone as hard as he could directly into the ocean. Undoubtedly, one of the more stupid moves he'd made.

But not the stupidest.

That, he was beginning to realize, was letting Madeline walk out of his house.

If the thought of another man in her life, giving her babies, taking care of her and the kid, taking over as Cassidy's father—was enough to cut his guts to ribbons, and drive a knife through his heart...he needed to rethink his choices. Rethink his reasons for letting them go.

He'd never been a selfish man. Why was he being one now? Madeline deserved all the best things life had to offer, and that included a man she loved and one who loved her.

Except...he wanted to be that man.

He wanted to have that life.

With a deep, raw breath, he closed his eyes and forced himself to go deep, to assess his reactions through a neutral lens. Instantly, he identified the con he'd been running on himself.

He hadn't walked out on her, and then let her walk out on him, because he was worried about betraying another child. Fuck no—he'd done it because he was a coward. The thought of giving his heart to another child—hell, even another woman—had terrified him. It was easy to risk his life. Much harder to face the possibility of losing someone he loved...again.

He'd barely survived losing Gracie...putting himself in that position again...? Yeah, that took true courage. But what were the alternatives? From his reaction, it was clear as a bell that he already loved them. Losing them to another guy...yeah, that would hurt like a bitch. Maybe even more than losing them to death. Because there wasn't much he could do when death came knocking...but he could prevent another guy from stepping in.

He could man up and claim them for himself—if they would have him—and save himself a lifetime of regrets.

His decision made, he spun and started running. He had things to do, and not much time to do them. God only knew how long he had before Tex carried through with his threat.

* * *

It was almost ten p.m. when Madeline's doorbell rang.

She looked up from the work report she was reading on the living room couch. She'd taken a month's leave of absence from the Best Western Corporation when she'd gone into the cult to retrieve Cassidy, but that month had stretched into three. On returning home, it had been a huge relief to find that corporate headquarters had kept her job open for her. She was playing catch up now, so every night, after Cassidy went to bed, she plowed her way through another company report.

The doorbell rang again. Frowning, she straightened against the oversized, cream pillow cushioning her back and glanced at the wall clock. It was awfully late for anyone to be visiting—even Margie. Besides, her twin would call before showing up.

Maybe there was an emergency out on the street. Her door was the closest to the intersection. But when she reached the door and checked the peephole, the face staring back at her was all too familiar, and completely unexpected.

What was Devlin doing here? She pulled back, her fingers shaking as she unlocked the deadbolt and opened the door.

Don't get your hopes up. It's been two weeks. If he were really interested in a future with you and Cass, he would have come sooner.

"Devlin?" Her voice emerged in a trembling whisper, because —yep, she was getting her hopes up.

Until she saw his face. His flat, implacable face. There was no warmth there. No intimacy. He looked frustrated and angry.

"What's wrong?" she asked. There was obviously something wrong.

"Can I come in?" Something flared in his eyes.

Maybe he was getting the same sense of déjà vu as she was.

But unlike that night a month ago, when she'd showed up at his place, she stepped back and held the door open for him.

He pushed his way past her, his big body tense. She followed him into her living room and watched him methodically scan the space. His gaze touched on *everything* before moving on—her cream and white couch, the television stand, the oak knickknack case against the wall, the peach walls and white window shutters. His focus as he surveyed her house was every bit as thorough as it had been back in the jungle, like he was expecting a horde of rebels to be lurking in the corners.

Maybe he was always this intense, even on his downtime. Maybe SEALs didn't have off buttons. When he finally turned to face her, some of the tension had left his face.

"Why are you here?" Madeline asked, fighting the giddy rush of excitement just seeing him again brought.

A frown touched his flat face. There was an obvious hesitation before he finally responded. "Have you heard from Tex?"

Tex?

He was here because of Tex? The disappointment was instant and immense.

What did you expect? He made it clear you weren't important enough for him to push past his ghost.

"No." Her response was more clipped than she liked. She tried to smooth it out. "Why?"

More hesitation. He was looking uncomfortable now. "He said he was going to call you."

"Me? Why?" Confusion pushed aside the disappointment.

Why would his friend call her? She'd never met the man. Heck, other than that one short conversation in Cassidy's hospital room, she'd barely talked to him. But then that last conversation jumped into her mind. He'd tried to set her and Devlin up. Maybe that's what Tex wanted, to talk her into confronting Devlin again.

She unconsciously tensed. She'd already tried that and gotten burned.

Was that why Dev was here? To warn her not to take Tex's matchmaking to heart?

When the uncomfortable look on Devlin's face climbed into

pure awkwardness, Madeline was sure she was right. Devlin was here to warn her off.

Great.

He could have called instead of showing up at her door.

"Tex didn't call to talk to you about Squish?" Devlin asked, his face hardening again.

It took her a second to process the name. Squish? As in his teammate? The one who'd infiltrated the cult compound with him? The last she'd heard, the SEAL team that had met them at the evacuation site had been on their way to find him.

"Why in the world would Tex want to talk to me about him?" Her voice rose, only to fracture as embarrassment set in. Heck... she could have expressed some concern for the guy's welfare. "I take it your teammates found him?"

"Yeah," Dev said slowly, back to frowning again.

She shook her head, trying to read his mind, which was impossible. "Why did Tex want to talk to me about him?"

He grimaced, his gaze flickering to her face and away again. "Tex thought you and Squish might have...things...in common."

It took a few seconds for his meaning to register, but when it did, heat exploded in her face. Good God. Did Tex think she was so pathetic, so incapable of attracting a man, that he had to set her up with one? First Devlin and now Squish. Or...did he think she was desperate to nab herself a SEAL? Someone to take care of her and Cass.

Either way, talk about humiliating.

"Thanks for the warning." Her voice was tight.

"So, are you going to take him up on Squish?" His voice was guarded now.

"No. Why would I?" she snapped. "I wanted you, Dev. Not Squish. Do you and Tex really think that you SEALs are interchangeable?"

"Wanted?" he pounced on the word.

"What?" Boy was he full of conversational switchbacks tonight.

"You said *I wanted you*. Past tense." His face was still, but his eyes were searching.

"Are you asking if I still have feelings for you?"

He nodded.

Madeline scowled. He expected her to throw herself at him? Again? Without giving her anything concrete in return? Well screw that. She was tired of being the one to always put herself out there, only to watch him walk away.

She folded her arms and glared at him. "Why are you here?"

He hadn't told her that either, although from what little he had said, she could guess.

"Because Tex told me he was sending Squish down," he growled, his voice gruff and gritty.

"And you didn't like that." It wasn't a question. His growl had made that clear.

She wanted to believe his reaction meant something, but she was tired of fooling herself. Jealousy had spurred him to Phoenix, but possessiveness didn't indicate love.

He shoved a tense hand through his hair and scowled. "Let's just say I wanted to break Tex's damn neck and gut Squish."

Her mouth rounded at his bluntness. She hadn't expected him to admit even that much.

"So, let me get this straight." Her teeth clicked together in annoyance. "You don't want me. But you don't want anyone else to have me either." She flapped her hands toward the door. "You can go now."

He shook his head and stared at her with a retrospective glint in his eyes. "I'm forty years old. I was married for eight years. There have been plenty of sexual partners before and after my divorce. But I have never, not once, wanted to rip someone's eyes out for just looking at someone I was dating. Or gut another dude at the thought of them touching—" He broke off to take a deep breath and seemed to force the next words out. "Until I met you."

She took that in, and some of her mortification lifted. He'd just said she was special to him…hadn't he? And if that didn't liquify every muscle in her body…

"Really?" she breathed.

"Yeah. Really." The breath he took visibly lifted his chest. "What I feel for you, in even the short amount of time we've spent together..." He shook his head. "I haven't felt like that since Gracie."

"Who you lost," she said, suddenly understanding why he'd been so resistant to taking a chance on them. His opposition hadn't been about guilt, it had been about fear.

"Yeah," he acknowledged in a whisper. "I couldn't survive going through that again."

He could. Madeline was certain of that. Devlin was the strongest man she knew. He might wrap himself in solitude and loneliness like he had after Gracie's death, but he'd survive. It wasn't in him to give up.

"I can't promise that nothing will ever happen to Cass or me," she told him quietly. "Nobody can promise that. Accidents and illnesses happen. What I can promise is that we will never take unnecessary risks." She paused, watching his face, seeing the hesitation there. "Cassidy and I face the same risks with you, Devlin," she added gently. Even more, I'd wager, since your job puts you in harm's way far more often than life endangers us."

A surprised look flashed across his face, as if he hadn't thought about it that way.

"What are we talking about here?" Madeline finally asked.

He hadn't said he was willing to take a chance on them now. Everything he'd told her was about why he'd walked away.

"We see where this leads. No more backing away." Uncertainty flashed across his face and settled into his eyes. "If you still want to."

Giddiness rose in waves. "Are you kidding?" She laughed. "Of course I still want to."

Well not quite. She wanted the whole shebang. His love. A wedding ring. A shared house. Entwined lives. But she'd take this for now. The rest would come in time.

With a quiet smile, he linked their hands and pulled her in for a long, sweet, kiss. When it turned ravenous, he pulled back. "I'll come up as much as I can."

The euphoria still bubbling away inside her, Maddie grinned. "Cass and I can come down to San Diego, too."

"Ace has three kids close to the little monkey's age. We'll set up some play dates when you guys come down."

If the floaty feeling got any stronger, she'd drift right up to the ceiling. "I could move down, you know. Save us all this travel."

He couldn't move. There weren't SEAL teams in Phoenix. And while she liked her job, there were plenty of other jobs down in San Diego. Maybe Margie could even move down, although she'd just bought her condo…

"Let's wait on the moving." The fact he pulled her in for another kiss eased the sting from the rejection. "And make sure this is going to work before disrupting your and Cass's life," he whispered against her lips.

This time their kiss drove straight past chaste and into hungry. She pressed against him, her arms twining around his neck, arching into the hard length of his body, smiling as he grabbed her hips and pulled her against his pelvis until she felt the hard length of his penis pressing into her belly.

Way before she was ready to let him go, he pulled away and rested his forehead against hers. She could hear his heavy breathing, feel the hard rise and fall of his chest against her breasts.

"Before this gets out of control, I better go. I'll be back first thing in the morning."

"What?" She jerked back her head to stare up at him in disbelief. "Don't be silly. You'll stay here. My bed is big enough for both of us."

He frowned down at her, concern warming his dark eyes. "Is Cassidy ready for that? Maybe we should ease her into the relationship."

He was worried about Cass's reaction. Good lord had she ever hit the jackpot with this man.

"Trust me. Cassidy will be thrilled to find you here in the morning. She talks about you constantly."

"She does?" He sounded surprised.

"You made her feel special, Dev. Safe. Yes, safe," she emphasized at the flicker in his eyes. "She talks about those two days in the jungle to anyone who will listen. Repeats everything you told her. She even asked if we could get some of that insect repellent you used. When we did, she sprayed it around the house and yard to keep the ghosts away. Then she gave the rest to her friend Mandy, the one with the ghost video." She paused to laugh. "Which was the Blair Witch Project, by the way. Apparently, Mandy's older sister brought it home and hid it in the video cabinet. Their mother didn't even know it was there."

"You're certain she won't feel like I'm pushing her father out of her life?"

Some of the effervescence fled. "Ronnie is dead. The FBI found his body in the woods behind the Montana compound."

She'd had the very sad task of identifying Ronnie's remains and breaking the news to her sobbing daughter.

The hand roaming up and down her spine shifted to comforting. "I'm sorry. I know you were close to your ex."

Madeline simply nodded.

The gunshot wound to his head proved that Ronnie had tried to get Cassidy out, once he'd recognized the cult for what it was. He might not have been the most intuitive man. He might have acted on impulse more often than not. But he'd loved his daughter so much he'd given his life to protect her.

"You're certain Cass won't be uncomfortable to find me here come morning?" he asked, his tone shifting from supportive, to hungry.

Yep, she knew where his thoughts were headed. Her thoughts were headed there too. Instead of answering, Maddie grabbed his hand and tugged him across the living room and down the hall. She bypassed the master bedroom in favor of Cassidy's room and stopped at the partially closed door. A nightlight, on the small table next to the bed, cast a warm glow over the slight lump beneath the comforter.

Madeline slipped into the room, with Devlin beside her. Cassidy was sleeping on her side, half in, half out of the covers, surrounded by an army of stuffed animals—most of them old and treasured, but a couple of them new. She had her favorite, a giant penguin, clamped against her chest.

Madeline let go of Devlin's hand long enough to draw the blanket and sheet back up to her daughter's neck.

"Momma?" Cassidy rolled onto her back and sleep hazed eyes fluttered open.

"I'm here." She leaned over, brushing a kiss across Cassidy's soft, clean cheek. She would never take clean for granted again. "Go back to sleep, baby."

"Okay." With a soft sigh, her daughter rolled back onto her side and fell back into sleep.

Grabbing Devlin's hand again, she led him back out of the room, only to pause next to the open door.

"She is doing okay since you two got home?" Devlin whispered, his gaze locked on the bed, with its army of plush guards.

"She's still a little insecure and she misses her dad, which the therapist I took her to said is normal," Madeline said as she led him back down the hall. Her pulse picked up speed with each step toward her bedroom. "But she's eating good. The nightmares are sporadic instead of constant. *And*," she shot him a sensual look, "she's sleeping in her own bed again and sleeping the whole night through."

Thank God for that.

The dry look he sent her indicated he knew what she was thinking. The quirk to his lips told her he was thinking it too. He yanked her against him and ran a palm around her ribs to cup her breast.

"Good to know," he said as he flicked her nipple with his thumb.

Even through her t-shirt and bra, she could feel the heat of his hand. It scorched through her, shooting straight between her legs, where it set off an explosion of hunger.

"We'll need to be quiet," she added. "Cass is a deep sleeper. So, we should be fine... But just in case, we should keep it down."

"What?" he raised his eyebrows and pulled her against him for a deep kiss. "Does that mean I can't make you scream?"

Once he let her up for air, she scoffed softly. "I certainly don't mind you trying..."

But then seriousness touched his face. "Look, we don't have to do this now. We can wait."

Madeline's lips quirked. He might be able to wait...but she wasn't sure *she* could. She'd been dreaming about him for months. Time to see if the dreams and memories lived up to the real deal.

"Timing-wise, this is about as good as it gets when a child's in the house. We'll need to grab the ...intimacy... when we have a chance. After she's in bed. When she's in school. Weekends with her friends. Or when Margie takes her for their special time together."

She'd have to see about sending her to Margie's more often.

He paused beside the master bedroom door. "I need to grab my go bag from my truck. If you give me your keys, I'll lock up when I'm back inside."

"They're on the hook in the entry way. Lock the bedroom door too when you come back. We don't want Cass walking in on us." She paused to smile. Slowly. Sensually. "While you're grabbing your stuff, I'll change into something more...appropriate.

He raked her with burning eyes and lifted his eyebrows. "Why bother? You won't be wearing it long. Hardly worth the effort of putting it on."

"Trust me. It will be worth the effort."

His scoff was amused. "Sweetheart, nothing you wear is gonna turn me on as much as your skin."

She smirked back at him. They'd see about that.

As he backtracked to the living room, she raced to her wardrobe and grabbed a red lace negligee, and the matching panties. She'd bought the pair on a whim over a year ago and never had the chance to wear them.

From there, she retreated to the bathroom to wash her face, brush her teeth, and change. She kept an ear out for Devlin's return as she pulled on the negligee and crimson panties.

Upon hearing his quiet footsteps in her bedroom, she threw open the bathroom door and leaned against the doorjamb, posing seductively. "Like what you see, sailor?"

He straightened from the open duffel bag on her bed, a brand-new box of condoms in his hand. With slow deliberation, he placed the box on the nightstand, picked the duffel up and tossed it onto the armchair behind him.

Her skin tingled as he prowled toward her, his gaze glittering with hunger, his pupils dilated. The heat built slowly. It started in her belly, a slow, warm spread that infiltrated her chest and throat. Before he'd even reached her, the heat spiked and shot to her clit in a scalding rush of excitement.

Without realizing it, she squeezed her thighs together to soothe the building ache.

Devlin, of course, noticed.

"Anything I can help you with there?" he asked, bracing a hand on the doorjamb above her head and leaning in.

But rather than plastering himself against her as her electrified flesh craved, he held himself a hairsbreadth away, his heat singeing her from thighs to breasts. With each breath, their chests brushed, but the pressure was ephemeral, more suggestion than weight, which somehow cranked the desire into the stratosphere. Her legs quivered. Her nipples peaked. Her clit throbbed.

And that was before his free hand went wandering.

He started at her thigh, slowly gliding his fingers to the inside and up. She spread her legs to give him room. Not that he needed the encouragement. Her breath caught as he slid his hand beneath the elastic of her soaked panties and rubbed her slit.

A choked cry broke from her.

"Shhh," he whispered against her mouth. "Wouldn't want to wake the kid." He nipped at her lip and moved to the right, sipping his way to her neck for a long, slow, erotic suckle.

Her arms, which had been frozen by her sides, jerked up to circle his ribs, to pull him closer, to bring his heat and weight flush against her. He didn't budge. At least his body didn't. His hand though, it moved faster and faster against her clit.

Her legs spread wider, wanting more of him…wanting all of him. A choked, demanding cry trembled on her tongue. He swallowed the cry with his mouth as he pinched her clit and then rubbed it even harder.

When he slipped a finger inside her soaked sheath, pulled it out and thrust it in again, she shook from toes to shoulders.

"Look at how wet you are for me." His smug chuckle brushed her lips. Her gaze snapped up to his face and fought to focus. He looked entirely too satisfied with himself.

Time to even the playing field.

Her hands slid down to his muscled butt and squeezed, then moved around to his zipper. She stroked the outside of the metal, rubbing the hard length of his penis before easing the button free and slowly drawing the tab down. He froze as the zipper went down and then slipped a second finger inside her. Closing her eyes, her soaked pussy clenching, she forced herself to concentrate on her task, rather than what he was doing to her. Driving each other crazy was a two-way game.

Slipping her hand down the inside of his white boxers, she grasped his swollen cock. She gently squeezed the base, then stroked him slowly and firmly until she reached the head. She lightly scraped the sensitive tip with her thumbnail and slowly reversed the stroke down again. He hardened even further in her hand, and she heard his breath catch. His big body stilled—but he never stopped pushing his fingers in and out of her drenched pussy.

He knew how she liked to be stroked—just as she knew how he liked it.

Those two days in Dark Falls had taught them a lot about each other, their likes and dislikes, what pushed them over the edge.

They'd also developed a bit of an orgasmic rivalry, so to speak. Whoever came first lost—or won—it depended on how one looked at it. It was the only contest Madeline had ever been in where the loser was also the winner. Which made it a heck of a lot easier to lose these battles. Plus, holding the moment off as long as she could made the eventual release even stronger... sweeter...longer.

From the way her muscles were quivering and her pussy was tightening, she was about to lose another battle to the man playing her body like a master fiddler. His mouth moved back to her neck and sucked—hard enough she was going to have a bruise.

Good God...you're a thirty-three-year-old mother of one, and about to sport a hickey.

She was so distracted by his sneak attack on her neck, she didn't realize he'd yanked down the bodice of her negligee until he pinched her nipple.

She jolted against him, her head falling back—so close to flying she knew she wouldn't last much longer.

And then he dropped his mouth from her neck to her nipple and sucked.

That did it. Her entire body clenched, her pussy spasmed, euphoria rolled through her, and she went flying. His head rose and his mouth slammed down over hers, swallowing her scream.

Good thing too—she'd completely forgotten about being quiet.

She was in his arms and headed for the bed while the quivers were still shaking her. He kicked his shoes off, dropped her on the bed and ripped her negligee over her head. Her soaked silk panties shredded as he dragged them down her legs. She wasn't sure when he shoved his jeans and boxers off, or rolled the condom into place, but suddenly he was spreading her legs and entering her with one, hard thrust.

The tension which had exploded and started to fade, quickly built again once he started to move. God…he felt so good inside her—that hard length of him surging and withdrawing. The thrust of his hips. The way his butt flexed beneath her hands with each thrust. The way his muscled chest, with its light dusting of hair, rubbed against her nipples. She wrapped her legs around his hips, dug her fingers into his ass, and matched his rhythm, her hips surging forward and withdrawing. The hard, hot length of him was inside and outside of her, surrounding her in every direction.

Groaning, she squeezed him harder, the tension coiling through her like a loaded spring. She fought it off, wanting to fly *with* him—not before, not after. But all it took was one look at his face to push the tension to its peak. His hard, driven face, with the red flags painting his cheeks and his dilated eyes. The knowledge that he was as turned on by her, as she was by him hurled her over the edge.

She came so hard her entire body shook and shimmied, and tried to fly apart.

With a guttural grunt, followed by a deep, raw groan, he froze and then collapsed on top of her, his face buried in the mattress beside her head. Their hearts hammered in unison as their bodies quivered and cooled.

Eventually, Devlin rolled over and sat up.

"Don't move one muscle," he ordered, leaning down for a slow, thorough kiss. Rising to his feet, he crossed to the bathroom.

When he came back out the condom was gone. He crawled back onto the bed beside her, stuffed a pillow under his head, and settled on his side. Immediately his hand fell to her breast.

"I take it you liked the negligee?" she asked, her voice raspy and breathless. Wallowing in her contentment, she pressed her hand against his chest, feeling the hard beat of his heart beneath her palm.

"I like your skin better," he drawled, and bent his head to lick her nipple. "And I believe I won our little contest…again."

"I wouldn't be so sure about that." Her smile was blissful. "I came twice. You only came once."

He laughed, and rolled over on his back, pulling her on top of him. His eyes closed, but his hands never stopped moving—stroking her from her shoulders to butt and back up again.

His face was softer with his eyes closed. Content. The warmth in her chest spread out, engulfing her whole body. But it wasn't a sexual heat this time, it was an emotional one. The sense of coming home.

Of belonging.

"Just so we're clear." His voice was quiet, almost solemn. "I love you. Took me a while to figure that out. But I do. This—" he waved his hand over their bodies, "isn't an any-old-body will do hookup. It never was. Not even back in Dark Falls. I've never felt like this before, not for any other woman. Not the way I feel about you."

Madeline's breath, which had caught when he'd said I love you, escaped in a whoosh.

"Good, because I love you too." She strove for a matter of fact tone, but the declaration came out wobbly and weepy. But soon the curiosity rose. "Didn't you love your wife?"

His palms stopped their back and forth glide.

"Not the same way I love you," he finally said, his hands

settling on her butt and squeezing. "We married because of Gracie. And I loved her for that, for gifting me with my daughter. But if Sharon hadn't gotten pregnant, the relationship wouldn't have lasted. We were too different. Without Gracie, there was nothing to hold us together."

"Is that why you divorced? Without your daughter there was nothing between you?" Madeline asked hesitantly and held her breath. Maybe he wasn't ready to talk about this yet.

"That and the blame." His voice was quiet and reflective. "She blames me for Gracie's death. So do I." He shrugged, his eyes opening.

There was so much pain and regret in his gaze, Madeline's eyes stung with tears. But that wasn't what he needed from her. He needed her support, but also her strength. If she cried every time he shared his grief, he'd stop sharing. So she wrapped her arms around his waist and hugged him instead. Hard.

"She's wrong. So are you." She pushed herself up to stare down at his face. "I'm sorry about your little girl, Devlin. But there is no way you were responsible for her death." She hesitated, before adding softly, "Tex said you weren't even in the country. Your ex-wife is wrong to blame you. And you're wrong to blame yourself."

She half expected him to push her away like he had the last time they'd discussed this. But he drew her closer instead.

"Yeah. I was offshore, which is exactly why Sharon blames me. I spent a lot of time offshore back then. In Afghanistan, Iraq, Iran—wherever HQ1 sent me. I was gone more than I was home. If I'd been home more often, spent more time with Gracie. Disciplined her more—" He swallowed so hard his Adam's apple bobbed. "She wouldn't have ignored Sharon and snuck out. If I'd been home, I could have found her in time. Stopped her from jumping into that fucking pool."

For a moment, his hands tightened so hard on her butt they burned. She winced, and his grip instantly loosened.

"She drowned?" Madeline asked tentatively, putting the clues together.

"Yeah." His face tightened and then went still.

But she could sense the agony churning beneath the stillness.

"Our neighbors, the Caseys, had invited Gracie to swim in their new pool. But Sharon was busy. Gracie begged and begged, but Sharon said no. So Gracie snuck out her bedroom window, climbed the neighbors' outside fence and the fence around the pool, and went swimming on her own—while the Caseys were in town. When they returned, they found her towel and floaty on the patio and Gracie at the bottom of the pool."

He recited the events woodenly, like he was recapping a movie or book.

Where had his ex-wife been? Hadn't she checked on their daughter?

But she swallowed the questions and simply hugged him tighter. There was nothing she could say that would take the guilt and pain away. But she could support him. Get him to talk about it. Maybe if he brought that grief into the open, some of it would eventually leach away.

"How old was she?"

His hesitation this time was longer…much longer.

"Seven," he finally said.

She jolted up. "Seven? Holy—" She broke off with a shake of her head. Cassidy was seven. That coincidence must have been excruciating.

From the look in his eyes, he knew exactly what she was thinking.

"Yeah." The acknowledgement was quiet, but serene, like he'd accepted that particular pain and moved past it. "They look a lot alike too. Same dark hair. Same dark eyes. Gracie got my coloring. But she was taller than Cass. Guess she got my height too."

She digested that, realizing for the first time just how much he'd had to push past when it came to her daughter. How much he'd had to put behind him.

"Cassidy must be a constant reminder of what you lost." The words emerged without thought, as an insidious fear infiltrated her. What if he couldn't handle those similarities long term? What if they piled up and he had to break free?

"She was—at first. Every time I looked at her, I saw Gracie. But Cass has her own personality, a completely different personality. By the time we left the tunnels, she'd set herself apart in my mind. After a while I didn't see Gracie, just the little monkey."

A big chunk of that insidious fear subsided. "And now?"

He threaded his fingers through her hair and tugged her head down until he could brush her mouth with his lips. "And now—all I see is Cassidy. A sweet, strong, funny little girl, a carbon copy of her mother. Gracie doesn't haunt me anymore… at least not when it comes to your daughter."

With a relieved sigh, Madeline settled back down on top of him, burrowing into his hot, hard body. His response made it clear that he still carried a boatload of grief and guilt when it came to his little girl. She'd work on that. She had time now…a whole lifetime to help him come to terms with his loss and perceived failure.

She'd make it her life's ambition…to free him from his ghosts.

Devlin deserved that kind of effort. He deserved to be completely, one hundred percent happy, with no shadows lurking in his mind.

CHAPTER 23

Six Months Later

With the sweet scent of flowers surrounding him, Devlin waited beneath the red rose and white carnation studded wedding arch for his bride and new daughter to join him.

Madeline, along with the Hotel Del Coronado wedding organizer, had done a stellar job of organizing the event, which had ballooned from an intimate fifty guests to over two hundred.

He couldn't think of a better place to launch his new life than here, on the Windsor lawn, with Coronado Beach and the Pacific Ocean spread out below them. With the cry of seagulls and the salty ocean breeze climbing the air. Some of the most important events of his life had taken place on this beach—BUD/S, beach boat training, PT... it was only fitting he'd start his new life while looking out over the waves.

"You still haven't thanked me," Tex drawled from Dev's right, looking spiffy as shit in his black tux, with his dark hair slicked back and his brown eyes amused.

"Why the hell do you think you're standing up beside me?" Dev drawled back.

The fact Tex had tracked Madeline and the little monkey to

the Amazon, and orchestrated an entire team into going after them, had gone a long way in securing his position as Devlin's best man. But that last phone call, when he'd threatened to send Squish down to Madeline, which had sent Devlin hurtling down to Phoenix, had cinched the role in his favor.

Madeline believed that sending Squish to her had been an empty threat. Devlin wasn't so sure. Tex had sent Max Brown to Eva Dawson. And Riley Ashland to Maria Moretti. The dude fancied himself as some kind of spec ops matchmaker.

"How long were you going to give me before sending Squish to Madeline?" Devlin asked curiously.

"A week." Tex shot him a snarky grin. "You'd already wasted two. I figured if you didn't claim her within the week, you didn't deserve her."

He didn't deserve Madeline and the kid now, but he'd take them. And by the end of the day they'd belong to him, as he'd belong to them.

Not that he was about to go all bleeding heart on the bastard beside him and tell him any of that.

"Asshole," he said instead.

Would he have gone to Madeline without Tex's interference? Absolutely…eventually. It had been getting harder and harder to stay away from her—from them. But he would have fought the impulse to the very last breath, and he could have lost them by waiting too long. If life had taught him anything, it was to seize the moment and never assume there would be a tomorrow.

Never assume that the people you loved would always be waiting around for you.

A wave of sorrow went through him, and he wished, with every fiber in his heart, that Gracie would be joining the other two loves of his life as they walked down this white aisle with its border of flower pots.

"Gracie would have loved Madeline." Tex, being Tex, picked up on Devlin's thoughts after one look at his face.

"Yeah." Dev cleared the hoarseness from his voice. "And Cass. Hell, the two would have been inseparable."

Although, if Gracie had lived, there would be an eight-year difference in the two girls' ages.

"Like Hope and your little monkey." Tex offered a wry grin. "Can't turn around without tripping over one and then the other." He paused before adding with a laugh. "You know Hope is insisting on a nickname now? Since it's your damn fault, I'm going to leave it to you to come up with one that will satisfy her."

Dev turned to take another look toward the Windsor entrance. It was hard to believe how anxious he was to start this new life.

"Did I tell you Ace and Piper are taking Hope for the week too? Akilah's going to stay with Melody's friend Amy, which leaves Melody and me free to take a long anticipated second honeymoon." Anticipation glittered in his eyes, turning them more bronze than brown.

"No shit?" Devlin's eyebrows shot up. "Is he crazy? Five girls at once?" Although he was seriously indebted to the guy and his wife for offering to watch Cassidy during his and Madeline's honeymoon.

They'd considered having Margie watch her, but Madeline was still a little insecure about letting the kid out of her sight. Then they'd discussed bringing Cass with them, along with Margie to watch her when they were otherwise occupied. But that would have meant adjoining rooms...and yeah, they were looking forward to some alone time, along with we-don't-need to-be-quiet time.

Ace's offer had been the perfect solution. Madeline was comfortable with Cassidy spending time over there. Fuck—the place was like SEAL command with Ace's men constantly in and out. There was no dearth of protective alpha males hanging around. Plus, Cass had been thrilled with the prospect and had begged for weeks to be allowed to go.

A rising murmur of awed voices rose from the guests sitting to the right and left of the wedding aisle. Devlin turned, only to freeze in awe at the sight of his girls approaching. They were both wearing white. Matching floaty dresses that fell in lacey layers to their knees in the front and brushed the top of the grass in the back. Their sandals matched too, and with each step, the crystals studded across the sides, front, and toes caught the sunlight and shimmered. He flashed back to when Madeline had first rocked his world, and how her crystal studded tennis shoes had caught his eyes.

The woman certainly liked her rhinestones.

Their black hair had been braided along the sides and pulled back, then wreathed with tiny white and yellow flowers.

His soon-to-be bride glided across the bright green grass toward him, each stride full of confidence. While his soon-to-be daughter, her right hand tucked into her mother's left, bounced toward him with airy effervescence. Excitement and happiness propelled every lift of her legs.

His chest clenched beneath a wave of suffocating emotion. Christ they were beautiful. The woman he loved more than life itself and the little girl who'd smashed her way into his heart.

When the pair joined him at the altar, he reached for their hands and they formed a circle. Just as they'd practiced the night before.

He smiled at Madeline before turning to the child on his right.

"Are you ready, little monkey?" he asked her softly, smiling at her suddenly shy, but enthusiastic nod. He leaned down. "You look beautiful." When he straightened, his gaze locked on his glowing bride. His throat tightened. Fuck, gorgeous didn't come close to describing her. "You both do," he added gruffly.

The first set of vows—the ones between him and Madeline—were traditional fare. The kiss they shared after being declared man and wife was long, and sweet, and full of promise.

The second set of vows though, the ones he and the kid had been practicing—on their own—for weeks, were less traditional, but just as heartfelt. He was already set to adopt Cass after the wedding, so he knew Madeline wouldn't have a problem with what he and their daughter had planned.

As soon as he'd finished kissing the bride, Devlin turned to Cassidy. When he took the little monkey's hands in his, he caught the flicker of confusion across his bride's face.

"You ready, baby?" His voice was rough. Tight with emotion.

Cass nodded with such enthusiasm a couple of the white flowers in her hair fell over her eyes. He pushed them back up and nodded at Rear Admiral Creasy, who'd offered to officiate both ceremonies.

"Do you, Devlin Raymond Russo, take this child, Cassidy Jacqueline Roux, to be your chosen daughter? To have and to hold, to love and protect, from this day forward?" Rear Admiral Creasy intoned with the same solemn, reverent tone he'd used when Devlin and Madeline had exchanged their vows.

Soon, Cassidy would take the Russo last name, instead of Ronald Roux's. Just as Madeline would take his last name too.

"I do," Devlin said solemnly, as he reached into the breast pocket of his tux for the much smaller, but matching ring to the one he'd just slipped on Madeline's finger. He lifted Cassidy's hand and slid the ring onto her middle finger. It fit perfectly, glittering fiercely against her freshly painted pink nails.

He heard a sob to his left and swung around to find Madeline with her hands over her mouth, tears streaming down her face. Leaning forward, he grasped her wrists and kissed one wet cheek, and then the other.

Suddenly a hand tugged at the hem of his tux. "It's my turn now."

The kid's voice was the opposite of timid and compliant. In fact, the demand rolled down the aisle and brought a whisper of laughter.

He let go of Madeline and turned to the other female in his life and heart. "It sure is, little monkey. You remember what to say?"

She nodded, her eyes sparkling as brightly as the crystals on her shoes.

"You got the ring?" She nodded again, her hand diving into her pocket. "Okay. Just hang onto it for a second." He leaned over to kiss her warm forehead and whispered. "Just like we practiced."

Straightening, Devlin nodded at Creasy, who smoothly continued with the ceremony. "Do you, Cassidy Jacqueline Roux, take this man, Devlin Raymond Russo, to be your chosen father? To have and to hold, to love and protect, from this day forward."

"Yes." Her voice was so emphatic it startled a seagull floating overhead. With a squawk and a dip, it soared off.

Another whisper of laughter rolled through their guests. But it died as Devlin held out his hand and spread his fingers so Cass could slide his ring into place. She took hold of the side of his hand with her tiny left fingers and carefully pushed the ring up his middle finger. Her tongue caught between her teeth and peeking through her lips, she focused completely on her task until the ring was in place, nestled next to the ring Madeline had given him minutes ago.

"With these rings, I bind you as father and daughter, to have and to hold. To love and protect, from this day forward." Creasy turned to Devlin and he could swear there was a wet sheen to the guy's stern eyes. "You may kiss your daughter."

Leaning over, he peppered Cassidy's radiant face with kisses. She giggled and squealed but made no attempt to break away.

When he straightened, he tucked Madeline's hand into his left arm and Cassidy's into his right and escorted his two girls off the stage. A cheer broke out as they walked down the aisle.

"You asshole," Madeline leaned up to whisper in his ear. "You made me cry. My mascara is probably running all over the place. This stuff isn't nearly as waterproof as the label claimed." But there was no heat in her voice. Only love.

He glanced down at her. Yep. Her eyes looked like drowned raccoons, and there was a smudge of black on each cheek. But Christ, nothing and nobody came close to her beauty.

"Not one woman here holds a candle to you." Which might not have been the most politically correct thing to say as Ace's wife Piper, along with Rocco's wife Caite, converged on them. But hell, he meant every word.

"Let's get you to the bridal room and repair the waterworks damage," Piper said, linking her arm with Madeline's free one and wresting her away from Devlin.

Before Devlin had a chance to protest at the kidnapping of his bride, the women swept Madeline and Cassidy away. Leaving him untethered and alone. Which was just fucking crazy. He'd been alone for years without feeling adrift.

Ace walked up to him with a beer in each hand. He handed

Devlin one, and held out his right hand. "Congratulations, brother. I'd wish you the same happiness I found with Piper, but it's pretty clear you already have that."

He reached out for the guy's hand and gave it a hard shake. "No debating that, brother."

Lieutenant Taggart, Lieutenant Trammel, and Detective Addario were the next to waylay him as he waited for Madeline to return. After the back thumping and hand shaking was over, the bullshitting began.

Taggart studied him with cool blue eyes and then lifted his chin. Completely dead pan he asked. "What? Not even a thank you for introducing you to your bride?"

Dev's beer froze on its way up. He scoffed, shoveling as much derision as he could into his reply. "When was that? While you were unconscious and bleeding all over her?"

"Got you together, didn't it?" Tag drawled without missing a beat. "You wouldn't have met her if I hadn't taken that round." He paused and leaned heavy on the bullshit. "But hell—anything for a brother."

"Fucking yeah," Trammel agreed, his eyebrows rising. "And don't think we didn't know what the fuck you were up to during those extra days you hung around Dark Falls. You sure as hell didn't do much sitting by this asshole's bed." He lifted his chin toward Tag.

Devlin shrugged. It wasn't like he'd tried to be subtle about his interest in Madeline, not even back then.

Rio stepped in to take his own swipe. Only this time it was directed at his two former teammates. "Can't tell you how refreshing it is to not have to clean up the mess when things go south with one of your women."

Rio had been an ST7 operator, way back. He'd left the teams eons ago and joined the SFPD, where he'd quickly climbed to his current rank of detective. And yeah, he'd smoothed things over a couple of times when Tag and Tram had acted like the possessive, protective, cavemen they were at heart.

But that was team life—former or current—your brother always had your back.

The reception and dinner passed in a blur. He had no fucking clue what they ate, barely remembered the toasts, and then it was time for their first dance.

Madeline grabbed his arm as she kicked off her shoes and followed him onto the beach. The hotel staff had sprayed and packed down the sand and ringed the area with jeweled stake lights. The effect was magical.

But the woman clinging to his arm was even more magical.

Christ—she was beautiful. So gorgeous she took his breath away.

Their path to the dance floor was suddenly blocked by a swarm of shrieking, giggling children—the girls in church dresses, and the boys in dress pants and button down shirts. As they flew past, he caught a glimpse of a white asymmetrical dress, braided hair, and glittering sandals.

Cassidy, had been assimilated.

"I have to admit..." Madeline smiled up at him as they swayed to *Always and Forever,* the song they'd chosen for their first dance, "I'm impressed. Cassidy has never been able to keep a secret. How long did you two practice to pull that stunt off?"

"Two weeks." He pulled her closer, his steps matching hers, his breathing matching hers, fuck he was pretty sure his heartbeat had even slowed to match hers.

They were that in sync. Two halves of the same soul.

By the end of the night, she'd danced with virtually all their male wedding guests, except for one.

"Did you hear that Margie dragged your assistant onto the dance floor?" Madeline asked without bothering to lift her head from his chest. "And not just once, but twice."

"She's got some guts, that twin of yours. Anderson's a pro at reducing people to ashes with just one look. Hell, after he's finished with them, even the cockiest special operators walk out of my office with their egos in a thimble." His palms roamed down to her ass and squeezed. "She reminds me of someone else I know." He leaned down for a deep kiss before pulling back.

As the lights dimmed and their guests wandered off, and the music finally fell into silence, a bare footed Devlin and Madeline swayed around the beach dance floor, locked in each other's arms.

Cassidy had long ago piled into Ace and Piper's SUV along with Sinta, Kemala and Rani. So far there hadn't been a panicked phone call from Cass begging to be picked up. But Madeline had taken to checking her cell phone obsessively since their daughter had left.

She sighed, her eyes drifting closed. "When does our flight leave tomorrow?"

"It doesn't." Devlin stopped in the middle of the dance floor.

He pulled back long enough to scan her face and recognized the exhaustion in her eyes. Taking her hand, he led her from the empty dance floor. Time to put his princess to bed.

"I thought we were flying out tomorrow?" Madeline murmured as they stepped onto the prickly grass.

"I switched to plan B and booked us a suite here for the weekend. We fly out on Monday," he said nonchalantly.

"Devlin! That must have cost a fortune!" she protested.

His arm tightened around her shoulder as he steered her through the Windsor entrance and toward the elevators.

"I figured we'd need some time to relax, without the stress of rushing to the airport." He paused, before adding quietly. "Plus, this gives us a chance to make sure Cassidy is good with being away from you for more than a day. If things go south in the next two days, we'll still be around to step in and make new arrangements."

She stopped in her tracks and turned to face him. Cupping his face, she went up on her toes and brushed his mouth with her lips. "Thank you."

The look of love in her eyes pierced his chest, filling it with heat. Christ—he loved this woman. But then she yawned.

Draping his arm around her shoulders again, he urged her toward the elevators. He needed to get his woman to bed. To sleep—damn it. They'd have plenty of time for all those groans and shouts and screams that they were looking forward to.

A soft, romantic glow spilled from the stained-glass lamp in the corner of the living area as they entered the signature suite. Devlin scanned the room—plush carpet, gray upholstered sofa with matching arm chairs, marble desk, ocean scenes on the walls, but he was much more interested in the two bathroom features the suite had to offer—according to the hotel's website. The oversized shower and jacuzzi had sold him on the suite, rather than one of the beach cottages.

He had big plans for that shower and jacuzzi...loud, urgent, sexually explicit plans. Madeline yawned again. Which would have to wait until morning. With a shrug, he followed his bride's stumbling, half-awake steps into the bedroom, where a king-sized bed stretched from wall to wall.

They had the whole weekend to test out that shower and jacuzzi and bed...he could wait.

Hours later, Devlin jolted awake to hot, wet, suction surrounding his hardening cock. He pushed himself up on his elbows, staring down his suddenly rigid body, watching his brand new wife's head bobbing up and down on his dick while her dark hair swirled around his pelvis.

His heartbeat sped up like a jackrabbit.

Christ—

Threading his fingers into the cool, silky strands of her hair, he arched up, burying his dick deeper in her mouth. The glossy, soft strands of her hair as they caressed his overheated skin, and the hot, wet pull of her mouth as she sucked her way up and down, electrified him. Each time she paused at the head and swirled her tongue around it, his balls tightened even more. Holding off release for as long as he could, he let the tension build, while his heart tried to thump its way out of his chest and the need for release climbed to an agony and pleasure. When tingling hit the base of his spine and his balls jacked up, he knew he was about to come.

"You're about to hit the motherlode, babe," he groaned, dropping his head back to the pillow and letting himself go.

The orgasm hit him like an earthquake, rattling every bone in his body and tooth in his mouth. When he came back from oblivion, he found Madeline lying on top of him, her chin propped on her clasped hands, and wicked satisfaction on her face.

"That's one for me. Zero for you," she sassed.

His lips twitched. He may—or may not—have created a

monster by instigating their orgasm challenge. Not that either of them had any intention of calling it quits.

"Give me a few minutes to recover and I'll see about evening the odds." The long, soapy, sexy shower he had planned would reel the game back in his favor.

Once he was certain he could move without dropping her, he jackknifed up, grabbed her around the waist and tossed her over his shoulder, hauling ass to that oversized shower the suite boasted.

The website hadn't lied. The damn thing was huge. It had six shower heads—two up front, as well as two on both sides. By the time they emerged, soaking wet, squeaky clean and so weak and satiated, they could barely stand—he'd upped his game, three to two. Hell, her cries of satisfaction were still ringing in his ears. He felt all puffed up and ten feet tall. There was something about making your woman scream—repeatedly—that brought the macho out in a man.

Arms around each other, they staggered back to the bed and collapsed.

Fuck…this game of theirs might just kill them both, but at least they'd go together.

When she reached out and picked up her phone for the second time since they'd returned to bed, he took it from her and kissed her forehead. "Babe. It's only five-thirty. They aren't even awake yet."

According to Ace's text, the girls had been up half the night, watching movies, and playing games, and running around the house shrieking over nothing. They'd probably sleep for hours yet.

From the conflicted look on Madeline's face, she was having separation anxiety. He turned toward the window looking out over Coronado Beach and smiled. He had just the distraction, something he'd wanted to share with her since she'd moved down to San Diego. And now was the perfect time.

Rolling out of bed, he held out a hand to her. "Let's take a walk."

She huffed out a breath, her eyebrows shooting up. "A walk?

Now? As you pointed out, it's five-thirty...in the morning," she emphasized, as if he didn't know exactly what time it was.

But she still reached for his hand and let him tug her out of bed. They dressed quickly and headed out the door.

Sunrise was just starting to paint the sky with its patented array of orange, yellow, and purple as they walked through the Windsor entrance and down to the beach.

He didn't tell her to look up, or point out the skyline, he let her discover Coronado's secret treasure on her own. He'd traveled the world twice over, and few things rivaled the sheer beauty of a Coronado Beach sunrise. It was one of the reasons he'd wanted to stay the weekend at the Hotel Del Coronado. He'd wanted to share this moment with her...watch her soak in the beauty.

It took her a few minutes to notice what was happening across the brightening skyline. But when she did, she stopped dead and stared.

"Oh my God," she whispered, reverence in her voice as well as her face. "That has to be the most gorgeous sunrise I've ever seen." Her gaze dropped to the calm water spreading out before them and her breath caught. "Look at the way the water reflects the colors back. I've never seen anything like it."

When he shuffled in behind her and wrapped his arms around her shoulders, tugging her against his chest, she tucked the back of her head into the hollow of his neck.

They stood there like that for what felt like hours, listening to the seagull's cries riding the water, watching the new day dawn in brilliant bursts of purple and orange as their new life loomed before them, with the same wonder and brightness as the sunrise painting the sky.

The End

Dear Reader,

Thank you for purchasing Hero Under Fire! I hope you enjoyed Devlin and Madeline's story!

If you're wondering what happened to Lucky and Squish—their stories are on the way. Look for Luck Under Fire (Lucky's story) to release in the winter of 2021. This book's preorder will not go live until approximately two weeks before the book releases. If you'd like to be alerted when the book releases, sign up for my newsletter!

You can find the entire Hot Spot Series lineup here:

For those interested, there is a glossary of military terms after the excerpt. 😊

Have you read Trust Under Fire? No? Check out this short excerpt!

Trust Under Fire
Excerpt

"That's your new home up there, fourth house on the righ—" Emma's voice fractured at the sight of the black Jeep Renegade parked alongside the curb in front of her house. Every muscle in her body tensed.

Don't be an idiot. There are plenty of people in San Diego who drive a black Renegade. That's not Lucas's car. He proved two dozen phone calls ago that he has no interest in visiting you. It's a coincidence, that's all.

Still, her foot automatically eased off the gas as she scanned the area surrounding her home.

A surprisingly loud and menacing growl erupted from the dog sitting beside her. Emma shot Cuddles a look of astonishment. The depth and threat in Cuddles's growl could have come from a Rottweiler. The dog's attention was solidly fixed on the Jeep. She must have sensed Emma's sudden anxiety upon spotting the vehicle. Perhaps she'd make a good watch dog after all.

"It's okay, baby." Emma's eyes darted back to her house. "I'm sure it's not him."

After all this time? No. It's not him.

She eased her Accord in behind the black Renegade, turned off the engine, and twisted in her seat, craning her neck for another look around. The vehicle in front of her had tinted windows—like Lucas's did—but through the dimness it looked empty and there was no sign of a tall, lean, athletic God wandering around her property.

Relief whooshed out of her. Revisiting the destruction someone had unleashed on her home was going to be bad enough. But it wouldn't be nearly as painful as facing Lucas after the ass she'd made of herself over him. Three months of distance hadn't come close to easing that particular humiliation.

Another long, slow look around. Still no sign of that libido stirring masculine swagger.

"What did I tell you?" Emma's voice rose with forced cheerfulness. "Nothing to worry about. It's just a coincidence."

Yanking her key out of the ignition, she scrambled out of the sedan and walked around the front of her car. She pulled open the passenger door just enough to slowly reach inside for the leash, using her body to block the open space until she had the lead firmly in hand. Although the dog hadn't shown any aggression toward her, she'd be wise to move cautiously until they'd acclimatized to each other.

With the leash held tight, she stepped onto the sidewalk, and opened the door wide. "Come on, baby, time to investigate your new home."

Cuddles stood up, hopped out of the car with regal grace only to suddenly stop and let loose with a series of body shakes hard enough to whop-whop-whop her ears against the sides of her head. Once finished, she stood calmly at Emma's side with her tail slightly wagging. Emma shut the passenger door and tightened the slack in the leash in preparation for leading her new housemate to her new home.

"What the hell?" a deep, frustratingly familiar voice thundered from somewhere above Emma. "Rio said you were getting a dog. What the hell is *that*?"

Emma froze and then slowly turned, finding Lucas Trammel, in all his six feet-three inches of overbearing glory barreling down the porch steps toward her in his customary worn jeans and t-shirt. His hair was wet, as though he'd just stepped out of the shower. She scowled as he headed toward her with that limber, far too sexy walk. The gait of a man in peak condition, in the prime of his life.

Her traitorous body went weak kneed and hungry. Her muscles heated, her skin tingled, her mouth watered. Sexual attraction revved her heart and respiration.

Not going to happen. Not ever again. Like ever.

"Lucas." She schooled her voice and face to ambivalence. No hurt. No anger. No embarrassment. Nothing to show how much he'd wounded her with his abrupt abandonment. "What are you doing here?"

His stride checked at her tone and the eyes locked on her face turned wary. "Rio called me." He stopped and cocked his head, apparently noticing her lack of familiarity with the name. "Dante Addario, the officer who responded to your 911 call? He's an old friend." He shrugged and ran a palm across the back of his thick neck. "He told me what happened."

Emma fought back a sour smile. Of course Officer Arctic was Lucas's buddy. She should have known from his surly disposition and lack of people skills.

"What do you want?" She let a hint of impatience creep into her tone. Better annoyance than hurt, or even worse—interest. He stepped back slightly, as though her attitude surprised him.

"I thought you could use some help," he said after a long pause.

"Thanks. I appreciate the offer, but I've got it handled." She forced a smile, but suspected from the sudden crinkle to his brow that she hadn't sounded all to sincere in her appreciation.

Another awkward pause, even longer this time, and the dark brown eyes watching her narrowed. "Rio's concerned whoever's responsible may return."

Concerned? Really? Officer Arctic? She swallowed a derisive snort.

"If they do, I'm prepared for them," she told him with all the confidence she could muster. "I've taken steps to protect myself."

Her eyes were desperate to soak in that long, lean body she remembered so well, far too well after thirteen weeks of abstinence, so she locked her gaze on his jaw. That chiseled chin, with its hint of a dimple, was about as safe as it got when it came to the man in front of her.

"Steps?" he repeated, his gaze dropping to the dog sitting patiently at her side. "Is that one of your *steps*? When Rio told you to get a dog, he meant an actual dog, not an oversized rat."

Emma bristled. Nobody made fun of her Cuddles. *Nobody*. Before she had a chance to force feed that disparaging description down his arrogant throat, the animal he'd maligned exploded into another of those deep, vicious, Rottweileresque growls.

Lucas did a double take, his eyes widening.

Ridiculously pleased with Cuddles's response, Emma bent over to give her an appreciative petting. "Good girl. You showed him who's boss."

"Right," Lucas drawled, with a shake to his head. He stepped back and appeared to reassess. "I just meant that when it comes to dogs and protection, the bigger the better." He glanced down at Cuddles who was still snarling at him and his eyebrows climbed so high they merged with his damp, mocha colored hair. "And it sure as hell helps if they have some *teeth*."

"Cuddles will do just fine," she said stoutly. Setting her jaw, she narrowed her eyes and glared, daring him to argue. "She'll bark and alert me to strangers on the property, which will give me a chance to protect myself."

...hopefully...

"Cuddles?" He snorted and rubbed the back of his neck again. "Yeah, that name just inspires fear."

"Look, go away, alright? I don't need your help." The request came out much sharper than she'd intended. Something he'd obviously picked up on since that earlier wariness returned to his square face.

Ambivalence, Emma. No hurt. No anger. No embarrassment. No emotion.

He said something softly beneath his breath. Although she hadn't heard it clearly, she was pretty sure it was a swear word. With a frown, he ran a tense hand through his hair leaving it tousled and sexy and unbearably reminiscent of those nights in his bed. Unwelcome memories flashed through her mind.

Burnished shoulders arched above her...his hard, tight face dripping sweat...the sleek skin and rippling muscles of his back beneath her hands...

Whoa! She pulled back hard from the memory, praying it hadn't blazoned itself across her face. She was over him damnit —she was!

"Look..." An awkward, uncomfortable look dug into his face. "I should have called you back sooner. I'm sorry, okay? I was out of town and—"

"Sooner?" she interrupted in pure disbelief. *"Sooner?"* Her voice climbed. "This unwelcome visit does not count as a call back!"

And there went her mask of ambivalence.

"Emma—" Gentleness touched her name. Regret flashed across his face.

She flinched. "Don't. Just don't." She took a deep breath, and regrouped. "How long have you been back in town?"

He scowled, and rolled his corded shoulders. She could see the play of muscles through his gray *American Sniper* t-shirt. "I don't see—"

"How. Long?" she snapped.

He studied her face and swore beneath his breath again. Yep —definitely a curse word.

"Two months, give or take."

Two months? The breath huffed out of her. "See? We have nothing to talk about."

He squared his shoulders and set his jaw. "Regardless of how things ended between us, I still consider you a friend."

A friend? Really? *Really. He's playing the we can still be friends card?* And here she hadn't thought things could get more humiliating.

"And friends help friends," he continued doggedly.

Was the man insane?

"So we're friends?" Her tone emerged perfectly cordial. Nothing there at all to cause him to back up a good solid foot, but he did. "So friends ignore each other for three damn months, they abandon each other for no good reason, they turn into cowardly weasels who don't have the guts to return one phone call? A quick sorry, I'm not interested would have sufficed. Or there's that old standby—it's not you, it's—"

She broke off, reining herself in. Apparently she had some unresolved issues with him after all. She gulped down a huge breath, which got stuck in her tight throat, and tried to asphyxiate her.

"Look," she said, her voice raspy with the urge to cough. "I don't want you here. That's about as clear as I can make it. *Go away.*"

* * *

If you'd like to try **Trust Under Fire** absolutely free, sign up for my newsletter and you'll receive a download link.

If you enjoyed Hero Under Fire, I'd appreciate it if you'd help other readers find this book by sharing the title and book description with your friends, reader's groups, book clubs, and online reading forums.

Additionally, leaving an honest review on Goodreads, Amazon or any other retail site would be appreciated. Reviews help cue readers into what they might like or dislike about a book. They also enhance book discovery.

. . .

As always, thank you for reading!

Your support is appreciated!

All the best,

Trish

Find Me

Trish is on Facebook!

Join Trish's Red-Hot Readers!

Trish is on Twitter!

Sign up for Trish's newsletter!

Looking for Trish's Website!

GLOSSARY

Military Terms

Beach Boat: A Rigid Hull Inflatable Boat, (RHIB) high-speed, high-buoyancy, extreme-weather craft.

BUD/S: (Basic Underwater Demolition training/SEALs): A twenty-four-week training course that encompasses physical conditioning, combat diving, and land warfare.

BDU: Battle dress uniform.

CQB (Close Quarter Battle): A battle that takes place in a confined space, such as a residence.

Deployment: Active combat or training; deployments last generally between six and ten months.

FUBAR: Slang, means fucked up beyond all recognition.

HQ1 (Naval Special Warfare Group 1/the West Coast Command): HQ1 has naval bases in Coronado, California; Kodiac, Alaska; Pearl Harbor, Hawaii; and Mare Island, California. Among other naval units, HQ1 houses SEAL Teams 1, 3, 5, and 7.

HQ2: (Naval Special Warfare Group 2/the East Coast Command): HQ2 has naval bases in Dam Neck, Virginia; Little Creek, Virginia; Machrihanish, UK; Rodman NAS, PM; and Norfolk, Virginia. Among other naval units, HQ2 houses SEAL

Teams 2, 4, 8, and 10, and DEVGRU (also known as SEAL Team 6.)

IED: An improvised explosive device, commonly used in roadside bombs.

Insertion: Heading into enemy territory, whether it's a house or a territory.

JSOC (Joint Special Operations Command): A joint command that encompasses all branches of special operations. This command ensures that the techniques and equipment used by the various branches of the military are standardized. It is also responsible for training and developing tactics/strategy for special operations missions.

Klick: Kilometers.

LC: A rank of lieutenant commander.

NAVSPECWARCOM (Naval Special Warfare Command or NSWC): The naval command for naval special operations. This command is under the umbrella of USSOC and is broken into two headquarters: HQ1 and HQ2.

NVDs/NVGs: Night Vision Devices/goggles.

PST: (Physical Screening Test): The physical test a prospective SEAL has to pass. Minimum requirements: 500-yard swim in twelve and a half minutes, rest ten minutes, fifty pushups in two minutes, rest two minutes, fifty sit-ups in two minutes, rest two minutes, ten pull-ups in two minutes, rest ten minutes, 1.5-mile run in ten and a half minutes.

SEAL Prep School: A crash course in preparing to take the BUD/s challenge. Prospective BUD/s candidates are put through a physical training program meant to prepare them for BUD/s. This includes timed four-mile runs and thousand-meter swims. If the candidates are unable to pass the final qualifications test, they are removed from SEAL candidates lists and placed elsewhere in the navy.

SEAL Teams: Each SEAL team has 128 men, of which twenty-one are officers and 107 are enlisted. Each team has ten platoons, and each platoon has two squads. There are sixteen men per platoon and eight SEALs per squad.

SQT: (SEAL Qualification Training): Follows BUD/S. SQT teaches tactics, techniques, and special operations.

MRE: Meal, ready-to-eat—a individual field ration.
Sitrep: Situation report.
ST4: SEAL Team 4
ST7: SEAL Team 7.

OTHER BOOKS BY TRISH MCCALLAN

Series: Operation: Hot Spot

These are military romantic suspense. There are no cliff hangers and each book has a HEA. The books can be read and enjoyed in any order.

Books in the series:

Hearts Under Fire

Trust Under Fire

Loyalty Under Fire

Future Under Fire

Hero Under Fire

Series: The Red-Hot SEALs

This series is complete. These are military romantic suspense. The first three books end with plot cliffhangers, but the main romance for each book is resolved and each couple gets their HEA.

To follow the plot and for full enjoyment, these books do need to be read in order.

Book One- Forged in Fire

Book Two- Forged in Ash

Book Three- Forged in Smoke

Book Four- Forged in Ember

Series: Dark Falls, CO

This is a multi-author series set in Lori Ryan's Dark Falls CO world. Each book is a standalone and features a law enforcement hero or heroine. There are no cliffhangers and the books can be read in any order. My two contributions to this series are:

Dark Legacy

Dark Tidings

Are you interested in new release news, and information on sales and contests? Then sign up for Trish McCallan's newsletter!

ABOUT THE AUTHOR

Trish McCallan was born in Eugene, Oregon, and grew up in Washington State, where she began crafting stories at an early age. Her first books were illustrated in crayon, bound with red yarn, and sold for a nickel at her lemonade stand. Trish grew up to earn a bachelor's degree in English literature with a concentration in creative writing from Western Washington University, taking jobs as a bookkeeper and human- resource specialist before finally quitting her day job to write full time.

Forged in Fire, the first book in her Red Hot SEALs series, came about after a marathon reading session, and a bottle of Nyquil that sparked a vivid dream. She lives today in eastern Washington. An avid animal lover, she currently shares her home with four golden retrievers, a black lab mix and two cats.

There are many more books in this fan fiction world than listed here, for an up-to-date list go to www.AcesPress.com

You can also visit our Amazon page at: http://www.amazon.com/author/operationalpha

Special Forces: Operation Alpha World

Christie Adams: Charity's Heart
Denise Agnew: Dangerous to Hold
Shauna Allen: Awakening Aubrey
Brynne Asher: Blackburn
Linzi Baxter: Unlocking Dreams
Jennifer Becker: Hiding Catherine
Alice Bello: Shadowing Milly
Heather Blair: Rescue Me
Anna Blakely: Rescuing Gracelynn
Julia Bright: Saving Lorelei
Cara Carnes: Protecting Mari
Kendra Mei Chailyn: Beast
Melissa Kay Clarke: Rescuing Annabeth
Samantha A. Cole: Handling Haven
Sue Coletta: Hacked
Melissa Combs: Gallant
Anne Conley: Redemption for Misty
KaLyn Cooper: Rescuing Melina
Janie Crouch: Storm
Liz Crowe: Marking Mariah
Sarah Curtis: Securing the Odds
Jordan Dane: Redemption for Avery
Tarina Deaton: Found in the Lost
Aspen Drake, Intense
KL Donn: Unraveling Love
Riley Edwards: Protecting Olivia
PJ Fiala: Defending Sophie
Nicole Flockton: Protecting Maria
Alexa Gregory: Backdraft

Michele Gwynn: Rescuing Emma
Casey Hagen: Shielding Nebraska
Desiree Holt: Protecting Maddie
Kathy Ivan: Saving Sarah
Kris Jacen, Be With Me
Jesse Jacobson: Protecting Honor
Silver James: Rescue Moon
Becca Jameson: Saving Sofia
Kate Kinsley: Protecting Ava
Heather Long: Securing Arizona
Gennita Low: No Protection
Kirsten Lynn: Joining Forces for Jesse
Margaret Madigan: Bang for the Buck
Trish McCallan: Hero Under Fire
Kimberly McGath: The Predecessor
Rachel McNeely: The SEAL's Surprise Baby
KD Michaels: Saving Laura
Lynn Michaels: Rescuing Kyle
Wren Michaels: The Fox & The Hound
Kat Mizera: Protecting Bobbi
Keira Montclair, Wolf and the Wild Scots
Mary B Moore: Force Protection
LeTeisha Newton: Protecting Butterfly
Angela Nicole: Protecting the Donna
MJ Nightingale: Protecting Beauty
Sarah O'Rourke: Saving Liberty
Victoria Paige: Reclaiming Izabel
Anne L. Parks: Mason
Debra Parmley: Protecting Pippa
Lainey Reese: Protecting New York
KeKe Renée: Protecting Bria
TL Reeve and Michele Ryan: Extracting Mateo
Elena M. Reyes: Keeping Ava
Angela Rush: Charlotte
Rose Smith: Saving Satin
Jenika Snow: Protecting Lily
Lynne St. James: SEAL's Spitfire

Dee Stewart: Conner
Harley Stone: Rescuing Mercy
Jen Talty: Burning Desire
Reina Torres, Rescuing Hi'ilani
Savvi V: Loving Lex
Megan Vernon: Protecting Us
Rachel Young: Because of Marissa

Delta Team Three Series

Lori Ryan: Nori's Delta
Becca Jameson: Destiny's Delta
Lynne St James, Gwen's Delta
Elle James: Ivy's Delta
Riley Edwards: Hope's Delta

Police and Fire: Operation Alpha World

Freya Barker: Burning for Autumn
B.P. Beth: Scott
Jane Blythe: Salvaging Marigold
Julia Bright, Justice for Amber
Anna Brooks, Guarding Georgia
KaLyn Cooper: Justice for Gwen
Aspen Drake: Sheltering Emma
Alexa Gregory: Backdraft
Deanndra Hall: Shelter for Sharla
Barb Han: Kace
EM Hayes: Gambling for Ashleigh
CM Steele: Guarding Hope
Reina Torres: Justice for Sloane
Aubree Valentine, Justice for Danielle
Maddie Wade: Finding English
Stacey Wilk: Stage Fright
Laine Vess: Justice for Lauren

Tarpley VFD Series

Silver James, Fighting for Elena
Deanndra Hall, Fighting for Carly

Haven Rose, Fighting for Calliope
MJ Nightingale, Fighting for Jemma
TL Reeve, Fighting for Brittney
Nicole Flockton, Fighting for Nadia

As you know, this book included at least one character from Susan Stoker's books. To check out more, see below.

SEAL of Protection: Legacy Series

Securing Caite
Securing Brenae (novella)
Securing Sidney
Securing Piper
Securing Zoey
Securing Avery
Securing Kalee
Securing Jane (Feb 2021)

SEAL Team Hawaii Series

Finding Elodie (Apr 2021)
Finding Lexie (Aug 2021)
Finding Kenna (Oct 2021)
Finding Monica (TBA)
Finding Carly (TBA)
Finding Ashlyn (TBA)

Delta Team Two Series

Shielding Gillian
Shielding Kinley
Shielding Aspen
Shielding Jayme (Jan 2021)
Shielding Riley (Jan 2021)
Shielding Devyn (May 2021)
Shielding Ember (Sept 2021)
Shielding Sierra (TBA)

Delta Force Heroes Series

Rescuing Rayne (FREE!)
Rescuing Aimee (novella)
Rescuing Emily
Rescuing Harley
Marrying Emily (novella)

Rescuing Kassie
Rescuing Bryn
Rescuing Casey
Rescuing Sadie (novella)
Rescuing Wendy
Rescuing Mary
Rescuing Macie (Novella)

Badge of Honor: Texas Heroes Series

Justice for Mackenzie (FREE!)
Justice for Mickie
Justice for Corrie
Justice for Laine (novella)
Shelter for Elizabeth
Justice for Boone
Shelter for Adeline
Shelter for Sophie
Justice for Erin
Justice for Milena
Shelter for Blythe
Justice for Hope
Shelter for Quinn
Shelter for Koren
Shelter for Penelope

SEAL of Protection Series

Protecting Caroline (FREE!)
Protecting Alabama
Protecting Fiona
Marrying Caroline (novella)
Protecting Summer
Protecting Cheyenne
Protecting Jessyka
Protecting Julie (novella)
Protecting Melody
Protecting the Future
Protecting Kiera (novella)
Protecting Alabama's Kids (novella)

Protecting Dakota

New York Times, USA Today and *Wall Street Journal* Bestselling Author Susan Stoker has a heart as big as the state of Tennessee where she lives, but this all American girl has also spent the last fourteen years living in Missouri, California, Colorado, Indiana, and Texas. She's married to a retired Army man who now gets to follow *her* around the country.

www.stokeraces.com
www.AcesPress.com
susan@stokeraces.com